A NOVEL

# Ratcatcher, Be Still

Dennis Anthony

SANDPIPER PRESS PENSACOLA, FLORIDA

**Sandpiper Press**
**Pensacola, FL 32501**
**www.dennis-anthony.com**

Publisher's Note: This is a work of fiction. Names, characters, places, and incidents are a product of the author's imagination. Locales and public names are sometimes used for atmospheric purposes. Any resemblance to actual people, living or dead, or to businesses, companies, events, institutions, or locales is completely coincidental.

**Ratcatcher, Be Still/ Dennis Anthony**. -- 1st ed.
EBOOK ISBN 978-0-9897375-6-2
ISBN 978-0-9897375-7-9

**Other Books by Dennis Anthony**
***the Debunker Trilogy***

*Debunker: Independence Day*
*Debunker: Psychic Storm*
*Debunker: Scream of the Valkyrie*

*http://www.dennis-anthony.com*

*To Patricia Wiegand and every teacher*
*who whispers inspiration*

*"I am terrified by this dark thing*
*That sleeps in me;*
*All day I feel its soft, feathery turnings, its malignity."*

—SYLVIA PLATH

# { prologue }

*Northern Ohio, 1967*

Thousands of earthworms driven to the surface by a heavy spring rain clogged roads, driveways, and the sidewalk to Emily Laudicina's home.

Rice Channon tried to step around the lethargic clumps but ended up squashing them by twos and threes under the soles of his shoes. He thought the stink of them smelled like death.

As Mrs. Laudicina held the door open and Rice dragged his slime-covered feet over the doormat before stepping inside, he watched as the ghost of a dead soldier hovered near the glass doors of the oak sideboard in the dining room.

He had no doubt what it was. A stack of white plates and saucers in the sideboard were visible through the spirit's filmy torso.

Once inside, he watched a chestnut-colored field mouse run across the floor toward the apparition. The little rodent stood on its hind legs, whiskers animated as though chewing on food or considering this odd vision.

The *Goodwater Tribune*, a daily and Sunday newspaper with a circulation of thirty-five thousand, ran a major local news or feature article on page one each Sunday. Rice, the new general assignment reporter, was selected to speak with family members of servicemen killed in Vietnam more than six months ago and then write about it.

He'd done similar interviews before, usually right after the Defense Department released news of a local death. There were tears, yes, but they were often accompanied by smiles as friends and family related special memories that Rice always included in the death announcement.

Talking to loved ones who'd had months to consider their loss was a different experience entirely. Mothers and wives were over the initial shock. Instead, they cried for prolonged periods, head in hands, tears raining through splayed fingers. Huffed sighs. Apologies for their behavior.

The reporter let them be until they composed themselves. He simply watched their faces turn pale while the round of sorrow and tears and sadness rolled over them like a summer squall off Lake Erie.

Mrs. Laudicina, whose son had been killed in a perimeter firefight at his combat base in South Vietnam, was unable to hear or see her boy's ghost behind her. Rice said nothing.

As she told her story, he watched Mrs. Laudicina's son sit down at the dining room table as though waiting to be served meat loaf and gravy.

The ghost didn't speak and seemed to be waiting.

As Rice was leaving with the man's photo, the dead soldier turned to look at him. Instead of being empty, his eyes were now warmer and less angry than before.

Rice hoped he would end up far away from war in some gentler place.

Three more interviews followed with three more brokenhearted families.

At each home, he spoke to tearful family members and endured long uncomfortable silences.

And he watched the ghosts of the deceased servicemen circle around him at a distance, like timid house cats.

Sometimes, he thought he heard their words. Or the sense of their words. Questioning. Confused.

Lost.

# { 1 }

*Northern Ohio, 1972*

Rice parked his Fiat 850 in front of the Goodwater Police Department headquarters, stubbed out his Hav-A-Tampa cigar into an overflowing ashtray, then considered the man standing by the door, hands in his pockets and head down.

The guy didn't see him. The streetlight illuminated his weariness.

"Get here early," Rice said as he approached the man. "You'll need the time if there's a lot on the blotter."

The twenty-seven-year-old veteran police reporter—no longer called wiry or skinny, but still slender—had thick brown hair, a comma of which often dropped across his forehead. Rice had given this speech many times before, even though he himself *always* arrived late. He trusted his speed and experience to get the stories written before deadline. But on weekends—his days off—a substitute police reporter from the general assignment pool took over his duties. And he had to be trained.

"Mr. Channon," the other man said, alert now. He was about five years younger than Rice and wore a new double-knit blazer that seemed way too bright this early in the morning. He pulled out a reporter's notebook and a pen, then wrote something down.

Rice cocked his head and looked at him. Stylish haircut. Off his collar but over his ears.

He hadn't been called Mr. Channon very often, and he was trying to decide if he liked it.

"Call me Rice," he said. "Who are you?"

"Joyce. Mitchell Joyce."

"Mitchell," Rice said, stretching out the name, as if tasting a new flavor. "Let's start with the basics. Bring a pencil—a couple of them—not a pen. Leave a few more in your car."

Mitchell stammered. "I got a pen."

"Don't worry about it this time. Problem is pens leak, they run out of ink, and sometimes, they don't work for their own goddamn reasons."

Mitchell started to make a note in his book when Rice grabbed the pen.

"Don't write down everything I say. Especially around the cops. You'll look like an asshole and cops hate assholes."

"I'm not an asshole," Mitchell said.

Rice put a light hand on his arm. "Of course you're not. But don't *look* like one. That's all I'm telling you."

Not much happened on lazy Friday mornings like this one. But Saturdays, when the fill-in cop reporter was on the job, were unpredictable and often deadly. Traffic accidents on dark stretches of two-lane country roads resulted in frequent Saturday morning fatalities. Fights including shootings, stabbings, and wife beatings were also common as workers drank away Friday paychecks at local watering holes.

If that wasn't enough, the substitute police reporter had to deal with the city editor, David Paul Billard, cranky as a harridan on Saturday mornings. Having to work with a stand-in didn't improve his disposition.

"On Saturdays, you're looking for fatal car crashes," Rice said. "That's the most important thing. Usually, the officer on duty will tell you before you even check the blotter. But check it anyway. Plus, the cops sometimes fuck with new guys. Any murders, you call me. If you can't get in touch with me, call Billard right away. Got it?"

"You're the Ratcatcher," Mitchell said, grinning. "You caught three murderers."

"Four," Rice said. "And I didn't catch them. Not any of them. I … helped."

Mitchell grinned sheepishly, like a little kid meeting a television cowboy.

"You're the reason I got into journalism," he said. "We passed around your clippings at school. Everybody read 'em."

"Don't let Billard hear you call me that name," Rice said. "He'll smack you so hard that pretty plaid tie will spin off your neck."

Mitchell held up his hand defensively.

"Check and double-check all the details about a fatal. Names are the most important," Rice said. "You screw up a name, you'll never hear the end of it. Not just from the family of the recently deceased, but from Billard."

"He's a little guy."

"So's a dachshund but they're meaner than hell. Are you listening?"

Mitchell nodded.

"You're going to need to get photos from the family to use with the story," Rice said. "This can be the hard part. You have to get them fast. The good news is the families are usually in shock, so it's easier to talk to them the day after the fatal. Easier than a week later anyway."

"Can't we get somebody to do that?"

Rice put a hand on Mitchell's shoulder. "This is not a glamor job, Mitchell. Maybe a copy girl will get it for you. Maybe not. But it's up to you to do the dirty work—the calling, the request. Be sure to apologize for the intrusion and express your regrets."

"Of course."

"But don't pretend you're someone you're not. Don't act like a grieving family member. It's best and simplest to be professional. Most people understand that."

Mitchell followed Rice as he walked into the police headquarters, down a narrow dingy hallway with a row of old auditorium chairs lining one wall. Rice stopped before they got to the desk sergeant. "You want to make everything better, am I right?"

"I want to fix what's wrong," Mitchell said without irony. "I want to help, anyway."

"Stick it to the man?"

"He's got it coming most times."

Rice rubbed his eyes hard with a thumb and forefinger but refused to sigh.

At the front desk, he pulled the blotter off a wall spike. He introduced Mitchell without looking at the desk sergeant sitting there. The cop muttered something, might have been "G'morning."

"Look here," Rice said. "This report says a high-school kid was walking naked down the median on Broad Street at two o'clock this morning. According to this, he was drunk and took a swing at a cop. Arrested and charged with drunk and disorderly, indecent exposure, resisting arrest …" Rice flipped the page over. "Some other stuff. What should we do with this?"

Mitchell took the report and looked it over. He shrugged.

"I'm guessing stuff like this happens all the time," he said.

"Yeah, it does," Rice said. "Read it again." Mitchell did. Then he shook his head once more.

"It doesn't seem worth the ink," Mitchell said. "Kids do dumb shit every day. I wouldn't report it."

Rice gave a dismissive chuckle. So did the sergeant at the desk.

"Bobby Holmes is the son of City Council President Loretta Holmes," Rice said. "Her kid is an underage drunk, belligerent, and regularly skinny-dips through town. None of this will be featured in her re-election brochure."

"How could I know who he is?"

"If you read our newspaper every day, you'd learn who our elected officials are. When they or their families do something stupid or get hurt or killed, we do a story."

"To embarrass them?"

"That's just a bonus," Rice said. "The people who elected her have a right to know about her and those close to her."

The desk sergeant harrumphed dismissively but still didn't look up.

"You want to change the world?" Rice said. "This is the way we do it. One naked kid at a time."

That brought a big laugh from the desk sergeant who turned to share his amusement with Rice. The cop's face was a roadmap of red lines from too much drink and red eyes from too little sleep.

"You've got to read *all* the paper," Rice said. "Not just your stories, your beat, the sports pages, and the funnies. Read the women's pages, the courthouse and city hall news."

"You do that?"

"And the business pages. And the obits too," Rice said. "When people die, there's a stringy chain of events. It pays to keep an eye on them. On everything."

The desk sergeant studied Mitchell, wearing something like a wily grin. "So you're working with the Ratcatcher now?"

"Christ, Logan. I'm tryin' to break him in right."

"Just be nice to all the men in blue, and we'll be nice to you," Sergeant Logan said, making it sound like a jingle he just made up.

Rice tossed the blotter in front of Logan. "That's bullshit. It's better to fuck 'em over every chance you get but send a birthday card to their mothers."

Logan laughed again and shook his head, his smile dying slowly on his lips.

When they were outside, Mitchell said, "Do you really fuck over the pigs every chance you can?"

"They're good guys. Most of them," Rice said. "They do the right thing, even when nobody's looking."

"Really?"

"Most of the time."

Mitchell snorted and looked at the bottom of his right shoe, like he'd just stepped in something.

"But if I hear you call them pigs again," Rice said, "I'll make sure you die screaming. Let's head back."

# { 2 }

David Paul Billard's fingers worked his editing pencil like a scalpel, cutting away layers of bullshit to reveal the truth of things.

Thirty years ago, those fingers lifted bombs into the bellies of B-17s where they fell on German cities and factories, exploding over concrete, wood, and flesh.

He was annoyed at the current generation's hatred of the military, law and order, civilization. And bathing. That one especially.

Rice and Mitchell walked quickly into the newsroom and stopped in front of the city editor. Billard looked up expectantly.

"No fatals," Rice said. "A break-in at the old coal company off Cleveland Street. And Council President

Holmes' son was caught dancing naked along Broad Street and took a swing at the arresting officer."

Billard's desk was at the far end of the open bay newsroom, near the rattling teletypes and half-circle copydesk.

"How much?"

"I think four or five grafs should cover it," Rice said. "Maybe eight if I can get some comments from mom."

"Okay," Billard said.

Rice turned to Mitchell who stood behind and mostly out of sight of the city editor. "You do the straight story," he said. "I'll call Councilwoman Holmes."

Mitchell, seemingly relieved, scurried to his desk and threaded a sheet of newsprint into his typewriter.

"Well," Billard said. "What do you think?"

"He needs to learn some respect for law enforcement," Rice said. "Other than that, it's just a matter of time."

"He smells okay."

"Yeah, I think he's a regular bather," Rice said.

"Did he catch the Holmes kid story?"

"No," Rice said. "But he now understands the importance of reading everything in the paper and not just the cop beat."

"I had lunch with the mayor last week," Billard said. "He told me he doesn't like you much."

"We have some history. Stupid shit."

"He'll get over it," Billard said. "But the safety-service director. He's a fan."

The Goodwater safety-service director, Phillip Fortunato, oversaw police and fire for the city as well as maintenance and sanitation. He reported directly to the mayor.

"Why are you telling me this?" Rice said. "Are they throwing me a party?"

Billard rubbed his long narrow fingers along the ridge of his nose. Then he took off his glasses, crossed his arms on the desk, and looked up at Rice.

"Are you taking the city hall job or not?" he said. "I've got to make a selection by Monday."

"Why do you keep asking me?"

"Because it's a good fit," Billard said, looking exasperated. "You're our best reporter. City hall is our most important beat."

Many years earlier, when Dave Billard was the *Tribune*'s city hall reporter, his coverage and weekly column won state and national awards for the newspaper.

"I like the cop beat."

"You like …" Billard looked left and right and lowered his voice. "You like being the Ratcatcher. Listen. If you wanna be a cop, then quit and go to cop school. If you want to be a newspaperman, you need to get serious about your job."

Rice leaned forward. "Leave me alone, Dave," he said. "I know what I want."

Billard moved back in his chair. "I could *make* you take the job."

"I'm going to call Loretta Holmes now," Rice said, walking away. "I'm going to let Mitchell do the coal company break-in too. You want me to check it over first?"

"No," Billard said, putting his glasses on again. "Let me see what the kid's got."

—

Mitchell's typewriter screeched as he yanked out the newsprint and tossed it on Rice's desk. "Our streaker exposed," Mitchell said when Rice dropped into his chair. The copy floated down in front of him.

Rice pushed out his bottom lip. "Okay," Rice said after reading it over. "Give the copy to Billard. Don't tell him you showed it to me first. I'll include whatever I get from Holmes after I talk with her."

Mitchell grinned and winked.

Rice pulled out a desk drawer, pushed aside an electric razor and two new-baby cigars he never got to, then flipped on his police scanner. Billard had one at his desk, but Rice thought he never paid enough attention to it. There wasn't much. Traffic stops, patrolmen breaking for breakfast, a suspicious man prowling around somebody's backyard.

He turned down the volume and dialed Councilman Loretta Holmes.

"Mrs. Holmes," he said. "This is Rice Channon with the *Tribune*."

She said nothing for a long time. "Yes?"

"Your boy, Bobby, was picked up by the police last night," Rice said.

He could almost feel her stiffening. "You're not … You're not going to put it in the newspaper, are you?"

"Oh, we have to," Rice said, like it was out of his hands. More chatter on the scanner. Many voices. "Any incidents involving public officials go to ink. That's the rule."

"Bobby isn't an elected official," Loretta Holmes said, chuckling uncomfortably. "He's just a boy."

"He's nineteen," Rice said. "If he was seventeen, we wouldn't cover it. If you were just a councilman and not the president of council, we'd probably leave it be. If he hadn't taken a swing at a patrolman … Well, you get the idea."

"I don't want to talk about it."

"Sure, I get that," he said. A police car, siren blaring, raced by outside, and most of the newsroom scrambled to the windows. Rice stood up and stretched his neck to see what was happening. "Sometimes that can look like you're hiding something."

"I'm not … "

"Is Bobby living at home?"

Another pause from Councilwoman Holmes, followed by a cough. "He's going to school at Mosopelea County Community College."

"My alma mater," Rice said. "What's he studying?"

"He's in the business curriculum," she said.

"Smart," Rice said, making a few notes on the bottom of a fire chief feature story he was writing. "Is he graduating soon?"

Mrs. Holmes coughed again nervously and didn't bother to shield the phone. Rice jerked the receiver away from his ear.

"I'd like to talk with your editor," she said.

Rice put her on hold and dialed Billard. "Loretta Holmes doesn't want to talk about her son. She doesn't think it's anybody's business."

"So?"

Rice could see Billard across the newsroom digging into his desk drawer. He pulled out a tube and shucked off a lozenge with his thumb. Probably an antacid.

"She wants to talk to you."

Billard shook his head.

"Or I could just go with her no comment."

"Find out what's going on," Billard said, giving a vague wave toward the window. "Officers are being dispatched to the east side. Couldn't copy the address."

"Fire?"

"No," Billard said, pulling another antacid from his packet. "But there was a call for an ambulance."

Rice transferred the call to Billard, then dialed Earl Sugarman, Phil Fortunato's assistant.

"What's going on?" Rice said.

"I don't know," Sugarman said. "Phil ran over to the PD."

"You must know something," Rice said. Sugarman was one of the few people he felt comfortable bullying. The man never got ugly and always felt bad for not knowing more.

"Somebody important got hurt," Sugarman said. "That's all I know."

"Got hurt how? Accident. Cooking fire? What?"

"Not sure…"

"Was it the mayor? County commissioner? Dogcatcher. Come on, Earl."

"Nobody in politics. That's all I can tell you."

Rice hung up.

Billard looked over to him, and Rice shrugged, held up a finger. Billard lifted his wrist and tapped his watch. First deadline was ten minutes away.

Rice dialed Colonel Quincy Markle, Goodwater's chief of police. He was about to give up when he finally picked up the phone.

"Markle," he said.

"Colonel, it's Rice Channon. I'm two minutes from deadline and I'm hearing sirens all over town. You gotta give me something."

"I don't give a damn about your deadline, Channon."

"A community leader? Sports figure? Who is it?"

"Who told you it was anybody?" Markle said.

Rice took a breath. "I know somebody important is hurt, maybe hurt bad," Rice said. He took a chance with the last embellishment. Markle didn't correct him. "But that's not much of a headline. I need a name and a few details."

"We haven't even called her family yet," Markle said, voice rising. "Assuming there is one." The man was quick to anger, but Rice didn't care.

"People in the public eye don't get that luxury," Rice said. "You know that. The public's right to know supersedes ..."

"Yeah, Channon," Markle said. "I remember your lecture from last time. Did you learn that in journalism school?"

"I was a liberal arts major," Rice said. "Come on, Colonel. I need something now."

"You're going to have to wait," Markle said and hung up.

Billard was at his desk. "Talk to me," he said.

"Somebody important," Rice said, starting to dial again. "And it's a woman. Hurt bad or dead. I don't know which."

"Five minutes," Billard said.

"Sugarman."

"Earl, I know what her name is and I know what happened," Rice said. "What I don't know is if she's alive or dead."

"Who gave you her name?"

"I just got off the phone with Markle," Rice said, knowing full well he was playing a dangerous game here. "I reminded him how figures in the public eye don't get the same privacy protections as regular folks."

"Is that so?"

"Yep. That's what our lawyers tell me."

No lies so far. Not exactly.

"You should go back to Markle, then," Earl said. "He knows more. He was at the scene."

Rice ran his hands through his hair. "I'm sure you're right, Earl. That's why he's in such demand right now. Listen. He's chasing down murderers and you're scheduling trash pickups. Who do you think has more time to talk with me?"

Anyone else would have taken offense, but not Earl. And Rice knew he was taking a big chance bringing up murder as a given. If he was wrong, this would be a short conversation.

"Who said anything about murder?" Earl asked, immediately suspicious.

"Well, what would you call it?" Rice said, ripping off the wrapper from one of the two "It's a Girl!" cigars in his drawer.

"Look, nobody knows if she's dead," Earl said.

"Okay, attempted murder," Rice said, lighting the dry stogie and taking two quick, unsatisfactory puffs.

"This is all I got, okay?" Earl said. "Annike Eichel was found inside her home. In the kitchen, I think. She was stabbed multiple times. Lots of blood."

"Jesus," Rice whispered.

"You know all this, right?"

"Go on, go on," Rice said. Annike Eichel was a widely known and sometimes despised atheist activist in Goodwater, the state of Ohio, and to a lesser extent, nationally. She was angry. She was vocal. And she was gorgeous.

"One of our patrolmen found her this morning," Earl said. "She was supposed to be on a panel at the college about the war and religion. When she didn't show, a friend knocked on her door, then called the cops when nobody answered. That's all I know."

Rice could hear the hesitancy in Earl's voice. "You might as well give it all to me," he said.

"She may have been sexually assaulted," Earl said.

"May have been?"

For the first time, Earl seemed relieved. "It was ugly, Rice. They told me somebody did things to her insides I didn't know you could do to a woman."

"I need details, Earl."

"Looked like wounds from a butcher knife," Earl said. "Used by someone who knew what he was doing. Somebody who hated her real bad, from what the on-scene guys said."

"I need to know if she's alive or dead, Earl."

"I don't know," Sugarman said. "The cops tell me the amount of blood at a crime scene can fool you sometimes."

"She at Goodwater Memorial?"

"I guess. I don't know."

"Okay."

"If I knew, I'd tell you," Earl said. "You know that."

"Yeah."

Rice looked over to Billard who was standing, hands open expectantly. Rice gave him a thumbs-up, and the city editor quickly picked up his phone and began barking to someone at the other end. Then he rushed off toward the pressroom downstairs.

Rice fed a sheet of newsprint into his typewriter.

"Here comes Phil," Earl said. "Maybe he knows something."

The spectral form of Annike Eichel appeared across the newsroom behind David Billard's now-vacant chair. She had the sad, empty eyes of someone both ashamed and confused. She stared directly at him. Rice had seen the look before.

"Never mind," Rice said. "I'm pretty sure she's dead, Earl."

Then he hung up the phone.

# { 3 }

On Memorial Day, Phil Fortunato cooked up burgers and hot dogs for his family and about a dozen others.

And like last year, he invited Rice Channon.

Two metal tricycles—one turned on its side so rainwater pooled in the fender—were pushed against the fence, next to a corrugated trash can.

"Where's the cute gal you brought last time?" the Goodwater safety-service director asked as he flipped a burger, black as the grill lid. He wore a wife-beater T-shirt, black shorts, and black socks. On his head was a white chef's toque with the price tag flapping merrily from its peak.

Rice looked toward a cooler dripping with condensation. He could see the tops of Colt 45 beer cans.

"I'm not sure how's she's spending the holiday," Rice said, wincing as he stared into the sun.

He and Stacey Ann Lattermore had bonded over the poetry of John Keats while in junior college. She went off to Kent State for her baccalaureate, then took a job teaching in a local elementary school. Rice went to work for the *Goodwater Tribune*. For five years they had stayed together. Last year, she ended their relationship.

Phil held up both hands defensively, grease dripping down the spatula. "Didn't mean to pry. I hate busybodies," he said.

Rice dug into the ice and pulled out a can of Colt 45, a favorite beverage during his college days. Super fortified with alcohol. Same low price. He yanked the pull tab and returned to Fortunato.

"We went in different directions a while back," he said.

Phil's wife brought over a tray of piled hockey-puck burgers alongside another pile of fat tomato slices. She wore a blue, front-slit dress that was way too formal for the crowd. "Sorry, store-bought tomatoes," she said with an affected southern drawl.

Phil gestured with the greasy spatula. "This is Rice Channon," he said. "The boy I told you about."

His wife had been unable to make last year's party. "Had to deal with lady problems," Phil had told him.

Sally pulled back theatrically. "He is no boy," she said, batting her eyes in an over-the-top manner while extending a soft white hand. "I'm Sally."

Rice shook her hand and nodded.

She turned around, kissed her husband on the cheek, and carried her burned beef to another gaggle of guests.

Rice looked around. He recognized a few officers, a couple councilmen, and the sanitation director.

"Where's the mayor?" he said.

Two hot dogs slid off the grill and fell onto the concrete patio. Phil cursed and kicked them against a low brick wall.

"He's over at the VFW, pressing the flesh and drinking free bloody marys," he said. "He likes hanging out with the older vets. And he likes the free drinks. The cheap bastard."

"Is that on the record?"

Phil laughed and didn't even pretend to take Rice seriously. "You decide," he said. "But I can tell you this. It's not news to anybody who knows the guy. Am I right?"

They touched beer cans, and Rice tried to choke down the rest of his dry hamburger.

The safety service director was appointed by the mayor, usually for political or other favors. Phil had run the mayor's first successful campaign and, by anyone's standards, did a good job as the city's second-highest official.

The two leaders communicated every day, but they didn't like each other and everybody knew it.

City councilmen trying to take advantage of this enmity by driving a wedge between Phil Fortunato and the mayor, however, usually ended up bloody and apologetic.

Phil's assistant, Earl Sugarman, stumbled uncertainly in Rice's direction and pushed his face in a little too close.

"You got any ideas on the Eichel murder?" Earl said. He was already slurring his words and trying to speak *sotto voce*. But he was drunk, so everyone standing nearby heard him.

"Mooshies," sang out Sally Fortunato. She held up a tray carrying square slabs of meat topped with tomato slices, cheese and something round, skewered with a toothpick. Rice couldn't tell if it was an olive, a pickle, or maybe a rolled-up piece of bacon.

She made an elaborate gesture of stopping in front of him so he could choose one. He bobbed a thank-you and smiled. The *mooshie* meat had no flavor but it was mercifully moist. The tomatoes were good. He tossed the raw bacon into the trash.

"No," he said to Sugarman. "I'm going to talk with Markle next week."

"He won't tell you anything."

"I know that," Rice said. "But after he tells me nothing, I can approach the guys who *will* talk."

"I'm not talking to you either," Earl said.

"You don't know anything," Rice said. "So you don't have to worry."

He smiled when he said this, but Earl didn't seem to care one way or the other.

Rice ate some pretty good mustard potato salad, flirted unsuccessfully with a girl who was probably still in college, and started drinking another Colt 45, a little slower this time.

His head was buzzy from the malt liquor as he started considering excuses for departing early. Then Colonel Quincy Markle, in full uniform including eagles on his epaulets, walked into the party and scanned the crowd as though looking for someone. His expression was grim, and with the reflective sunglasses, he appeared almost robotic. When he spotted the safety service director, he headed over to him.

Phil grinned and pushed a hot dog into his hand. His expression sobered when Markle leaned over to whisper in his ear. Fortunato shook his head as he pretended to take new interest in the burned burgers on his grill. Then he put down his spatula and took a long swallow of his beer.

Markle stepped clear and stared off into a neighbor's yard, one arm behind his back, the other holding the uneaten hot dog. Rice approached.

"Happy Memorial Day, Colonel," he said.

The police chief turned toward him slowly, seemingly surprised the reporter was here. "Nothing happy about this holiday, Channon," he said. "It's a day to honor the good men who have died—who *are* dying—and not an excuse to guzzle piss that passes for beer."

"Is that why you're in full regalia?"

"I'm not a goddamn king," Markle said, not raising his voice at all. "I'm on active duty serving my country."

"I thought you were the head cop," Rice said.

"Don't say cop to me," Markle said, turning to face the reporter so Rice could see his reflection in both reflective sunglass lenses. "You don't know me well enough to call me a cop. I'm the chief of police."

"You said you were on active duty. When Phil's face dropped after you talked with him, I thought maybe you were going to join up and finally straighten out the mess in Vietnam."

"There was a ceremony downtown on the square," Markle said, turning away again. "I was there in uniform representing the city at a wreath laying. Hardly anybody showed up, of course. People don't give a damn about our soldiers being killed every day. Or for the ones who died in earlier wars."

"People are tired of Vietnam."

"And I'm tired of chasing down thieves, burglars, and murderers," Markle said. "But I keep at it. How'd you avoid the service?"

"High draft number," Rice said. "Have you chased down Eichel's murderer yet?"

Now Markle took off his sunglasses and actually smiled. "We'll get along better if you understand something, Channon," he said. "I don't dislike you personally. Don't really care about you one way or the other. But you stick your nose in too far, and that troubles me. You know a little bit and think you know a lot."

"I wouldn't be asking questions if I knew anything, Colonel."

Markle huffed a chuckle and put on his sunglasses again. "The Ratcatcher," he said, shaking his head and smiling. He took a bite of his hot dog, then reached out with it. Rice thought he was going to toss it in the trash can behind him.

He was wrong.

Colonel Markle grunted as he pushed it hard through Rice's teeth and into his mouth. Mustard and hot dog juices dribbled down the reporter's chin.

The chief of police executed a sharp about-face, then walked past the overturned tricycles and the other guests, and returned to his car.

# { 4 }

When he leaned his hand against his head—fat face on a skinny neck, white teeth, open grin—Arnie Corso looked exactly like the father in the television commercial peddling Life cereal.

Arnie was neat and clean. He had a fondness for collared checked shirts. He always wore pressed trousers instead of jeans, and shoes and socks instead of the more hip sandals. His fellow students wore wide muttonchop sideburns and shoulder-length hair. Arnie's haircut looked like something from an FBI recruitment poster.

Rice watched him from his open apartment door. Arnie was studying an array of pale-yellow objects on a large cutting board and mumbling to himself.

"Anybody here?" Rice said.

Arnie turned to him and frowned. "There's always somebody here," he said. "Close the door, will ya?"

He was cutting the yellow ribbons—they looked like fat, twisted wood shavings—into thin strips and then dicing them.

"What's this about?"

"What's it look like?" Arnie said, never taking his eyes from his work, a little sweat on his brow. "I'm getting these dried banana skins ready for smoking."

"The recipe you found in *The Anarchist Cookbook*?"

"Yup. Uh-huh."

"It's a hoax, Arnie," Rice said.

"I don't think so."

"If you hadn't quit the dish-washing job at Rizzo's, you could buy some good, honest weed and save yourself a lot of wasted work."

"I got tired of getting up at six every morning," Arnie said. "I fell asleep in psych. I'll make my own shit."

"Anybody here?"

"I told you, yes," Arnie said, his hand shaking a little as he did the fine work of cutting the dried-out banana skins.

"What do you do next?"

"I'll soak it all in lighter fluid for a couple of days. Then alcohol for another two," Arnie said. "I'll dry the mush out and smoke it in my pipe."

"And it really works?"

"That's what everybody tells me."

"So who's here right now?" Rice said, looking around, knowing he would see nothing.

Arnie sighed heavily, dropped his knife, and turned to face him. "My guardian angel, spirit guide, a few others I don't know. There were more but they left when you showed up."

"Not very neighborly," Rice said, taking a seat across from him.

"About five went out, and a bunch more came in with you," Arnie said. "It evens out."

"Did you hear about Annike Eichel's murder?"

"That hot atheist? She's dead?"

"Don't you read the papers? It was even on television."

"I had to sell my television."

Rice ran a hand through his hair and looked around the room. No dirty dishes in the sink. An unopened can of Campbell's Soup next to the stove.

"I don't know how you live," Rice said. "Do you need some money?"

"Can you spot me a twenty?"

"Here's ten," Rice said, folding and holding it toward him with two fingers. "And I want it back."

"Pop's sending me money at the end of the week," Arnie said, putting the bill in his front shirt pocket. "It doesn't feel right spending it on weed. That's why the bananas."

"I'm seeing her," Rice said.

Arnie raised his eyebrows and looked over Rice's head. "The dead atheist? She's not here now," he said. "You sure you're seeing her?"

"I'm never sure," he said.

"The mind can do strange things, man," Arnie said. "It could all be in your head. That's really more likely."

"I guess you want to be the only guy in your spook-seeing club."

"You don't want to be in my club," Arnie said. He returned to the meticulous cutting work. "She talk to you?"

"Not so far," Rice said.

"Probably a vision then."

"You think I'm hallucinating? If that's the case, you must be *seriously* zappy."

"The simplest explanation is usually right," Arnie said, grinning with the really white teeth. He used the knife edge to slide the diced-up banana skins into a corner of the cutting board.

"Let's pretend we're both normal and just have this … gift," Rice said.

"Yeah. Merry Christmas."

"So what do I say to her?"

Arnie got up and pulled open a kitchen drawer, fumbled around inside for a while, and finally pulled out a Zippo lighter fluid can. "Excuse me," he said to nobody but, presumably, one of the spirits populating his kitchen. He grabbed a cereal bowl and returned to the table. Then he started squirting lighter fluid into the bowl. "I guess that depends what you want. Do you want to help her or do you want to find her killer?"

"Can't I do both things?"

Arnie's smile widened and he shook his head. The Zippo can sucked air noisily as he squeezed another long stream. "You gotta have priorities, Rice," he said.

"Okay, I want to learn who killed her."

"Do you think that's more important than showing her how to escape from this dimension?"

"I can't help her with that," Rice said.

Arnie tipped the chopped-up banana peel into the lighter fluid without losing a crumb. "Don't go lighting any cigars here," he said, looking up abruptly.

"What are you doing?"

"I'm making a nonpolar-polar extraction of the banandine," Arnie said, stirring the mush with his finger.

"Oh, yeah. I can see that now."

"A couple days steeping in this stuff, and we can go to the next step."

"You're such a smart guy," Rice said. "It doesn't seem fair that you haven't been able to get out of junior college in four years."

"I keep changing my major," Arnie said, carefully placing the bowl on a shelf and laying a saucer on top. "Did you ever meet her when she was alive? Annike Eichel, I mean."

"I once went to a speech she gave at the Unity Church across town," Rice said. "When she wasn't ranting, she was funny and self-deprecating. Had to run a gauntlet of Holy Rollers just to get into the church hall. Lot of folks don't like her."

"Wasn't she in *Time* magazine?"

"Yeah," Rice said. "They did a piece on free love. She mostly talked about that in the article. Not so much about religion."

"So you really never had much to do with her, and yet after she's murdered, she knocks on your door," Arnie said after sitting down and interlacing his fingers behind his head. "Why you, I wonder?"

"Do you have a personal history with all the spooks in your house?" Rice said.

"No. But they think I can help them."

"Are you saying she looked me up because she thinks I'll help her?"

Arnie shrugged. "You've done it before," he said.

"Why do dead people care who killed them?"

"Don't ask me," Arnie said. "I've been in junior college for four years. I'm just a dumbass, Mickey." He said the last sentence with the voice of the cartoon character, Goofy, complete with guffaws.

"Maybe you should stop sniffing lighter fluid."

"I don't sniff it," Arnie said, unoffended. "Talked with Stacey lately?"

"We talk every once in a while."

"I saw her new boyfriend at the bank last week. He takes long steps when he walks. It's like he doesn't want to wear out his expensive wingtip shoes."

"You go to the bank?"

"Pop sends me checks. I keep a little cash in a savings account so they think I'm stable."

"So should I ask Annike Eichel who killed her?" Rice said.

"I don't know," Arnie said. "There's no manual for this shit. Some ghosts like to communicate. Some just like the company."

"That's not helpful," Rice said.

Arnie shrugged again. "Some aren't really there at all, of course. You could be talking to your subconscious."

"Yeah, he's probably lonely."

"I gotta pack of cheese crackers," Arnie said. "Wanna split 'em with me?"

"They're all yours," Rice said, getting up and heading for the door. "And don't forget that ten you owe me."

# { 5 }

When he was investigating a crime, especially a probable capital crime, Detective Edwyn Kadish's palms itched and rashes bloomed on the back of his neck.

He paced in front of his desk while Rice Channon read the narrative of the Eichel homicide. The other pages of the fat file lay scattered across Kadish's desk like a jigsaw puzzle where none of the pieces fit together.

The first time Rice assisted in a murder investigation, no one had paid much attention. But Kadish recognized that, in a department with only one investigating detective, Rice could be a useful if unofficial assistant.

He ended up being far more. Using his access to the *Goodwater Tribune*'s morgue of past newspaper stories, his doggedness—and not being a cop—Kadish had been able to arrest a small-time drug dealer who had unloaded a twelve gauge into the belly of a liquor store owner.

Rice picked up the report and looked at Kadish. "I've got a question for you," the reporter said and then started reading off the narrative. "The body of a woman was found lying against a cupboard on the kitchen floor surrounded by a brownish-red liquid."

Kadish scratched his right palm with his left hand and waited. "Yeah? What?"

"Why do you see brownish-red liquid?" Rice said. "Why not just say blood? Was she leaking transmission fluid?"

"Maybe she was," Kadish said. "That's up to the lab guys to decide. I just say what I see."

"Yeah, but you went into some detail about the"—Rice turned back to the narrative—"apparent stab wounds inflicted by a large edged weapon to the deceased's abdomen and vaginal area."

"The coroner got there fast," Kadish said, stopping his pacing and pointing at the narrative. "I'm just quoting him. He also said she probably died of multiple stab wounds."

"But you couldn't make that leap?"

"It's not my job," Kadish said. "Or the coroner's for that matter. He said it *appears* she died of multiple stab wounds. Maybe she was poisoned first. Or she was drowned and brought back to her house."

"So the stabbings might have been meant to cover up something else?"

"I didn't say that," Kadish said, scratching his neck and looking frustrated, like he wished he could stop. "It's just that we can't make any assumptions."

"But unofficially ..."

"Unofficially, somebody stabbed this woman to death with a butcher knife and jammed it up her cooch repeatedly for good measure. I don't know if this was premeditated," Kadish said. "But it sure looks like a crime of passion."

"Any indication of sexual activity?"

"Besides the knife?"

"Come on, Ed."

"I don't know," Kadish said. "We'll have to wait for the autopsy report. No fingerprints, though. No footprints either. And, of course, no knife."

"You said in the narrative that many books on her bookshelves were pulled down. Was the killer looking for something?"

"We don't even know if the killer did it," Kadish said. "Maybe she was doing spring cleaning."

"Do you *think* he was looking for something?"

"Maybe. It's possible the killer didn't like her choice of reading material."

"You know what I think?"

"Tell me."

"I think somebody wants it to *look* like he's making a statement about her religious views," Rice said. "It's kind of ham-fisted is all I'm saying."

"You can jump to conclusions like that. I need proof."

Rice grinned at him. "You got that weird splotch on your neck," he said.

Kadish reddened. "You going to help me or not?" he said, dropping his voice.

"How does Markle feel about me assisting? He's kind of a dick," Rice said.

"That's *Colonel* Dick to you," Kadish said. "He'll leave us alone. He pretends he doesn't know."

"Real professional," Rice said. "Same deal as usual. I get the exclusive on the arrest and ridealongs on promising leads."

"Goddammit, Rice, I can't promise that."

"I can't promise I'll help then," the reporter said, flipping absently through the paperwork. "I got a boss too, you know. He doesn't like me playing cop. I might convince him otherwise if there's a big story or an exclusive in the future."

"Now who's the dick?"

"I want to help you, Ed. I'll even do legwork on my days off. I want to catch this guy too."

"Yeah," Kadish said. "I'm already feeling the pressure. Mayor stopped by. He wants to know if there's anything he can do."

"Should've told him to get off your ass."

"It crossed my mind, believe me."

"What would you like me to do?" Rice said.

"You're the man with the gift," Kadish said, dropping hard into his chair. "Let me worry about the forensics. You sniff around your low-life friends and see if you can come up with anything. Might help."

"The public is going to figure this is some kind of holy reprisal for Eichel's godless views."

"You think I haven't heard that yet?" Kadish said. "So all we need to do is find some God-fearing murderer with a bloody butcher knife."

"Somebody's gotta know something."

"Somebody *always* knows something," the detective said. "The trick is finding that person and getting the sumbitch to talk. If you can help with that, go for it."

Rice nodded and closed his notebook. Kadish raised a warning finger.

"But don't go off thinking you're Efram Zimbalist, Jr. and can solve this murder on your own. You check in with me every day," he said. "Or every other day, anyway. I appreciate your help, but I can't have you going vigilante on me. Understand?"

Rice nodded.

"Sure would like to solve this one on my own," Kadish said. "The colonel thinks you're just lucky."

"Markle said that?"

"Yeah, and a lot more," Kadish said. He chuckled. "Heard about him hand-feeding you lunch at Fortunato's party."

"I guess he doesn't appreciate my gift. Where were you, by the way?"

"You're shittin' me, right? I'll be working holidays and Saturdays until this case is solved." Kadish pushed some of the papers around on his desk, and a smile slowly floated across his face. “Did you have to eat a mooshie?”

“Sounds dirty when you say it.”

“Like chewing on a quarter-inch block of sandpaper. I hate those fucking things. Did she at least cook the bacon this year?”

“Nah. The bacon was raw,” Rice said, getting up to leave.

“You should have fed it to the chief.”

“Yeah,” Rice said. “Good one.”

# { 6 }

The photo of Domenico Sartor, infamous Goodwater bootlegger, hung crooked under a struggling fluorescent, an ancient drip of grenadine staining the picture.

Sartor loved reporters, which is why he'd often stopped in at the Tribune Grill during his heyday in the twenties. The press loved him too. After Prohibition was repealed, he bought everybody drinks, talked freely, and only occasionally unleashed venom-filled rants against the law.

The visits stopped when Domenico was found one morning in the back alley with multiple 45-caliber bullet holes in his double-breasted fur coat, a cigar still clenched in his teeth.

These days at the Tribune Grill, reporters were the only steady customers. Sometimes they stopped in for lunch after deadline and stayed until closing, drinking hard and wincing when someone opened the door to let the outside light in.

Stacey Lattermore walked in wearing a red skirt, bright yellow top and a multicolored sash tied loosely around her waist. She looked like she was in a hurry, but when she plopped onto the bench seat across from Rice, her big eyes were wide, as though waiting for him to say something clever.

Even in the dim light, he saw the glow of affection in her face. He saw the acceptance of their distance. She blew her nose and shook her head at the same time.

"I worry about you," she said. "I don't want to."

"I'm sorry," he said. "Is that why you wanted to meet me here?"

She looked at him, shook her head. Her eyes were red.

"I'm fine," he said. "Billard said I had to make a decision about taking the city hall job today."

"What'd you tell him?"

"I said I want to stay where I am."

"I see." Stacey looked off, knowing she could no longer press him on taking the more prestigious, higher-paying city hall job. Now that they were no longer a couple.

Rice started to slide out of the bench seat. "Is that it then?" he said.

"Sit down, please, Sweet."

She used to call him Sweet. Back then. Now she looked embarrassed for accidentally saying the word.

"This is Father Pete Growden," she said. "He's a friend."

The priest, a short man with the body of a wrestler and an easy handshake, seemed to appear out of the dark. Rice didn't know if he'd just come from the restroom or had been hiding in a booth nearby. He carried the weary frown lines of a man used to offering sympathy and consolation.

Rice turned to Stacey, her eyes wider than ever. Father Growden drummed his fingers, smiling, waiting.

"Stacey thought we should talk," the priest said. "She thinks I can help you."

"Oh?"

"Are you a Catholic, Rice?"

"I'm a nothing," Rice said. "And I'm not hurting."

Growden held the weary smile. "First, recognize that people close to you are worried. And even if you don't agree with them, respect their concern."

"Okay," Rice said, leaning forward, arms on the table. It was an aggressive gesture but it made him feel better. "I just remembered who you are."

Nothing from Father Growden.

"You and Annike Eichel put on a good-cop-bad-cop show about faith and belief last year at the Unity Church," Rice said.

"Which cop was I?"

"Can't remember," Rice said.

"So you are at least interested in matters of faith?"

"I was interested that night," Rice said. "My editor needed someone to cover it at the last minute, and I was the only one in the newsroom. So I got tagged."

"What did you think?"

"I thought the lady was beautiful," Rice said, looking over at Stacey. "I asked her to join me for a strawberry sundae at Isaly's."

"What did you think about what she said?"

"I can't remember that either," Rice said. "I did go to Isaly's. I ate alone, though."

"I understand you spend time with her now," Father Growden said, arching one eyebrow, "or think you do."

Rice shot a glance at Stacey who held his gaze unashamedly.

"The Lord does not want us to speak with spirits, to dabble in the occult," Growden said, his smile just a shadow now. "This is not a Catholic belief. It's God's law."

"Fine with me," Rice said, pulling his eyes away from Stacey's gaze.

"And yet you continue to …"

"Dabble?" Rice said.

"It's dangerous," Growden said.

"Ghosts are mentioned in the Bible, aren't they?"

"Are you a student of the Bible?"

"I've flipped through it," Rice said.

"The church fathers—Saint Augustine, particularly—rejected the idea that the soul could return."

Rice heard a guy at the far end of the bar slurping at his empty glass.

"I don't know what Stacey told you," Rice said. "And I don't know *why* she told you. But I bristle when people direct me to think what they think."

The grin was back in full. Sad. Knowing. "Tell me this," the priest said. "Have you seen ghosts all your life?"

He said the word *ghosts* like he was trying to cough up a gnat from the back of his throat.

"I never saw spirits at all," Rice said. "Until I lost my virginity."

Stacey ignored him and squinted at the far wall, as if suddenly interested in reading the sign posted there. But the priest didn't look at her.

"It's true I see people—men, usually—who were killed in violent circumstances. Soldiers. Murder victims," Rice said.

"How do they look to you?" Father Growden said, reaching across the table but not quite touching him.

"Surprised, at least at first," Rice said. "Then sad. Confused."

"Do you ever think these visions could be in your head?"

"Sure, I think about that a lot, as a matter of fact," Rice said. The man at the bar spun around on his stool and considered the three of them, a slight grin starting to grow. It annoyed Rice. "Excuse me a minute."

He slid out of the booth and walked to the slurping man at the bar. "Why are you looking at me?" he said.

The guy was slim with even features and long hair that fell almost to his shoulders. "You're Rice Channon," the man said. He had great teeth. "I've read some of your stuff. Spare.

Short, powerful sentences. Very Hemingway. I'll bet your editors love you."

"Not at all."

He thrust out his hand, smirking. "I'm Tom Janousek with the *Cleveland Chronicle*."

"And yet, here you are in Goodwater."

"I'm doing a piece on the Eichel murder," Janousek said. "I figured we'd run across each other sooner or later. So I thought I'd look you up."

Janousek had recently returned from Vietnam where he'd written a series of articles about incidents of cruelty and torture reportedly inflicted by US soldiers. The stories had already gained national attention. There was talk of a Pulitzer. He had an almost mythical stature in the journalism community, even though he was only a few years older than Rice.

The bartender—a new guy, Rice didn't know him—strolled over, white towel slung over his shoulder. "I got five people in the bar and so far all anybody's ordered is a bottle of pop," he said.

"Bring us a couple coffees," Rice said. He couldn't recall if Stacey took it black. The priest could get his own. "I'll see you around."

When he returned to the booth, Father Growden was gone.

Stacey looked unhappy. "I got you a coffee," Rice said. "I couldn't remember if you took cream and sugar."

"Father said you aren't going to change and I was wasting my time to try," she said.

Rice frowned. “He gave up awful fast. Makes me think he doesn’t like me.”

“And I don’t drink coffee. I like tea.”

“I forgot,” he said. “It’s been a while.”

“You could have been nicer to him,” she said, her look harder now.

“You bushwhacked me. Both of you,” he said. “I wasn’t comfortable.”

She shrugged as though it didn’t matter anymore. “He was a chaplain at Mosopelea’s Newman Club when we both went there. That’s how I met him.”

Rice shook his head. “I’ve never been much of a joiner,” he said.

“It’s not that kind of club,” she said. “It’s a place for Catholics on a secular campus.”

“Didn’t even know you went to church,” Rice said. The bartender dropped off the two coffees, and Stacey pushed hers away.

“I’ve started attending Mass again. Trying to get my life in order.”

“First Roger, then church. You’re not going to stop drinking too, are you?” Rice began toying with his cup.

“This business about seeing ghosts frightens me. It always has,” she said. “But Father Growden says you don’t care. Not yet.”

“So that’s why he didn’t say goodbye?”

"He was going to help you if you were open to it," Stacey said, tapping a nail on the edge of the coffee saucer. "You weren't. So he left."

They hadn't noticed Janousek's approach. He slid in next to Stacey, smiled at her, and pulled her cup over. "I don't think she wants the coffee," he said. He smelled of English Leather aftershave.

Stacey shot Rice the wide-eyed expectant look.

"Join us," Rice said.

Janousek drew back his lips briefly after sipping the hot coffee.

"I know the look of true love," he said. "It's like the look of lust, but with the edges filed off."

"That's beautiful," Rice said.

Janousek brushed at the lapel of his tan sport coat. "So when's the wedding?" he said.

"You saw the priest," Rice said. "So you decided we were discussing arrangements for a wedding. Here. In a bar."

Janousek smiled, took another sip.

"I asked him here to talk to me about Annike Eichel," Rice said. "The two of them used to appear on panels discussing faith and religion."

"I don't care that you're trying to bullshit me," Janousek said, staring into his coffee. "But it annoys me that you think I'm stupid."

"Didn't mean to step on your feelings."

"You weren't taking any notes," Janousek said. "And here you are with this pretty woman. You have some kind of relationship."

"Will I see it mentioned in the *Chronicle* like the other stuff you make up?"

Janousek finished the coffee—still steaming—with one long pull. The vinyl squealed a little as he slid off the bench. Then he stood up, hands on hips, surveying the bar like he was Alexander the Great and this was Persia. He took a deep breath and slapped his sides.

He offered a toothy smile to Stacey. "Off to see the mayor," he said.

# { 7 }

"I wanted to tap that white piece of tail first time I saw her," Star Lightman said, sucking on a twig, wincing like it hurt him a little.

His name wasn't really Star. It was a street name. Nobody knew his real name. He had a gold star inlaid into his right incisor. His last name probably wasn't Lightman either. Two of his whores stood behind him looking like they cared about nothing.

"How'd that work out?" Rice asked.

"Shee-it," Star said.

Annike's diaphanous form floated behind but at the same level as the two hookers.

On the way over, she had sat in the passenger's seat of Rice's Fiat wearing a dull expression but radiating anxiety.

Like someone late for an appointment. A drunk on his way to a drink.

"Who killed you, Annike?" he had asked her. She turned slowly to look at him, as though surprised he recognized her at all. When her mouth opened, it was all blackness inside.

"Did you ever meet her?" Rice asked.

The pimp rubbed his chin and feigned little-boy shame. "Once I went to one of her meetings," he said. "Remember that ruckus when her God-haters met at the library?"

Last year, in a heavily publicized gesture aimed at proving her organization—Right Thinkers for a New America (RITNA)—enjoyed the same rights as any other civic group, she demanded access to the public meeting room at the library. Her RITNA group held one meeting there before the library board ruled that hers was a political and not a civic organization.

"Yeah," Rice said. "I remember. Lots of smoke. No fire."

Star shook his head angrily. "No," he said. "Nobody was smokin' nothin'. There was almost nobody there."

"Yeah," Rice said, rubbing the back of his head. "That's what I meant. So did you meet her or not?"

"I stood in the back," Star said. "Although there were lots of empty seats. Figured I might scare these good white folks with their ponytails and their serious faces and shit."

"Were you wearing that?" Rice asked, pointing at Star's wide-brimmed Panama hat, open-necked scarlet shirt with faux gold chains and medallions swinging over his hairless chest.

"I dressed nice," Star said, pulling on the wide shirt lapels to make his point. "And I was quiet. Stood by the coffee table figuring I'd meet that fine piece of white flesh during the break."

"So did you?"

Star made a sad face and sighed heavily. "I might have been a little nervous," he said. "Being around smart white folks does that. I got close to her when she reached for one of those little butter cookies and my arm brushed hers. She felt good, but I was wet and she moved away fast. Didn't even look at me."

"You were sweating."

"That's what I said. Didn't take any cookies. Didn't have any coffee. I didn't want her to think I was there for the free treats, you know?"

"Sure."

"Some of the others, including a big guy who looked like a Marine, kind of blocked me from the treats," Star said. "Like I didn't belong."

"Not very welcoming."

"Hey, I don't mind. This wasn't my scene. I knew it. They knew it. They were just protecting their shit. You gotta protect your shit," Star said. "Am I right?"

He reached back and squeezed the left tit of one of his hookers. She gave a halfhearted slap at his hand and he laughed at her. Annike's eyes remained empty.

"So you brushed your sweaty arm against Annike Eichel, but you never ate her cookies."

The whore whose tit had not been squeezed leaned over and whispered in Star's ear. He shook his head and waved a finger in space.

"Deena thinks you're funny and wants to give you a free one," Star said. "You want a free one?"

"No, thank you."

"Good, 'cause you're not that funny."

"Did you ever see her again?" Rice asked.

"I watched her house for a while," Star said. "I loved the way that woman walked. She waved her ass like she was a flag and it was the Fourth of July."

"What did you see?"

"Just watchin' her walk ..." Star said, lifting his head, remembering. A dramatic sparkle reflected off the gold star in his tooth. The smile was back.

"When she wasn't walking, what did you see?"

Star thought about this a while. "Why should I tell you?"

"We're friends," Rice said. "Aren't we?"

"We ain't friends. You have a little juice with the pigs. You helped me out last year. That's it. That's what we got."

"I told you about the sweep along Toledo Avenue," Rice said. "I didn't have to do that. I kept you out of the slammer. Gave you a monopoly on the action downtown for a few days. I probably broke the law in the process."

Rice pulled out his pack of Hav-A-Tampas and popped out a cigar.

"What's that?" Star said. "Give me one."

Rice tapped out another cigar and gave it to Star. Without dropping his gaze from Rice, he handed it over his shoulder to Deena, the generous hooker. She unwrapped it, tossed the refuse in the street, and handed it back. She had carefully maintained fingernails, just long enough to begin curving down at the tips.

Rice held out a lighter, and Star inhaled in short puffs to get it going. "Shee-it," Star said. "It's got a wooden nipple."

He turned his head so quickly the Panama hat didn't have a chance to follow and remained facing forward. Star held out the wooden cigar tip to Deena.

"See?" he said. "This is what your tit's going to look like if you let that sick bastard, Tommy Frankson, suck on your blinkers a half hour at a time."

"He's a nice man," Deena said, pretending to be hurt. "A real gentleman."

"He wears a diaper."

Deena shrugged. "Always pays first and tips me good later," she said.

"Don't you be tellin' me that," Star said. "You get any extra, you pat the kitty. You know that."

Deena turned away and Star puffed at the cigar uncertainly.

"Have you seen anything that looked suspicious?" Rice said, trying to get the vision of local dirtbag Tommy Frankson nursing at Deena's breast out of his mind.

"Suspicious? Now you sound like a goddamn cop."

"People hanging around who look like they don't belong."

Star tilted his head back and took a long, slow draw. The whore standing next to Deena looked impatient.

"I saw something funny," Star said after a bit. "Don't know if I'd call it *sus-pi-shush*. Just odd."

Annike seemed fascinated by the rising smoke clouds. "Yeah," Rice said, finally getting impatient himself. "What?"

"You know that big church over by the college?" Star said.

"Faith Bible Church?"

"Yeah, yeah, that's it," Star said. "They have this big motherfucking van I guess they use to haul old biddies to church and—I don't know—prayer trips."

"Prayer trips?" Rice said, wondering but not pushing it. "I haven't seen it, but I know the kind of van you're talking about. It can carry about twenty people or so."

"Yeah," Star said. "I saw it over here."

"So what?" Rice said. "Some people around here go to church, I'm guessing."

"I imagine," Star said, rubbing his chin again, enjoying the theatrics. "I never met them, I can tell you that."

"Except as customers."

"Clients," Star said, correcting him quickly. "But nobody in the house of that woman is going to church in that big van. Yet it was parked under the oak tree across the street for an hour or so at a time. And more than once."

"Anybody in it?"

"No," Star said. "It drove itself here."

"Did you *see* anyone inside?"

"Not sure," Star said. "Looked like a man. Couldn't be positive."

"Maybe the driver enjoys watching her walk. Like you. "

"Maybe."

"Ever thought he wanted to do business?"

"Well, sure," Star said. "But when I slid over there, he drove off. Twice."

"Interesting."

"So do I get another cigar?"

"I only got the one left," Rice said. "But if I hear anything about another sweep on Toledo Street, I might let you know."

"The cops have been pushier than ever lately," Star said. "Must be the hot weather moving in."

He withdrew the cigar from his mouth and admired it in the dim light. "It doesn't taste completely like shit," he said.

Annike Eichel's spirit watched the pale smoke rise, and Rice imagined a smile on her face, as if she felt comfortable here.

# { 8 }

A short county worker wearing a gray shirt and blue dungarees washed the blood and brains of Ike "Sticky" Samuelson from the east sidewalk of the county courthouse in Goodwater's downtown square. The worker directed a water stream at the greasy gore and washed it all into the tulip bed.

Bleating blue jays hushed up and watched from an overhead power line, only moving to chase away the occasional Carolina wren.

Ike had been escorted into Courtroom Two to face justice after being arrested once again for burglary and larceny. The escorting officer—an overweight, overaged sheriff's deputy—was probably half-asleep or not paying attention when *Sticky* pulled away and dove through the second-floor window leading into the courtroom.

He had probably figured he'd fall into the grass or the boxwoods just one floor below, and make his escape. Even with the cuffs on, he might have pulled it off if his aim had been better.

Instead, he hit the sidewalk with the crown of his head, and according to the groundskeeper now flushing the man's brains into the flower bed, his head popped open like a ripe watermelon. So *Sticky*—the unimaginative moniker coming from his predilection for grabbing anything not his and not nailed down—would no longer be rifling empty homes for cash and silverware.

Rice had been on his way to work when he heard about the courthouse incident on the radio.

"He looked small, but he was a strong little bastard," the sweaty deputy explained to Rice. "And slippery."

Rice nodded, not caring much. He'd write a couple grafs, and as much as he'd love to use the "ripe watermelon" comment, it would never make it past the copydesk, even if Billard let it go through.

The *Tribune* was "a family newspaper." He'd heard it more than once.

He could include the escort's name, but it would only embarrass the old man and piss off the law enforcement folks he worked with every day. Rice did it when he had to, but he always weighed the value of such a disclosure against the kickback from the sheriff's department.

"How long 'til retirement?" he asked the deputy.

"Two months," the deputy said, eyes wide, still shaken. "Wife and I are going to head south. Go camping. See New Orleans."

An old guy in a porkpie hat was tossing peanuts on the ground so the blue jays flew off to squawk and beg. Even they weren't interested in Ike's demise any longer.

The reason Rice had wandered over—in addition to getting out of the newsroom—was because he knew Ike Samuelson. They used to play shooter together when Rice was still in college and thought he could pick up easy change off the downtown street gamblers.

Ike and some of the other street hustlers disabused him of this naive notion pretty quickly. That's how he'd made Ike's acquaintance. And Star's. And more than a few others. The contacts became useful later when he worked the police beat.

Rice watched Ike's spirit float back and forth over the sodden tulip bed like he was looking for something. Once when the gardener waved his hose around, a little rainbow shimmered through the spectral body. Rice caught Ike's eye but there was no recognition in the dead man's gaze.

Finally, Ike "Sticky" Samuelson shuffled off slowly in the direction of the new coffee shop on the square and disappeared, and Rice knew he'd never see him again.

After nine, he stopped by the squad room at the Goodwater PD. Nobody was there but Detective Ed Kadish, and that was fine with Rice.

"Checkin' in with my parole officer," Rice said, despite knowing it was too early in the morning for cute.

Kadish scratched his neck. His eyes were puffy and he looked awful. "I wish I *was* your parole officer," he said. "I'd toss you in the sneezer first time you were late."

Rice shrugged. "I didn't stop in because I had nothing to tell you."

"Then tell me that. That was our deal. You touch base every day."

"You said I could check in every other day," Rice said. "By the way, you look like crap."

"I saw Phil Fortunato this morning," Kadish said. "Don't need you telling me what I already heard from him."

"Faith Bible Church," Rice said. "What do you know about it?"

Kadish's eyes were blurry, almost rheumy. "I don't know. They got faith. They read the Bible."

"They didn't like Annike Eichel very much," Rice said. "The pastor told the congregation it was no accident that the Lord dropped her in their backyard. He expected them to deal with her."

"Deal with her? Were those his exact words? You hear this firsthand?"

"I don't know the exact words. I wasn't there," Rice said. "A guy in my building attends the church with his wife. I talked to him last night while we took turns using the clothes dryer in the basement. He said the pastor made everybody think it was their job to silence Eichel."

"That's pretty thin," Kadish said, leaning over to open a desk drawer. "Secondhand information. Vague threat. It could mean anything. Maybe it didn't even happen. Perhaps your friend thought you'd put his name in the paper."

"He's not a friend. He's just a guy. I don't think he wants that kind of publicity."

"Oh, yeah. You don't have any friends," Kadish said, smiling for the first time. "Anyway, people are the shits. I had a man tell me last year he robbed First Northern downtown. Found out later he just wanted to impress his gal who thought he was unexciting."

"There's something else," Rice said. "The church van was spotted in front of Eichel's place on more than one occasion. Not too long before she was murdered."

Kadish cocked his head. "Do tell," he said. "The driver jump out and plant a flaming shit bag on her porch?"

"Nope. Just watched, apparently."

"What time?"

"Night," Rice said. "And the driver didn't want anyone knowing about it. He took off if the van was approached."

"Didn't want anyone knowing about it," Kadish repeated. "But he's driving a van with the church's name on it?"

"Yeah."

"You figure he's making some kind of statement?" Kadish said.

"I don't know," Rice said. "But you put the two things together and it's suspicious, don't you think?"

"It's odd."

Colonel Markle walked into the squad room, eagles on his collar, buzz cut on his head. His eyes scanned Rice briefly, but no closer than if he had been an old cup of coffee starting to grow mold. He narrowed his eyes when he looked at Kadish.

"You look like hell," Markle said. "Your puppy run away again?"

"I got allergies, Chief."

"Oh, yeah," he said. Markle looked at Rice and his lip actually curled. "What's he doing here?"

"I'm the police reporter for the *Tribune*," Rice said, standing up, reaching his hand out. "Have we met?"

"I'm not talking to you, Channon," he said. "Sit down."

"I'm looking for leads on the Eichel killing," Kadish said. "Sometimes Rice hears things. I'm desperate, Chief."

"Uh-huh," Markle said. "Well, I don't want him working with you on this case, and I don't want him in my squad room. The place stinks bad enough."

Colonel Markle grinned wide enough to show teeth. Rice laughed out loud, like the chief was Red Skelton.

"It's the First Amendment, Colonel. I'm allowed to talk to people and then write about it," Rice said. "I keep a copy in my desk if you want to read it."

Markle squatted down in front of Rice. He looked around as if searching for another hot dog to feed him. Then he went nose-to-nose—the noses actually touching—and his tone was quiet.

"*My* first fucking amendment is no fucking reporters in my squad room," he said. "You want to talk with anyone on the force, you do it downstairs."

"But it's cold and musty down there," Rice said, trying to pretend he wasn't intimidated. "And Ed's got the allergy thing."

Markle stood up. Rice had expected worse. "Just leave," he said. "Before I lose my temper."

Rice stood up. "I think I'll be on my way now, Ed," he said. "I'm gonna stop in and chat with the safety-service director. I'm going to talk to him about getting you some more detectives."

Markle grinned wide again, and for the first time, Rice could see laugh lines around his eyes, like any normal person would have. "Yeah, go talk to Mr. Fortunato," Colonel Markle said. "That's a good idea."

The chief, laughing now, did an actual military about-face, and walked from the squad room. He stopped at the door and turned around again.

"Come down to my office and give me a report, Ed," Markle said. "The mayor wants to know why we haven't found the killer yet. And you're going to tell me."

Kadish pulled his papers together and looked even more frazzled than before. "Don't piss him off, Rice," he said. "He can do a lot worse than force-feed you a tube steak."

"I'll be careful."

Ed started shaking his head and chuckling as he put the papers under his arm and stood up. "Ed's got the allergy thing," he said. "Where do you come up with this shit?"

"I'm the guy with a gift, like you said."

Kadish leaned close to Rice and whispered to him after looking around again. “Autopsy report came in,” he said. “Annike Eichel was two months pregnant.”

# { 9 }

In 1964, when Rice had still been in high school, he bet two hundred dollars—every penny he owned—on Cassius Clay to beat the street thug Sonny Liston for the heavyweight boxing championship.

Nobody was betting on Clay. He was loud, boisterous, and rumored to have purchased a plane ticket out of the country before the fight.

So Rice got eight-to-one odds. He placed his bet through a part-time teller who worked at his father's bank. He figured it was unlikely an employee of his old man would stiff him if he won.

And he did win. The teller mumbled something about paying processing costs and made up some bullshit about state taxes, but he handed over fifteen hundred dollars and Rice decided to let it go.

His mother seemed to know what he'd done, but she just winked in that special way of hers, never telling his father. This was in spite of her desperate attachment to the man.

Over a glass of wine, she told Rice how it was. "If anything happened to you," she said. "I'd feel awful. But if something happened to your father, I'd be devastated."

Rice had nodded, respecting her honesty. He avoided women for a long time afterward, but continued betting. At first it was boxing. Then championship games. He just about broke even.

But, while his gambling days were largely behind him, Rice found his ability to read people and detect their *tells* had remained. Sometimes it wasn't very hard. Like when he stopped into the safety-service director's office.

"Hey, Rice," Phil Fortunato said as he pushed his chair back and stood up. "I've got a meeting with the sanitation folks right now, but stop by tomorrow and we'll talk."

Rice said nothing. Something was going on but he didn't know what. He found out quickly.

—

"You're covering city hall starting tomorrow," Billard said without looking up as Rice handed him the story on Ike Samuelson's swan dive from the courthouse. "Joyce is taking over your beat. Give him your files. Brief him. Then let him be."

Rice acted unsurprised. "So I guess with the pay bump, I can buy those new tires I need."

Billard wasn't laughing. He dropped his pencil loudly and looked up, his face dark with rare anger. "There is no pay raise. You're not getting a promotion. You're being fired and I've found another position for you."

"So I should just be grateful and shut up?"

Billard wore a tight smile. "That's good advice for you," he said. "Not just now, but always. And when you talk with the mayor tomorrow, don't ask him about the Eichel murder investigation. That's not your concern anymore."

"Are you going to tell me what this is about, or should I just ask the mayor?"

"You know what it's about."

Rice walked back to his desk, aware that most of the eyes in the newsroom followed him across the floor. He pulled out a half-dozen files regarding open cases, a laminated contact sheet with law enforcement phone numbers, and unplugged his scanner. He put it all in one pile and dropped it on Mitchell Joyce's desk.

"It sucks," Joyce said, shooting a furtive glance toward Billard. "I didn't ask for this."

"Yeah," Rice said. "Most of your job is grunt work. Do that part well and you'll be fine."

"But you're still handling the Eichel killing."

"No," Rice said. "You got that too. Stay away from Markle. Talk to Ed Kadish about progress on the investigation. But maybe you should stay out of the squad room for the time being."

A copy girl dropped a batch of files on his desk related to the city hall beat. He saw tabs with names of each councilman, a fat file on the bypass project being hotly debated, and another with clippings of the last twelve months' council meetings.

"I told you they'd put you on city hall," she said, sashaying away, her short skirt snapping at her thighs.

He shoved the stack to the far corner of his desk. The council meeting file slid off the top and dropped into the trash can. Rice debated whether to dig it out. Out of the corner of his eye, he could tell Billard was watching him.

Rice picked up the phone and dialed.

"It's me," he said.

Kadish sounded wearier than usual. "What?"

"I'm off the police beat, effective now."

"Yeah. Markle told me right after he bit off my ass."

"I figure *der führer* went to Fortunato."

"Why would you think that?"

"Couple of reasons," Rice said. "Fortunato seemed to be in a big hurry to get rid of me when I dropped in on him today. And, second, when he first saw me, he looked like a puppy I just got caught pooping on the new sofa."

"Why would your editors give a damn what Fortunato wanted?" Ed said. Rice could tell he was cupping the phone so no one in the squad room could hear.

"They've been wanting me to quit playing cop for a while now," Rice said. "Phil calls my boss—maybe the publisher, I don't know—and tells him I'm interfering with the investigation. Plus, Billard gets to make a statement by giving me a beat I don't want. Anyway, new job for me. Starting right now."

"Comes with a raise though, right?"

"I'm still poor. Billard made it clear that I'm lucky to have any job. He's pretty pissed, so no raise."

"That's not fair."

"Yeah," Rice said. "Usually, it's all truth, justice, and the American way here in the newsroom. Doesn't matter. I'm going to hit them up for a raise in a few weeks."

"And you say you don't care about money."

"I care a little," he said. "But this is about the principle."

"Ahh," he said. "The principle. Well, shit."

Rice smiled and hung up the phone. Then he reached into the trash can and withdrew the errant file. He waved it at Billard who shook his head and went back to his work.

After a stop in the newspaper morgue to read a folder on the Faith Bible Church, he left the building and headed for the parking lot.

# { 10 }

This was a funny thing about Star Lightman.

If coddled, pressed, praised, or threatened, he'd usually produce useful information. But if you came back twenty-four hours later after letting his brain percolate for a day, he'd invariably do better.

So on his way to Faith Bible Church, Rice stopped by the Call & Call Drugstore where Star often discussed business and perused the magazine book rack. Rice found him sitting outside on a bus stop bench reading a Superman comic.

Star didn't even look up when Rice approached. "Lois Lane," he said. "What I wouldn't give to wax that ass."

"You should take something for your hormones," Rice said.

"I really should," Star said, rolling up the comic and waving it like a classroom pointer. "You know what I hear works? Saltpeter. Salt. Peter. *Shee-it*, I love that word. It's supposed to make your dick sleep, and it's called saltpeter."

"Sure. You should try some of that stuff."

"You got any more cigars for me?" Star said.

"I gave you my last one."

"Then move along, white boy," Star said, unrolling Superman once again. "You're blocking my light."

"I wanted to ask you about Annike Eichel."

"Now that's interestin'," Star said, affecting a studious air. "I hear you're not even the cop reporter no more. So you must just be nosy."

"Who told you that?"

Star laughed. "You're not the only one with secrets. You've been fired, so bye-bye." He looked up quickly. "Unless you got cigars."

"Will you take an IOU?"

"Do you know how many johns have asked me that same question?"

"But I'll deliver," Rice said. "You know I will."

Star shrugged. "It's not much," he said. "But I remembered something after you left. The guy driving that big church bus wasn't the only person stalking that lady's pad. One of my black brothers—light shadow and looked like an ugly Harry Belafonte—paid late-evening visits and sometimes I didn't see him leave."

"He spent the night?"

"Or slipped out the back. I don't know," Star said. "But kind of unusual for a brother to be visiting the home of a pretty white lady with a reputation for trouble."

"I'll get you some cigars," Rice said.

Star nodded and shifted in his seat, like he was planning to stay awhile. "So why'd they fire you?"

"I wasn't fired," Rice said. "I just got promoted to covering city hall."

Star laughed and waved a long, skinny finger at him.

"I'm still investigating the Eichel murder."

Star tapped lightly on the gold star in his tooth, then studied his finger as though he expected to see gold flecks there. "I don't think so," he said. "But I'll forgive you for lying to me when you drop off a few stogies."

"You know, you could buy a pack if you like them so much," Rice said. "They don't cost much."

"I can't be seen going into a store and buying things," Star said. "Folks on the street might think I'm weak."

"What about the comic book?"

Star smiled wide, the gold star blazing mightily in his mouth. "Mr. Call and I have an understanding. If anybody's in the store, I just take what I want and pay him later."

"Like an IOU," Rice said.

"I guess."

"But they keep the tobacco products behind the counter."

"So now you see my problem," Star said. "Bring me a few of them *Have-a-Tampaxes,* and we'll be straight."

"I'm looking out for you," Rice said. "I still have friends on the force."

"So you say, so you say," Star mumbled, letting the words fall off as he picked up the story about Superman on the hunt for Lex Luthor.

—

The Faith Bible Church parking lot was empty except for the twenty-passenger church van and a pumpkin-colored Ford Pinto.

Rice pulled on the handle of the wooden doors to the church, but they were locked. Floor-to-ceiling red and green glass windows marked what appeared to be the church offices. When Rice cupped his hand to look, he saw no one inside although the lights were on.

Behind him he heard a noise that sounded like a balky old motor continuing to chug after it was shut off. Except this sound wasn't coming from the engine.

The church van was rocking left and right as if buffeted by a stormy wind.

Rice climbed up the step and opened the passenger-side door. On the long bench seat in the rear of the van, a man with his trousers around his knees held apart the legs of a young woman and pummeled her with hard, abrupt thrusts, grunting with each motion.

Rice took a seat, regretting having given Star Lightman his last cigar. As it turned out, he wouldn't have had the chance to light it before the two players on the wide bench seat finished up.

"You wouldn't be Pastor Stanley Crawn," Rice said, intentionally looking away from the action, out the front windshield.

The man came toward him, face red, breathing hard but smiling in an easy manner that suggested no shame. He buckled his belt and reached out a wet hand.

"I am Stan Crawn, pastor of the Faith Bible Church of Goodwater, Ohio," he said. "And who might you be, sir?"

A short woman with a bad complexion and a tight green skirt walked past them both without stopping, and carefully stepped off the van.

"I am Rice Channon, a reporter for the *Goodwater Tribune*," he said. "I was hoping I might have a few words."

"I would have preferred if you'd called first," Pastor Crawn said. "But it probably wouldn't have mattered. I recently lost my secretary and I'm seldom in the office. Let's go inside."

Rice shot a thumb over his shoulder toward the woman who was unlocking the door to the orange Pinto. "Maybe you should have had your counseling session with the young lady inside as well," he said.

Pastor Crawn pursed his lips and shook his head resolutely. "No, sir," he said. "The church is a sacred place."

Rice raised his eyebrows and the pastor noticed.

"The spirit indeed is willing, but the flesh is weak," the pastor said, sighing. "That's from Matthew, Chapter 26. Not sure of the verse. I've come to accept my weaknesses and move on. Try to do better. That's all a man can do."

"So submitting to your weakness, does that make you more understanding of the burdens of your congregation?"

"I believe you mock me, sir," Crawn said.

"I'm just curious," Rice said, looking down at his notes. "It seems there's a Mrs. Pastor Crawn. What if she had walked in? Or a member of your congregation? Or a reporter looking to write a story on the hypocrisy of the clergy."

Pastor Crawn smiled broadly. "Come on inside," he said.

Rice took a seat on an opulent brown leather couch while Crawn reset his tie and shrugged on a tan sport coat. He looked young for being pastor of such a large congregation. His fine features made him look girlish and callow, but he wore an air of confidence as comfortably as the jacket.

"Are you a man of faith, Mr. Channon?"

"I spend my Sundays catching up on sleep. Occasionally, I spend the day reviewing the sins of the previous night," Rice said.

Crawn's features pinched, but his look was condescending. "I don't think you're such a bad boy as you'd like to portray yourself," he said. "I've seen your byline and read your stories. You're resolute and hardworking and a little wet behind the ears. That's my read."

"Read away."

"I asked if you're a man of faith because I wanted you to understand how the members of my congregation, my friends, my family would accept your claims."

"You're saying they wouldn't believe me?"

"Their faith is strong," said Pastor Crawn. "Truth doesn't come from rumormongers or," and he opened his eyes wide to reinforce the point, "newspaper reporters. It comes from the heart place deep inside. It's the place where truth resides."

"I guess that means you can do whatever you want."

The pastor made a dismissive gesture with his lips and moved some papers around. "It allows for order and continuity," he said.

"Isn't there something in the Bible about pride going before the fall?"

"Pride goeth before destruction and a haughty spirit before a fall," Crawn said, acting bored now, ready to move on. "It's from Proverbs. Miss Shanley, who you met briefly in the bus, was here to discuss that very book of the Old Testament. Ironic, no?"

"Sure."

"Exactly how can I help you, Mr. Channon? I have a lot of work to do."

Rice felt the anger rising up in him. He decided to take a chance. "What were you doing outside the home of Annike Eichel a few days before she was murdered?" he said.

"I'm not sure what you're talking about."

"You were seen in front of her house in the church van. You seem to spend a lot of time in the van."

Pastor Crawn spread his arms wide and smiled, interest restored. "She intrigues me," he said, interlocking his hands behind his head and leaning back in the chair.

"Were you planning on peeking in her windows? Maybe you'd see her prancing about in her unmentionables."

"She invited me."

"That so?"

"We met on a number of occasions," Pastor Crawn said. He drove his knuckles together. "The coming together of extreme positions creates tension. It creates interest. People loved seeing us clashing about matters of faith and the True Word."

"Good theater?"

Crawn sat up straight. "That's it exactly," he said. "She and I are both in show business, preaching in different tents. She's a professional and so am I. It's only natural that we would … get together."

"Like with Miss Shanley?"

Pastor Crawn pursed his lips again disapprovingly. "It stirs the spirit to do battle in the open. It creates a kind of fraternity between the combatants. I wouldn't expect you to understand."

"Enlighten me."

"It's kind of …" The pastor tapped his fingertips together looking for precisely the right word. "Arousing."

"So you had sex? The two of you?"

Pastor Crawn winced at the word. "We had coffee two times after our sessions. She was charming. Not the harridan I expected."

"And a looker."

"Quite attractive, true," Crawn said. "But she's the one who suggested I stop by. She said to come anytime. Night was better."

"And that's why you drove the church van and parked it in front of her house?"

"I was warring within myself, I won't deny it," he said. "Driving the van made it less likely I would actually go through with a … private meeting."

"She was kind of a mess when the police got to her," Rice said. "A real butcher job on her lady parts. Like something a man warring with himself might do."

"That doesn't surprise me," Crawn said. "But if you're suggesting I might be that man, you are quite mistaken."

Annike Eichel was sitting in the passenger seat when Rice returned to his Fiat. Her hands were flat on her lap, and she looked straight ahead.

It was the only time he had been frightened by her. By any spirit.

Annike looked him in the eyes—they were wide and innocent like Stacey's—and her mouth opened wide. At first, he thought she was going to scream as he stared into the black maw under her nose.

Then something that grew large as a pea shot out from the open O of the mouth. Not a scream. The projection of the tongue? A word?

The third time it appeared Rice fell into the blackness and when he shook himself free, he was driving down the road like everything was fine. The sun was high in the sky.

And the spirit of Annike Eichel was gone.

# { 11 }

Jeanie Loughlin wore her black hair straight and just off the shoulders, her eyes flicking left and right as she typed.

The mayor's office, where she worked as his secretary, was in a small building off the town square. When Rice walked in she didn't even look up.

"He's in a meeting," she said.

Pretty girl.

"Think we could start over?" Rice said, dropping into a tattered Naugahyde chair.

Jeanie stopped typing and looked over at him as if this simple gesture exhausted her. "He's going to be a while," she said.

Rice hadn't said anything to Billard—not that it would have mattered—but the mayor's secretary and the *Tribune*'s new city hall reporter were not on good terms. They used to be.

In the police beat job, he seldom dealt with the mayor, but he liked to stop by from time to time. In the good old days, he would flirt with her and sometimes make her blush.

Then her dad, a notable in the local Democratic Party, was picked up for drunk driving after he was caught weaving between lanes on Columbus Avenue following a victory party last November. Since then, it had been all business between him and Jeanie Loughlin.

"Who's in there?"

She ignored him.

"Should I come back?"

Nothing.

"I was just doing my job," he said. "I can't be doing favors for people just because I like them."

Jeanie's simmering anger caught fire. "You destroyed the reputation of a good person. Everybody makes mistakes."

"I know that."

"He's the sweetest, kindest man I've ever known," Jeanie said about her ward-heeler father who was notorious for manipulating cash and promises to win elections. He was also an eminent drunk, although he stayed clear of the Tribune Grill.

"I like him too," Rice said, lying. "So it was hard writing the story. But it's my job."

She leaned over her typewriter, glaring, her face ugly and dark, her smile wicked. "But you ended up getting fired anyway," she said, jabbing her finger at him like a knife. "So much for doing the right thing."

"I wasn't fired," he said weakly. "I was promoted to the city hall job."

Jeanie pursed her lips and blew derisively. She returned to her work, the electric typewriter clacking away with renewed crispness.

The door to the mayor's office opened, and Tom Janousek walked out grinning. He was followed by the mayor who was laughing heartily, his right arm on Janousek's shoulder. When the mayor saw Rice, he sobered at once, and Rice almost felt bad for tossing cold water on the partiers.

"Hey, Channon," Janousek said, wiggling his fingers in a mocking wave. He winked at Jeanie who shot a quick glance at Rice before returning to her typing.

Mayor Leonard "Sandy" McMillan, serving his second four-year term as Goodwater mayor, took a drag from the Marlboro cigarette in his fingers, tapped the ash from the butt and ground it into the gray carpet with his toe. "Stop by anytime, anytime at all," he said.

"Thank you, Mayor," Janousek said.

"It's Sandy," the mayor said, his teeth white in a broad smile, the same one he'd used to sell Chevrolets uptown before his election.

The Cleveland reporter slapped the mayor's arm like they were old fishing buddies. "I think you may be right about the riot thing," he said, shaking the mayor's hand before leaving.

Rice watched him walk past the Navy recruiting poster urging passersby to “Lead the Bold Ones,” at the foot of the stairs.

“What’s the riot thing?” Rice said.

“I wish he hadn't mentioned it,” the mayor said. He tapped off another ash wad from the end of the cigarette.

“I'm glad he did. Didn’t sound like you were going to tell me.”

“Did you know the *Cleveland Chronicle* has a bigger circulation than the *Tribune* in Goodwater?”

“I did not.”

“Tom Janousek’s a first-class journalist,” the mayor said, pointing the burning cigarette tip at Rice, wincing from the swirling smoke. “You could learn something from him.”

“I already know how to make stuff up.”

McMillan shook his head, as if some kid had just tried to lowball him on a Chevy Camaro. “If you’re talking about the Vietnam torture series, I think you’re wrong. The military has been lying during this whole damn war. Of course they’re going to deny it. Maybe when he wins the Pulitzer, folks will start believing him.”

“I won't be among them.”

Mayor McMillan shook his head again, stubbed out the unfinished Marlboro. “Before you ask, there’s nothing new on the Eichel investigation. This is the same thing I told Janousek. A bad business.”

“You going to be bringing in outside help? Maybe the FBI?”

The mayor looked up, surprised. "That's what Janousek asked," he said. "I'm going to wait a little while longer. See what we can uncover on our own."

Rice scribbled in his notebook. "Now tell me about the riot thing."

The mayor narrowed his eyes and studied Rice at length. He tapped his ballpoint against Jeanie's desktop for a long time and never said anything.

"I spoke with some of the people in the ghetto recently," Rice said. "Back when I was investigating the Eichel murder. They told me the Goodwater PD seems to be cracking down in the neighborhood."

"There's no ghetto in Goodwater," McMillan said, raising his voice.

"Sorry," Rice said. "I talked to folks in the part of town with only Negro citizens, churches, and clubs. They don't understand why you're cracking down."

"In the summertime, people get rowdy," the mayor said. "Nothing to do. They sit outside, talking to each other and coming up with crazy ideas. We're just trying to let them know we're not going to stand for any mischief. I've got no patience for outside agitators."

"Who's agitating, Mayor?"

"I don't have names yet," he said. "Communists. That's what I'm hearing."

"From Colonel Markle?"

"It's his job to keep me informed."

“Not sure how he can do that,” Rice said. “You’ve got just two Negro police officers on the force, and they never patrol in the ghet … in that Negroes-only part of town. I think you’d want to know where he’s getting his information.”

“Thanks for the advice, Mr. Channon,” the mayor said, his face darkening for the second time today. “I’m glad I will have access to your advice from now on. Whether I want it or not. Maybe I should tell the chief and the safety-service director to take long vacations now that you’re on the job.”

“Markle could benefit from some time off.”

The mayor stood up. “We’ll talk again, Mr. Channon. Tomorrow, I guess.”

“It's okay to call me Rice.”

The mayor just smiled.

“The *Chronicle* may have a bigger circulation in town, but people don't read it to find out what's going on in Goodwater,” Rice said. “They read it to learn why the Indians are losing and if Leroy Kelly is going to be playing another season with the Browns. Janousek is just using you.”

The mayor's smile faded slowly. “Tomorrow,” he said.

# { 12 }

Tomorrow didn't happen. That night a summer cold clawed up the back of Rice's throat, and when he awoke the next morning, it was ripping his chest apart.

"I can't breathe," he rasped over the phone to Billard next morning.

"Where'd you catch it?" the city editor asked. "You get it from here?"

Rice could almost see the little newsman's head swinging around the newsroom, looking for secretive snifflers and coughers.

"I don't know," Rice said. "I'll be out of action for a few days, though. Will you be okay?"

"Yeah, yeah," Billard said. "You just take care of yourself. And stay the hell away from here."

Annike Eichel's form hovered in place at the foot of his bed. No expression. No movement. Just waiting.

He wondered if he'd imagined that incident in the car when he thought her mouth had tried to form a word. She didn't seem interested in talking now, though. Neither did Rice.

Sometimes when his dreary sniffling or explosive coughs awakened him, he would see her form like a dim lighthouse at the end of the bed. Once when he padded back from the bathroom, he thought her eyes followed him, but he wasn't sure.

Back in the world of the healthy, no one seemed to miss him.

City council had slipped into summertime scheduling, so they held only one meeting each month. He'd probably be well enough for the next one.

Mayor McMillan went on vacation the same week, despite his promise to talk to Rice about his conversation with Tom Janousek. His office shut down. Rice wasn't expecting any wish-you-were-here postcards from him or his secretary.

Billard called once three days in and seemed almost kind. When he discovered Rice was neither dead nor near death, his gruffness returned.

"That guy from the *Cleveland Chronicle* stopped by yesterday," Billard said.

"Janousek?"

"Yeah. The Boy Wonder," Billard said. "He was looking for you."

"Christ. You didn't tell him where I live, did you?"

"What's he want?" Billard said.

"I'm not sure," Rice said, hacking once into the phone for effect. "He and the mayor act like they're doing each other's hair now."

"McMillan's always been a media whore."

"Except when it comes to the *Tribune*."

"Yeah," Billard said.

"By the way, I thought I was the Boy Wonder," Rice said. Billard hung up.

Stacey Ann came by the same afternoon. Rice stumbled across the room in his undershorts and T-shirt to answer the door. When she saw him, she pretended to be cheery.

"When's the last time you shaved?" she asked.

"Can't remember."

She yanked open the blinds. When the sunlight streamed in, Rice groaned.

Stacey opened the light-blue canvas bag she brought. "I made you some sandwiches," she said. "Bologna and cheese on rye. And I made up a thermos of cherry Kool-Aid."

"My two favorite food groups," he said, surprised he was hungry. "If you brought me a case of Twinkies, you get the Clara Barton Award."

She wrinkled her nose. "I brought you some apples and oranges."

"Thought you could trick me into eating healthy?"

"Your idea of eating healthy is getting a tomato on your hamburger."

Rice got into bed. “I like hamburgers. I don’t like veggies.”

Stacey shook her head.

“Is anyone here?” she said.

“No. Just us.”

Stacey wrapped her arms around herself, and looked around anyway. “Did you ever ask her who killed her?”

Rice erupted into a short sneezing jag. He apologized, wiped at his sore nose, and dropped the Kleenex into the overflowing trash can next to his bed.

“She’s not much of a conversationalist. I tried when Arnie said I should make the effort.”

Her face lit up at the mention of Arnie’s name. “How’s he doing?” Stacey asked. “I haven’t seen him in a while.”

Rice fell back against his pillow and took a sip from the thermos of Kool-Aid. “Yeah, he asked if I heard from you. Says he saw your boyfriend at the bank.”

“What was Arnie doing at the bank?”

“It turns out he has an account there. I couldn’t believe it either.”

“Does he see her?” she asked. “The atheist, I mean.”

“Not yet,” Rice said. “He thinks she might be an hallucination.”

“So you’re not psychic. You’re just crazy.”

“Those seem to be the two options.”

After Stacey left, Rice dropped off to sleep again. When he awoke at five, his face clammy, his hair wet, Tom Janousek was sitting in the only chair in the room. He sported a new shorter haircut and an open-necked shirt. Tan Cuban heel cowboy boots poked out from his bell-bottom jeans.

"How you feeling?"

Rice slid up on his pillow and tried to croak something, gave up, then got out of bed and walked into the bathroom. When he came out, he pulled on some pants and started looking for Stacey's bologna and cheese sandwich.

"How'd you get in?" he asked.

"Door was open," Janousek said. "What say we go down the block and pick up something to eat? My treat. If you're up to it."

Rice was feeling weak, but he was hungry. He nodded and got cleaned up. He pulled on a new shirt, brushed his teeth. Shaved.

At the nearby Sage Family Restaurant, Rice ordered an open-faced roast beef sandwich with mashed potatoes, the whole concoction smothered in thick gravy. As an afterthought, he also ordered a bowl of green beans. Janousek selected a rib eye cooked rare and a small salad.

After two bites of the roast beef, Rice poked his fork at Janousek. "You ready to tell me exactly what you're doing here?"

"We might be able to help each other."

Rice decided the roast beef was stringy, but the gravy was first-rate. Potatoes were too salty. He noticed Janousek wince when Rice tipped his plate so gravy cascaded into the bean bowl, almost to the top.

"Do you know what a hypothesis is?" Janousek said.

Rice speared two gravy-laden beans with his fork tines and lifted them to his mouth. “A guess?”

Janousek shook his head adamantly. “It’s a statement of expectations,” he said. “I stick my head out the window and see that it’s dark and getting darker. So I hypothesize that it’s going to rain.”

“Okay. So if it doesn’t rain, what does that mean? Your hypothesis is incorrect?”

“Why would you think that?” Janousek said, chewing on a piece of romaine with the delicacy of a little girl biting a tea cookie. “It’s going to rain eventually.”

“If that works in your world, okay.”

“When I went to ’Nam, I went with a working hypothesis.”

Rice dipped his spoon into the remaining gravy and slurped it loudly. “That American soldiers torture prisoners?”

“That’s one of them. It’s the one I stuck with. It’s the one that brought me home.”

“A lot of people think it’s shit,” Rice said. “A lot of people think you made it all up. Including me.”

He was surprised when Janousek laughed. “I don’t have that kind of imagination,” he said. “I just tested the hypothesis. Kept asking questions. Kept poking around.”

“People actually admitted to it?”

Janousek shook his head, a tomato wedge dangling from his mouth. “You’d be surprised what people admit to. A Marine gunnery sergeant told me he killed a Charlie sniper, chopped him up, skewered the parts, and cooked them on a grill with onions and potatoes. True story.”

"But soldiers barbecuing the enemy wasn't one of your working hypotheses, I'm guessing."

"I'd never been to a war zone before I went over there," Janousek said. "It's startling how quickly you can become dehumanized to death, suffering. Nothing surprises you after a while. I had to keep reminding myself of my hypothesis so I could stay on task and limit the scope of the ugliness I wrote about."

"So that stuff really happened?"

"Beatings, starvation, a couple of brandings, slow dehydration," Janousek said. "Lots of testimony and some pretty revealing photos. Haven't you read my stories?"

"No. I don't like you so I ignored them."

"Well, you're in a big club," Janousek said, letting his fork clatter loudly into his salad bowl. "But this is my point. I could have gone over there with any working hypothesis and proven it true. Sooner or later, it's going to rain."

"So you *did* make it all up."

"You're missing my point. *Everything* is true. Everything. My little spotlight on the truth may be a small spotlight, but it illuminates a little bit of the bigger picture."

"You hate the men fighting the war, so you make them look like thugs and murderers."

Janousek sighed. "It's a stupid war fought by stupid people for stupid reasons."

"So demeaning the poor bastards sent to fight and die there makes it all better?" Rice's head was throbbing.

"It's not that simple. I found guys building schools and churches," Janousek said. "Young kids just out of high school risked their lives to get medicine to people they didn't know and would never see again. Incredible sacrifices. It broke my heart sometimes."

"But you ignored it," Rice said. "Because you wanted to write the other story."

"Different truths," Janousek said, as if that explained it all. "The more outlandish, the more interesting. Dig into it and discover that truth. It'll make you famous."

"Why are you here?"

"You don't really think Annike Eichel was killed by angry churchgoers," Janousek said.

"I don't know."

"You spoke to Stanley Crawn at Faith Bible. The man's a moron who can't keep his fly zipped. He's no killer."

"He might inspire a killer."

"He's no Charlie Manson either."

"So what's your hypothesis?"

"I don't think Eichel's death had anything to do with her activism or her beliefs."

"And you're going to keep asking questions until you can prove that's true," Rice said.

Janousek shook his head. "Both of us are," he said.

# { 13 }

"Might have been better if you died," the copy girl said to Rice when he returned to the newsroom next morning. He coughed once but forgave her attitude because she had full hips and wore short skirts almost every day.

Plus he half agreed with her.

She dropped a folder on his desk with clippings from the *Cleveland Chronicle* about the Eichel death. Each one carried Janousek's byline.

Janousek had been busy. Stories about Goodwater's history, speckled with lots of folksy quotes from the mayor, accompanied photos both old and new. He wrote about the city's beginnings as a mill town and its growth into a small industrial center. He also suggested that recent exits by long-time companies were signaling a downturn in economic prospects.

"Goodwater is the Gateway to Progress," Mayor McMillan was quoted in one article. "Just like it says on the sign coming into town."

Rice sighed. The mayor's monumental ego was blocking out Janousek's attempt at irony.

Billard squatted alongside his desk, but a little more distant than usual. He drummed his fingers and looked around. "How are you feeling?" he asked.

Rice raised the folder. "This isn't helping," he said. "I may relapse."

The city editor forced a smile and gestured at the hallway leading to the front office. "Let's talk."

They went into a small conference room. The room was empty, but the coffeepot was full. Rice grabbed a cup and looked back to Billard, raising an empty mug.

"No, thanks," Billard said. "Have a seat."

The hot coffee felt good on Rice's throat.

"Okay, here's the deal," Billard said. He looked nervous. "First of all, you get a raise for the city hall job. Congratulations."

"If I stay home another week, maybe you'll bump it up again."

"Yeah," Billard said, frowning. "That's funny. You're also going to be working full-time on the Eichel murder."

"So who's handling city hall?"

"Nobody's handling city hall," Billard said, his voice rising briefly. "Everybody in government is out catching trout or sailing over to Put-in-Bay. For at least another couple of weeks."

Rice nodded as if this all made sense. "So the folks at city hall won't mind that you've put me back on the police beat," he said. "Because they won't know about it."

"That's not their decision to make," Billard said, eyes narrowing. "And you're not back on police beat. You're on special assignment."

"Now I get it," Rice said. "Markle calls and next day I'm off the police beat. Tommy Janousek stops by, and next day I'm working with him on special assignment. What if Dick Nixon wants me? You going to send me to Washington to be his press secretary?"

"Who said you're working with Janousek?"

"Tell me I'm wrong or stop fucking with me, Dave," Rice said.

Billard pressed his thumb and forefinger against his temples. "Christ. Sometimes I hate this job," he said.

"At least you know what your job is."

"The editor from the *Chronicle* called while you were out," Billard said. "He wants us to work together on the Eichel murder. The editors and even the publisher talked it over. To put it mildly, they were pleased at the prospect of teaming with the mighty *Cleveland Chronicle*. They were so giggly I thought it was Christmas morning and everyone was getting their own Barbie doll."

"Markle's not going to be happy that I'm working with his boys again."

"You're not allowed to work with the cops," Billard said. "Leave that to Janousek."

Rice was surprised to see his hand was shaking. He took a long sip of his coffee. "Gonna make it hard to do my job, Dave."

"There'll be plenty for you to do."

"Like what? Janousek's laundry?"

"He's got the lead, Rice," Billard said. "I don't like it either, but that's the way it is. You'll share the byline but he's calling the shots."

"I wonder whose name will go first."

"He's not a bad reporter," Billard said. "He's got attitude issues that bleed through once in a while, but I can't help that. Maybe the two of you can work some magic."

Rice coughed up a loogie and spit it into his coffee cup. Billard got up, disgusted. "Take something," he said. "You're not well yet."

When he returned to his desk, Rice found a copy of the morning's *Cleveland Chronicle*. A small story below the fold on page one carried Janousek's byline: Goodwater Cleric Preached Venom Against Murdered Atheist. The subhead said Preacher's Personal Behavior Questioned.

The story quoted numerous congregation members from the Faith Bible Church explaining how Pastor Stanley Crawn tried to incite a "battle against Satan" in the person of Annike Eichel. He wanted protests, letters to the editor, marches, and more.

The "more," according to increasingly uncomfortable churchgoers, could also include physical attacks from the Goodwater church family or, as Crawn called them, "the arm of the Lord."

"Not true, not true," Crawn said in the article when asked to respond to the charges. Rice could almost see the fat beads of sweat breaking out on the minister's forehead. "I urged a confrontation of her godless ways in a public setting in such a way as to embarrass and discredit her falsehoods. It is our duty as Christians for, as the Lord said to Moses, 'How long will you refuse to keep my commandments and my laws?'"

Janousek interviewed a twenty-two-year-old man and former congregation member. At Crawn's urging, he put on his best white shirt and tie and stood outside a restaurant where Eichel and a friend were having dinner. There he preached about salvation coming through grace alone while railing against her godlessness. When she left the restaurant, Annike shook the young man's hand and presented him with a small club sandwich and a Coke.

So moved was he by this simple gesture that he returned to Faith Bible Church at once. There he discovered his bride of a month in a position he would only characterize as "unfortunate" and "inappropriate" with Pastor Crawn.

The pastor suggested they all hold hands, fall down on their knees, and pray together for a stronger faith, according to the story. Instead, the young street preacher tossed his Bible at Crawn and went sobbing to his mother's house. He began annulment proceedings against his wayward wife the next day.

Other anonymous churchgoers said Pastor Crawn was "obsessed" with Eichel and "fixated" on her in a way that seemed "inexplicable" and even "unnatural."

Maybe it was the lingering fever making Rice's mind wander. But he felt a notion growing into a hunch that needed dealing with.

His shirt was slightly damp as he jogged down the stairs to the parking lot. On the way, he thought about Janousek's article and his hypothesis approach to journalism.

It didn't take hypotheses or much reportorial skill to flush out the hypocrisy and licentiousness in the Faith Bible pastor. Still, Janousek had put some effort into representing both sides, which made the big hole Crawn had dug for himself even more satisfying.

When he was just about to open the door to his Fiat, a red Ford Maverick pulled in behind him, blocking his departure.

The driver's side window rolled down. Stacey's boyfriend, Roger Ranscombe, stuck his head out. Rice could see himself reflected in the other man's mirrored aviator glasses.

"How you doin', ace?" he said. "Off to a fire?"

Rice walked over to him. "Not chasing fire engines these days, Roger," he said. Rice rubbed the top of the car like it was fine leather. "New wheels?"

"Yup," Roger said. "A made-in-America Ford. Brand new. What's that you're driving?"

"A rented Fiat 850," Rice said. "Made in Italy. When the US starts making decent cars again, I may buy one."

"Uh-huh."

"I kind of need to get going, Roger," Rice said, pointing at his open door.

Roger dropped his smile and whipped his glasses off like he was Clark Kent turning into Superman. He had a pleasant, nondescript face. His hair was unfashionably short.

"Stacey and I are getting married," Roger said, sticking out his chin.

Rice felt his heart drop. "Congratulations," he said.

"Thanks," Roger said, putting the sunglasses on again. "I wanted you to be the first to know."

Rice felt sick to his stomach. *Was it the illness or the news?* He wasn't sure. "I gotta get going," he said.

Roger rolled up the window and managed to coax the little car into throwing up a respectable spray of gravel as he pulled away.

Annike was sitting in the passenger seat when he got in. Smiling. She turned to him and her lips moved. The openmouthed *O* revealed a velvet blackness inside that looked like eternity. Tip of the tongue sticking out. Then the *O* again. The last part was new.

Her figure fluttered momentarily in the seat, as if the effort to communicate had drained whatever battery powered her manifestation.

Maybe it wasn't Arnie, but someone had to understand what was going on here.

DENNIS ANTHONY

# { 14 }

The Church of the Sacred Heart rose above the squalor of the surrounding neighborhood, its sandstone blocks suggesting strength and permanence, its twin spires pointing resolutely at the heavenly reward.

The edifice was constructed in the late 1800s to serve the spiritual needs of a growing population of central European immigrants. These days, the second- and third-generation progeny had moved out of the heart of the industrial city and into the suburbs. Many of the homes surrounding the church were in disrepair, or vacant and boarded up. According to the sign outside the entrance, only one Sunday Mass—10:00 a.m.—was now offered.

Rice rang the bell at the rectory. While waiting, he watched paper and a few beer cans blow down the street before falling into a clogged storm grate. Father Peter Growden finally came to the door.

"I didn't expect we'd be talking again," the priest said, directing him to a ratty corduroy-covered armchair. His eyes were bright, as though pleased to see him. "I had the sense you weren't much interested in what I was selling. Was I wrong?"

Rice spotted a foot-high statue of Jesus that stood on a bookshelf overlooking the priest's desk. His hand rested on a blood-red depiction of his heart in the center of his chest. Rice pointed at it.

"The Sacred Heart of Jesus," Growden said. "It represents Christ's divine love for all humanity."

"Would that include Annike Eichel?" Rice asked.

"Of course." The fingers on the priest's powerful hands looked as though they could crush walnuts.

"You do weddings, funerals, and Sunday services mostly?"

Father Growden sighed. "More funerals than weddings in recent years," he said.

Rice nodded, looked around some more.

"You seem uncomfortable," the priest said. "Do you want to talk about Miss Eichel? Or is there something else on your mind?"

"Let me ask you this," Rice said. "Would you say Annike Eichel was a hard-boiled atheist or an agnostic who simply didn't understand the meaning of faith?"

Growden scratched his mostly bald scalp with a little finger, as though afraid he might pull out one of the few surviving hair strands. "It's an interesting question," he said. "I didn't know her well, like I told you earlier. On the surface, her outlook was almost radical. She didn't believe. She didn't want you to believe. That was the public face."

"Did she have another?"

"I caught a ride with her back to church once after some kind of symposium. I think your friend Stacey was involved."

"I never knew."

"Yes, well, when we were alone, Miss Eichel asked me to explain the meaning of the sacraments, how the saints acted as intercessors, and similar matters."

"I don't even know what those questions mean."

"It has to do with very specific aspects of the Catholic faith, but that's not my point," Father Growden said. "She seemed genuinely interested in understanding how it all fit into the larger church doctrine. Her questions were not adversarial. It was surprising. And quite touching, actually."

Rice spotted a pile of magazines on the table next to the chair. Willie Mays looked out from a recent issue of *Sports Illustrated*. "Did she ever show up in church?"

Growden pursed his lips and shook his head adamantly. "No," he said. "But I remembered her because of her hearty curiosity. And then more recently, of course, because of her unfortunate death."

Rice began flipping through the *Sports Illustrated* magazine and said nothing for a while.

"What's on your mind, Rice? Why are you here?"

"I see Miss Eichel," Rice said, tossing the magazine on the table. "Or a shadow of her or her spirit or her— "

"Her ghost," the priest said, cutting him off. He pronounced it *gust*, as though he couldn't quite bring himself to say the word. "I remember."

"She's not the first," Rice said. "There have been others. Most of them murder victims."

Father Growden fell against his chair back, and it screeched wildly. He put his fingers together under his chin. "The ghosts of the dead tell you who killed them?"

"They don't tell me, exactly," Rice said. "I pick up a sense when I'm headed in the right direction. Ghosts aren't very chatty in general, I've discovered."

"And Miss Eichel?"

"An unusual woman, as you mentioned," Rice said. "And a strange ghost. I forgot. You don't believe in ghosts."

"I don't think I used those words," the priest said. "I merely suggested it was unwise to prowl in ghostly domains."

It smelled musty in the office. Rice shook his head.

"What do you want exactly?"

"I'm not a religious man, Father. Not even a particularly spiritual one. But I don't know where else to turn right now."

Growden laughed and it startled Rice. "Half the men who come in that door tell me the same thing. Their wife dies or their child runs off to live on a commune or they coughed up blood while eating toast. Then they want to talk to me."

"Must piss you off."

"Not at all," Growden said. "I'm here to help when I can."

"And do you, Father?"

Growden spread his hands wide, and Rice saw that he had heavily muscled biceps to go with the vicelike fingers. "Sometimes. Sometimes not," he said.

"Annike Eichel is trying to talk to me."

"Is that unusual, in your experience?"

"Pretty much unprecedented," Rice said. "It makes me think it's really important that I hear what she has to say."

"Do you expect she'll tell you who murdered her?"

Rice simply shook his head like none of this made sense.

Father Growden pursed his lips. "What role does Stacey play?"

"She brought you into this. I don't like it, but there it is."

"I can tell she's worried about you," Growden said.

"We were pretty serious for a number of years," Rice said. "But she wanted the whole white picket fence, Ozzie and Harriet lifestyle. Now she's engaged to a guy who will give it to her. I don't blame her."

"I've seen her in church on Sundays. It's a long way for her to drive, but she's been showing up the last few months. Just about my youngest parishioner."

"Yeah," Rice said. "Something else I didn't know about her."

The priest took a deep breath. "Do you want to know what I think?" he said. "I think you're the one looking for answers and all this business about ghosts and murdered people is just a smoke screen."

"That doesn't help me much," Rice said.

Father Growden shrugged broadly. “You want to learn about discovering peace in this life? You want to join the Lord in eternal bliss in the next? Come to Mass next Sunday.”

“You’re going to lead me to salvation, is that it, Father?”

“That’s not up to me, thank God,” the priest said. “That’s up to you.”

“Why are you leaving the priesthood?” Rice said. “You got salvation locked in already?”

—

Two years earlier, Mary Shanklin, parish secretary at St. Mary’s Church, was arrested for embezzling just under ten thousand dollars from church collections over a period of three years.

Rice had taken down the information from the police blotter, and when he got back to the office, he placed a call to the bishop of the diocese for comment. He ended up talking to Father Roy Carson, secretary to the bishop.

Father Carson, who was quite familiar with the case, pleaded with Rice to keep the story quiet. St. Mary’s was a poor parish with a rich history, he said, and if the theft was made public, the few wealthy donors who were keeping the parish afloat, would drop their support.

He knew it was wrong, but Rice loved the big, old church with its tall stained-glass windows and its well-kept flower garden next to the rectory. When he passed the church on the way to work, it reinforced his belief that some things in this life were solid and real.

The embezzlement story never ran.

Rice had never met Father Carson face-to-face, but when he'd stopped by the diocese offices on his way to see Growden, he had been welcomed warmly.

"The bishop's out of the office today," Father Carson said. His florid complexion made him look like he had just come in from the cold. "Maybe I can help you."

Rice didn't think there was any reason to remind the priest about his smothering the news of the St. Mary's embezzlement. The guilty secretary had been convicted, spent a year in prison, and was making restitution at a new job. St. Mary's may not have been thriving, but it was hanging on.

"What can you tell me about Father Growden at Sacred Heart?" Rice said.

Father Carson rubbed his chin and the bright, welcoming light in his eyes dimmed some. "Can I ask why you want to know?" he said.

"He knew Annike Eichel."

Father Carson stood up and paced a couple of steps, arms behind his back. "You're not telling me he's a suspect?"

"I don't know," Rice said. "I don't think so. Let's just say I'm curious about him."

The priest turned around, pressed his hands together, and raised them up and down as though praying fervently. "I'm telling you this because you're a fair and honest man," he said. "But you've got to promise me it will go no further."

"Promise."

"Father Growden is planning to leave the priesthood," Carson said.

"Can he do that?"

"Well, yes, of course," Father Carson said, eyebrows rising. "The Catholic Church is not a prison. It's unfortunate, but priests leave all the time. And it seems to be happening more and more often these days."

"Do you know why?"

"Usually, it's a woman," Carson said. "But in his case—" He shrugged. "I don't know. When he was an assistant pastor at—well, never mind where—he had a personality conflict with the pastor. The pastor was an old-school fire-and-brimstoner, and Growden wanted to preach about forgiveness. He brought a folk group in for Sunday Mass. He was active in youth ministries. He even tried to get a semipro football team to play their games at the stadium behind the church. The old priest didn't like it. Made his life …"

"Hell?"

Father Carson smiled.

"What's your best guess why he … fell away?"

"It's called laicization," the red-faced priest said. "A reduction to the lay state. Of course, the ordination itself can never be undone, but sometimes, a priest can lose his faith, just like a layman. It takes great spiritual will to serve in the clergy. It's lonely. Doubts arise. Most persevere. Some don't."

"It can't be an easy decision to make. To leave, I mean."

"It takes a special kind of courage, I guess," Father Carson said.

"When will it happen?"

Carson sighed again. "He's found a position with some kind of athletic club run by the city in Cleveland. He's leaving in a couple of weeks. A number of priests—me included—will be filling in at Sacred Heart masses until we find a permanent replacement."

"Do you know anything about any relationship he might have had with Annike Eichel?" Rice said.

Father Carson thought for a moment, then shook his head adamantly. "No," he said. "But that doesn't mean much. I know very little about our priests' personal lives."

Rice nodded, stood up.

"You're not going to print any of this?" the priest said. "That information was—what do you call it?—confidential."

"Off the record," Rice said. "No, I won't be writing a story, if that's what you're asking. The religion editor will probably do something when Growden finally leaves though."

—

"What makes you think I'm leaving the church?" Father Growden said, holding his stare. Almost challenging.

"If I said it was a hunch, would you believe me?"

Father Growden shrugged as if he was indifferent to the matter. "I guess it was bound to get out," he said. "It just sounds so odd when you say the words. It's like you're talking about someone else."

"But I'm not. Am I?"

"No."

When the priest stood up and walked around, wringing his hands, he looked more than ever like a worried wrestler. He huffed out an explosive burst of air that ended with a weary smile. "So hard to believe. The church has been my whole life," he said.

"So why?" Rice asked, a part of him wondering why he cared. "Why now?"

"The world is changing, Rice," Father Growden said, once again assuming a consoling air. "The secular world leaks in then explodes like a bursting dam. When it does, it washes away everything you thought you were. It happens fast. One day you wake up, and you're not the person you thought you were."

"Did Annike Eichel have anything to do with your decision?"

The dead atheist's ghost floated behind Father Growden like a shadow. Her mouth was unmoving.

"Do you think I had anything to do with her death?"

"Did you? Maybe she was part of that secular dam that exploded over you."

"She was a beautiful woman. Could tempt a saint."

"So you gave in to temptation," Rice said. "And now you feel guilty."

Father Growden smiled again, dropped his head, and shook it. "No. Nothing like that. But it's true she made me feel guilty."

"Even priests must feel the longings of the flesh."

"Of course we do," Father Growden said, a slight snap in his tone. "We're not made of stone. But every sin is not a sexual one."

"A lot of them are."

Annike looked worried as she followed the priest. She began slowly shaking her head and something about the simple gesture sent a chill through Rice. But he said nothing to the priest.

"Sexual matters are part of that flood I was talking about," Father Growden said. "That's true. But faithlessness, disloyalty. They are worse. Far worse."

Annike looked like she wanted to stroke his head.

"I told you about our ride home together," the priest said. "What I didn't tell you was how I revealed my doubts to her. I had begun questioning my faith, the prayers, the arc of it all. When she asked me to illuminate some aspects of my faith, I couldn't do it. Wouldn't do it."

"How did she react to that?"

"I thought she would laugh at me. Maybe taunt my hypocrisy. But it was nothing like that."

"What was it like?" Rice asked.

"She cried with me," Growden said. "Right there in her car in front of the rectory. As the two of us realized my faith had washed away."

“And then?”

“And then I said goodbye.”

# { 15 }

Tom Janousek didn't have a glue pot, so he snatched one off the desk of the business reporter. Then he lifted the business reporter's ruler too.

He was frustrated, and the petty thievery made him feel better. He'd been unable to find anything new on the Eichel investigation. Nobody in the Goodwater PD would talk to him, and Rice Channon couldn't be found. They had, in fact, not spoken since they'd been officially teamed up on the story.

Janousek ripped a strip of copy he wrote yesterday, slathered some glue on the top, and pasted it onto his lead paragraphs. It wasn't much, but it was something.

"Keep the news boil bubbling," his Cleveland editor told him once. "As long as you keep the heat on, things will happen."

Unfortunately, not much bubbling was going on except at Faith Bible Church where Pastor Stanley Crawn was in his own kind of hot water. The church's governing council was taking a hard look at his ministry in light of the recent article about him.

Crawn flatly denied he had spoken to Janousek, and even dragged out the old chestnut that "outside extremists" trying to "tear down the faith" were responsible for the lies.

It wasn't too hard for Janousek to find two women in the congregation—one married, one not—who, after some maidenly hemming and hawing, spilled the beans on Crawn's extracurricular doings with church ladies. They pretended they weren't involved and Janousek allowed them the lie. But the editors were convinced otherwise, and the *Tribune* winked at its longstanding policy of disallowing second-party testimony.

When Janousek called Crawn seeking his response to the claims, the preacher hung up on him.

That was pretty much the whole story. It wasn't much, but it was all Janousek had. He folded it up—just ten grafs long—and walked it over to the city editor's desk.

"What?" Billard said. He didn't even bother looking up when he snatched the copy.

"A piece on Pastor Crawn," Janousek said, looking off as if the AP wire machine pounding away in the corner might be printing out something more interesting.

"You haven't found anything new on Eichel?" Billard said, tossing the copy into his basket.

"I can't find your golden boy," Janousek said. He tried to act annoyed because he was forced to work with this two-bit newspaper. Billard was having none of it. He assumed a crooked smile and leaned forward on both forearms. The city editor motioned Janousek to squat down to eye level.

"I thought *you* were the golden boy," Billard said. He studied Janousek's silk tie and tailored yellow shirt. Half his general assignment team didn't even wear ties.

"Does he *ever* come to work?" Janousek asked.

"Don't worry about him," Billard said, dropping the grin. "He's got a gift. That covers a lot of sins."

"That so?"

"It is," Billard said. "He's got an unusual insight. Cops talk to him. Street hoodlums. He seems to know where to be when something newsworthy is about to happen. So he gets lots of leeway."

"That's interesting," Janousek said. "I'm told I have a gift."

"Being pushy is a trait. Not a gift."

"How's he do it?" Janousek asked.

Long pause. "There are rumors about his … special abilities."

"So he's mad."

Billard shrugged. "Go find him," he said. "Then you decide."

Janousek went to the Tribune Grill at eleven and stayed until almost two. He tried to make nice with the reporters, editors, and printers he had been ignoring all week.

Most were unreceptive. A few were friendly but had no useful information. Or if they did, they weren't willing to pass it on.

He nursed his hamburger for about two hours and refilled his Coke glass three times. Coming out of the men's room with its dingy condom dispensers and yellow walls, he spotted the pretty copy girl with the great legs standing at the bar. She was sorting through five greasy brown bags.

"You going to eat all that?" he said, grinning broadly.

"It's my turn to make the late lunch run," she said. She stuck two fingers in her mouth and emitted a wicked whistle which caught the bartender's attention. "This one's supposed to be onion rings. Not fries." She held out the bag like it was someone's dirty laundry.

"Attention to detail," Janousek said. "Very impressive."

"I'll be back here again if I don't get it right."

"You see Rice Channon lately?" he asked her.

"No," she said, still holding out the bag with one extended arm until the barkeep finally grabbed it and pushed it through the window to the kitchen. "Maybe his feelings are hurt because he was taken off the police beat. Maybe he's sick again. We don't share our schedules."

"A pretty thing like you," he said. "I thought he'd tell you everything."

"What's my name?" she said.

"What?"

"Tell me my name."

Janousek shook his head, tried to look ashamed.

"He likes to watch me carry copy when he thinks I don't see him," she said. "Not like you, who stares right at me like you have expectations. But you don't even know my name."

"Forgive my big-city lack of manners."

She shrugged. "I don't care. As long as all you do is look." She smoothed what there was of her skirt. The bartender brought another greasy brown bag, and she unfolded it, checked it out then folded it back up.

"Meet me here after work and I'll buy you a scotch and soda. I'll share the dark secrets of Cleveland," Janousek said.

"Can't drink legal yet," the girl said, smacking her gum audibly for the first time.

"So come by and I'll buy you a Shirley Temple. I'll tell you about my favorite zoo animals."

The copy girl offered a teasing smile. She was older than her years, even if she was too young to drink.

"You might try Martelli's. I've heard Rice goes there sometimes. Cops hang out in the place. It's a gentlemen's club," she said, sneering her way through the word *gentlemen*. "Ugly men in the dark watching half-naked women. It's very popular, I'm told."

"You think Rice is ugly?" Janousek asked.

The girl scooped up the five bags with practiced ease and started walking for the door. "I don't know," she said. "I never thought about it."

# { 16 }

At three p.m., Rice watched the out of work, the loafers, and the losers shuffle out of Martelli's Lounge while strippers languidly swung on poles to the almost empty house.

Rice was in the back, in the darkest part of the bar near the heavy black entrance door. He sucked on a lukewarm longneck Carling Black Label while Roberta Flack sang about the first time she saw someone's face.

The sticky vinyl bench cracked and groaned like an old man swearing every time he shifted in the seat. Rice looked down as he rolled the neck of the beer bottle in his fingertips. He never heard her slide onto the bench across from him.

"Hey, darlin'," she said. "Haven't seen you in a while."

Rice looked up. Smiled. "Been sick," he said.

Tulips Kissin'—real name, Pearl Clinton—had coffee-colored skin, almond eyes, and legs that just went on and on. Rice got a good look at the whole package a few years back when the sports editor thought it would be fun to buy the police reporter a table dance one Friday night.

So Tulips and Rice had retired to a back room, and she'd strutted those great legs, pursed the pretty lips, and shook her moneymaking ass while B. J. Thomas sang about raindrops falling on his head. It was the longest five minutes of Rice's life.

"Well, sweetheart," Tulips had said afterwards, a light sheen of sweat on her naked chest. "I think you're blushing."

That made it worse, of course.

"I've had men try to grab me. I've had 'em whoop and holler," she said. "But never saw a white man get red before. You look crunchy. And I think it's sweet."

Tulips was so tickled she ran off to tell her colleagues. The boys from the Sports Department overheard the story and laughed so hard they tipped the table and all their half-filled Black Label bottles onto the floor.

After that, every time he passed the sports desk, he would inevitably be greeted with "How ya doin', Red?" and a chuckle. Mercifully, they kept the story to themselves.

Tulips realized what mischief she had uncorked. Now, every time he stopped in at Martelli's, she made it a point to sit with him while drinking a glass of ginger ale, no ice.

She reached out to touch his hands as she always did. Her hands were cold as they always were. "Feelin' better now?" she asked.

"You *do* make me feel better, Pearl," Rice said.

She used to insist he call her Tulips, but she didn't bother anymore. She patted his hand. "Sometimes, I don't think you take care of yourself. You need to find a woman."

"Think that would fix things, do you?"

She smiled. "Fix some things," she said. "Unfix some others. But that's the way, isn't it?"

Rice nodded. "That's been my experience," he said.

A tall, powerfully built black man walked in with a much smaller, bespectacled white man who bumped into two chairs while his eyes adjusted to the darkness.

Tulips furrowed her brow. "Early crowd's coming in," she said. Then she looked back at Rice, her eyes softening. "I'm going to find somebody for you, you'll see."

Rice checked out the big man again. He looked familiar.

"Do you know that guy?" Rice said, poking his chin in the man's direction.

Tulips sighed, smiled. "I don't know his name, but he appreciates exotic dancing," she said, singing the last two words. "Most guys slip me singles, if they give me anything at all. He gives me fives. Sometimes more. Thinks that gives him permission to slap my bonbon. I let him."

"That so?"

She nodded and slid off the bench. "Don't be a stranger, honey," she said, patting his hand one more time. She waved her generous ass as she sashayed away, looking back once with a naughty grin. Rice had never seen her outside of Martelli's. He wondered what she looked like in the daylight.

Guys cutting out early from work began streaming in. Most of them sat up front, closest to the strippers. The early crowd tended to be beer drinkers. Later would come the mixed drink crowd. Then the straight shooters.

Rice didn't expect any customers in the darker corners until around eight. By then he would be long gone. It wasn't just the solitude that appealed to him. It was the cave-like darkness that hid him from the cleaner, real things outside.

That's what the guys here called it. Outside. This was the hiding place. This was the tree fort for boys only. That other world of school and doting mothers and chores stayed elsewhere for a while. Outside.

"What are the odds?" Tom Janousek said as he slid into the bench across from Rice, the same seat that only moments ago had supported the large and expressive ass of Tulips Kissin'.

Rice took a sip of his beer.

"You get a lot of work done here, do you?" Janousek asked, studying the arrival on stage of a tall, skinny dancer who seemed unsteady on her high heels.

Rice said nothing.

"So where you been lately?" Janousek pointed to Rice's warm beer when a waitress came over, and held up two fingers.

"I went to church," Rice said, pushing his beer away. "I was talking to a priest."

"You talk to the clergy a lot?"

Rice didn't reply. He half turned to watch the unsmiling dancer go through her routine while a heavy jungle beat played behind her.

"Me, I don't go to church," Janousek said. "I go to titty bars. They are my place of worship. Like-minded sinners sitting in the dark praising nature's gifts. I even slip money into the collection if the gal sidles up to me. So I guess you and I are members of the same congregation."

"I just come here to get away," Rice said.

The waitress was already back with two cool bottles of Black Label.

"Anything on tap?" Janousek asked.

She shook her head. "Just the bottles. Who's paying?"

Janousek raised his hand, took out his wallet, and dropped a five.

"Billard tells me you have a special gift," Janousek said, taking a long suck on the bottle. "That's why you get to come and go as you please. In case you ever wondered."

"I never thought much about it," Rice said, finishing the warm bottle of flat beer in front of him.

"He thinks pretty highly of you," Janousek said, turning his attention back to the stripper who received a few unenthusiastic claps after her routine ended. "I haven't seen any miracles from you yet but, hey, it's early. Right?"

Rice was annoyed when his hands shook as he unwrapped a cigar. He lit it and offered the pack to Janousek who shook his head.

"Hav-A-Tampas are like smoking sweet hay," he said.

Rice tapped the cigar ash into the old beer bottle between sips from the new one. A little hiss seeped out.

"I heard the cops even have a special name for you," Janousek said, grinning and shaking his head. "I can't wait to hear what you know."

"I don't know anything," Rice said. "Not for sure. I'm swimming in murky water just like you. Shapes. Movement. I'm just trying to make sense of it."

"Is that why you went to the priest?"

Rice nodded.

"Is there a story there?"

"No," Rice said, blowing out a sigh with the cigar smoke. "I don't think so. He's just a good man as confused about things as everyone else. But Annike felt an affinity for him. People are fucked-up."

Janousek nodded as if that made perfect sense. Then he pulled out his notepad and flipped through the pages.

"Did you know Annike Eichel had lots of money?" he asked. "Hundreds of thousands. Maybe more."

"I'm surprised being an atheist pays so well," Rice said.

"I know. We live in this 'one nation, under God,' but lots of folks believed in what she was doing, even if they didn't like to talk about it publicly very much," Janousek said. "And her organization, Right Thinkers for a New America—very catchy—brought in a lot more. She was married once to a banker or stockbroker—I can't find out for sure—in New York. No children, but she still got alimony. Speaking engagements brought in some coin. Not here, not in

Goodwater, but in the big cities. She could command top dollar."

"That explains it, then."

"Seems there was a true money-grubbing heart beating inside that gorgeous, cold atheist breast," Janousek said. "She shook down fat cats in Cleveland left and right. I talked to some of them—had to be off the record, unfortunately—and got the impression that our dead hell-raiser was not above balling a high roller then hitting him up for a donation. And not just once."

"Why you telling me this?"

"We're a team," Janousek said.

"So she whored herself, then blackmailed the victims?"

"I wouldn't exactly call these guys victims, and nobody would use the word blackmail. Not even off the record."

"I knew she was no Girl Scout, but I'm surprised."

Janousek finished off his beer. "Doesn't sound like the kind of person who's going to visit a priest and ask him 'What's it all about, Alfie?' More likely she wanted to rob the collection plate."

The large black man who came in earlier wore a big grin as he slipped a rolled bill into a dancer's garter, then allowed his hand to linger along her calf. She smiled but looked uncomfortable and tippy-toed down the bar and out of his grasp.

"Why does he look familiar to me?" Rice said. He slid off the bench into a pool of light. When the big man saw Rice, his smile fell away, and he gently elbowed his partner. Both of them took a last swig and exited in a hurry.

"Seems to know you," Janousek said. "Even if you don't know him. But he could take some lessons in hiding his guilt."

The two reporters followed the men outside in time to watch them speed away in a government vehicle. "That's cheeky," Janousek said. "Taking a city vehicle to a strip club. Or was it county?"

"No," Rice said. "Those are city wheels."

Standing in the dust of the truck was Annike Eichel, glum as usual, but staring off at the truck as though it was carrying away her favorite purse. She returned her gaze to Rice.

"Let's go back to the office," he said. "I want to check something out."

# { 17 }

It was four thirty when Rice and Janousek returned to an almost empty newsroom.

A reporter at the sports desk threw a halfhearted wave in their direction but was apparently too busy to do any "Red" taunting.

"What kind of hours do you guys keep?" Janousek said, looking around. "I mean the regular, nongifted newsmen."

Rice pulled open a desk drawer and started riffling through files. "Most of the reporters cover local government meetings or other afternoon and evening events," he said. "As soon as the paper comes up after one o'clock, most of them work on stories or go home until their meeting starts."

"Or go to the grill," Janousek said.

Rice plucked out a booklet from the file and smacked it with the back of his hand. "This is what I was looking for."

Janousek crouched closer. “The 1972 Goodwater Municipal Report,” he said. “What’s the hurry to read that?”

Rice flipped through the pages, snapping them sharply until he found what he wanted. “Take a look,” he said, handing the book to Janousek. “Anyone you recognize?”

Janousek put on a pair of glasses then squinted down at the page. “Foster Ebner. You got a Negro running the Public Works Department?” he said. The heavyset man had light-colored skin with an ugly face that looked like a crushed throw pillow. “He was the guy in the bar.”

Rice took the book back and flipped through various city departments before slapping the book again and throwing it on his desk. “And there’s his sidekick,” he said, pointing to a small photo of the assistant city finance director. “Frank Lalley. I only met him once. Mousy guy who won’t look you in the eye.”

Janousek shrugged. “He wears a green eyeshade all day and works with numbers. Probably doesn’t know what to do when he sees actual people.”

“But why were the two of them at Martelli’s together?”

“Thirsty? Lovers of exotic dance?”

Rice shook his head. “I got a hunch about something,” he said, turning to Janousek as though considering whether to say the next thing. “You interested in meeting one of the city’s more disreputable citizens?”

“Sure. Scum of the earth. They’re my favorite people.”

—

When they located Star Lightman, he was sitting on a bus bench sliding a twig along his heel.

"Dog shit?" Rice said.

Star looked up, brows furrowing when he saw Janousek. "Cat shit," he said. "It smells worse, if you can believe it." He held out his free hand toward Rice. The reporter fumbled in his pocket and handed over a Hav-A-Tampa.

"Who's your sidekick?" Star said.

Rice made introductions. Star studied him for a while and held up his cat shit twig, looking for a moment like he was going to pick his teeth with it. He threw it into the gutter at Janousek's feet. "I don't give tours to out-of-town visitors," he said. "And I don't imagine you're bringing me business."

"Loan shark," Janousek said.

Star eyed him again and wasn't pleased. "Pimp," he said. Janousek snapped his fingers, as if he'd just missed the sixty-four-dollar question.

Rice held out a match, and Star hurriedly undressed the cigar, puffing while holding his gaze on the Cleveland reporter.

"What do you want?" he finally said to nobody in particular.

"Do you know this guy?" Rice asked, holding a folded copy of the city's municipal report in front of him.

Star's eyes narrowed as sweet cigar smoke swirled around him. He blew the next puff right into the photograph of Foster Ebner.

"I'll be damned," he said. "My brotha has a gummit job. That accounts for the nice car."

"That's the guy you saw going into Annike Eichel's place some evenings, right?" Rice said.

Star looked at one reporter and then the other. "Why we talking about this?" he said. "You thinkin'—" he leaned over the photo to read it again—" Mr. Ebner cut up that pretty white gal after kertanging her?"

"It's a possibility."

Star shrugged. "What about the church bus? Did you ever find out who was driving that?"

"We did two stories on that guy," Janousek said. "Don't you ever read the paper?"

Star smiled, showing off his gold tooth star and a fine line of spittle on his lower lip. "Sometimes, when I don't want to get any grit on my threads I fold up a newspaper and put it on the bench," he said. "I might look at the headlines when I do that."

"The bus guy was a nobody," Rice said. "You won't see him around anymore."

Star nodded, puffed on the cigar, and studied the book photo again. "Should be a handsome guy like me running that department," he said. "Ebner's got the light shadow, but he's too ugly to pass."

"But that was him, right?" Rice said.

"You know it was."

"And you saw him at her home multiple times?" Janousek said.

Star looked Janousek up and down. "Love the tie," he said.

The reporter undid his mint-green necktie and handed it to Star.

"That's real silk," the pimp said, pursing his lips. He wrapped it around his neck like a scarf. "Yeah, he was there lots of times. Came out the front some times. Came out the back some times. 'Course I'm not always here, but I'm guessing he was paying house calls pretty regular. Spending the night more than once."

Janousek turned to Rice and shook his head.

"I know," Star said, catching the exchanged look. "Ugly motherfucker like that."

"Anything else come to mind since we talked last?" Rice said.

"I was thinking some more about that church bus," Star said, toying with the tip of his new tie. "And I remembered seeing somebody else visiting Miss *Eye-Kill* a couple times. He was dressed in black but had his collar on backwards. Little white thing on his throat. Looked like another church guy."

"Are you telling me you saw a priest visiting her house?" Janousek said.

"I don't know what he was," Star said. "He came more than a few times. Always during the day. Stayed a couple hours. You tellin' me he was a priest?"

"What'd he look like?" Rice said.

Star shrugged. "I never saw his face. If he came in a car, I never saw that either. Do you think he was tapping her too?"

Another look between Rice and Janousek.

"Do you recall anything else about him? Anything at all?" Rice said.

"He was low to the ground and moved smooth. Like a ballplayer," Star said. "I wouldn't want to get in his way."

# { 18 }

Rice told Janousek to go away. He wanted to think.

He wondered how much Ed Kadish knew about the murder he was investigating. Would he be willing to talk now that Markle had planted a stink finger on Rice's forehead?

Phil Fortunato had always liked Rice. Stop by anytime, he'd told the police reporter more than once.

Rice was pretty sure it was Markle behind the effort to get him off the police beat. Had he somehow talked Fortunato into it? The police chief didn't have enough juice to do it on his own, did he? The biggest surprise was Billard buying into it. He couldn't believe he wanted him on the city hall beat *that* badly.

He picked up the phone and dialed.

"What are you doing?" Rice asked when Stacey answered.

"I'm doing my nails," she said. "Going out tonight."

"With whom?"

"How are you feeling, Rice?" she said. "All better now?"

"Yeah," he said. "Thanks to my raise I buy fresh fruits and vegetables all the time and drink lots more milk. I think it's helping."

"I don't want you starting about Roger."

"My love is selfish. I cannot breathe without you."

"You're just being annoying," she said.

"Keats wrote it in a letter to Fanny Brawne."

"Sounds like him."

"So you don't care about Keats anymore?" he asked.

"He's all aromatic flowers and sunlit butterfly wings," Stacey said. "I've grown up since college."

"I'd like to see you again," he said.

"Why?"

"I need to talk to you."

"Talk to me now," she said. "But no more Keats."

"How well do you know Father Growden?"

"Pretty well. I was surprised he left while the two of you were talking about ghosts."

"No, no, that's fine," Rice said. "He could tell the conversation was going nowhere. I was a little mad at you for sharing my secret with him. I got over it, though."

A pause and then her voice rose an octave. "Well, I'm sorry for trying to help you," she said. "Roger says you're troubled. That was his word. So I thought you could use some professional guidance."

"Roger knows too then?"

"Of course not," she said. "But he reads your stuff."

"Did Growden ever talk to you about personal things?"

"Like what?"

"I don't know, if he was happy or depressed. Where he was going on vacation. His favorite saint. Personal stuff."

"Priests don't get depressed."

"Did you know he's leaving the priesthood?"

Rice heard her stifle a gasp. "I don't believe it."

"He's going to work for some boy's club in Cleveland. Says his faith is gone. He told me himself."

"Sometimes he seemed … distracted. But this …"

"Yeah."

"It's like you just don't know what to believe in anymore," she said. "These days it's all changing. All the time. It's sad."

"But you still believe in Roger?"

"I don't want to talk about him."

"Did Growden ever talk to you about Annike Eichel?" Rice said.

"He did say something about her once that I remember," Stacey said, and Rice was able to picture her warm lips next to the phone, her eyes wide and childlike, and he felt awful for a moment. "He said she had a kind of faith, just like believers. And she questioned it just like believers do. He thought that kind of openness to doubt was attractive."

"Attractive? Is that the word he used?"

"Yes," she said. "I remember because I thought it was unusual too. An odd thing for a priest to say."

"Do you think there was anything between them?"

"He seemed more amused than anything else when her name came up," Stacey said. "I don't know. That could mean anything."

"He was seen leaving her house," Rice said. "More than once."

A little sniff from her end. Nothing else.

"And he wasn't the only one. A Negro city supervisor spent a lot of time with her too. Left late. Sometimes the next morning. And there might have been others. I don't know yet."

"Roger knows Father Growden. Maybe he can help you."

"Tell him nothing. Understand?"

"Yes. Okay."

"I'm just bouncing things off you," Rice said.

"Off the record," Stacey said. He could almost see her nodding.

"Yeah. Like the ghost thing was off the record."

"You never told me I couldn't talk about it," she said. "It scared me every time you brought it up. It still does."

"Annike Eichel may have been sexually blackmailing some Cleveland big shots. So with that history, you can understand why I wondered about her relationship with Growden."

"It's all getting pretty complicated."

"And she was two months pregnant when she died."

"What … What color was the child?" Stacey said.

"They can't tell. Religion wasn't clear either."

"Why do you talk like that?"

Rice didn't say anything for a long time. His mouth was dry and he smacked his lips once. "Remember that time we went to Oberlin? We saw a play together. Theater of the absurd, I think. The actors ended up screaming the alphabet at each other."

"I remember some of it," Stacey said. "I fell asleep."

"Afterwards, we went to Foster's and had a root beer float and some hot dogs. Then we drove around on country roads for a long time. Do you remember what we talked about?"

"I remember the root beer float. And sitting next to you, holding your arm while you drove on dark roads. A train came through a crossing, and there we were in the middle of nowhere. Just the dark and a noisy train going by."

"And I asked you if you got anything out of the play at all."

"Yes," Stacey said. "The world has turned upside down. White is black. Left is right. And we can't talk to each other about it."

"Do you really love him?"

"That …" Stacey started, ready to defy him, to summon up vitriol. Then sighed instead. "I've matured, or tried to. I'm working on being responsible. I'm thinking about the future. I think love—mature love—is mixed up in that soup somehow."

"Do you love me?"

"Yes."

"Maybe in an upside-down world our kind of love is the only thing that makes sense."

"I said no more Keats."

"What's wrong with poets?"

"They die young. And heartbroken," she said. "And usually penniless."

"Would you want me if I had lots of money? Don't tell me if the answer is yes."

Nothing for a while. "Father Growden touched my arm once," Stacey said. "We saw each other before a Josh White concert at the college so we sat together. When Josh sang 'Early Mornin' Rain,' Father reached over and touched me on the elbow."

"So … Did that mean something to you?"

"You get enough touches from enough men in your life, you learn to read them. Sometimes, you don't need anything else. That's what I meant about maturity."

"So what did his touch tell you?" Rice asked.

"It said 'Listen. Attend to this.' I think something about the song's theme of loneliness got to him."

"And you pretend not to care about poetry," Rice said. "He read your own loneliness."

"Probably," she said. "The point is he never tried to make a move on me. Not then. Not ever. It wasn't his style."

"So?"

"I don't care how beautiful and seductive Annike Eichel might have been," Stacey said. "He never had a sexual relationship with her. The poor dead child was not his."

"I think you're right."

"I have to get going," she said.

"Tell me," Rice said. "Was this concert before you met me?"

"Yes," Stacey said. It sounded like she was digging something out of her purse. "Please don't call me again."

# { 19 }

Foster Ebner scowled when Tom Janousek picked up the model of a three-masted schooner from his office shelf.

"How can I help you boys?" the Goodwater director of Public Works said as he watched Janousek carefully replace the ship model on its stand.

Ebner's thick body looked unnatural in his sport shirt. He holstered two pens in a pocket protector, but his shirt was stained with ink anyway. His desktop was covered with an uncurled map of the city that he held in place with a tape dispenser and three sports-themed paperweights. A variety of loose-leaf folders were piled up on the shelf next to the ship model.

Janousek plucked out one and began leafing through it. "You a Navy man, Foster?" he said.

The director looked uncomfortable. He shifted his gaze between Rice, sitting on a chair in front of his desk, and

Janousek, who was flipping through his technical library like he was the curator. "I served in the Navy during Korea," Ebner said. "Listen, what is—"

"I like Navy guys," Janousek said, putting the book back, smiling. "I spent many happy hours with PBR crews on liberty in Saigon. They couldn't hold their liquor and they sure liked the ladies. Especially after they were stewed."

Ebner offered an uncomfortable smile, then seemed to pull himself together. "You serve in 'Nam?" he said.

"We're looking into the Annike Eichel murder," Rice said, and Ebner's head snapped in his direction. "We're hoping you can help."

The Public Works director sat down and his chair groaned. "I'll do what I can," he said. "I've got a few minutes. Shouldn't you be talking to the GPD, though?"

"Sure, sure," Rice said, waving his hand. "We're talking to them too, of course. But your name came up, so we're trying to close the loop."

"I don't know why," Ebner said.

"Have you spoken to Ed Kadish yet?" Rice said.

"The name sounds familiar but, no, I don't think so."

Rice exchanged glances with Janousek who pushed out his lower lip. "He's the detective investigating the case," Rice said. "Of course, he might bring in the state boys to help him. There's lots of pressure to solve it."

"I imagine," Ebner said.

"Kadish will be by soon enough to talk to you," Janousek said. He started to toy with a Cleveland Browns paperweight on the desk. "Or maybe one of the state boys. Or the FBI."

"The FBI? Why would they want to talk to me? I take care of streets and storm sewers."

"Murder investigations are funny that way, Foster," Rice said. "I've been involved in a number of them. You wouldn't believe the direction they take sometimes. Two years ago, Ed Kadish interviewed an eight-year-old schoolgirl while investigating the shooting of a drug dealer uptown. Maybe you remember it."

"I don't follow the news much."

"Too bad," Rice said. "It was pretty interesting. She ended up fingering the killer personally. Of course, they had to move out of state after ..."

"We saw a guy looked like you feeling up the talent over at Martelli's the other day," Janousek said. "About three, four o'clock. Taking a late lunch, Foster?"

"What's my lunch schedule or where I choose to eat it have to do with a murder investigation?" Ebner said. "You guys are starting to push bad buttons."

"Relax, Foster," Janousek said. "You're a bright guy. Can't be easy for a Negro to become head of Public Works. And we really don't care where you spend your spare time—even if it's in the middle of the afternoon—or who you spend it with."

"Little Frank Lalley, the city's assistant finance director," Rice said. "It just looked odd. That's all. But that's another story for another time, right?"

"Look, I saw you at Martelli's, Channon," Ebner said, leaning forward. The hardness in his face was back. "I'll admit I felt guilty. Hell, I was in a city truck. Middle of the afternoon."

"You needed a smoke break," Janousek said. "Nothing wrong with that."

"Fuck you," Ebner said. "Do you have any idea how many Saturdays I work off the clock? And Sundays sometimes too."

"So you set your own hours," Janousek said, looking over Ebner's head. "I'm cool with that. You're the man. Do what you want."

"Except folks see a Public Works truck in front of a strip club," Rice said, holding out his hands in a pleading manner. "It looks bad. For you. For the city. Somebody drops a dime on the mayor, and he may not care for your logical explanation."

"People got long memories," Janousek said.

Ebner looked like he wanted to hit something. The creases in his face deepened and his coffee-colored skin grew darker. "Like you?" he said. "You going to tell the mayor I was in a strip club?"

"Hey, I don't care where you spend your time," Janousek said. "I don't pay your salary. I live in Cleveland."

Ebner turned to Rice. "What is going on here?"

"We're just trying to clear some things up, Foster," Rice said, forcing an ingratiating smile to his lips. Judging by Ebner's face, it wasn't working. "The city cops are going to stop by eventually to ask the same questions. You can practice on us. Get your story down."

"I don't have a story."

"Fine," Rice said. "All the better. It works best if you tell the truth. That way you don't have to remember so much."

"Are you calling me a liar?" Ebner asked.

"Oh, hell, Foster," Janousek said. "Everybody's a liar. We're people. We can't help ourselves."

This time, Ebner squinted hard in Janousek's direction. "I'm going to take you out behind the parking lot and beat your head into the concrete. Then I'll toss what's left into the burn barrel."

If Janousek was worried, he didn't show it. "See, that's what I mean," he said. "You're not going to do that. You've got a witness."

"Let's stay away from words like liar, head, and concrete," Rice said, still smiling and pretending he wasn't uncomfortable. "We just want to know why you spent so much time at Annike Eichel's home."

"What's it to you?"

"Because she's dead, Foster," Janousek said before slapping his head. "Oh, yeah. Forgot. You don't read the papers."

"I'm amazed nobody has busted up that pretty white face," Ebner said. He turned to Rice. "Who said I was there?"

Janousek got up and actually moved closer to the huge Public Works director. He made an ugly squawking sound like a game show buzzer going off. Ebner winced. "Wrong answer, Foster," he said. "The cops are going to ask you that question because they already know the answer. You pretend you weren't there and you become murder suspect number one."

"I didn't do anything wrong," Ebner said.

"You wouldn't believe how many bad guys say that," Janousek said, staring out the window like this conversation was starting to bore him. "The cops are going to want more."

"The police know why I was there?"

"They might," Rice said, surprised the tension had fallen off some. "But they know for sure you were in her house. They're going to want details."

"Are you going to put them in the paper?"

Janousek toyed with his shirt sleeve. "His paper *and* my paper. You're going to be famous."

Rice shrugged. "It's a murder, Foster. You were seen at the dead woman's house. A lot. People are going to want to know why. If you don't want to talk about it, well, that makes you look guilty. Even when you're not."

Janousek sniffed loudly at the last comment.

"You don't think I killed her."

"Me?" Rice said. "No. But it doesn't matter what *I* think."

"I think you did it," Janousek said. "Big strong man chops up a little bitty woman who nobody liked. It makes sense to me."

Ebner ran a meaty hand through his hair. "Christ," he said. "I'm going to need a lawyer."

"I think that's a good idea, Foster," Rice said. "A real good idea. So how would you characterize your relationship with Miss Eichel?"

Ebner looked left and right across the map of Goodwater on his desk. "I hardly knew the woman," he said. "I met with her a few times, but I didn't know what she was about. And I didn't kill her. That's all I'm going to say to you."

"Then that's what we'll write," Rice said, closing his notepad. "If you remember anything else, give me a call. Anytime."

Rice placed a business card next to Ebner's fingers, which were drumming on the map over the planned expansion of Highway 42 to four lanes.

"What's the deal with you and Frank Lalley?" Janousek said, acting like he wasn't going anywhere. "The Public Works director and one of the city's top money men stuffing bills into ladies' underwear during working hours."

Ebner looked at Rice, his face softening like a child caught stealing cookies before dinner. "If I think of anything else, I'll call you," he said. "Now I want you to go."

Rice nodded. Janousek smiled and followed him out of the office.

"He doesn't like you much," Rice said.

"He's dirty," Janousek said.

"Oh yeah."

# { 20 }

Tom Janousek walked into the office of Frank Lalley, a little man with a little office containing neatly stacked ledgers and not much else. He wore a short-sleeved gray shirt that used to be white, and a clip-on striped tie that hung uneasily over his unbuttoned top buttonhole. Some two-dozen pencils of varying lengths stood inside a cup bearing the name of the Ohio Municipal League. A cheap metal plate announced that this was Frank Lalley, Goodwater assistant city finance director.

Janousek picked up the nameplate and began studying it before Lalley even noticed him.

"Can I help you?" the little man said, staring past Janousek to the door at the vacant desk of his secretary. He only scanned Janousek's face once before looking away again. His glasses were filthy with fingerprints.

"Have you ever seen a woman's tits close up while alone" —Janousek paused and pretended to study the nameplate— "*Frank*? Or is it always on a stool in a seedy bar with a beer at your elbow?"

"Who are you?" Lalley said, looking again at the secretary's empty desk. "And how did you get in here?"

"I'm sorry," the reporter said. "My name is Tom Janousek. I thought you might remember me from yesterday when you and Foster Ebner bolted from Martelli's. You looked right at me."

Lalley's face turned red. He pulled off his glasses by the lens and looked around nervously again.

"I went with Mr. Ebner because he invited me," Lalley said. "He wanted to talk over some matters."

"Ah," Janousek said. "So it was a business meeting."

"Are you with the state?"

"What would a state auditor be doing in a titty bar at three o'clock in the afternoon?"

"I never saw you," Lalley said. "Mr. Ebner saw somebody he knew and said we should leave."

"So you're not a Martelli's regular?"

"No," Lalley said, dropping his pencil into the Ohio Municipal League coffee cup and sliding his glasses around on his desk. "Of course not."

"Why didn't you just talk things out in this nice office?" Janousek said, looking around like the place was Versailles.

"Lots of nosybodies around here," he said. "They hear things they shouldn't or things they don't understand, and then they blab them to their friends." He made a hand gesture that was supposed to look like a woman's flapping mouth.

"Like your secretary?" Janousek said, looking back at the still-empty desk.

Lalley leaned over the desk and Janousek did the same. "Even low-level employees—after they've been on the job for a lot of years—you can't get rid of them," he said, trying to whisper, his breath stinking of coffee. "Even if they're undependable. Or indiscreet."

"You could try closing the door."

"Mr. Ebner wanted to talk about this outside the office," Lalley said. "He told me it would be fun. I thought we were going to the park."

"Sure. Feeding the birds. That's enjoyable."

"He's an important man," Lalley said. "So I went with him."

"The two of you talking together outside the office," Janousek said. "Suspicious people might say that looked like conspiracy."

"Conspiracy? We weren't doing anything wrong. Besides, I wasn't the one doing the talking."

"So what did he want?"

Lalley picked up his glasses and put them back on his face. "This sort of thing happens sometimes," he said. "Public Works sent over an especially large monthly reimbursement request. Accounts payable wasn't sure all the items were appropriate. Some lacked documentation. I asked the mayor about it, and he told me to do whatever needed to be done."

"The mayor. He's a good guy," Janousek said.

"Uh-huh. But all he really cares about is making sure everything works smoothly. He's not interested in the details."

"Where the devil lives," Janousek said.

"Exactly. So I decided to call Mr. Ebner directly. That's when he invited me to the, um, meeting."

"Did you get a chance to talk at all?" Janousek asked.

"We talked in the truck on the way over a little," Lalley said. He reached into the pencil cup and carefully flipped all the pencils that were eraser end up to pointy end up. He sighed loudly like he'd just discovered his favorite daughter was pregnant.

"Yeah?"

Lalley ground the blunted pencils in a pencil sharpener across the room. He blew off the wood dust from each one and daintily slid his finger along the points. Then he blew on them again.

Janousek stood up, smiled, walked over to Lalley, and ripped the glasses off his head.

"Hey," the little man said, reaching out for the spectacles that Janousek held high over his head.

Next, Janousek grabbed Lalley's other arm—the one holding the newly sharpened pencils—and snatched the pencils from his fist. These he smashed hard against Lalley's desktop. Then he put them back into the pencil cup.

"Sit down," Janousek said, directing Lalley to his chair. "What did you talk about in the truck?"

"Give me my glasses back," Lalley said.

Janousek shook his head and his smile faded. He ripped the pencil sharpener from the wood table it was bolted into, a chunk of wood still clinging to the sharpener's screws. He placed Lalley's glasses on the busted-up desk and held the sharpener's heavy cutter assembly over them.

"You've got five seconds to tell me what you talked about or I turn your specs into shards of greasy glass."

Lalley nodded and sat back. He spoke quickly. "He kind of threatened me."

"Threatened you how?"

"He said I didn't understand how urgently his office needed certain supplies. That it would cost the city far more if he waited and went through channels. Those were his exact words. If he went through channels. *Proper* channels, I think he said."

"And what did you say?"

"I told him that, while that may be true, I still needed the paperwork. I reminded him that government isn't always efficient, but its dealings have to be transparent."

"Well, you got a gold star coming your way," Janousek said. "Now, tell me how he threatened you and maybe you'll get your glasses back."

Lalley took a deep breath. "He said the mayor appreciates my cooperation. He said it would be unfortunate if the mayor had to dismiss me."

"And what did you say?"

"I didn't say anything," Lalley said. "We were at the … at Martelli's by then. So he threw his arm around me, and we walked in. Then he saw you and we didn't talk again."

Janousek tossed his glasses back to Lalley. Then the pencil sharpener. Then he sat down. "Were those the first almost-naked women you ever saw, Frankie?"

"I don't want to talk with you anymore."

"What were the supplies for?"

"Tires. Lots of tires. Other truck parts."

"Go on."

"Tell me who you are again," Lalley said.

"I didn't tell you the first time."

"There's a sheriff's deputy in the building. I'll call him."

Janousek scowled while he flicked a busted pencil point off his jacket. "Why?"

"Misrepresentation," Lalley said.

"I'm just a guy off the street who wants to know how the city's money is spent," Janousek said. "I'm from out of town, but is that against the law here?"

"I don't know."

"Jesus, you're dumb," Janousek said. "Go ahead and call security. I've got to get going anyway. I have a story to do."

"What?"

"My name is Tom Janousek, and I'm with the *Cleveland Chronicle*. We're working with the *Tribune* on a series of articles. I think I can get your name in the paper, Frankie."

Lalley gulped, and Janousek chuckled.

"I've been sitting here trying to come up with a lede. How does this one sound? The Goodwater assistant finance director was intimidated by the Public Works director, the city's first colored man serving as department head, into authorizing suspect expenditures and charging them to the municipality."

"That was off the record," Lalley said. "Everything I told you was off the record."

"I don't do off the record," Janousek said.

"You'll ruin me," Lalley said, falling against the chair back and managing to seem even smaller in the process.

"Could happen."

"The mayor told me to do whatever Ebner wanted," Lalley said.

Janousek stood up when he saw lots of pencil shavings on his pants. He talked while brushing them onto Lalley's carpet. "I doubt it," he said. "Mayor is a little too smart to say something like that. Besides, he'll deny it. Your word against his."

"That's not fair."

"No, it's not," Janousek said. "But I've got good news. I'm not here to do a story on embezzlement."

"Embezzlement?" Lalley said. His mouth fell open, which showed off his mostly yellow teeth.

"It's about murder. The murder of Annike Eichel."

"Murder?"

"That's good. If I say dumb ass, will you repeat that too?"

"I've got nothing to do with a murder."

"I don't know," Janousek said. "Maybe you're right. Maybe you'll just go to jail for being stupid."

Lalley didn't repeat the last word this time. Janousek looked disappointed.

Lalley gulped again. "I'll help you in any way I can," he said.

# { 21 }

Kleavon Hayes yanked the starter cord of the busted-up lawn mower. It coughed once, twice, then nothing.

"Here's the thing about running a scam," the tall black man said, sweat dripping from his brow onto the rusted red mower chassis. He gave a twist to the spark plug and adjusted a set screw on the engine. "You gotta make sure you pay everybody involved. Somebody gets left out, they feel like a sap."

Rice Channon nodded. He'd spent two days tracking down every Public Works Department employee who had recently retired, been fired, or quit. He posed just one question: do you know of any illegal or inappropriate transactions that took place in the Goodwater Public Works Department during your time working there?

No one said a thing. Rice learned early on that mentioning Foster Ebner's name ended the conversation pretty quickly. Three men closed the door on him without saying a word.

A half-dozen others made it clear they didn't want any trouble or wanted to protect their pension or weren't interested in cooperating with an official investigation. When Rice assured them this was not an official investigation, most of the men said they weren't interested in cooperating with an unofficial investigation either.

Until he talked to Kleavon Hayes.

Hayes had retired from the city last year, apparently on good terms. Now he ran a shop out of his garage that repaired mostly lawn mower engines, although he claimed to be doing a brisk business working on go-cart engines as well. He wanted to make sure Rice included that in his story.

"Everybody knew what Ebner was doing," Hayes said. "He made sure city contracts went to shirttail relatives—a stepson, a half brother—and that he got a cut. That's the way it started."

Hayes pushed a spring under the motor, and the smell of gasoline briefly filled the air.

"Those kinds of arrangements are pretty simple," Hayes said, wiping his hand on his spotted jeans. "If the department does good work, nobody much cares. It ain't right, of course, but you want to hang around to get your retirement so you keep your mouth shut."

"But you knew what was going on?"

"Mostly rumors but, yeah, we knew," Hayes said. "Ebner was pretty good at keeping what he was doing quiet. You don't want to flaunt that kind of shit in front of people. It's insulting."

"What else happened?"

"If things were quiet in the carpentry shop, he'd have them stop by his house to repair a leaking roof shed, gutters, shit like that," Hayes said, looking up to the garage ceiling, reflecting. "He ended up getting a whole new back deck and a greenhouse, courtesy of the citizens of Goodwater, Ohio."

"You know this for a fact?"

"Yeah, I know it, but I can't prove it," Hayes said. "Hell, it's still going on. I think a supervisor has a new addition on his house, and I'm pretty sure none of those guys mow their own lawns."

"Don't the neighbors say something when they see city trucks doing lawn and repair work at these homes?"

Hayes shook his head adamantly while biting his bottom lip. "Like I said, Ebner doesn't throw it in your face. He's got unmarked trailers and vans. Sometimes, they're used for city jobs too, but mostly they're hauling unidentifiable city equipment to private homes."

Rice wanted to ask the big question, but he held off. A thousand interviews taught him to let the information torrent flow. Wait until it became a trickle.

"Sounds like nickel and dime stuff," he said.

Kleavon Hayes had the big grin. He looked like a guy anyone could shoot the shit with. "I guess that's why nobody much cared," he said. "At least that's what folks told themselves. Ebner's a man you don't want to poke. So they pretended he was just skimmin' cream."

"They?"

"All of us. You know that joke?" Hayes said, laughing. "Don't make a wave. It's easier that way. Lots of strains in people's lives."

"But something happened."

Hayes frowned and began rolling the lawn mower carcass back and forth like he was testing the wheels for squeaks. "Before too long, he was using all that city equipment to do other jobs. Safe jobs. Jobs nobody would think twice about if they saw it going on."

"Like what?"

"The city contracts out a lot of road repairs. So does the county. A big storm drain project a few years back went to a company in Columbus. Ebner helped them out. Unofficially, if you get me."

Rice shook his head sadly. Then he looked up as though he really didn't want to hear any more.

"Hey, wait," Hayes said. "This is where it gets interestin'."

Rice studied his face. Hayes with the big smile again. He interlaced his fingers. "It was about this time that Foster Ebner figured something out," he said. "Why chew on the crumbs of those big out-of-town companies who won the contracts? He could make lots more by overseeing the work himself. And he could mix in city Public Works workers with the out of towners. More money. Pretty soon, he's splitting the contract money, putting about half in his pocket, and paying off his own supervisors with the rest. The work gets done. Nobody notices. Everybody's happy."

"Not everybody," Rice said. "Or we wouldn't be talking about it."

"Yeah, well ... It's like sweeping the floor of a barn loft," Hayes said. "Do you know what I mean?"

"I have no idea."

"City boy," Hayes said, smirking again, but his look was paternal this time. "You sweep up the floor, and it looks fine when you're done, but pieces of straw and rat shit float down through the seams. It can't be helped. If anybody's downstairs watering the horses, they get crap in their hair and wonder what's going on."

"Pretend I'm stupid and don't know where you're going."

"You're making it easy," Hayes said, this time slapping Rice good-naturedly on the shoulder. "The bean counters, the secretaries, the janitorial crew. All of them are feeling the straw dropping on their heads. Equipment is breaking down faster than it should. Tires are wearing out. Maintenance costs are going up. The ditchdiggers putting in the storm sewers are working overtime but not getting paid extra for it."

"Ebner must have realized that wasn't going to work."

Hayes rubbed his chin, picked up and considered the monkey wrench on his workbench for a bit. Put it down. "My guess is he didn't want that bag of money he was receiving to get any lighter," he said. "So the man started cutting corners.

Supervisors still got their cut, sure, but the little guy—the truck driver, the ditchdigger—they got squat."

"Why didn't they talk?" Rice said. "Or did they?"

Hayes smiled like he was talking to a deaf man. Or a child. "You're not getting it, are you? Ebner started with the threats. He probably just got frustrated one day, but once he started telling his workers they would lose their jobs if they didn't shut up and do what he said ..." Hayes chuckled, spread his arms. "That worked pretty good so he figured out a way to *guarantee* their silence. He threatened them physically. Have you ever met the man?"

"Yeah, a big guy," Rice said. "Like King Kong in a dress shirt."

Hayes grimaced a little. "The word got out anyway. State auditors showed up."

"Bound to happen."

"Ebner was cool as an icebox tomato during the audit," Hayes said. "Everybody in his department backed his story. Costs were up, but these days, the city was expected to do more with less and blah-blah-blah. The state bought it."

"And Ebner felt more comfortable than ever."

"Yup."

"Did anybody get beat up?"

Hayes shook his head. "Not that I know of. Turns out, it wasn't necessary. He used ... What do ya call it?"

"Intimidation."

Hayes jabbed a confirming finger at Rice. "Yeah. Intimidation. He used intimidation. That kept everyone in line."

"Except you."

"With me, he used something else," Hayes said. "He pretended he liked me. Maybe he did. I don't know."

"So you'd go along with whatever he wanted, you and he being tight and all."

"He was the boss and I was nice to him, but I knew better," Hayes said. "I was supervisor of one of the bigger city park work crews. We mulched around trees, repaired broken swings, that kind of thing. One day, he stopped by and pulled me off under a red oak tree and told me all the good things he heard about me. He shook my hand and thanked me."

"And then what happened?"

"That was the funny thing," Hayes said. "I heard all the stories. I knew what to expect, so I was waiting for the other shoe to drop, get me?"

"Sure."

"But he got back in his car and drove off. Honked when he left. Waves. Never asked me for anything."

"I'll be damned. He came back, though, right?"

"I haven't talked to him since," Hayes said, wincing as though the memory hurt. "A little later I learned I have cancer. It's in the lungs but slow growing. I guess that's a good thing, right?"

Rice was surprised. He smiled weakly.

"Moved into my back so I can't do any heavy work. It hurts when I bend over. I was a supervisor, but I always jumped in to help my crew. I wouldn't do it any other way. Most folks don't understand that."

"So they fired you?"

"Retired early," Hayes said. "My doc told them my back problem was partly due to the work I did for the city, so I got a little disability too. He was trying to take care of me. He knew it was the cancer."

"The motor repair work doesn't hurt?"

"It hurts like hell," Hayes said. "And it's getting worse. But I've got a couple good years left, I figure. I put in eight hours most days. And the work's fun."

Hayes pushed the lawn mower chassis with his foot, and it rolled smoothly across the garage floor. He laughed. "Sometimes all you need to make these things work is a little 3-IN-ONE Oil."

"Did you ever see or hear anything about a woman named Annike Eichel?" Rice asked.

Hayes looked up, seemingly caught off guard for the first time. "That woman on television who was killed?"

Rice nodded.

"What's she got to do with Foster Ebner?"

"I don't know," Rice said. "They seem to have known each other."

Hayes grunted as he rolled a bright-green lawn mower back to his work area. It looked almost new. "This one's froze up. I think the guy drained the oil for some reason. It's gonna cost him."

"Why you being so open about Ebner, Kleavon? Nobody else will talk to me."

Hayes grunted again as he lifted the mower onto his workbench. "Nobody but me, huh?"

"So far."

"I could tell you it's because of the cancer or that I'm tired of being afraid or wanting to make amends or some shit like that. And you'd probably believe me."

Rice shrugged, nodded.

"Here's Foster Ebner, a colored man who's got a big city job. Lots of people work for him. He gets paid pretty well too. Whoo-ee! Have you seen his house?"

Rice smiled.

"So the way I see it, he's got an obligation not just to the city. He owes something to his own people. He's got to be better than a white man doing the same thing. And he's got to keep his hands clean. But the thing that bugs me most is that despite all the out-of-work colored folks in this town, he will almost always hire a white man over a black one. That's not right."

"Why does he do that?"

"He doesn't want to look like he's leanin' too hard to the black side, if you get me. So he leans hard the other way."

"And that's the reason you're telling me all this."

Hayes rubbed his chin again, this time leaving some grease behind. “Yeah, I guess,” he said. “But mostly it’s just because I don’t like the son of a bitch.”

# { 22 }

Rice watched Glenna Cowser study the Tribune Grill's lunch menu like it was a crossword puzzle she was determined to finish.

She sat, as usual, in the booth farthest from the front door, just outside the ladies' room and completely out of sight of whoever was working the bar. She sat there often, especially in summer and winter.

"Tell me the truth, Sal," Rice called out to the bartender. There were no waitresses. They left at two and returned at five for the dinner crowd. "Are these homegrown? They actually taste like real tomatoes."

Rice kept an eye on Glenna who didn't even pretend to care about the conversation. Sal shrugged and drew a short Coke for himself. He wasn't a talker.

By the time the Grill's owner showed up—usually after seven—Glenna would be long gone. She was small with matchstick legs and a chest that looked consumptive, but that didn't stop the owner from throwing her out if he saw her in his place.

Sal didn't care. She pretended to hide and he pretended not to see her.

Glenna didn't smell bad. She never created a ruckus. Her short-cropped gray hair was kept in place with a thick brown headband. If the place was full, she would go outside or retreat into the restroom. Patrons coming and going would acknowledge her with a wave or a nod, but she never made eye contact. She only spoke with other street people, and only outside the bar, usually in the alley.

Rice brushed his fingers together to knock off the hamburger bun crumbs. He ate the last fry on his plate and slurped up what remained of his Coke. Glenna turned over the menu to check out the dessert options on the back.

Nobody knew where she went at night. In the summer, if the St. Francis shelter was filled up, it wasn't so bad to sleep on the streets. In the winter, it could mean death.

Rice took his empty plate to Sal. He wasn't used to his customers doing cleanup.

"How about another burger, fries, and a small Coke?" Rice said. He reached into his pocket and pulled out a handful of coins.

"Better hold the fries," he said. Sal nodded and returned a few minutes later. He put the plate down on the bar, drew a Coke.

"Buck and a quarter," he said.

Rice lifted the bun. "Is that slice from a runt tomato?" he said. "And slather a little more mayo on that, would ya?"

Sal's eyes narrowed as though his honor had been questioned. But he slid a larger tomato slice on the burger, then slapped on another dollop of mayonnaise.

Rice smiled sheepishly when Sal returned. "It's just that I said all those nice things about your tomatoes."

Sal grunted.

Rice took the plate and the Coke over to Glenna's table. He gently placed it in front of her while she reviewed the pie options on the menu.

She put the menu down, regarded the burger, then Rice.

"You look hungry," he said.

She sipped the Coke gracefully, wiping her mouth after each sip with the deliberateness of a cat preening itself. She ate the burger with small, tentative bites, and never said anything until it was half-gone, the fat tomato slice dripping juice onto her plate.

"Thanks," she said. "I missed breakfast today."

"How have you been?"

"I got a cough that's hanging on," she said, taking another bite.

"There's a free clinic on Cleveland Str—"

"I know about that," she said. "I'll go there if I have to."

"I could give you a ride now, if you like. I'm not doing anything."

She giggled, and it turned into a short coughing spasm. Then she wiped her mouth and smiled at him. Her teeth were white but more than a few were missing. “Me either,” she said.

Rice nodded, returning her grin.

“Heard you weren’t feeling too well yourself,” she said. “Didn’t see you in here for a while. Worried they might have finally fired you.”

“Not yet.”

“Well, good.”

“I told Sal to give you extra mayo,” Rice said.

Glenna nodded briskly. “I can taste it,” she said.

“You figure on seeing your family before the weather turns cold?”

Glenna shrugged, her face turning darker. “Billy’s usually drunk or in jail. Haven’t seen him in a while.”

Rice nodded.

“But he brought me a flower on Mother’s Day,” she said. “He always remembers me on Mother’s Day.”

“Sounds like a thoughtful son. Don’t you have a brother?”

This time she spoke with a cheekful of hamburger. “Moved to Columbus. Told me I could come with him, but I didn’t want to go there. Too many people.”

“Do you have a phone number for him?”

She looked at Rice, surprised. “Why? I don’t have a phone.”

After lunch he drove her to the Goodwater Community Free Clinic located in the showroom of the old Myer Chevrolet dealership downtown. That company now sold its

Impalas and Novas at a new place closer to the Westside Mall, next to the popular Kmart store.

Now the largely deserted streets of downtown Goodwater contained storefronts for two jewelry stores, a family-owned camera store, Mac's Shoe Repair, The Tux Shop, and a Woolworth five and dime where Rice used to order egg-salad sandwiches for lunch. The old Capital Theater that premiered *The Sheik*, a silent film starring Rudolph Valentino back in the twenties, now served as the home of The Praise Tabernacle. A small Sears outlet still serviced customers from the more rural areas who came into town for tools, wire fencing, and saddles.

"I think you check in over there," Rice said, pointing toward a desk on a riser that used to showcase the hottest Chevy of the year. An older woman with an open face and thick glasses nodded encouragingly at Glenna.

Glenna grunted. "Okay," she said. "But they're not putting me in a hospital."

Most of the clientele, Rice observed, were hippies wearing ragged bell-bottom trousers and dull, vacuous expressions. Skinny, dirty, and, he suspected, stinking of the streets. Black mothers sat in a smaller group and chatted while their children scurried under chairs or pressed their noses against the showroom window, ogling the few passersby.

Rice was trying to recall if the *Tribune* ever did a story on the clinic when he saw Roger Ranscombe walk out of one of the exam rooms. He was studying something in his hand—possibly a prescription—when he saw Rice.

"Don't tell me," Rice said. "You wanted to trade in your Maverick for a new Chevy Vega, and just found out the dealership had moved."

"What are you doing here?" Roger said, balling up the paper and stuffing it into his pocket. He tried to make his grin look wicked. "I heard you were sick."

"No, I'm feeling fine," Rice said. He ran his finger along the window ledge and made a great display of wiping away the dirt. "Does Stacey know you come here to get your checkups?"

The wicked grin fell away. An empty look of sadness replaced it. "I don't know," he said—barely audible—as if talking to himself. "Does it matter?"

"You tell me," Rice said, feeling like a cat playing with a lethargic mouse. "You a little short of cash, Roger?"

Roger looked through him, out to the street where only an occasional car drove past.

"No. Not now," he said, grinning in that mirthless way of the dead, or the profoundly depressed. "Not yet, anyway."

Roger dropped into a chair and held his head in his hands, his handsome features looking old now. Rice expected sobs to come next, but he just sat there, saying nothing.

"Lost my job. And my health insurance," Roger said. "Then the headaches came."

"The headaches?"

"I get these tension headaches. Sometimes I almost black out from the pain. I need really strong meds to deal with them. Prescription. That's why I came here."

Rice said nothing.

"Now you know everything."

"Not everything. A lot though," Rice said.

Roger lifted his head, his look accusatory. "What's that supposed to mean?"

"Did your boss find out about that stretch in Mohican?" Rice said. "Is that why he fired you?"

"You told him, didn't you?" Roger said.

"I didn't tell him anything," Rice said. "And I didn't tell Stacey."

Roger swallowed hard and took a deep breath. "Why not?"

Rice rubbed his chin and watched as Glenna went into one of the old sales offices followed by someone in white.

"You seem to have pulled yourself together," Rice said. "I don't care about your boss. And I just assumed you'd tell Stacey when the time was right."

Roger smiled and rubbed his hands together. "I was pretty wild as a kid," he said. "Would you believe it?"

"You broke a bunch of windows at the old men's store on the square," Rice said. "You're not exactly Dillinger."

"I do these exercises now when I'm angry. Started reading the Bible while I was in juvy. It's helped. Sometimes I still vent my anger in stupid ways though."

"Does Stacey know all this stuff?"

Roger clasped his hands, leaned over, and looked at Rice. "She knows about my past. We don't keep anything from each other."

"The secret to a good marriage," Rice said. "So I'm told."

"How'd you find out about it?"

"I checked up on you. I understand you know Father Pete Growden."

Roger's expression turned hard for an instant, the way it must have done when he was a wild child ten years ago. Then it softened. "Stacey wants me to become a Catholic before we get married. I talked to Father Growden about it. He set me up with some classes. He's a nice guy. Kind of sad."

"Did he ever say anything to you about Annike Eichel."

"We never talked about her," Roger said. "Not that I can remember."

"Does Stacey know you're shopping for a job?"

Roger paused and looked away. "I know you're in the business of asking people questions," he said. "I'm just a little uncomfortable the way they keep coming at me."

"I understand," Rice said, looking past him toward the examining room that had swallowed up Glenna. "I'm just passing the time, waiting for a friend. Like you said, I get paid for being nosy."

"I guess you can't turn it off."

Rice laughed. "I guess you're right."

"Stacey wants the whole Eisenhower-America-*Leave-it-to-Beaver*-family thing," Roger said.

"Yeah," Rice said. "She missed Woodstock and everything that went with it. Now she wants the new house with an edged lawn and well-dressed neighbors over for a barbecue."

"All that stuff costs money," Roger said, playing this is the church and this is the steeple with his fingers. "She wants solidity. That's what she told me once. That I was solid."

"Uh-huh."

"She said it was my best trait," Roger said. "I was thinking I shouldn't tell her about losing the job until I get a new one."

Roger turned his head to look at Rice. Then he looked down. More finger playing. "What do you think?" he said.

"I think you should have more faith in your fiancée," Rice said. "She understands things can't always be perfect."

"Yeah. Well, I don't like to disappoint her."

"Probably won't be the last time."

"You know, now that I think about it, Father Growden did bring up Annike Eichel's name once."

"When?"

"He was trying to explain how confession, or what's now called the Sacrament of Penance, works. You tell your sins to a priest. He gives absolution. Now you can't be condemned for those sins. They're forgiven."

"Sounds like a good deal for the faithful."

"Yeah, but I said 'What if I come back next week and confess the same sins?' I wondered if the same priest would forgive them again."

"What'd he say to that?" Rice asked.

"He told me Annike Eichel asked him once if some sins were just unforgivable. And he told her, no, every sin could be forgiven. You just have to take responsibility for it and make an honest effort not to do it again. Even if you keep committing the same sin, you've got to make the effort."

"He mentioned Eichel's name?" Rice said.

"This was after she was murdered," Roger said.

Glenna had walked over to them so quietly, neither man heard her approach. She looked at Roger and sniffed. "I'm ready to go now," she said to Rice. "They gave me some vitamins is all. Said I had a cold and would probably be fine in another couple days. Told me I should stay in bed."

Rice chuckled. Roger looked confused. Glenna blew her nose in a ratty-looking handkerchief.

When Rice stood up and reached into his pocket for his car keys, Roger put a hand on his wrist. "I asked him if Annike Eichel's murderer could be forgiven, and you know what he said?"

Rice shook his head.

"He said, 'I hope not. I hope he burns in hell'."

# { 23 }

Rice stared through the murky window in his bedroom and watched an army of raindrops envelop the dirt huddled in the corner of the windowsill.

The window was so dirty he could barely make out the outline of the Goodwater Bank Building at the end of the street. Rice couldn't remember the last time he'd seen a window washer outside his apartment building. Outside any building, for that matter. Maybe nobody washed windows anymore.

He sat backwards on an old wooden chair that used to serve as his nightstand when he was growing up. It was the only piece of furniture he'd brought into the apartment, but he never understood why. Sentimental reasons, he guessed.

Now he could see the beacon blinking relentlessly at the top of the WCGN radio tower, situated on top of the bank building, the highest point in the city.

The weather outside wasn't even trying hard. It was a third-rate rain shower. Alligator tears and not real rain at all. Not a storm with lightning and thunder that would rattle the dirty glass. It was like the sky couldn't work up the enthusiasm for a good late-spring rain.

He dropped his chin to the back of the chair. Everything looked so dull.

Rice wondered what Annike Eichel thought of the gloom. He could ask her. She was standing directly behind him, looking out over his head.

Staring at something, maybe. Or not.

She seemed less anxious these days, and he couldn't figure out why. She showed up infrequently, usually when he was asking questions, researching morgue files at the newspaper, or writing stories at his desk.

He hadn't been writing many stories on the dead woman's murder investigation. His editor reminded him frequently, in case he forgot.

"You're not for shit since I put you on the Eichel murder full-time," Billard had told him this morning, squatting next to his desk. He said it in that flat way that was more intimidating than screaming.

"So put me back on the cop beat," Rice said.

"I'm going to put you on general assignment pretty soon. Where's Janousek?"

"Pissing people off all over town," Rice said. "I'm probably his best friend, and I'd run him over quick if I caught him off the sidewalk."

"He knows you don't have to be liked."

"Yeah, well, he doesn't have to live here."

Billard tapped Rice's desk twice. "I want something tomorrow," he said.

Eichel's spirit had been waiting when Rice returned to his room. He turned and tried to look up into her face. He saw nothing. Like the rain, she was barely there at all. He could feel her behind him as a subtle coolness on his back. But he could only see her if he stood up and looked at her straight on. The phenomenon was typical of all the ghost victims he'd known.

"What do you think of this weather?" he said.

Nothing.

"You don't have to tell me who killed you, but I'm curious about your relationship with Father Growden," Rice said. "Throw me a crumb."

He felt a slight vibration along his back when he mentioned Growden's name.

"Foster Ebner?"

There was a knock at the door.

When he opened it, Detective Edwyn Kadish stood there stooped over, like he was still outside huddled against the rain. Or maybe trying to appear smaller and less visible.

"Thanks for coming by," Rice said.

Kadish pushed inside and closed the door behind him. He pulled off his double-knit olive sport coat and shook the rain from it, leaving a small puddle at his feet.

"Could've done that in the hallway," Rice said, dragging a throw rug over to sop up the water.

Kadish's brow furrowed. "And I could have stayed in my office. You're not the most popular guy right now."

"Yeah, why is that?" Rice asked.

Kadish shook his head. "I don't know, but I'm guessing Markle is at the bottom of it. I don't think he likes you."

"He said it wasn't me. It's just the business I'm in."

Kadish frowned as he squeezed a little more rainwater out of his sleeve. "I just bought this jacket. It's supposed to last forever."

"It's very smart. Try to drip over the rug, will ya?"

Kadish ignored him but spread the new puddle around with the toe of his shoe. Then he scratched an ugly red patch on the back of his neck. "The mayor doesn't like you," he said. "That I know for sure."

The ghost of Annike Eichel sat on the bed and looked at Kadish expectantly. "What do you got for me?" Rice said.

Kadish huffed out a laugh. "I didn't come over here to brief *you*," he said. "I'm taking my career in my hands just talking to you, even behind closed doors."

"Markle's got X-ray vision now? Like Superman?"

Kadish put on his sport coat, muttered a curse, and took it off again. "Wouldn't surprise me," he said. "So tell me what you know, and I'll try to put in a good word for you to those cops who've been directed to shoot you on sight."

"Father Growden," Rice said. "What do you know about him?"

"Goddammit, I'm the one asking the questions," Kadish said. "What do *you* know about him?"

"And Foster Ebner. You know he's skimming money off city contracts?"

Kadish looked down and scratched his neck again. "That's just a rumor."

"It's more than a rumor, Ed. We talked to him and we talked to Frank Lalley. And some other people too. Ebner's been a bad boy. You can read all about it in a series we're going to be running."

At that, Kadish looked up. "Who's *we*?"

"Me and Tom Janousek from the *Cleveland Chronicle*."

"The guy with the attitude problem?"

"So you've met him."

"Yeah, but I never talked to him at any length. And he never mentioned anything to me about embezzlement. Are you sure about this?"

Rice spread his hands. "When have I been wrong?"

"Lalley's that creepy guy in Finance?"

"That's him."

"And he knows about this … this embezzlement thing?"

Rice nodded.

"And you're going to run stories telling everybody the Goodwater PD doesn't know a thing about it?"

"I guess we could hold off until you start an investigation," Rice said. "But if we did that, I'd expect you to let me interview someone about what you've uncovered."

"Christ," Kadish said. "I thought you were assigned to the Eichel killing full-time. What's this embezzlement thing have to do with that?"

"I tripped over it on the way," Rice said. "Back in the good old days when we were pals, I would have told you about it."

"I talked to that Father Growden," Kadish said. "He's clean. He's a priest, for god's sake."

"If you say so."

"I hate when you do that," Kadish said. "How did Ebner's name come up with regard to the Eichel murder?"

"He was seen going into her house a lot."

"On the night of the murder?"

"I don't know, but a lot of other times. And sometimes when he left, he was picking pieces of breakfast bacon out of his teeth."

"Are you trying to tell me that Eichel's dead baby is his?"

Rice shrugged.

"Christ," Kadish said again and scratched his neck, harder this time.

"You're going to get an infection and then you'll have real trouble."

"Who told you all this?" Kadish said.

"Star Lightman."

"The pimp?" Kadish said, and he laughed with what looked like relief. "Now him I could see being good for this."

"Everything he told us checked out," Rice said. "Starting with Pastor Stanley's late-night visits outside Eichel's place."

Kadish sniffed. "Stanley Crawn's a Peeping Tom, a creeper. He's no killer."

"So who do you like for the murder?"

"Lightman hangs out around her place," Kadish said. "Odd neighborhood for a pimp to set up his office."

"Star Lightman is afraid of the downtown girls. Hell, I've known him since we used to play shooter behind Benny's. He's sneaky," Rice said. "But he's not mean."

"Didn't know he was your friend."

"We don't take long hot showers together, but we share an understanding."

"You should watch who you pal around with," Kadish said.

"I used to pal around with cops."

"Yeah, well ..."

"You going to talk to Ebner?" Rice said.

"I'm sorry, colonel," Kadish said, not bothering to disguise the mocking tone. "I thought you wanted me to solve the murder. We've only got the one detective, as you know."

"Because if you or somebody at GPD can't give me something, anything—and I mean today—the story runs in both the *Trib* and the *Chronicle* tomorrow. It'll be page one for us. I don't know where the *Chronicle* will put it."

"You can be a Grade A bastard sometimes," Kadish said.

"I wonder what the mayor will tell me when I call him on deadline tomorrow and ask for his reaction to our investigation into Ebner's embezzlement."

"After he stops sputtering, you mean?" Kadish said.

"Yeah, after that."

"He'll probably say 'For one thing, I'm firing Kadish,' " the detective said before arching one eyebrow and looking into Rice's eyes. "Everybody knows we've worked together in the past. Why are you threatening me? Now, of all times?"

Rice looked away, feeling like the kind of bully he always despised. The spirit of Annike Eichel was gone.

"I want somebody to talk to me about the progress on the Eichel case," Rice said. "I don't care who it is. You give me that today and we'll hold off on the other story. I need something."

"Why are you telling me this?" Kadish said. He put on his jacket, not caring that it was still wet. "Why not talk to the mayor or Phil Fortunato?"

"I'm on the mayor's shit list or we wouldn't be having this discussion," Rice said. "His safety-service director is going to follow his lead."

Kadish rubbed his jaw. "The mayor's got his own reasons for not talking to you, but when he hears about your … deal, he might rethink it. No reason Fortunato couldn't talk to you. I'll go see him."

"And now you know why I talked to you first."

Kadish chuckled for the first time. "You don't look very bright, but sometimes you got your shit together," he said.

"I'll look forward to Fortunato's phone call," Rice said. "I wonder what he'll tell me."

"He'll probably say," Kadish said, "that he wishes you were working this thing with me. And also that he wishes you weren't such a son of a bitch. You might even get a call from the mayor."

"Wow. I can't wait to tell my mother."

Kadish was at the door. "You know, this Ebner business really messes up things," he said. "Do you really think it might be related to the Eichel murder?"

Rice looked around the apartment again, but Annike Eichel's ghost wasn't there. "It wouldn't surprise me," he said.

# { 24 }

Janousek/Channon
Eichel
Weds

by Tom Janousek and Rice Channon

The Goodwater Police Department is investigating a connection between the murder of well-known atheist activist Annike Eichel and recent evidence of widespread embezzlement in the city's Public Works Department.

According to Goodwater Mayor Leonard McMillan, his office had been investigating rumors of wrongdoing in the Public Works Department for some time. As of this morning, the head of the department, Foster Ebner, has been placed on administrative leave and McMillan said formal charges may be forthcoming.

> Phil Fortunato, safety-service director, said police have learned Ebner made frequent visits to Eichel's home, although the reason for the visits isn't clear.

—

Rice sucked in a last puff from his cigar, tilted his head back, and watched the cloud ascend to the yellow fluorescents overhead. "Are you sure you don't want one?" he said to Janousek, sitting at the facing desk.

"It smells like Kool-Aid," Janousek said. "Hell, toss one over here."

Everyone in the newsroom left them alone. Billard looked like he wanted to walk over, but fought off the urge. He did tap his watch nervously and made sure both Rice and Janousek saw him do it.

Rice flipped Janousek a cigar and read over his first three grafs. "We did all the work and they look like the experts," he said. Janousek harrumphed and started typing. "You know what? We should write a screenplay. I'll bet Hollywood would be interested."

"Don't think I haven't considered it," Janousek said, drawing on the cigar tentatively like he was sucking on a lemon. "Of course we've got to come up with the killer first."

"True."

"Doesn't mean we can't start the work," Janousek said. "We could fill in the names later."

"I'm going to act like I didn't overhear you guys talking about working for Hollywood when you haven't written your first decent story for us," Billard said, scowling down at both of them, after finally wandering over to their desks. "I'm sorry we don't have the bright lights and friendly starlets, but right now, we're the ones paying you. Try to remember that."

Janousek waved his cigar like it was a prop he'd been using all his life. "This story is practically writing itself, Dave," he said. "We'll have it to you a half hour before deadline."

Billard squatted down at his desk and assumed the trademark crooked smile. "But what if I don't like it?" he said, practically whispering. "What then?"

"I don't see that happening," Rice said while continuing to type. "My head's busting with this story. It's flowing like honey."

"Christ, Channon," Billard said, getting up easily for a middle-aged man. "No poetry, please. Not today."

Then he tapped his watch again.

Rice had returned to the newsroom yesterday after his meeting with Detective Ed Kadish. Before he could scoot his chair in, the phone rang. It was Phil Fortunato.

"You trying to make my boys look bad?" he said. Rice couldn't tell if he was serious, but he was tired of rolling over.

"Do they need my help for that?" Rice said, and the safety-service director laughed.

"It's about time we talked," Fortunato said. "Let's call a truce."

"I never declared war, Phil," Rice said. "You guys started it."

"Hotheads," Fortunato said. "The mayor's got a bug up his hiney, and Markle, well, he's being Markle."

"I'm tired of taking crap when I'm just doing my job."

"I know, I know," Fortunato said. Rice could hear the exasperation. "Everybody's on edge. You come over and talk with me. We'll sort this thing out."

"Aren't you afraid the mayor will catch us together?"

"Don't you worry about Sandy," Fortunato said. "You and I got to be the levelheaded ones."

"Does this mean you're going to call my boss and tell him it's okay to put me on the police beat again?"

"That's up to your guys," Fortunato said. "Since when has that goddamn newspaper ever taken orders from city hall? Tell me."

"I'm coming over," Rice said. "And I want to talk to Markle too."

Fortunato chuckled. "One mountain at a time," he said.

—

> The possible embezzlement includes misuse of city maintenance equipment for personal use by city employees, the taking over of some city contracts awarded to private bidders, and skimming of funds from contracts carried out by winning bidders.

According to Goodwater Safety-Service Director Phil Fortunato, the illegal activities included intimidation, payoffs, and kickbacks.

Mayor McMillan said formal charges will be forthcoming as soon as prosecutors complete their investigation and prepare charge sheets.

"No one is above the law," the mayor told the *Tribune*. "A breach of the public trust by city employees will be prosecuted to the full extent of the law and as expeditiously as possible to ensure everyone's rights are properly respected."

Annike Eichel, president of the atheist activist organization Right Thinkers for a New America, was found murdered in her home ten days ago. Local law enforcement officials and the coroner's office have released only minimal information about the murder.

While city officials and detectives investigating the embezzlement admitted a possible tie-in to the Eichel murder, they were not prepared to explain how the embezzlement of city resources and the death of the atheist activist were related.

—

Dave Billard held up the copy in his hand almost defiantly as Rice and Janousek stood over his desk.

"This is it?" the city editor said.

"I can't get confirmation on anything else," Rice said. "We know Ebner's been stealing thousands from the city, but everyone who knows anything clammed up when we talked to them."

"Don't fuck with your boss this way," Janousek said, looking down at a speck of something on the shoulder of his jacket before flicking it off. "We got Ebner admitting to going to Eichel's place—"

"But he said he didn't kill her," Rice said.

Janousek sniffed. "We got Foster Ebner asking little Frank Lalley to cut corners. The big guy told him things would go better for everyone if he didn't have to fill out pesky paperwork when he wanted something."

Billard dropped the copy and pinched his nose wearily. "Yeah, Lalley over at Finance. He called me. Said you misrepresented yourself."

"That's bullshit," Janousek said. "I didn't represent myself at all. I just started asking questions and he answered them."

"He said something about a busted pencil sharpener. What was that?"

"Look, Dave. The guy's a weasel," Janousek said. "I've got a page and a half on what he did. It could be part of the bigger story, or a sidebar."

"You didn't hit him, did you?"

"No, I didn't touch him," Janousek said, studying his other jacket shoulder for other errant lint specks. "I just got his attention. The worst that happened is maybe he pissed himself."

"And we got the two of them going to Martelli's in the middle of the afternoon," Rice said.

"That's odd, but kind of gratuitous," Billard said. "Why should I care?"

"You guys talk pretty out here in the sticks," Janousek said. Billard scowled. "It's important because that's where Ebner was trying to put the big squeeze on little Frankie."

"Christ," Billard said. "You sound like Walter Winchell."

"That is, until Ebner saw us," Rice said.

"Ebner barely had time to slide a few bills into a dancer's unmentionables before he spotted us," Janousek said.

"Did you ask him what he was doing there?" Billard said.

"He gave us some bullshit about a little downtime for him and Frank," Rice said. "Reminded us of all the hours he gives away to the city when he has to work on Saturdays."

"He ran," Janousek said, "because he was in a city vehicle and thought it might look bad if it was found in the Martelli's parking lot."

"All right, so he's full of shit," Billard said. "What's that got to do with anything?"

"Because it reinforces what Lalley told me," Janousek said.

Billard sighed and looked at his watch. "I'm going to have to hold page one, aren't I?"

"Why?" Rice said. "I've got, maybe, five more grafs on the embezzlement, including more quotes from the mayor and Fortunato. And Tom's got another page and a half, like he said."

"If this is your pitch, it stinks. You guys couldn't sell shoes to Thom McAn," Billard said. "Okay, Foster Ebner's a crook. Frank Lalley is a lackey. The mayor doesn't know what's going on in his city. Fine. Good stuff. But what's any of it got to do with the murder of Annike Eichel?"

Rice and Janousek looked at each other.

"Do you think it's a coincidence that Foster Ebner is stealing from the city and spending time with a white woman who ends up murdered?" Janousek said.

"It is until I see the connection," Billard said.

"But the city is looking into their relationship," Rice said. "That's got to count for something."

Billard dropped his forearms on the desk and hunched over them. "The city is over its head," he said. "They're desperate and will jump at any crumb that falls their way. And where did the crumb about the Eichel-Ebner connection come from?"

"From us," Rice said.

Billard shook his head and handed the copy back to Rice. "Rewrite this," he said. "The embezzlement is the story. Throw in everything you've got about Ebner and Lalley and all the other evildoers. But leave Annike Eichel's murder out of it. For now. I'll hold page one until you finish, but don't make me wait long."

"My boss at the *Chronicle* isn't going to be happy," Janousek said. "I told him we had a big break on the Eichel murder today."

"Sorry," Billard said, reaching into his basket for other copy. "That's the way we do it here in the sticks."

# { 25 }

Detective Kadish's sport coat looked like an old dishrag, probably because he dragged nervous fingers over the lining repeatedly.

"You guys at the *Trib* and half the city probably think we sit around our offices drinking coffee and eating donuts," he said. "Our thumbs up our ass, waiting for payday. Tell me I'm wrong."

"I can't speak for the citizens," Rice said. "I know you work hard. You do drink a lot of coffee, though."

Kadish rubbed his red eyes. "They should give it to us for free," he said. "I'm on the job even when I'm not."

"I know," Rice said. "Why am I here?"

Yesterday, Phil Fortunato had told Kadish the Goodwater PD headquarters was no longer off limits to Rice Channon. "But," the detective added, "I wouldn't go tooting any horns when you walk in the front door."

The desk sergeant and a few patrolmen greeted Rice with feeble waves when he returned. Colonel Markle saw him but acted like he didn't.

"Phil said we should work together," Kadish said. "Keep you up to speed on what we're doing."

"Just like the old days," Rice said.

"Nobody said that, but I'm going to act like they did. Maybe we could, you know, help each other."

"I show you mine. You show me yours."

"I know you need stuff to write about," Kadish said. "And maybe if I let you know what we've been doing, it might trigger something to help the investigation."

"It might work that way," Rice said. "Tell me what you have."

Kadish kept his gaze on Rice for a long time as if trying to determine his worthiness. "Some of this stuff I don't want you to write about," he said. "But I tell you what that is so there's no confusion. I can't risk letting important information out that might help the killer. That's my condition for discussion."

"I don't like off the record," Rice said.

"I know that," Kadish said, looking almost warm with his squinty eyes and rumpled coat. "But this is an unusual circumstance. Do we agree?"

Rice nodded.

Kadish sat up straight. "Okay. This is on the record. Whenever I investigate a death scene, one of the things I look for is the presence of insects. One of the reasons I've got to get to a scene fast is to keep well-meaning patrolmen from destroying insect evidence."

"Like what?"

"Out of respect for the dead, they'll shoo away flies or pick maggots off the wounds. Most cops aren't the cold, laugh-in-the-face-of-death machines people think we are."

"Just sweet guys with guns," Rice said.

"But the presence of blowflies, maggots, and ants can tell us a lot about the time of death. That's why they're so important."

"This is the first I heard about that."

"I don't tell you everything," Kadish said. "Blowflies usually arrive first. They'll be on a body in minutes, maybe seconds. If I see them flying around, I know the death was pretty recent. Of course, it also depends upon the temperature, whether the deceased was inside or outside, and some other variables."

Rice made a few notes. "What did you find at the Eichel death scene?"

"I'll get to that," Kadish said. "Let's stay on the record for now. Agreed?"

"Okay."

"The blowflies and houseflies will lay eggs in open wounds, eyes, ears, and genital openings, among other interesting places. Maggots show up later. At some point, wasps start feeding on the flies. When maggots appear, you might find ants hauling the little worms back to their nests. It all follows a pretty definable schedule."

A uniformed policeman carrying a file walked past them, and Kadish stopped talking until he was out of earshot.

"Must be hard to keep from spilling your lunch when you come upon something like that," Rice said.

Kadish's eyes widened and he nodded. "I tossed my cookies the first time," he said. "I'm not ashamed to admit it. I gagged a lot too. But after a while I came to appreciate my buggy friends."

"Can I quote you on the 'buggy friends' thing?"

"I'd rather you didn't but …" Kadish shrugged.

"So what happened when you got to the Eichel death scene?"

"Hold onto your goddamn horses. Can you do that?"

"I'm getting some coffee," Rice said. "Do I need to give you a dime or something?"

"Somebody stole the coffee money last week," Kadish said. "So we don't leave money in the open anymore. Just write my name on the yellow pad next to the pot."

Rice walked over to the coffee stand next to the fingerprint station. He found a paper cup that looked relatively clean. When he raised the coffeepot to fill the cup, he caught the reflection of someone standing just outside the doorway.

It was Goodwater Chief of Police Colonel Quincy Markle.

When Rice returned to Kadish's desk, he immediately began talking while writing on his notepad. "Any other critters help you in your investigation?" Rice said as he continued to write. Kadish's brows furrowed. "Moths? Honeybees? Hummingbirds?"

Rice turned his notebook toward Kadish so he could read it.

*Markle's hiding outside the door. I'll play along if you want to end our discussion.*

"Hummingbirds?" he said. "You think this is funny, Channon? You may find it hard to believe, but I've developed something of a reputation in this state on the subject of forensic entomology."

"Big name for the study of bugs."

"Sometimes you're dumber than shit," Kadish said. It didn't sound like he was acting any longer. "You probably don't know it, but there are a whole range of critters, as you call them. Each one provides more information about the time of death. There are blowflies, the little green bastards. Then there are houseflies, cheese flies, coffin flies."

"I guess you know the guy is long dead when the coffin flies show up."

Kadish's face reddened, and he looked like he was going to begin sputtering.

Rice walked over to the door and looked out. "He's gone," Rice said. "I think he made us."

"He *made* us," Kadish repeated. "So now you think you're an undercover cop."

"I could be," Rice said as he searched the hallway in both directions. "Was he checking on you or checking on me?"

"Both of us. I'm glad I never got to the off the record stuff."

"You're going to have to give me something, Ed. I can't do a story on cheese flies and your bug expertise."

"That's your problem," Kadish said. "You can publish a little story that makes me look good or simply write off the afternoon as old friends drinking cold coffee together. Your choice."

"So we're old friends," Rice said. "Does that mean our relationship is in the past tense?"

Kadish decided to check the hallway himself, then looked around the rest of the squad room. He seemed weary when he sat back down.

"You're trouble for anybody who knows you too well," he said, spreading his hands as if admitting an infidelity. "That's just a fact."

"Mad, bad, and dangerous to know."

"What?"

"Folks used to say that about Lord Byron," Rice said.

Kadish shook his head. "Never knew the guy," he said. "Here's my point. I gotta be careful how much I talk to you and how often we hang around together. I'm counting on your discretion. It could mean my job otherwise."

"You going to tell me what you found at the Eichel scene?"

Kadish looked around some more, then scratched his neck. "What I'm telling you now is off the record, do you follow?"

"I don't want you to lose your job," Rice said. "Who else would buy my coffee?"

"First of all, I knew Markle was out there. He told me he was going to listen in."

"Sorry I scared him off. Makes me wonder if you trust me," Rice said.

"Well, I do," Kadish said, looking seriously unhappy. "I have to. Markle wanted me to tell you we found nothing at the crime scene. No flies, no maggots, no ants. Nothing."

"But that's not true?"

"It should have been. Based on people who we can confirm met with the deceased, she was dead less than twelve hours when I first got a look at the body. It was a warm day, but she had air conditioning in her office and she liked to keep it cold. Conditions like that limit the likelihood of entomological evidence."

"I don't get your point," Rice said.

"Blowflies, maggots, wasps, and even carrion beetles. It was like a pack of Irishmen at an open-bar wedding. Her body was coated with hundreds of bugs."

# { 26 }

The big clock over the teletype machines clicked to eleven. Deadline.

Nobody moved. City Editor Billard unwrapped wax paper from an olive loaf sandwich and blew on his coffee, which was too hot for his taste. He was going to eat lunch early.

There had been no fatals, major crimes, political developments, or announcements this day. Most of the reporters were out of the office or reading out-of-town newspapers at their desks. All their work had been completed well before deadline.

Page one carried a photo of the fountain in the square. It had been recently cleaned and repainted for the summer. Children dipped fingers and toes into the pond or simply giggled as the water spray blew over them. Mothers laughed. A feel-good photo.

On page one of the local section, above the fold, was a murder investigation update that revealed nothing. Next to it was Rice's story about insect entomology and how Detective Edwyn Kadish enjoyed a statewide reputation for being a master of this forensic technique.

"Tell me you've got something else," the city editor had said after reading the copy. "Something that ties all this crap to the investigation?"

"Just wait, Dave," Rice told him. "Be patient."

"No. Goddammit."

"I'm spinning a lot of plates right now. Try to trust me."

"As long as Janousek doesn't scoop us," Billard said.

"He won't."

And now Rice was at his desk writing names on a piece of newsprint. The mayor. Fortunato. His assistant, Earl Sugarman. Colonel Markle. Detective Kadish. Star Lightman.

The last name he crossed out. Then he wrote it down again.

Foster Ebner. Frank Lalley.

He crossed out Lalley's name, thought for a while, then drew a second line through it. The city's assistant finance director wouldn't cross the street against the light. Rice couldn't see him butchering Annike Eichel.

Rice wrote down Dave Billard's name. He wasn't sure why. Probably because he was still annoyed at being jerked around and told who to talk to and who not to talk to. And then being reminded to keep the stories coming.

Pastor Stanley Crawn. If he was going to be charged with murder, the cops better hurry. He was on his way out as pastor of Faith Bible Church. Crawn was no killer. But Rice didn't cross out his name.

Father Growden. This name he underlined. Then he wrote down Roger Ranscombe's name and then Stacey's name. Then Tom Janousek.

The *Trib*'s new police reporter, Mitchell Joyce, folded up the newspaper he was carrying and squatted down on the far side of Rice's desk like he was trying to hide from Billard's view.

"You need any help with the Eichel thing?" Mitchell said. "I've got some time this afternoon. I've made a few contacts at the police station, and they might have something for you."

Mitchell scanned the list of names on the desk. Rice placed a phone book over them. Mitchell looked back at him, smiled.

"One of them the killer?" he asked.

"How would I know?"

"Because you're ... Because you know that stuff."

"Yeah," Rice said, instinctively looking over at Billard to see if he overheard. "Thanks for the offer. I'm allowed back at GPD as long as I pick up after myself. That's the deal for now. How are you doing on the job?"

"I'm having fun," Mitchell said. "There are some good guys over there."

Rice nodded, then lifted the phone book and took another look at his list. "I gotta go," he told Mitchell.

He needed to buy some ice cream.

—

"How'd you know I'd be home?" Stacey said when she opened the door. She wore beige shorts and a tie-dyed top that looked new.

"School's out for the year," Rice said, the vanilla custard cone beginning to drip along his hand. "Where else would you be?"

She took the cone and loudly licked its circumference, never dropping her gaze. "So you figured I'd be hungry?"

"I've never known you to turn down a cone."

Stacey took a big bite and greedily slurped the ensuing spillway of cold vanilla cream. "I haven't had an ice cream cone in so long …" she said, daintily dipping her tongue at a drop that had fallen on her hand.

Rice pulled the list from his pocket.

"What's that?" Stacey said.

"Some names."

"Suspects?" she said. Stacey was making short work of the cone.

"When I started it this morning, I wasn't sure what it was," he said. "Now I think it's just a list of people I might discuss the murder with."

Stacey briskly wiped her hands before reaching out. "Lemme see," she said.

She scanned it while wearing a serious expression. Then a smile broke across her face. "You wrote Roger's name down," she said.

"Yeah, but he didn't make the cut."

"But you considered him. That's sweet," she said, staring at Rice with a look that swallowed him whole. "You two should get to know each other. I think you'd get along."

"Yeah. He's a peach."

Her smile faded as she looked away.

"Congratulations, by the way," Rice said. "Roger told me the news personally."

Stacey didn't look at him. Two red dots on her cheeks grew into full bloom. Then she turned back to face Rice but didn't look at him directly.

"So why you showing this to me?" she asked, holding the paper out.

"You're the only person I'm comfortable talking with," Rice said. When her brow furrowed, he added quickly. "About this case, I mean. I can still talk to you, right?"

"And that's it?"

"Yeah," he said. "And I trust you. I can say something stupid and you won't laugh at me."

He provided her with more details about the murder, information that hadn't appeared in the newspaper or on television. He explained about the gruesome nature of the murder and the tenuous connection with the city's embezzlement scandal. He told her about being promoted, demoted, and shuffled sideways. He complained about the way his access to officials was restricted, and reiterated his problems with the mayor's office. He mentioned the strange and unlikely appearance of flies, maggots, and beetles on Annike Eichel's body.

"Is that *Cleveland Chronicle* reporter any help?"

"He's smart and pushy. It's not my style, but he's coming up with stuff," Rice said. "I think some of the city hall folks get stars in their eyes when he asks them questions."

"Big city reporter talks to them so they must be important," she said. "Is that it?"

"Might be."

"Are you sharing all this information with him?"

Rice tried not to look guilty. He wasn't sure he was succeeding. "Not all of it," he said.

"And I'll bet you're not telling Billard everything," she said.

He didn't answer her question.

"So you can probably assume they're not telling you everything either," she said. "I have the feeling your new sidekick would walk over you if it would further his career."

"That's kind of harsh."

"Do you think I'm wrong?"

Rice looked off, then back at Stacey. He smiled. "Pensive they sit, and roll their languid eyes," he said.

At this, Stacey rolled her own eyes, but there was fire in them. "And now you commence with quoting me Keats," she said. "I guess that means our discussion is over."

"When did you begin hating John Keats?"

"He can be a tedious bore," she said and actually looked at her nails as if disinterested in the discussion. "He moans about love and eternity and things that children care about."

"Children care about those things?"

She turned to him, defiant. "Childish, then. A child believes that snowmen, a favorite toy, youthful friendships, and summer will last forever."

"But nothing does."

"That's right," she said.

"Are we still talking about Keats?"

"No," Stacey said, biting at her words. "I believe we're talking about you. About your infatuation with me."

Stacey stood up, her legs looking fine and tanned perfectly, even this early in the season.

"You run away from love the way you run away from Keats," he said. "What's your hurry?"

She turned back to him, her eyes softer now. "Did you really think you would win me over with an ice cream cone?"

"No," he said. "I wanted to talk. Our talks together were always good, weren't they?"

She said nothing.

"But I remember the feeling of your cold tongue in my mouth after a snack at Isaly's. In the dark. Just us and the lights from the ice cream store turning your face azure, your eyes closed. Those memories were in the back of my head. With Keats. They both spilled out when I saw you again today."

"I hate that you can do this to me," she said, returning to the stoop, sitting on her hands. "This is why you shouldn't talk to me."

"I can't help it."

"Which is why you shouldn't see me," she said. "It's never going to happen again. I won't let it."

He grinned at her. "I've got more Keats. You once told me he made you feel all pudding-y inside."

She stood up and brushed her hands together. "I'm growing a thick skin over the pudding. It's Roger I care for now," she said. "Two roads diverged and I took his path."

"You always hated Frost."

She turned to him, angry again. "I do not. He uses beautiful imagery."

"You said he was a cranky old Yankee more interested in building walls than bridges," he said. "I think I'm quoting you exactly."

"You remember too much," she said, and for a moment he thought she was going to use an endearment, but she didn't. "Think more about the future and less about the past."

Rice looked down. It was time to go. "Yeah."

"And be careful around that Cleveland guy," Stacey said, eyes warm again. Caring. "I don't trust him."

# { 27 }

At a new hamburger drive-in serving indifferent burgers and fries, Rice Channon fell into something like sleep in the shade of a redbud tree next to the Dumpster.

His Orange Crush drink with extra ice fell out of his hand and spilled over the floor of his Fiat, making a mess that would be hell to clean when he awoke. The toasted hamburger bun fell into the slop too. The burger itself fell into some grit in front of the accelerator.

But Rice saw none of it. He was someplace else, although his body remained sitting up, eyes closed, fingers clutching empty air where his lunch used to be.

It started when he left Stacey. A kind of lightness. It made him feel like a child's helium balloon, bouncing off the roof of his little Italian car, likely to float away if a window opened.

After one bite of the burger, two fries and one long slurp of his drink, a window did open, and off he went.

He was walking along a plaza in a place he didn't recognize. He heard a kind of whimpering, like the crying or mewing of a puppy stuck someplace it didn't want to be.

No one was around, but the sound grew louder as he walked. Then he was seemingly over it, and he looked down at brick-sized slabs of rock at his feet.

A dog seemed buried beneath the rocks. It was hoarsely barking and panting. Rice dropped to his knees and yanked up the rocks, which gave way easily. Then he clawed at the dirt, which had the consistency of sand. As soon as he did, the sound stopped.

"Where are you?" he called out. "Where are you, boy?"

The crying began again. But this time it wasn't a dog's howls under his feet. The sound was coming from a house about fifty yards away.

The same desperation lingered in the voice, but now it took on a rolling *eww, eww, eww*, the sound of something lost and near despair.

It wasn't a puppy's yammering any longer. It was a child's crying. Or a woman's.

Rice began running toward the house, which sat by itself in a weedy lot, a gray sky behind it. Police barricades surrounded the house, but he was unable to move them. He jumped over one, running toward the front door where the crying sound grew in volume and desperation.

Rice worried that the door would be locked, and as he ran, he searched for some other door or window, or anywhere he could get inside.

But the door wasn't locked. And the moment he touched the handle he knew where he was.

It was Annike Eichel's home.

He pulled open the door but was unable to turn on the lights.

The sound was different now. The voice seemed to be saying "Oh, oh, oh," and there could be no doubt it was a woman's voice. Like someone in a nightmare pleading for assistance.

A puddle of light lit the end of the hallway where Rice assumed the kitchen must be. He walked toward it, his legs moving slowly as if marching through molasses.

It was a kitchen. And it was a woman.

Annike Eichel sat in a chair, bloody hands outstretched toward him, her face flushed with terror.

"Help me, help me, help me," she said, her form not ghostly now.

Rice was unable to move any closer. He waved his hands impotently. "How can I help you?" he said.

Annike Eichel stopped her pleading cries and pointed to the far corner, above the cupboards, where a strip of harvest-gold wallpaper butted against a yellow painted wall.

A creeping black mass as smooth as newly poured ink spread across the ceiling and congealed into a dark, humanlike form that crouched in the corner. It vibrated as if aching to burst into movement.

The mewing was back. Maybe there was a dog, Rice thought.

He looked again at Annike, but in the place of the handsome adult woman was a girl—maybe ten years old—wearing a child's green-checked taffeta dress with puffy sleeves. She wore a matching green bow in carefully coifed blond hair.

The girl's mouth was open and seemed to be screaming, but only the kind of pleading mew he heard earlier came out. She stood on the chair, seemingly unable to move away, and pressed both hands to her cheeks, her eyes wide.

Rice drew closer, but she seemed unable to see him. In the corner, the dark shape jostled its shadowy shoulders, as if dancing to otherworldly music.

Rice moved away from Annike—he guessed it was still Annike—and toward the shadow shape, surprised he wasn't more apprehensive. As he got closer, he felt cold for the first time during this nightmare.

The black shape seemed to be exhaling, and its shoulders continued to rock while it remained otherwise still. The sound of its breathing or pulsing became a long *hawww*. It seemed like a warning.

But he moved closer still.

He could see dimension to the thing now. It was thick, thick as a large man, but somehow bigger than any human and without human features. No eyes or ears. Where its mouth should have been was a quivering slit as though it were afraid or preparing to speak.

Rice reached out, and when he pushed into the smoky goo of its body, red eyes with unnaturally large black pupils popped into place. Ears sprung out at the same time, bat ears that twisted eerily at the tips.

The shoulder movement stopped, and the thing seemed to stand, its mouth no longer quivering but resolute to its purpose.

What that purpose was, Rice could not be sure. But he was fairly certain it involved the girl-woman Annike Eichel.

The shadow thing seemed uninterested in Rice. It moved past him and toward the girl who had stopped screaming, but whose hands remained pressed hard to her cheeks. When it got within arm's length of the girl, it squatted slightly and studied her.

Only when a line of pee dribbled down her left leg did the black shadow move again, circling her as she shook, terrified, in place on the chair.

One time the thing half reached out to her with its shadow arm that contained no definable shape of a hand or fingers. Before it touched her, the shadow pulled its arm back. The appendage disappeared against its flank like a wave dissolving into the nighttime sea.

Rice tried to run to the girl, to console her, to rescue her somehow.

But he was now completely immobile. He could smell the delicate scent of her hair and sense her fear as a fist around his heart.

But he couldn't move. Not even a little.

When the thing breathed on her with the long *hawww* sound, the girl became quiet and dropped her hands to her side and no longer seemed afraid.

In that same moment, Rice was back in his car. But just as in the nightmare or dream or vision, he still could not move. He smelled the onions on the hamburger at his feet. A whiff of french-fried potatoes. He saw a sparrow hop on the Dumpster, picking at flecks of food. Rice's hands were cold, even as movement returned to him.

But the sick hurt of the shadow fist around his heart remained.

Behind him, the restaurant's kitchen vent fan exhaled a continuous *hawww* that carried all the scents of whatever they were cooking inside.

# { 28 }

Rice returned to his desk in the newsroom and tried to calm the jitters sweeping over him in waves.

His right hand shivered visibly, and he snatched it with his left, wrestling it to the desktop as if it were a foreign attacker and not part of his body.

He heard Mitchell's police scanner squawking about a robbery at a downtown liquor store. A gang of kids had thrown bricks and a bicycle through the store's front window, then helped themselves to cases of Seagram's, malt liquor, and lots of sweet liqueurs in collectible bottles.

A brazen daylight robbery was pretty unusual, but it wasn't his problem. Not today.

Billard looked across the room at him and seemed ready to say something, caught himself, and instead, asked a passing general assignment reporter if he knew where Mitchell Joyce was.

Brazen robberies and other assorted mayhem fell under the purview of the new police reporter. Rice didn't feel the least bit guilty about ignoring the commotion.

Another squawk. A fire truck had been dispatched to the scene. Then another.

Billard looked over at him again, his lips working madly, but his motions easy and unhurried.

Rice could tell the city editor wanted to send him to the scene. Even a few weeks earlier, he wouldn't have had to say anything. Rice would have been out the door already.

Yeah. Billard wanted him there bad.

Rice's hand started flopping again. This time it behaved like a landed fish, noisily slapping the desktop before he could calm it.

More radio chatter. One arrest was made, but some of the locals were throwing rocks and bricks at arriving police and firemen. This was more than unusual. It was unprecedented.

"Go, goddammit," Billard said while casually picking up a phone. Rice knew he was talking to him.

It was just as well. He couldn't stay here and do nothing, but he had hoped for some time to think. He stood up.

"Photo's already sent somebody," Billard said. "I don't know who. When you get to the scene, find him and make sure he gets close to the action. And find Joyce, but don't spend a lot of time looking for him."

Rice scanned the newsroom for Janousek but didn't see him. On the stairs to the parking lot, he was able to hear the scanner report a head injury to one of the on-scene patrolmen.

Things were getting ugly. Rice smelled burning wood before he saw the flames.

The burgled store was located just outside an area called the East Town projects, a large tract of subsidized housing built after the Korean War. It was populated almost entirely with Negro families. Black men holding paper bags of hooch walked listlessly throughout the area, paying no attention to the thick police presence or the two fire trucks spraying water on the liquor store and an adjacent shop.

Rice spotted Janousek right away. He was standing by a patrolman manning one of the police barricades, seemingly joking and gesturing wildly amid the chaos. The cop's only reaction was a modest smile.

A gaggle of black youths behind the barricades looked on at the burning stores, occasionally tossing taunts at the firemen, but otherwise behaving. Rice looked for the *Trib*'s cameraman but couldn't find him. No sign of Mitchell Joyce either.

The fire slowly intensified, accompanied by a feral growl as smoke shot into the air. A minor pop from within the liquor store came next. It was followed by three or four more pops then the unmistakable sound of tinkling glass. A burst of flame shot forth from another part of the same building.

Firemen on an arriving fire truck took axes to nearby structures—a covered bus stop and a decrepit garage—in an attempt to establish a perimeter to keep the flames from spreading. Then they directed their hoses at exterior walls of the burning buildings and worked in from there.

An older black man—apparently owner of the empty garage—screamed at firemen to save the structure. It looked as though it might burst into flame at any moment.

A couple of twenty year olds approached the fire-fighting team and began yelling something, raising their hands high overhead to punctuate their anger.

Rice looked around for his photographer and finally found him with the police. He was a young kid—probably a summer intern—who looked quite comfortable well away from the action.

"What's your name?" Rice said when he reached him.

"Kenny. Bill Kenny," the cameraman said, his voice quavering. Excitement compounded with fear were etched on his features.

"Okay, Bill Kenny," Rice said, pointing at the black men harassing the firemen. "There's your story."

"I'm supposed to stay with the cops," Kenny said, looking around. "That's what Dave Billard told me."

"Knock off the bullshit, kid," Rice said. "Billard doesn't even know your name. If you want to last until the Fourth of July, do what I tell you. Go."

The photographer wore a cheap sport coat with a sizing tag still attached to the sleeve. "What if they attack me?" he said.

"Then get pictures," Rice said.

Another young black man burst free of the barricades and ran over to the duo screaming at the firemen. The firefighters began looking around nervously. They yanked back on the nozzle bale so the wide spray dropped off to a sorry dribble.

The crowds behind the barricades cheered, and the firemen spun the hose around and directed the nozzle toward the screaming crowds in what looked like a defensive gesture. Although the lead fireman kept a hand on the bale, he did not let loose the spray.

Another man leapt over the barrier and raced to the others, all of them berating the firefighters who began backing away as the fire blossomed into life behind them.

In the light of the resurrected fire, Rice saw an older man at the back of the crowd seemingly giving directions to young men who hopped barricades and harassed the firefighters from another direction.

Other firefighters joined their comrades and began pushing the harassers back toward the barricades. A couple punches were thrown, and Rice expected an all-out street rumble. But a cadre of patrol officers used their batons to press back the barricade jumpers, and a shaky peace was restored.

The firemen returned to dousing the flames. More police cars showed up. More firemen.

Tom Janousek worked his way through the crowd and began talking with the older man who looked like he was directing rioters at the firemen. The light from the flames was dimming, but enough remained to get a good look at the man. He was smiling and shaking his head at Janousek.

He was the retired city employee of the Goodwater Public Works Department Rice had interviewed earlier. The talkative one.

Kleavon Hayes.

—

"Do you know who that is?" Rice said when Janousek came over to him.

"Talk to me behind this pumper," Janousek said. "You go. I'll meet you in a bit."

It was quieter behind the truck. "Why the drama?" Rice said when Janousek arrived a few minutes later.

"I didn't want him to see us talking to each other," Janousek said. "He told me his name is Kelly. Something Kelly."

"That's Kleavon —"

"I know who he is," Janousek said. "But he doesn't *know* I know. The big question is what is he doing here?"

"Maybe he wanted to top off his hip flask," Rice said. "Can't think of any other reason a small-engine repairman would just happen to show up."

"Exactly," Janousek said, peeking over the hood of the fire truck in Kleavon Hayes's direction. "If he wanted a snootful, he didn't have to drive all the way across town to get it."

"So what did you two talk about?"

"When I walked up to him, he was shaking his head the way old folks do just before they tell you the world is going to hell," Janousek said, checking on Hayes from time to time. "I don't think he knows who I am, so I started a conversation, all innocent like. What happened, I asked him. How'd the fire start?"

"What'd he say?"

"He told me the young men in this town are angry. That they feel trapped. That they're on a bus headed for jail or perdition. That's the way he put it."

"He's blaming the kids?" Rice said.

Janousek rubbed his chin and narrowed his eyes as he looked out on the fire. "He didn't say it, but, yeah."

"So he'd have you think he's just an observer of the passing parade," Rice said.

"I think he'd like to be seen that way," Janousek said. "But I threw him a little when I asked him what those kids who jumped the barricade said to him."

"Yeah?"

"He told me they were just mad. Mad and scared. That's what he said."

Rice threw a glance at Hayes. The man was standing in the crowd with hands in his pockets, craning his neck to watch the fire, like he had nothing better to do. He saw a slight smirk cross the man's face and fall away in an instant.

"He was doing the talking, not those kids," Rice said. "He's no idle observer. He ordered those kids to taunt those firemen. I don't get it."

As the fire died to a few glowing boards hissing before the spray from multiple fire hoses, the harassers drifted away. Rice and Janousek watched them look over to Hayes. The older man shook his head and waved the back of his hand at them in a dismissive gesture. Then he turned his back and walked on.

Ed Kadish found the two reporters huddled next to the front tire. “You boys afraid of getting burned?” he said. “Fire's almost out.”

Janousek flashed his thousand-watt smile and slapped the cop on the shoulder in a way-too-familiar manner.

“You've got a real interesting town here, Detective,” he said. “I may never leave.”

# { 29 }

While the city baked in ninety-plus degree temperatures on the day of the summer solstice, an army of rangy black men in white ribbed tank tops prowled the streets of downtown Goodwater.

The mostly white shoppers watched packs of five or six men—all wearing grim expressions—stride defiantly along both sides of the street.

Some of the shop owners stepped onto the sidewalk to see what was happening, but the men said nothing to them. They walked around people, light posts, and trash cans but made a point of stopping to peer with hungry eyes through shopwindows of open stores.

The car fires were next.

In the parking lot of the former Goodwater Post Office, a grand edifice built in the Greek Revival style using sandstone from the nearby Ohio Quarries, someone threw a brick through the window of a Mercury Capri, then tossed a poorly designed Molotov cocktail through the resulting hole. The bomb maker didn't understand the mechanics of using a stopper in his homemade bomb. As a result, most of the gasoline spilled out as it was thrown, the glass never broke, and the resulting fire died away quickly.

Better bomb designs and improved tactics soon followed.

The bombers wasted no more time breaking windows with bricks. Well-designed gasoline bombs—with a little motor oil added for texture—could be thrown in quick succession under cars or against windshields. Done correctly, automobiles would become black hulks in minutes.

One raid on the largest of the downtown parking lots disabled fifteen shoppers' cars before the fire trucks arrived. When they did, another team of rioters slashed at fire hoses with machetes, hunting knives, and switchblades before arriving police ran them off.

Few arrests were made. Most were hose slashers in their midteens, although one was only nine. The Molotov cocktail artists were older, faster, and smart enough to get away before anyone in authority showed up.

Most of the shop owners closed up and hammered pieces of plywood over their display windows.

Stanley Crawn, ex-pastor of Faith Bible Church, had packed up his belongings and was waiting on the movers.

But fate gave him another chance.

When the movers showed up, he sent them home. At the Wednesday evening prayer service, he bullied his way back to the pulpit, explaining to a worried and confused congregation that the Lord had recently sent him a message. It had come yesterday during daily prayers.

The Lord, he said, told him the End Times were coming. They were coming to this community and this nation and this sorry, sorry world. Trumpets of sin and destruction presaged the end.

He raised his head and howled as fat tears fell. His own descent into sins of the flesh he blamed on a manipulating Satan. With the end coming, the God-fearing populous must not be left leaderless.

Stanley Crawn preached like he had never preached before. Great rivers of sweat flooded down his cheeks—the church's air conditioning was not working again—as he begged forgiveness and vowed a never-ending fight against the coming Armageddon.

Amid a shower of heartfelt *Amens*, Stanley Crawn was welcomed back as church pastor. Mrs. Crawn, not similarly touched by her husband's testimony, told Stanley she was moving in with her mother and suggested she would not be returning.

No one in the church's congregation, in locked homes around the city, in city hall, or the police department, was thinking about the murder of Annike Eichel. They were wondering if the city was going to burn to the ground.

They were worried that men of another race with weapons in their hands and hate in their hearts would be busting down doors to do them harm.

Rice walked the streets of the largely shuttered downtown. Nothing was here. No cars. No people. No angry demonstrators. It had never been like this. Soulless.

Annike Eichel was back. The ghost followed his movement from across the empty street, matching him step for step like a detached shadow. When he stopped, she stopped.

It was the first time he remembered seeing her full form like this. A lovely, lovely woman. A beautiful ghost.

But when she moved, it was more of a labored trudge than a crisp walk. Like she was a weary soldier bearing a heavy pack and moving toward an awful battle. Rice doubted she moved this way when alive.

He stopped in front of a fruit pie shop that closed last year just after the last summer pie had been baked. It never reopened. Rice turned to face Annike, and she looked toward him, her gaze somehow tolerant and questioning, her eyes as empty as the old pie shop behind him.

He began walking toward the town square and away from this dead place. Annike Eichel stayed behind, watching him but not following.

He would be at police headquarters within five minutes.

—

"Because it's a crime scene," Ed Kadish said, articulating each syllable.

"I know it's a crime scene. That's why I want to go there," Rice said.

"I can't take civilians to a crime scene."

"I thought a crime scene was only active a day," Rice said. "Two at most. Why's this one special?"

"The deceased is a notable person. We're being extra careful. That's one reason," Kadish said. "Normally, we cut up and haul away walls and carpeting, furniture, silverware, and anything else that may help us solve the crime."

"Did you do that?"

"No," Kadish said. "Would you let me finish? Eichel lived alone and has no surviving relatives. Nobody is waiting to move in. So we can take our time. Which is a good thing because the labs are backed up and they won't give us priority on this investigation."

"Why not?"

"Because they won't," Kadish said. "Who the hell knows why. Anyway, the crime scene is exactly the way we found it the day after the murder. We took photos, of course, but it's always better to have the real thing."

"I agree," Rice said. "Let's go."

"I'm still not sure it's a good idea."

"Whatever happened to helping each other? You said it was going to be like the old days, remember?"

"You're a pain in the ass," Kadish said.

"I'm not getting this," Rice said. "Fortunato said we should work together. The chief didn't throw anything at me when I passed him in the hall just now."

"He's got other things on his mind," Kadish said. "We all do. Mayor's thinking of calling in the state troopers if these riots escalate."

"Fine," Rice said. "Nobody cares about the Eichel home right now. They're all worried about the city burning down. Couldn't be a better time to look around."

"You know I'm investigating the firebombing of cars downtown. That's the priority for the department."

"How many people have died in the firebombings?" Rice said.

"What?"

"Give me a number. How many have died so far?" Rice said.

"Nobody," Kadish said. "So far. We're hoping to keep it that way."

"You've got one dead person at the Eichel house and her killer wandering the streets. Doesn't that bother you just a little?"

"When you take that tone, I want to beat you 'til you bleed."

Rice smiled. "You wouldn't talk to me like that if you didn't really like me," he said.

"Why do you want to go there?" Kadish said. "Why's it so goddamn important right now? Tell me."

"Call it a hunch."

"A hunch," Kadish repeated, mocking. "Your hunches don't count. You're not a cop."

He buttoned his top shirt button and tightened his tie. "I'm not taking that Cleveland guy with us," he said. "Just you and me."

"You and me. Got it." They stood up.

"And if we find anything, I told you about it later. I never took you to the scene."

"So you think we might find something too," Rice said.

"Christ," Kadish said.

# { 30 }

They entered the Annike Eichel's home through the back door.

Inside it was cold, despite the ninety-plus temperature outside.

"I'm not opening any windows," Kadish said. "You can turn a light on if you want."

Something was in here. Rice couldn't see anything, but he felt a heaviness and a kind of edgy energy. It made him a little sick to his stomach.

"You okay?" Kadish said, his look sympathetic. "It still stinks like a corpse. Being closed up so long hasn't helped."

"I'm okay."

"Here's where we found her," Kadish said, pointing against a cupboard in the kitchen.

Rice stared down at the floor. He could discern the outline of her legs in the dried blood, a thin trail of more dried blood led from the living room.

"You figure she was stabbed in the living room and dragged herself into the kitchen to die?"

"There's more blood in the living room next to the couch," Kadish said. "So, yeah, that's what we think."

"She didn't seem to be in a big hurry."

"You're kidding, right?"

"I'm just saying she didn't look like she was trying to get away," Rice said. "It looks like she was stabbed multiple times, then somehow crawled into the kitchen to die. Doesn't look like anybody chased her."

Kadish ran a hand through his hair. "We'd see footprints," he said. "We don't think the murderer followed her."

"Any footprints in the living room?"

"No, not anywhere," Kadish said. "Very competent."

"But the report suggested the killer acted in a kind of blood frenzy."

"He was one cold-blooded bastard," Kadish said. "I don't want to know him."

"You don't think this was a professional hit?"

"I'm not saying that," Kadish said, now looking around like he'd rather be anyplace else. "A professional is going to put three bullets in you and make sure you're dead. They don't generally get, you know, personal."

Rice pointed at a line of books—some open, some closed—on the floor beneath the bookcase. He reached down to pick one up.

"Don't touch, goddammit," Kadish said.

"Maybe footprints are under the books."

"That's the best you can do?" Kadish said.

Rice looked around. "Where are the bugs?"

"We, um, we took them when we removed the body," Kadish said.

"What do you mean 'um'? C'mon, Ed."

The detective took a deep breath and exhaled over fluttering lips. "The insects must have gotten out."

"Somebody stole your evidence bags?"

"No, that's not what I mean," Kadish said. "The bags were there, all labeled. The bugs were gone though."

"Bug parts left behind? Bug shit? Anything?"

"You could've put a ham and cheese sandwich in there, the bags were so clean."

Rice looked around. "Can I go into the bedroom?"

Kadish held out an upraised hand in an exaggerated be-my-guest gesture. The double bed was made up. A tiger maple chest of drawers was topped by a large mirror. A small photo of a much younger Annike Eichel was jammed into one corner.

It looked exactly like the little girl in his vision.

Rice got down on his knees and looked under the bed. Some shoes. Some dust. Nothing else.

"You seen enough yet?" Kadish asked.

The reporter opened the closet. Lots of suits. Tops, most of them pastel. Very neat, just as he expected. More shoes on the floor. He bent down and caught some movement near a box against the back wall.

It was a shoebox. When Rice dragged the box toward him, there was more activity. Next, he heard a skittering sound that caused him to draw back instinctively.

Kadish heard it too and moved closer.

"What?" he said.

He flicked on the closet light. Hundreds of beetles and maggots squirmed on the floor next to the wall. A flood of flies like smoke from an explosion arose with a noisy hum before settling down on the shoes, the clothes, everywhere.

Rice gingerly lifted the shoebox lid, but it contained only a pair of yellow shoes.

"They gotta be feasting on meat," Kadish said, dropping down and pushing shoes and boxes out of the way. Rice backed off and tasted a little bit of breakfast coming up.

"Shit. There's nothin' here," Kadish said. "They're just sitting there."

Rice belched into his fist before bending over to take another look. In the closet light, he could see a variety of insects squirming in place on the carpeted closet floor.

"Like they're waiting for you," Rice said.

From the living room, they heard the sound of something heavy dropping to the floor. Kadish jumped up so quickly his head unhooked a hanging apple-green cashmere sweater.

"Now what?" he said, his voice rising.

More thumps from the living room.

Rice got there first. He watched as large books fell off the bookshelf to the floor. It seemed like an unseen finger was pulling each one by its spine. The timing was unhurried. Mechanical.

"More bugs?" Rice said, pleased to hear his voice remain flat.

Kadish pushed him out of the way and watched as two more books dropped to the floor. The detective sprinted to the bookshelf and reached out to catch the next falling book. Then another.

Rice remembered his vision and searched for a shape prowling the room, but it was too dark. He yanked open the drapes and winced as light flooded the room.

"Hey," Kadish said. When he turned away from the bookshelf, another book dropped heavily to the floor.

Rice looked around, behind things. Nothing.

"What are you doing?" Kadish said.

Rice ran back to the bedroom, threw those drapes open, and looked around some more. Nothing unusual there, either.

Rice ran past Kadish into the kitchen. The books had stopped dropping off the bookshelf.

"Are you going to tell me …?" Kadish called out as Rice hurried by.

No drapes to open in the kitchen. There was a small curtain on the window over the sink. He turned the light on.

Rice squinted and looked around before directing a finger at a corner above the kitchen cupboard. "There," he said. "Right there."

Kadish joined him and squinted at where he was pointing.

"Christ," he said. "What the hell?"

A black cotton-like mass attached to the wall throbbed like a growing tumor, then seemed to become liquid and spread out along the ceiling, growing dimmer as it did so. Then it disappeared. It all happened in seconds.

Kadish fell into a kitchen chair. "The light is playing tricks," he said. "And I'm tired. So I didn't see that."

Rice walked into the living room. The books lay on the floor—some opened, some still closed—in a straight line. He went into the bedroom, opened the closet door. The light was still on. He squatted down.

"Hey, Ed."

Rice heard the kitchen chair scrape over the linoleum as the detective got up. Then his slow plod to the bedroom.

"No more surprises," Kadish said, trying to look over Rice's shoulder. "What?"

"All your buggy buddies are gone," Rice said.

Kadish pushed him aside and forced the hanging clothes into bunches on both ends of the clothes bar. He flicked off lids from the boxes on the floor, finding nothing but shoes, some still with paper wrapped around them.

"I should have bagged the goddamn bugs when I found them," he said, dropping down on his rear, legs splayed like he was getting ready to shoot marbles.

"Do you think it would have mattered?"

Kadish stared at him blankly, then stood up with some difficulty and returned to the bookshelf in the living room. "Okay, this is real," he said. "This happened."

Kadish carefully pulled the drapes closed and then did the same in the bedroom.

"Now it's getting warmer in here," he said, rubbing the back of his neck. He turned to Rice. "What the hell is going on?"

Rice pulled the drapes open slightly and peered out.

"This is all off the record," the detective said, his expression challenging the reporter. "You can't write about any of it."

Rice scanned the street and nodded his head when he recognized a man standing there. "Take me back to my car, Ed," he said. "I've got to talk to someone."

# { 31 }

Rice banged his fist hard against Arnie Corso's door.

Four doors down, a middle-aged man with long, curly hair and a tie-dyed T-shirt stepped into the hall. Rice stared him down until he returned to his apartment.

He heard Arnie unhook the chain and unlock the door.

"How'd your banana pot experiment turn out?" Rice said when he opened it.

Arnie shook his head and sighed. "Like smoking a Zippo lighter wick," he said.

Rice smiled in a way he hoped looked sympathetic. "Like you *imagine* what it would be like. You never, you know, actually *smoked* a Zippo lighter wick, did you?"

"What do you want, Rice?"

"It's about Annike Eichel."

"I can't help you," Arnie said, pushing himself farther into his couch. "Most spirits come and go until they finally figure things out. We can chase them away, but we really can't help them much. In the end, we're all alone."

"That's not very comforting," Rice said.

Arnie pushed out his lower lip. "I'm not your pastor and don't care if you're comforted."

Rice pulled out a cigar and held it up hopefully toward Arnie.

"Go ahead, smoke it," Arnie said.

Rice unwrapped the Hav-A-Tampa, lit it, and took two puffs before pulling out a kitchen chair and sitting down. "How long have we known each other?" he said.

"Four or five years, I guess."

"I've talked to you about my work. About Stacey. You've talked to me about your parents. Your studies. Right?"

"I don't have many friends," Arnie said, looking chastened and uncomfortable. "You opened up and that was something new to me. People hear stories about me and stay clear. But not you."

"That's right."

"You were scared," Arnie said. "You fell in love then started seeing ghosts. You heard I was spooky-crazy and thought I could help you. How am I doing?"

"I was confused," Rice said.

"But you were using me. Admit it."

Rice shrugged. "In the beginning, maybe," he said. "I wouldn't call it using you, though. I had questions and thought you might have answers. Is that using you? Most people would call that conversation."

Arnie looked down at his hands. "I'm not most people."

Rice raised his eyebrows.

"Everybody has spirit guides," Arnie said. "I just see them. Maybe you see something too."

"I don't know what I'm seeing," Rice said. "You taught me to be suspicious."

He told Arnie about the vision in the parking lot. About the visit to Eichel's home. The books. The bugs.

"And you want to know if it's real?"

"I had a detective with me," Rice said. "I'm pretty sure it's real. I'm just trying to figure out what it means."

"Your little dream-vision. You think that was real too?"

Rice lifted his head back and took two long draws on the cigar. "Yeah, I think it was," he said. "Does that surprise you?"

"So you have a dream in the parking lot, and next thing, you're seeing flying books and bugs in a dead woman's house."

"That's the chronology."

Arnie pushed himself forward on the couch cushion. He stood up, walked around, jammed his fingers into his back pockets. He really did look like a catalog model.

"You know, I used you too," Arnie said. "At first I just liked having someone listen to me. I don't get much respect, so it was nice."

Rice smiled. "I respect you. And I like you. So are we going to make out now?"

"It was when you talked to me about Stacey," Arnie said. "You told me about reading poetry and the long walks by the lake and all the things boys and girls do. You made me feel like I was there with you. That's how I used you."

"I don't mind," Rice said. "You won't be using me much anymore, though. Stacey wants a man with a firm jaw and a hand on the corporate ladder."

"I see her every once in a while. She still loves you."

"That isn't enough," Rice said. "Apparently."

He was surprised to see Arnie's face slowly redden, just before he turned around. "After you first had sexual relations with her, you began seeing spirits."

"I don't remember telling you …"

"I figured it out," Arnie said. "Do you think it was a coincidence that your world expanded after you first had sex?"

"That's a big leap."

Arnie watched Rice's smoke float against a window. "I don't know much about these things," he said. "I played post office once at a party when I was thirteen. That's the last time I kissed a girl who wasn't related to me."

"Who's fault is that?"

"Don't get pissy," Arnie said without venom. "I'm comfortable with who I am."

Rice looked around for an ashtray, then tapped the ash in his hand. "So getting laid unlocked the creepy locker in my brain," he said. "I don't care. It helps me in my work."

Arnie stood over him and smiled. "But these kinds of perceptions aren't a stagnant phenomenon," he said. "You're going to change and grow. Maybe you'll become a tulip. Or maybe you'll become one of those flowers that devours insects."

"That would be my preference," Rice said. "A bug eater."

"This Eichel woman's spirit isn't like the others you've seen," Arnie said. "Not like the dead Vietnam soldiers or the guy killed in the bar fight or the woman shot by her husband down by the river."

"So what kind of flower does that make me?"

Arnie walked into the kitchen and opened a cupboard filled with rows of cans. He stood on tiptoes, reached into the back of the upper shelf, and withdrew one. Chef Boyardee Ravioli. Arnie blew some dust off the lid and began scrounging in a drawer. When he found the can opener, he held it up with a cry of surprise like it was the first one he'd seen.

"You're a scary flower," Arnie said as he cracked the lid and plopped the congealed mass into a pan. It began to sizzle as soon as he turned the gas on. "You're a scary, evolving flower."

"Evolving how?"

Arnie turned the gas down and stirred the ravioli cubes with a fork. "More and more you seem to be attracting spirits and spiritual phenomena," he said. "They're lost and feel drawn to you because you're a little lost too."

"Maybe we just hang out in the same places."

Arnie plucked a piece of ravioli with his fork, bit it carefully, then dropped it back into the pan. "I'm not sharing these with you," he said.

"That's okay. I prefer SpaghettiOs."

After a few more minutes, Arnie dumped the entire pan of ravioli onto a plate, and they spread out like a beached jellyfish, sweet tomato steam rising up. "I wouldn't mind if you opened a window and put your cigar on the ledge while I ate," he said.

Rice smiled and complied.

"You should keep in touch with me about everything that happens with you," Arnie said as he pushed a napkin into his shirt. "Psychically, I mean. I'll try to keep you out of trouble. But you got to tell me everything."

"So far you haven't helped me much," Rice said.

Arnie nodded in agreement as he forked ravioli into his mouth. "That's because you haven't told me everything. So you go first."

"I thought you knew things."

"I do know things," Arnie said, wiping his chin with great care before returning to his meal. "I know, for instance, that despite what you said about not seeing her often, Annike Eichel was with you at her house this afternoon."

"She left me on the street. She didn't follow us in," Rice said.

Arnie grinned and poked his fork at him. "But she was there," he said, nodding and smiling as he cut a ravioli in half. "Wasn't she?"

"She wasn't following me."

"Okay, all right," Arnie said. "These are the kinds of things I need to know. She wasn't following you, but she was there. Right?"

"Yeah."

"So she was keeping an eye on her place," Arnie said. "Maybe worried about that thing you saw inside."

"I don't think that was it," Rice said.

Arnie was plowing through the ravioli. Now only some watery tomato sauce remained. This he inelegantly gathered with his fork.

"So?"

"She was with the priest from school, Father Growden," Rice said.

"This is coming out of nowhere."

"I'm trying to understand it myself," Rice said.

"So the priest was standing next to the spirit, Annike Eichel. On the street. Together. Did he know she was there?"

Rice shrugged. "Didn't appear to."

"What was he doing?"

Rice sighed heavily. "He had binoculars and was watching the house. Trying to watch Kadish and me inside, I think."

"Don't you think you should have mentioned this earlier?"

"Okay, I buried the lede," Rice said. "There's a lot going on."

Arnie carried his plate to the kitchen where he belched lightly and apologized to the curtained window over the sink. "I disagree," he said. "I think it's beginning to make some sense. Not all of it, but it's coming together. Do you know that feeling?"

"Not so much lately."

"You can get your cigar if you want," Arnie said. "I'm finished eating."

The cigar had gone out. Rice touched the tip tentatively, but it was cold. "I think she's trying to talk to me," he said, returning the cigar to the pack. "She moves her lips and tongue, but I can't hear anything and I can't make out what she's trying to say."

"It's hard for a spirit to make a sound, to physically move the air so you can hear their words," Arnie said. "Maybe she'll learn. I'd love to hear what she has to say. But she's already speaking to you."

"How's that?"

Arnie spread his hands. "Your dream. It was a mess, but she was trying to tell you something. And it must be important."

Rice reached down toward Arnie with both hands. "Let's get out of the house for a while," he said.

# { 32 }

At first Arnie wouldn't leave the car. He crossed his arms over his chest like a petulant child and shook his head.

It had taken Rice only a few minutes to convince Arnie to accompany him to Sacred Heart Church so both of them could talk with Father Growden. Arnie had seemed eager.

Now, not so much.

"You said you wanted to go," Rice said. There were so many empty parking spots, he was beginning to wonder if the church was closed.

"Take me home," Arnie said, casting a quick look at the church before drawing his gaze back inside the car. "I don't like it here."

Rice pulled open the door. "Come on, get out," he said. "Growden's probably not even here."

But he was. The priest welcomed them both into his office. Rice took the ragged corduroy chair, and Arnie stood behind him, shifting from one foot to the other while biting his lower lip.

More boxes were stacked on the floor and fewer books filled the shelves than last time.

"Father Growden is defrocking," Rice said after turning around to face Arnie, who looked around the cluttered office nervously, biting harder on his lip.

"I'm not being defrocked," the priest said. "That's forced laicization, still holding the wry smile. "I'm leaving voluntarily."

"Sorry I used the wrong words," Rice said. "Defrocking does sound kind of final. And a little naughty."

Growden stood at his desk. He was shorter than Rice remembered but solid and square as a chunk of sandstone. He wore a short-sleeved shirt with his clerical collar and sported battalions of wispy hair along his arms.

"What can I do for you?"

"It was something you said last time we talked," Rice said. "About how you and Annike sat in your car and how you said you were having doubts about the church and that the two of you cried about it. Remember telling me that?"

The priest nodded.

"And you kind of suggested the two of you met just that once."

"Did I?" Growden said. He had taken a seat on the edge of his desk. Crossed his arms.

"But you fibbed a little about that last part," Rice said, holding his finger and thumb about a half-inch apart. "Because you met with her privately a great many times."

The priest's eyes lit up briefly, and Rice could tell that fire lived there sometimes. But he began shaking his head and the grin returned. "You're a funny fellow, Mr. Channon," he said, using his surname, unlike the last visit. "I tell you something personal and even a little bit embarrassing, and you come all the way across town to tell me I'm a liar."

"That doesn't sound so funny."

Father Growden stood up. "I've got a young couple coming in for a baptism in an hour," he said. "First baptism of an infant in almost three months. So I want to prepare and do it right. Are you finished?"

"You told me she was a strange woman," Rice said. "She asked you questions about the church. You expressed doubts about your faith. All this in one or two car rides."

The priest said nothing.

"I'm pretty sure you saw her lots of times," Rice said. "Tell me I'm wrong."

Growden told him nothing.

Rice smiled. "When I was little and getting my tonsils out, I was surprised that a nurse on the floor got sick and had to go home. I thought that since she worked at the hospital, she enjoyed a kind of dispensation from illness."

"And because I'm a priest, I *can't* lie. Is that it?"

"Seems silly, I know …"

"We lie sometimes. Just like nurses get sick and cops break the law."

"So it won't hurt your feelings when I tell you I think you're lying about your relationship with Annike Eichel?"

Growden looked at his watch. "I told you I've got a baptism in a little while," he said. Rice opened his mouth to speak, but the priest raised a hand to stop him. "Parents—especially new parents like this couple—believe their child is the most beautiful thing on the planet. Sometimes they're a little nervous about the baptism. Many of them haven't been inside a church in a while."

He smiled paternally. "So to make them more comfortable, I often gush about the baby. About how beautiful she is or about the beautiful embroidery on the christening dress."

"You lie," Rice said.

"What would you tell your daughter waiting for her prom date if her face was blotchy, her dress was too big, and her arms were skinny?"

"You look beautiful, honey."

"Exactly," Father Growden said. "You'd lie and wouldn't give it a second thought. You'd know you did the right thing. Only children believe in absolutes. Are you a child, Mr. Channon?"

"Wow. That's the best defense of lying I've ever heard," Rice said. "You should skip the boys' club and jump right into politics."

Arnie tripped over a box of books as he moved closer to the only window. He mumbled an apology.

"You asked me if I lied to you about my relationship with Miss Eichel," Father Growden said. He spread his hands. "I might have misled you."

"Were you intimate with her?"

The priest moved from behind the desk and walked to the box Arnie tripped over. He pushed it against the wall. "Not that it's any of your business. Not that it's anyone's business. Yes, we shared a real intimacy. I will tell you this, but only because you seem fascinated with the subject. I was not intimate in a sexual way with Annike Eichel. I hope you're not disappointed."

"I'm in the word business," Rice said. "Intimacy usually suggests affection or a loving personal relationship."

"So my characterization stands," Growden said.

"Could you enlighten me?"

"I don't think so."

Rice twirled his finger in the dust on the end table. "Annike won't mind. She's dead."

The priest smiled.

"How come you were standing outside her home earlier today?" Rice said. "You had binoculars and everything. I feel bad we didn't open more curtains so you could see what was going on. It was pretty interesting inside."

Father Growden shrugged.

"Aren't you a little bit curious?"

The priest spread his hands and gave a tight-lipped smile. "You caught me watching you with binoculars," he said. "What do you think?"

"I think you've been there before," Rice said. "Maybe lots of times. Kind of proprietary, aren't you?"

Arnie turned around. Growden stood there like a mannequin in a Roman collar.

"Did you ever see anything unusual?"

"No," the priest said.

"Is this one of those times when it's okay for you to lie?"

"I think we've talked enough," Father Growden said. "I will tell you this. I'm really good at keeping secrets, Mr. Channon."

"So you admit you're keeping a secret."

"I never said that."

"Kind of, you did," Rice said. He smiled. "It's okay. I figured that out already. Remember when you talked with me about ghosts and you told me how I should steer clear of otherworldly things?"

"I do," Father Growden said, returning to his desk and sitting down one more time. He patted his fingers drumlike against the desk blotter and watched his hands as he did. Then he looked up at Rice. "How is Stacey, by the way? You two have a strange relationship. She told me she has feelings for you but doesn't want you in her life."

"That pretty much sums it up," Rice said. "I thought you didn't reveal secrets, Father."

"According to Stacey, it's no secret," the priest said, an edge in his voice now. "She thinks you're a little boy who plays around with matches and other things he should stay away from."

"She's becoming an adult. I'll catch up someday," Rice said.

Another tight-lipped smile from the priest.

"The last time I came to this office, I accused you of not believing in ghosts, and you quickly corrected me. Do you remember that?"

"Yes," Father Growden said.

"You said it was unwise to prowl in ghostly domains. I thought it was a nice phrase."

"Thank you."

"So here's my question," Rice said. "Did you see the ghost in Annike Eichel's home? Or did she merely tell you about it? Or both?"

The priest looked down at his fingers drumming against the desktop a little longer, then stopped. Looked up. "Do you mean her ghost? I thought only *you* saw that."

"I mean the ghost who rearranges books in her library. The one in the corner of her kitchen that looks like a big grease spot. That's the one I mean, Father."

"And you think I know about that?"

Rice was midlaugh when Arnie spun around. He practically leaped across the room, and placed two heavy hands on the back of the chair.

"It's not a ghost," Arnie said to the priest. "You're wrong if you think that. But you're right about not snooping around in ghostly … places."

"I'm glad you agree," Father Growden said, his mouth half-open in a surprised and amused way. "So can we all get back to our jobs? I have a lot to do."

"It's a poltergeist," Arnie said, whispering like it was a dirty word.

Rice leaned forward in his chair. "How do you know, Arnie?"

Arnie turned away from the priest and began pacing across the room. He made two circuits—carefully avoiding the boxes—before he spoke again. "You claim to see ghosts, Rice," he said. "Did this look like one?"

"No."

"And that dream-vision thing of yours," he said, continuing. "I think there was truth in what you saw. I suspected it even before you told me what happened in that woman's house."

"What kind of truth?"

"About the poltergeist," Arnie said.

"What the hell is a poltergeist, Arnie?"

"It's like a spirit with a Superman cape. It's a German word. It means noisy ghost." Arnie shifted his gaze between Rice and the priest. "But it can do a lot more than just make noise."

"Like what?" Rice said. Father Growden turned to listen and dropped the amused expression.

Arnie shrugged as if he were just picking and choosing from a long list. "Moving things. Like keys or your shoes or something like that. All of a sudden the things disappear from where you left them. A few days later, they reappear."

"There could be a lot of explanations for that," the priest said. "Forgetfulness. Mischievous children."

"Or grown-ups," Rice said.

"Sure," Arnie said. "That's the problem with all ghostly activity. Unstable houses, leaky windows, pranksters, liars. Nine times out of ten, that's the answer. Nothing paranormal taking place except an active imagination."

"So how are books flying off shelves?" Rice said.

"Oh, it's a poltergeist," Arnie said, his voice more confident now. "After your vision and then the books falling, I didn't have any doubt."

"What if Mr. Channon is lying?" Father Growden said.

"I'd know," Arnie said with a tight smile.

"If you're right, where did the spirit—"

"Poltergeist," Arnie interrupted gently. "It's not really a spirit. I shouldn't have called it a ghost. It's more of a Frankenstein's monster."

"So … Who's Frankenstein?" Rice said, momentarily confused by the interruption.

"I'm sure you can figure it out," Arnie said. "Maybe Father Growden already has."

The desk chair creaked loudly as the priest leaned back. "Annike Eichel had a troubled childhood," he said. "She grew up in a household of some means, but her parents were cool and distant."

"That's not unusual," Arnie said.

Growden rubbed the bridge of his nose. "No, unfortunately it's not," he said. "But Annike was a loving child. She was pretty and outgoing and everyone liked her. But her parents were suspicious of her warmth. Don't ask me why. They pushed her away. Like a lot of children—even those with loving parents—she created an imaginary playmate when she was at home. Over time, she even gave it a name: Alexander."

"And she told you all this?" Rice said.

"Over cups of Bao Zhong tea in the living room," Father Growden said. "She knows a lot about teas. That one was from China. Tastes a little like lilac."

"I've got to start drinking tea," Arnie said.

"As her parents grew more demanding and distant, Annike grew angry at everything they represented," the priest said.

"Were they religious people?" Rice said.

"No, not at all, apparently. They were sort of indifferent, according to Annike. But as she got older, her anger—she called it hatred—grew. She was able to develop relationships with people at school and at work, though."

Arnie looked agitated again. "But Alexander didn't go away like most imaginary playmates, did he?"

Father Growden raised his head. "No," he said. "She recounted a particularly ugly episode with her father when she was about twenty. She had come home for the Thanksgiving holiday. Somehow her father had learned of a relationship she had with an engineering student. Her father told her he wouldn't be paying to finance her fornication. That was the way he put it. And Annike's mother did nothing to defend her.

Neither parent even asked about the nature of her relationship."

"Which was?" Rice said.

"Which was over, according to Annike. But she never bothered to respond to her parents' charges. She told me she went into her room, locked the door, held a pillow against her mouth, and screamed into it."

"And then?" Arnie said.

"And then, for the first time, she saw Alexander for real."

# { 33 }

Rice sat in the parking lot overlooking Lake Erie, the dull wet sky mirrored in the lake water and its nervous waves. He lit a cigar and rolled the window down.

Even this early in the season, mothers and their kids would normally be here. The mothers would spread out blankets on the brown sand while the kiddies flirted with the water. They'd bring chicken sandwiches and thermoses of Kool-Aid.

Rice blew a smoke cloud toward the open window, but lake breezes grabbed it and tossed it back inside. The smoke cloud floated over the passenger seat before dissolving.

It was cold, overcast, and wet. Few places could be as gloomy as northern Ohio when the weather made up its mind to turn sour. It was not a beach day.

Rice turned on the radio and groaned when he heard Donny Osmond wailing about "Puppy Love." Frantically roaming the AM channels, he caught the opening riff of Deep

Purple's "Smoke on the Water" and left it there. The song's edginess fit his mood.

One good thing about crummy weather was it kept the rioters at home. Sure, they'd burn up buildings and cars, risk being shot or arrested by the police, but god forbid, they should go out when the sun wasn't shining.

The cigar wasn't burning well. Probably the humidity. He sucked harder, and a ring of red ash returned to the butt end.

Vietnam and the US had resumed talks about ending the fighting. Even the normally businesslike radio announcer sounded bored with the story. And disgusted. It looked like it would be a long time before that distant war with its questionable motivations and heartbreaking body counts would end.

The gray lake water with its empty strip of narrow beach looked like a sea of misery.

Rice got out of the car and found the concrete steps down to the beach. They could be slippery when it was wet like this, so he held the metal handrail which wobbled precariously. The county was supposed to maintain the beach facilities but was obviously behind in its work.

Maybe he would write a story about it.

*The power of the press*, he thought dismally. Rice flung his unhappy cigar into the river rocks behind the beach sand.

He started walking in the direction of the lighthouse off Perry Point. Rice had figured she would come from that direction. Before long, he saw a figure in a long wool coat with big buttons up to the neck.

"You look overdressed for a walk on the sand," he said.

To his surprise, Stacey leaned toward him and planted a chaste kiss against his cheek. She threaded her arm through his. "I'll keep you warm," she said. "Don't pretend you are."

The cool wind carried the scent of mothballs from her coat. Stacey must have smelled it too. "I don't know why I ever think I can put this coat in storage for the summer," she said. "There are days in August I could use it."

Rice didn't say anything.

"Thanks for meeting me," she said.

"Sure," he said. "Couldn't it have been someplace dryer? Someplace with a roof?"

"I didn't want anyone seeing us, getting the wrong idea."

"We should be safe here," he said, disappointed his intended sarcasm was so feeble.

"Roger lost his job," she said. "He's kind of down."

"Sorry to hear it," Rice said, feigning ignorance.

A young couple with two preschool-aged children walked in their direction. Rice guessed dad had promised the kids a day at the beach and couldn't get out of it.

Stacey turned around and began walking away from them, toward the lighthouse.

"I don't know them," Rice said, biting the words, feeling angry at her excess caution. "Do you?"

"I just don't feel like seeing people today," she said. "Do you mind?"

A rain squall or spray from an enthusiastic whitecap brushed over them, and she pulled him closer as they walked.

"He'll find another job, Stace," Rice said. "Bright guy like that. He'll land on his feet."

She turned her face to him, her look questioning. "I thought you didn't like him," she said.

"I like him well enough. Earnest. Clean-cut. Hardworking." Rice paused. "Celibate."

"It's wearing on me," she said.

"Celibacy?"

They walked along silently for a time, the wet sand mushing under their feet. "He's thoughtful, caring. Loving, in his way."

"The all-American boy," he said. "Just what you wanted."

"I'm seeing Tom," she said. "It happened before Roger lost his job but now it's … more frequent."

"Tom? Tom Janousek?"

"Do you know he's writing a screenplay?" she said, turning to Rice again, this time with a broad smile.

"Tom Janousek? From the *Cleveland Chronicle*?"

"Yes," she said, pouting. "I thought you'd be pleased."

Rice felt light-headed and couldn't get his brain around the idea. The two of them together. He couldn't see it. Refused to see it.

"You're putting me on."

"I am not," she said, withdrawing her arm from his. "I can see this was a mistake. I thought you'd be more mature."

"Mature like you?" he said. "Dumping your boyfriend, your fiancé, because he lost his job. That's real grown-up."

"We were drifting apart," she said, not looking at him.

"You just accepted his proposal of marriage."

"That was a week or ten days ago," she said, looking out at the lake, squinting like she expected to find the Canadian shore out there somewhere.

"How'd he take it?"

Stacey sighed. "Not well."

"I doubt he's ever been dumped before."

Stacey's eyes looked sad, confirming. "No, he hasn't been. I am—I *was*—his first serious relationship. So I broke his heart and there it is."

She looked up at Rice, seeking consolation. Forgiveness maybe.

"Why are you telling me this, Stace?" he said. "Don't you think this tears at me some?"

"I never thought about it," she said, sounding almost pleased. "You're my best friend. I needed to talk it out with somebody."

"I wish you'd picked somebody else."

"I thought you'd understand."

"I don't understand at all," he said. "Do you really think you can have anything serious with Tom Janousek?"

She played with the top button on her coat, rotating it as though she wanted to screw her collar down tighter. "It's not that kind of relationship, okay?"

"You're not reading Keats to each other."

"No. But he read me some of his screenplay. It's good."

"So who's the murderer in his movie."

"I don't know," Stacey said. "We haven't got there yet."

"I've been talking to your friend, Pete Growden. It turns out his relationship with Annike was more than a passing one."

"I can't believe he had sex with her," she said.

"Yeah, well, it can be surprising who has sex with whom," Rice said. "But I don't think it was like that between them. She'd been troubled by a spirit—maybe a real nasty spirit—for much of her life. She talked to Growden about it. A lot, apparently. They formed kind of a bond."

Stacey's cheeks were red and speckled with rain or lake spray. "So, who did it?" she said. "Who was the father of the two-month-old fetus?"

"They weren't talking about babies," Rice said, water trickling down his cheek and onto his shirt. "They talked about this thing chasing her."

Stacey laughed and stopped abruptly when she looked at his face, full of confusion. Then she laughed again. He'd forgotten how unfettered her laughter could be.

"What's so funny?"

"Father Growden and Annike Eichel talked about her experiences with ghosts?" she said. "Maybe many times?"

"Yeah. So?"

"Do you realize how hard it must have been for a dyed-in-the-wool atheist to admit such a thing to a Roman Catholic priest?"

Rice stuttered. "Well, they had this bond, like I said."

"Yeah," she said, smiling up at him. "They had a bond. You think she didn't tell him about the baby in her belly?"

Rice shivered. He thought it was the cold rain but wasn't sure.

Stacey stood on tiptoes and kissed him on the nose. "Some reporter you are," she said.

# { 34 }

Rice stood in the newsroom door and looked over at Tom Janousek typing at his desk, sleeves rolled up. A cigar burned in his ashtray.

When Rice sat down, Janousek eyed him briefly. "Where have you been?" he said. "Billard wants to talk to you."

"About what?"

"I don't know. He looks annoyed."

"He always looks annoyed," Rice said and nodded at the cigar. "What's with the stogie?"

"You make them look good," Janousek said. "Tastes a little like a lollipop you can smoke."

"So maybe your breath won't stink so much."

Janousek, who had been typing through the discussion, stopped and turned to face Rice. "What's your problem? Did you sit on something pointy?"

Billard came up behind and dropped a heavy hand on Rice's shoulder. "You didn't shave again today," he said. "And it looks like you took a shower with your clothes on."

"I was at the lake."

"So you decided to jump in?"

"I had some thinking to do," Rice said. "It was raining. Let's talk in the back."

Billard followed Rice to the telephone switching room next to the men's bathroom. It was cramped inside and relays clicked incessantly, but it was private.

"Tell me you've got something," Billard said. Now he looked hopeful, almost desperate. "I need something for today's paper."

"What's Janousek writing?"

"I don't know," Billard said. "He told me he was drafting a screenplay. But he doesn't work for me. You do."

Billard punctuated the last statement with an index finger to Rice's chest.

"I've got stuff, but I don't know if we can use it," Rice said, tapping on a relay until Billard brushed his hand away from it.

"If you're playing cop again, I'm going to hurt you."

Rice looked down at the short city editor and almost felt something like affection. He was so intense.

"I talked Ed Kadish into taking me into the Eichel home," Rice said.

"Okay. Good. What came of that?"

"We found lots of strange bugs in the house," Rice said. "It didn't make sense."

"We're not doing another bug story."

"These were the kinds of insects that chew on corpses. All different kinds. In different places."

"What did Kadish say?" Billard asked.

"He said they had to be feasting on meat."

"Terrific. So who or what were they eating?"

"That's the thing. They weren't eating anything," Rice said. "And when we came back later, the bugs were gone."

"How much later? The next day. Couple of hours?"

"A few minutes," Rice said.

Now it was Billard tapping at the snapping relays. He cocked his head. "What else?"

Rice told him about the books on the floor. The books shooting off shelves in front of the detective. The inky black mass in the corner of the kitchen.

Everything but the dream-vision in the fast food parking lot.

As he listened to his own words, Rice thought his explanation sounded detached and clinical. This seemed to please Billard, who smiled a little.

"What did Kadish make of it?"

"He tried to convince himself he was imagining it all. Said he's not sleeping well. At least at first," Rice said. "But he knows something weird is going on. Told me I couldn't write about it."

Billard grunted. "What could we say?"

"Exactly."

Rice explained about meeting with Father Growden and how he had been apparently counseling Annike Eichel about her experiences with apparitions. How she and the priest had grown close and that this was probably the reason for his regular visits to her house.

"How close?" Billard said, rubbing his chin.

"Not that close," Rice said. "But close enough to know her past history."

"What past history?"

—

Rice and Billard tromped through the newsroom as if they were returning from the war. Rice watched Billard sit at his desk, slip on his reading glasses and grab copy from his in-box.

Janousek leaned over his desk like he was going to tell a secret. "You talked to Stacey."

"Yeah. We spoke."

"We got a murderer on the loose, parts of the city are on fire—or will be when the sun comes out— and Rice is sad because his old girlfriend is making time with a new fella." Janousek made a pouty face.

"Have you started casting your movie yet?" Rice said. He pulled out his lighter and shook it, trying to look nonchalant.

Janousek looked down at the script in his typewriter. "I'm not the producer," he said. "But I'm going to recommend

Steve McQueen for my character. For you, I don't know, Woody Allen?"

"I gotta go."

"The things I'm hearing about you and what you're finding in your investigations," Janousek said. "You wouldn't believe it."

"I'm sticking close to Kadish and the priest," Rice said. "You've got the mayor, Fortunato, and Markle."

"Sure," Janousek said, shrugging. "But it seems my celebrity is wearing on the locals. I'm not getting much. I was hoping I could tag along with you."

"I'll do better on my own, thanks."

The haughty copy girl with the short skirt swished as she passed them on the way to Billard's desk. Rice thought he'd never seen such a bold leer as Tom Janousek threw in her direction.

"I don't have to see her, if you don't like," he said, turning back to Rice. "Stacey, I mean. I don't want it getting in the way of our relationship."

"Our relationship isn't going to change. Whatever's going on between you and Stacey, that's up to you."

Janousek smiled like he knew the truth. He held the smile while turning back to his screenplay. He stopped after a few pecks, leaned against the top of his typewriter and spoke to the air. "She's still got a thing for you," he said. "That's why I mentioned about backing off, if you'd feel better."

"Don't give it another thought."

"There's a club across town that plays classic jazz. I was surprised to find it. Piano bar. I think they have food. I'm taking Stacey there tonight."

"Enjoy yourselves."

"You're welcome to join us."

"I'm more of a Uriah Heep fan," Rice said. "But thanks."

Janousek said nothing more. He returned to his typing. Rice heard the rapid tapping of his keys joined by the harmony of rattling teletype machines as he descended the stairs out of the newsroom, two steps at a time.

# { 35 }

The radio reported that Foster Ebner, the suspended Public Works director, had been arrested and charged with embezzlement of city funds. He hadn't posted bail yet.

While driving past the free clinic, an empty bottle of Yoo-Hoo was thrown against Rice's fender and burst into pieces on the pavement. Three Negro kids—maybe twelve years old—ran off laughing.

The sun broke through every so often now. Steam rose from the sidewalks.

Rice felt in his pockets and realized he'd left his cigars behind, even though he'd made a point of grabbing a lighter. He reached over to pop open the glove compartment. Nothing inside but a notebook and pencils.

Tossing the city's highest-ranking black man into jail would almost certainly fuel anger in the black community.

With the return of clear weather and warm temperatures, there'd be trouble.

When he arrived at Mosopelea County Community College, Rice started looking for the car he'd seen parked in front of Sacred Heart Church. He prowled the faculty parking lot and finally spotted the same dented red 1964 Ford Galaxie. Rice knew it was Growden's regular day at the college and was pretty sure he would find him here.

Although he knew the school's security force was notorious for ticketing cars in the wrong lot, Rice parked alongside a new VW and relied on good luck to keep him ticket-free. He had just locked his door when he saw Growden walking along the sidewalk carrying a box. He dropped it on the hood of the tired old Ford, then pulled out his car keys.

"Moving day?" Rice asked.

Growden looked up and grimaced. Might have been the sun in his eyes.

The priest opened the back door and slid the box on the seat with two other boxes and a coatrack. He exhaled a big sigh.

"It is for me," he said. "Not enough Catholics to justify a priest for the Newman Club. So, yes, today is my last day. They were nice about it."

"And you were going to be leaving anyway," Rice said. "Right?"

Father Growden slammed the door and walked around the car where he leaned against the passenger-side fender and crossed his arms. "There are still lots of young priests in the diocese. It wouldn't have been hard to find a replacement."

"Still, you look a little disappointed."

The priest looked down like he was thinking about it. "More sad than disappointed," he said. "Kids don't take spirituality very seriously."

"Maybe if you told them about Alexander the poltergeist you'd stir up some interest."

Growden looked around. "I told you that in confidence," he said.

"I talked with my friend Arnie about Alexander after we left you."

"I never said anything about Annike's … spirit or demon apparition being a poltergeist," Growden said.

"Arnie's kind of strange. A little shy. But he helps me out with psychic questions," Rice said. "Probably best to leave it there."

"What did he say about … about Alexander?"

Rice scratched the back of his neck. "Arnie was in a hurry to get home. Getting anxious. He doesn't go out much."

"I got that sense."

"He said people—young people mostly, and usually women—are able to cause these beings to manifest. He wasn't clear if they were beings from some other dimension of reality or if they were creations of the person. A kind of psychic shadow."

"Or a childhood imaginary friend who took on a realistic form in a disturbed mind," Growden said, looking disgusted.

"Arnie wasn't too certain about the particulars, like I said. But he is pretty sure it's related to burgeoning sexuality. Whether that attracts beings or creates them—" Rice slapped his hands together and pursed his lips. "That part he isn't sure about."

"Sounds like your expert doesn't know much."

"He's cautious," Rice said. "I respect him for that. But he's convinced that a poltergeist is a real being with some kind of connection to a host. That would be Annike Eichel. I'm guessing you know most of this, though. You spent a lot of time talking together, right?"

Growden seemed like he wanted to get into his car and drive off to his new job in Cleveland without looking back. Like he wanted to leave his Roman collar spinning on the ground as he drove away.

"Why are you so uncomfortable talking to me," Rice said, trying to look cute and harmless, "when you were clearly comfortable talking with her? I don't get it."

"Chalk it up to a priest's appetite for confidentiality."

"I know all about the seal of confession," Rice said. "But Eichel wasn't Catholic. And your priestly days are numbered. And, of course, the woman is dead. So why not tell me a little more about her?"

Growden opened his car door—it squeaked loudly as he did, and drooped a little too—then he closed it. He massaged his forehead with his fingertips.

"This spirit or ghost or poltergeist—whatever it was—seemed to be growing stronger. That's what she told me. I could tell she didn't like talking to me about it, but her intellectual curiosity was so sincere. She wanted to know more. Wondered if I could help her."

"What did you tell her?"

"I told her what I told you," Growden said. "That there are certain realms people should stand clear of. She couldn't believe the Church actually bought into the idea of ghosts and demons harassing living people. She even laughed at me."

"There was a book about it. Came out last year."

"*The Exorcist*," Growden said, nodding. "I read it. She read it. We spent an evening in her living room talking about it. She tried to convince me it was just a fairy tale, but by the time we finished a bottle of some very good port, she admitted that a spirit followed her. She didn't ask me, but I knew she wondered if I could dispel the thing."

"What did you tell her?"

"I told her she'd have to talk with the bishop if she wanted an exorcism. It's an involved process. She didn't want any part of that. 'No bishops,' she told me. I agreed. We giggled. We were both a little drunk by then."

One of the school's white security cars slowly prowled the parking lot lanes like a lioness sniffing out a wounded gazelle.

"Did you see any evidence of a spirit?"

"If you're asking me if I saw floating bedsheets or hear disembodied moaning voices, then, no. I saw and heard nothing unusual. But when I looked in the eyes of this woman, Annike, I did see real terror. I saw a person who wanted help. But all I could do was be a friend. Listen to her.

So that's what I did. Maybe a dozen times or so we got together."

"Just you two and a bottle of port."

"We had tea a lot too," Growden said. "But she was less candid during those times."

"I guess she told you a lot of things," Rice said. The security vehicle stopped behind the priest's car.

"Everything okay here?" the guard asked. He had heavy jowls but alert eyes.

"I saw Father Growden here and wanted to talk to him for a few minutes," Rice said. "I'll move my car in a minute."

The guard nodded, his jowls flapping and his expression stern, as though a minute was all he'd allow. He pulled away slowly.

"We talked about a lot of different things, yes," Growden said. "She was intelligent and not nearly as cynical as I expected."

"Did you love her?"

Father Growden didn't miss a beat. "A priest offers a redemptive love," he said. "Like Jesus."

"But not the Hollywood kind?"

"No. The urge is there, but I keep a blanket over it. And I keep it tucked in."

"Did you know Annike Eichel was pregnant?" Rice said.

For the first time, Growden seemed uncomfortable. He looked across the parking lot, as though willing the security car to return. "She mentioned once that she could be. I don't think she knew for sure."

"Did she say who the father was?"

"Why should I tell you?"

Rice shrugged. "Then don't tell me. Tell the cops. They'd like to know."

The priest's features softened. "It doesn't matter," he said. "I don't know. She wouldn't tell me who."

"Did she say *why* she wouldn't tell?"

"She said it would put me in danger. And that's *all* she would say."

"Danger? Why?"

"I don't know."

The security car was back already. It was like the guy had nothing else to do. He pointed accusingly at Rice's Fiat, then jerked a thumb over his shoulder.

"Come on, Father," Rice said. "Help me out a little."

This time Growden got into his Galaxie and sat silently for a while. Rice was just about to move his car when the priest rolled down the passenger-side window.

"I'll tell you this," he called out to him. "Her conception was an act of violence, not love. She deserved better."

"Say it to me plain, Father."

"She was raped," Father Growden said, shaking his head. He put on his sunglasses and backed out of his spot at Mosopelea County Community College for the last time.

# { 36 }

Nelly, the fiftyish woman who oversaw the *Tribune* morgue, had wide hips, thick arms covered with wispy black hair, and a smile as warm as any grandma welcoming her favorite grandchild into the kitchen.

"Here's some of the older stuff," she said, carrying two files filled with newspaper clippings. Her forehead was damp, and her glasses had slid to the tip of her nose. "Buried behind the old Fair files and the Freeway clippings."

"I want to marry you," Rice said. "You always come through for me."

Nelly blushed and shooed him away.

"I was married once to my Henry," she said, eyes tearing as they always did when she mentioned him. "Once is enough."

"Let me know if you change your mind."

Nelly smiled as she left him there, taking her wide hips and sweet disposition somewhere else.

Rice and Janousek had both gone through the Annike Eichel clippings in the morgue more than once. Everything was in one fat file that couldn't hold another clipping. That's what made Rice think there might be more files holding more clippings somewhere else.

So he had asked Nelly to hunt around for any more Eichel files that weren't stored on the main floor. She had uncovered these two—neither as thick as the already reviewed file—that included older articles. One story was an interview conducted after Annike founded the RITNA organization.

In that interview, the religion editor had asked her what it was like to live life "without a light to guide the way."

Annike said she preferred the dark.

Other articles reported on debates in which she participated with students, clergy, and fervent believers. She usually kept the tone light but explained that she saw no evidence of a higher benevolent purpose. She proved herself a skilled debater, always arguing on the side of the shadow.

Her beauty coupled with the eager fierceness in her eyes drew attention. Her sharp mind and unrelenting assaults on the pious and the lazy drew followers.

Before long, Annike was a regular participant in the "God is dead" debate on campuses and elsewhere. She even garnered a mention in the famous *Time* magazine issue of 1966 bearing the words *Is God Dead?* on the cover.

Soon after the *Time* magazine issue, she shifted her strategy. Annike took on school boards throughout the state. She insisted on a strict interpretation of the Constitution as it related to religion. Under threat of a lawsuit, dozens of schools in the state canceled traditional prayer readings before high school football games.

"This is a day that will live in infamy," proclaimed one pastor in a vitriolic homily.

But the money poured in, mostly from anonymous donors. Much of it funded RITNA activities. Some of it paid for Annike's nineteenth-century three-story townhouse just outside the Goodwater downtown shopping district.

Nelly returned with two pieces of angel food cake and two plastic forks. She placed one of the slices and a utensil next to Rice.

"It's Marjorie's birthday," Nelly said. "She wouldn't tell us how old she is."

Rice thanked her and took a forkful of cake and a sip of lukewarm coffee. Marjorie was one of the reporters on the women's pages. She and Rice had spoken maybe once.

"How old are you, Nell?" Rice said before downing another bite of the tasty but too dry birthday cake. He liked teasing her and hoped he could coax another blush.

"I'm fifty-seven," she said, pushing out her chin. "I don't know why women—and lots of men too—keep their ages a secret. They're not going to live any longer by pretending to be younger than they are."

"Good for you."

She giggled. "I make allowances for young people who lie so they can order a beer," she said. "Nothing wrong with drinking beer. I've drunk it all my life."

Nelly was about to shovel in another piece of cake when Rice held up his hand. "Say allowances again," he said.

At first she looked confused, then grinned thinking it was a game. She said the word slowly and Rice watched as the *O* of her mouth was speared by her tongue when she spoke the second syllable.

"Now say the name Alexander."

Nelly looked like she would be perfectly happy sitting here all day articulating words. Her grin froze in place when she saw Rice's face turn white.

He stood up, left the cake, the lukewarm coffee, and the two Annike Eichel files on the table, and headed for his car.

Rice had never tried to summon a spirit before. They pretty much came and went as they pleased, in the same way as the sparrow now perched on his left front fender.

"I need to talk to you, Annike," he said while sitting in his closed car. The sparrow turned and cocked its head then flew off. "I don't know how these things work. I never really cared before. But I'm guessing you can't find a release from this life until we find your killer."

Nothing.

"I've seen other ghosts. Victims of other murders. But I never saw them again after their killers were brought to justice. I'd like to help identify your murderer, Annike."

More quiet. A strong gust shook the little car. His mouth was dry.

"I don't know what happens after we die," Rice said. "I'm pretty sure *something* happens. How can I think otherwise after what I've seen? I'm guessing we go home. Some new home. That's what I tell myself, anyway. I'd like to help you find your way there."

Annike appeared in the passenger seat, sitting primly, eyes straight ahead as if waiting for another sparrow to light. She didn't look like she wanted to talk.

"Is God in there? In that world you inhabit?" he asked.

The spectral figure dimmed.

"Is it hard being so alone?"

She turned to him, a weary sadness in her expressive eyes.

"Did Alexander kill you?"

For a while, Rice expected her to turn away again. Then the ghost of Annike Eichel nodded her head slowly, and she dissolved away.

The eyes—they looked like they had witnessed every kind of hurt—were the last thing to disappear.

# { 37 }

"Where's the other guy?" Foster Ebner said, standing large in his doorway. He peered over Rice's head and looked up and down the street.

Rice shook his head. "Oh," he said, getting it. "You mean Janousek. We're going in different directions."

Ebner seemed relieved but the hunted look remained. "I didn't like him and not sure I could deal with him again," he said, running a hand through unruly hair. "Not right now. Wanna come in?"

The living room was neat and looked like it had just been cleaned. Two empty bottles of Blatz beer and a big indentation on the couch were the only indications anyone lived here at all.

Rice pointed at the empty bottles. "Got one for me?" he said.

"No," Ebner said. "What do you want, Channon? I've got a meeting in a few minutes."

"I hope it's with a lawyer."

"As a matter of fact," Ebner said. "Same one who posted my bail yesterday."

"Good friend to have," Rice said, withdrawing his notebook.

"Don't you want to know his name?"

"Nah, not really," Rice said, feigning disinterest. He already knew the Josephus Patterson firm would be defending him. "You're kind of in a jam with this embezzlement thing. I understand Ed Kadish had a long talk with Frank Lalley. That won't help you any."

Ebner picked up the two bottles and carried them into the kitchen where Rice heard them drop into a trash bin. It was almost as if the ex-Public Works chief had nothing else to worry about. When he returned to the living room, he was smiling.

"Lalley's an unreliable witness," Ebner said.

"Seems to know a lot," Rice said. "And he's real chatty."

"The man jumps at his own farts. Nobody's going to believe him."

Rice made a few lazy circles on his notepad, and Ebner craned his neck to see if the reporter wrote down the *fart* comment.

"I'm going to tell you the truth, Foster," Rice said. "I'm not really here about the embezzlement issue. Are you guilty?" He shrugged, smiled. "Probably. I don't care. You've done a good job keeping the streets free of potholes. The storm sewers seem to drain real well. So you skimmed a little. I'm willing to overlook it."

Ebner slid his oversized butt to the edge of the couch and talked in low tones, as if afraid someone might overhear them. "So why are they after me?" he said.

"Well, like I said, it's just me talking. I don't care. But the mayor and the council and my publisher all think you're guilty and should go to jail. And they run the world, so ..."

Ebner sat back. "So you think I'm going to jail?"

Rice scowled. "No, I don't. It's just not politic, if you get me, to send the most important Negro in the city to prison."

"And I'm innocent."

"You keep saying that if you want," Rice said. "Your lawyer's going to tell you to plead, and you'll lose your job and find another one in some other town with sloppy bookkeeping. That's what I think."

Ebner's face darkened and Rice suddenly grew very uncomfortable. "I don't like you, Channon," he said. "Never have."

Rice tried to affect nonchalance. "I hear that so much, you'd think it would bother me more," he said. "But instead of throwing sticks and stones, I'd think you'd be more concerned about being accused in the Annike Eichel murder."

It was amazing how quickly the big man's expression changed. "I had nothing to do with that."

"You may be cleaner than clothes washed in Tide, like you're telling me," Rice said, feeling more confident, even smiling a little. "But while you're digging your way out of this embezzlement fuss, I'll bet somebody is getting ready to say you murdered Annike Eichel. If I were you, I'd prepare for it."

Ebner dropped his head into his hands. "I can't believe this," he said.

"It's a bad week for you," Rice said. "I understand that. Tell me what you told Detective Kadish when he asked about your late-night visits to the Eichel home."

Ebner's face was gray. "He … He never asked about that. He asked me where I was the night she died."

"Where was that?"

"I was at Martelli's for a while. I invited a … a friend to come home with me. But Kadish mostly talked about the embezzlement charges. That's all he seemed to care about."

Rice started chewing on his lower lip. "He's going to be back. And he'll want to know about the visits to the Eichel home. Believe me."

The big man stood up. "I gotta think. I gotta think."

"Think fast," Rice said. "Practice on me. What were you doing there? Buying? Selling? What?"

"We were just friends," Ebner said, spreading his hands like he was offering benediction. "We enjoyed each other's company."

"Yeah. Sure," Rice said. "The crooked Public Works director and the sexy atheist bust open a nice red Bordeaux, sit on the floor, and talk about their days. You tell her about bulldozers and macadam, while she discusses Bertrand Russell and why he isn't a Christian."

"We talked, yeah. What we talked about is nobody's business but ours."

"Then that's what you should tell the cops," Rice said. "But I'm guessing they're not going to buy into the interracial social club angle. They're going to wonder what you were doing there."

This time Ebner leaned back against the couch and spread his beefy arms along the backrest. He had a big toothy grin. "Maybe I got a ten-inch shlong and she likes making music with it."

Rice's laugh sounded like he was clearing his throat. "Maybe that was it," he said. "But I doubt it. You want to know what I think?"

"Talk."

"I think she wanted you to shoo away that big, ugly ghost that lives in her kitchen," Rice said. "I think she was hoping you might work some magic to chase it off."

"Do you get paid to peddle bullshit like that?"

"Not what I'm worth."

Ebner drew his hands together on his lap like he was going to pray. "Okay, I'll tell you this, but only 'cause I want you out of here."

Rice's expression said nothing.

"Yeah, she was afraid. A pretty gal out on her own, acting all tough in public cursing out the Lord God. But in her own home, she was like a little girl afraid her old man was going to beat her with a fat-buckled belt."

"What was she afraid of?"

Ebner's grim mouth flickered in the corners, and Rice knew he was going to lie. "I don't know," he said.

"And you never asked her?"

"We didn't talk much about personal stuff."

"I'd like you to stop for a minute, Foster, and think about how crazy that sounds."

"Okay," Ebner said, barely able to cross his huge legs. "We did some grass. That's what it was about. We didn't drink fancy French wines, and we didn't talk. We smoked pot together. She sat in the living room and sometimes I sat with her."

"All night?"

Ebner looked surprised. "Sometimes. Not often. Not lately."

"So where'd the grass come from?"

Ebner shook his head and smiled. He had big teeth that looked like they could chew rebar. "That's not part of this discussion."

Rice wrote in his notebook again, and Ebner glanced over at it, but the reporter was too far away. "Okay, so you brought pot and the two of you smoked it together."

"I never said I brought it."

"Didn't have to," Rice said. "What happened next?"

"Nothing. We just mellowed out."

"But you said she was afraid. How do you know?"

"She'd kind of huddle in the corner until the buzz kicked in. Then she'd smile and be friendlier."

"How friendly?" Rice asked.

"Wouldn't you like to know?"

"What would you do?" Rice said. "When you weren't being friendly."

"I might go into the kitchen."

"So you had the munchies?"

"Huh? Yeah," Ebner said. "Sometimes."

"See anything while you were in there?"

"Sometimes the walls would seem to puff in and out. And I'd feel energized once in a while. When I'd come back out, Annike sometimes looked like a flower or an angel. It was nice."

"Sounds like a pretty potent vegetable you guys were tokin'."

"I only get the good stuff," Ebner said and then cocked his head like he was going to spit. "Don't write that down."

"Like I said, I knew you were bringing the pot anyway. You've got bigger problems. Nobody's going to care that you're hauling around a little weed."

"Some people will care," Ebner said, half to himself.

"And some people will wonder what made her so special."

Ebner looked up as though he expected Rice to provide the answer. But the reporter left, leaving the question hanging in the air like a balloon both of them were afraid to pop.

# { 38 }

When Arnie Corso opened his apartment door, Rice stepped in without waiting to be asked.

"If you're hungry, I hope you brought something," Arnie said as he returned to his chair at the kitchen table.

"I'm fine," Rice said, but he prowled the kitchen shelves anyway. Lots of Chef Boyardee. Lots of Jell-O. Not much else.

Arnie was using a ruler to underline passages in a big American history book. "So, what's the buzz?" he said.

Rice told him about his meeting with Foster Ebner and the way his moods shifted quickly between intimidation and fear. He repeated what Ebner told him about their pot parties.

Arnie kept his head in his history book, underlining just about every other sentence. "Sounds to me like they were dropping acid," he said. "She was using it to get away from

Alexander. I don't know what the other guy was doing, but he's dipping into hinky."

"What does that mean?"

"I think he and Alexander were feeding off each other. Did he see anything?"

Rice shook his head. "He said the kitchen walls pulsed. He told me Annike looked like an angel. They took long walks sometimes when the sun came up."

"Typical LSD stuff. But it could be something else," Arnie said. He got up and went to the kitchen, carefully measured out some water and poured it into a pan."I feel like lime Jell-O. Gonna be a while if you want some."

"It's tempting," Rice said.

"It's got more taste than the other flavors."

"I've heard that."

"The thing about LSD," Arnie said, leaning over to turn on the range, "is that's it's a real gateway to superconsciousness. What you see when you're tripping is real. It's not an illusion."

"You're going to have to talk sense if you want me to keep up."

"When the yogis and gurus spend years contemplating their navels to rise to a higher level of being, they really do it. They see reality in a way the rest of us don't."

"Okay."

Arnie moved his hands to simulate a blooming flower or an explosion. "They grow into it. It stays with them."

"Tell me what this means to Foster Ebner."

"Be patient," Arnie said. "LSD also takes you to that superconscious place, but it's like standing on a stepladder to look over the fence. The yogis see over the fence too, but that's because they've *grown* tall enough to look over the top."

"What's on the other side of the damn fence, Arnie?"

"Let's talk about that some other time," Arnie said. "The important thing is if you grow, you're ready for the experience. When you take LSD, the experience can overwhelm you."

"Do you think that's what happened to Ebner and Annike?"

"I don't know," Arnie said, looking down at the Jell-O water. "But they weren't in control of the experience. And when you throw a poltergeist into the mix, things might get ugly in a hurry."

Rice walked across the living room while rubbing his chin with his index finger. "I remember something else. Ebner said he felt energized sometimes when he went into the kitchen."

Arnie returned to the table and dropped his pen into the pages of the history book.

"Alexander has got energy to spare," he said. "He's formed some kind of bond to this other guy. I'm guessing he's more malleable than your friend Annike."

"She's not my friend, for Christ's sake," Rice said. "Does this have anything to do with books flying off the shelf, or explain all the bugs we saw?"

"The bug thing I've read about," Arnie said. "Although I've never experienced it personally."

"Are you going to give me the book, Arnie, or tell me what was in it?"

"Think of Alexander as a sopping wet dishrag," Arnie said.

"I'll try. It won't be easy."

"If you don't wring out the dishrag, it will drip all over the floor as you carry it to the table or whatever you're going to clean up," Arnie said while looking over Rice's head at the pan. "It'll make a mess."

"Yeah."

"Alexander's the dishrag, like I said. This other guy …"

"Ebner," Rice said.

"Ebner is full of lust or anger or malice …"

"And he's hopped up on drugs," Rice said. "Don't leave that part out."

"All that stuff is like a fire hose feeding Alexander. He picks up on it. It makes him strong. It makes him confused. And it probably makes him angry too."

"When are we getting to the bugs and the books?"

"Alexander and this Ebner guy feed off each other," Arnie said. "Anything could happen."

"Are you telling me Alexander turned Ebner into a crazed, angry man? Ebner left that part out when he talked to me," Rice said.

"It's possible, that's all I'm saying," Arnie said. He went to the range and shut the gas off.

"Angry enough to murder Annike Eichel?"

"Maybe. I don't know." Arnie stirred in the lime Jell-O and poured the mixture into a glass bowl.

"What about the books flying off the shelves when Kadish and I walked in?"

Arnie put the bowl in the refrigerator. "Alexander was acting out," he said. "He misses his momma."

Rice said nothing for a long time.

Arnie closed the refrigerator door. "I'll add some peaches when it starts to harden. I can't wait," he said, grinning. He sat down, crossed his hands on the table, and waited.

"You need to get out," Rice said. "Really."

But Arnie held the grin, and Rice thought it was more frightening than any ghost or poltergeist he had ever seen.

"Bugs," Rice said.

"Oh, yeah. The bugs are kind of like Alexander drops. They're little bits of him, little pieces of, I don't know, malice, frustration that he can't hold inside. Like water dripping off the dishrag."

"I think you chose a bad metaphor," Rice said.

"The insects don't last long. They're just congealed ether held together by Alexander's will. They go away when he calms down. At least that's what I've read."

"Annike's ghost told me it was Alexander who killed her," Rice said.

Arnie leaned forward over the tabletop. "Now that's interesting," he said. "She's actually communicating with you?"

"Sort of," Rice said. "That's the name she was trying to form when I saw her mouth move. When I asked if Alexander killed her, she nodded."

"That's heavy," Arnie said, leaning back. "That's really heavy."

"Yeah."

"You've come a long way," Arnie said. "You're like a lighthouse. Psychic forces congregate around you. I wonder why."

"Jesus. I'm turning into you?"

"Nah, nah, not like me," Arnie said, grinning in that stupid way of his, like he'd just witnessed a river baptism. "They just huddle around me until they figure out where to go next. You're different. Don't get a big head about it, though. You could just be crazy."

"None of this is going to convince Ed Kadish to get an arrest warrant for Alexander the poltergeist," Rice said.

"Yeah, that's another problem entirely," Arnie said. "I'm sure glad I'm not you."

"That's not helpful, Arnie."

"I repaid you that ten, right?"

"Yeah," Rice said.

"Could I have it back? Or maybe a twenty?"

# { 39 }

Detective Kadish was alone in the squad room. Instead of his usual coat and tie, he wore a regular police uniform and a bulletproof vest. Next to his phone was a Little League batting helmet.

"You looking for a pick-up game?" Rice said, nodding at the helmet. Kadish looked up at him with a grim expression, his eyes red and his face unshaven.

"What are you doing here?" the detective said.

Rice picked up the batting helmet and put it on his head. It was a tight fit. "I wanted to talk to you about the Eichel case," he said.

Kadish stood and yanked the helmet off Rice's head. The reporter yelped as it ripped at his ears. "Nobody in this department gives a damn about the Eichel murder or anything else right now," Kadish said. "Didn't you hear what happened last night?"

"Is this about the riots?"

"Is this about the riots?" Kadish repeated, with a mocking tone. "Yeah, it's about the goddamn riots. Last night, rioters hit Ewer's Furniture store. Busted the display window and hauled off sofas and easy chairs by the dozen. It happened so fast, we weren't able to respond until it was too late. What they couldn't take, they set fire to. You must have smelled the smoke."

"Yeah, sure," Rice said. "I thought it was from the cars the day before. But you told me the guys were getting it under control."

"We're not," Kadish said, feeling on his belt for his service revolver.

"What about backup from the Highway Patrol? Didn't they show?"

"Yeah, they showed," Kadish said. "Last night troopers linked arms and marched down Ackerd Street, behind that old vacant foundry where a bunch of rioters were getting together."

Rice nodded. He knew the area well. He and Star Lightman used to shoot craps on the building's loading dock, underneath a gooseneck warehouse light.

"So they're walking down the street with billy clubs and all of a sudden, golf balls start flying through the air at 'em," Kadish said. "They're coming down like meteors or something. The troopers backed off and the rioters charged them. It was a near thing, but some of our guys showed up just in time and drove the bastards back."

"Where were you?"

"I was there. Everybody's been called in for this," Kadish said, blinking wildly as though smoke was still burning his eyes. "Some of the sons of bitches had busted into that sporting goods store just north of the foundry. They grabbed golf balls, some three woods, and started slapping them in our direction. Ever been hit by a golf ball?"

"Once," Rice said, but he could tell by the way Kadish looked at him that now wasn't the time to tell the story.

"Anyway," the detective said. "We shoved 'em back down the street, then some of us went into the sporting goods store and grabbed batting helmets to protect our heads from the fucking golf balls. They work pretty good, but they're a little tight."

Kadish rapped the helmet twice with his knuckles. " 'Course they don't help if you get hit in the face," he said. "Sweeney took a golf ball that broke his nose. Bled like a motherfucker. I thought he was going into shock."

"Don't they sell guns and rifles at that store?" Rice said.

"Yeah, that's what we were most worried about," Kadish said. "But the rifles and ammo are kept in a safe, so they couldn't get to them. They busted the display cases and grabbed some pistols, but they didn't get any bullets."

"A small victory."

"Yeah, I guess."

—

Where in the hell have you been?" David Billard said. He wore jeans and his eyelids drooped like they often did when he was exhausted.

"You don't look so good, Dave," Rice said.

The city editor lowered his voice. "The governor is calling out the National Guard. Fires are still burning in stores along Oswego Street. I've called everybody in."

"Just like the cops did."

Billard looked up. "Yeah. Except the cops showed up. Why weren't you here?"

"I'm off the cop beat," Rice said. "I'm working on the Eichel murder. I'll admit the smoke was distracting."

"Drop the attitude," Billard said. "You belong on the streets covering this thing. For Christ sake, Janousek has been on the frontlines since the start."

"What about —"

"Nobody gives a damn about the Eichel murder," Billard said, showing his teeth for the first time.

"It's starting to look that way."

"You know some of these people. Talk to them. Find out what's happening. But stay safe. I don't want you dead."

"It doesn't feel that way," Rice said. "How's the new cop reporter doing?"

"He's doing fine. But he doesn't know any damn people who know any damn thing. Not like you do," Billard said. He felt around inside his desk drawer until he found his roll of antacids. "Janousek is writing for the *Chronicle* now. He's using our desk and our goddamn phone to call his office to scoop us on these riots."

"I thought we were working together."

Billard shook his head, popped a lozenge in his mouth. "Not on this. Not on the riots. The arrangement only covers the Eichel investigation. That was the deal from the start," he said, then looked up at Rice. "Have you even read a newspaper today?"

"Not the *Cleveland Chronicle*."

"Well, don't," Billard said. "It'll break your heart. The guy knows how to cover a war zone."

"I think he does his best work in disasters."

Billard looked around the empty newsroom and exhaled loudly. "I need your help on this, Rice," he said. "Be a factor."

—

Black fire stains like demon fingers spread out above the entrance to the New Mission Redeemer Church on the edge of the riot area. The brick building, which used to be a grocery warehouse and, before that, a furniture factory, was gutted by flame yesterday. The fire leaked out doors and windows but did no major structural damage.

Rice kicked through the burned pews and the soggy heaps of hymnals watered down by the men of the Goodwater Fire Department last night. He jumped when he heard a sharp crack, but it was only a crumbling lintel. A few bricks tumbled down after it.

The streets were empty of people. Early this morning the police department installed barricades to keep automobile traffic out of the area. The only thing moving was a lazy swirl of smoke ascending from the burned-out church and a few curious wrens hopping amid the carnage.

“It stinks like old pussy,” Star Lightman said. Rice, startled, stepped into a defensive posture. This made the pimp laugh. “You white folks are all skittish as dumb mules today.”

“So you’d probably be wise not to go sneaking up on us,” Rice said. “Some of the white folks got guns.”

Star rubbed his chin and looked contemplative. “Yeah,” he said, sober for once. “Yeah, I think you’re right about that.”

“Thanks for meeting me.”

“Thought you might have another one of those honey-sweet cigars for me,” Star said. Not waiting to hear Rice didn’t, he walked over to the hymnals and tapped one lightly with the sequined toe of his boot. Water gushed out like blood from a new wound.

“Were you around for last night’s fun?”

“Always with the jokes,” Star said, kicking the water off his boot. He pulled a yellow and purple handkerchief from a pocket and wiped the tip to a gloss once more. “Is that why you wanted to meet me? ’Cause I’m not feeling yoyo funny.”

“Were you there?”

“It was hard not to be there,” Star said.

“But the riots weren’t even near your neighborhood.”

"If you mean my place of business, then you are correct," Star said. "Not the fire and the screaming. Not the pigs and troopers."

"Then what?"

"This is all putting a big dent in my *in*come," Star said. "The brothers and sisters are congregatin' and not copulatin'."

Star wasn't wearing his Panama hat. His Afro seemed tamer than usual, but it still jiggled when he shook his head. "And whitey ain't horny enough to risk running into what we got going."

"So what'd you do?"

"I sent the girls home. And I watched."

"Tell me what started it," Rice said.

"I don't know. Somethin' in the water, maybe. It's making people mean. Meaner than I've seen 'em in a long, long time."

"So you blame the water department."

Star Lightman threw his head back and touched a forefinger to his lip. "I'd say it all began when white sailors drove their boats up on those nice beaches in Africa and loaded up my great-great-grandfather. Took him on a cruise to America, where the livin' was easy."

"Your friends are burning up stores and homes owned by other Negroes," Rice said. "Does that make sense?"

"Well, it got your attention," Star said. "And you're pretty jumpy. Maybe that's enough."

"What's everyone talking about?"

"I think you might say the niggers are gettin' kinda uppity," Star said. "When the first fires started, a lot of *Ne*-

groes ran into the streets, even if they weren't involved in the actual rioting. That's where I was. We talked about the usual things, unhappiness with the stock market, country club dues, that sort of thing."

"You're not helping me."

"Maybe I'm not interested in helping you."

Rice looked at him. Star's narrowed eyes looked uglier than he could remember. "Uppity, how?" the reporter said.

The pimp's expression softened, and he wandered over to the pews for a while. "Sometimes when you kick at the wood of an old house, it'll crumble like dried mud. Then bugs—termites, ants, spiders, I don't know—will start running around all crazy like the ground was a skillet and they have to get off it in a hurry."

Rice nodded like he knew what he was talking about.

"So the pigs are like a big foot kicking at the neighborhood. And all the brothers and sisters are like those bugs hopping around, wondering what to do next. Where to go. They just know they're going to be kicked some more."

"What happens then?"

"I don't think anybody's sure, but here's one thing I do know," Star said.

"What's that?"

"They're not waiting around to be kicked again."

# { 40 }

Tom Janousek rubbed the gash above his left eyebrow and licked his fingertips clean of whatever liquid had been weeping from it. He stayed clear of his bruised right eye, which was shiny, black, and purple, like a ripe plum.

"Tell me about it," Rice said, not bothering with a preamble. He had crept into the office hoping to avoid attention, but with Billard's slight head tilt in his direction, he knew he'd been spotted.

"Axe handle," Janousek said, licking his lips and returning to his typewriter. The *Cleveland Chronicle* reporter noisily shuffled some papers and found his notebook underneath it all. Then he stopped and smiled way too wide at Rice, and even his half-closed right eye carried a mischievous glint.

"Ya missed a good time last night, laddie," Janousek said, employing a bad Scottish brogue for some reason. "All the fellas were there. It was a thing to behold."

Maybe it was supposed to be Irish.

"Axe handle, huh?" Rice said.

Janousek nodded and rubbed his head as though that hurt too. "It came flying at me from an open window in a building I thought was empty. Never saw who threw it."

"Were the cops around?"

"Yeah. They had a good laugh," Janousek said. "Promised to buy me a beer—I'm sorry, a *brewski*—after all the good times end."

"Maybe they'll tell you who killed Annike Eichel," Rice said, surprised at the pain he felt from this outsider's intimacy with *his* patrol cops.

Janousek returned to his typing. He was wearing glasses over his puffy eyes. "Nobody's talking much about Annike Eichel or who killed her," Janousek said. "Just you and Stace."

How Rice hated him for calling her *Stace*. It was like he was stepping into his clothes, cozying up to the few important people in his life. And making it all look so easy. He would have preferred if the man was *trying* to annoy him and not just oozing charm naturally like honest August sweat.

"Whaddya got?" Billard said. He was already squatting down at Rice's desk. Rice hadn't heard a thing. This was a man he could take sneak lessons from.

"Nothing specific," Rice said, pleased that Janousek acted like he wasn't listening even though he was. "Everybody's in a mean mood. That's what I'm hearing. There'll be more trouble tonight, I'm pretty sure of it."

"Where?"

"I don't know," Rice said. "Has the National Guard been called in?"

Billard stood up. "There's some truckers' strike in Akron and the governor's dispatched the guard there," he said. "Goddamn Republicans." Like that explained everything.

"I want a picture of you," Billard said, poking a finger in Janousek's direction, a smirk on his lips. "I don't usually like my reporters to be the news story, but I'll make an exception in your case."

All three of them knew Janousek wasn't writing for the *Tribune*. His copy about the riots was exclusive for the *Chronicle*. Rice really wanted to say something, but didn't.

"And after you get your picture took, go home and take a bath," Billard said. "You smell like a lumberjack in an old shirt."

Janousek nodded vigorously while staring at the copy on his typewriter roll.

"You," Billard said, looking at Rice and shaking his head sadly.

Rice had seen the gesture before. It said, "Damn it, I guess this is as good as you get." It said "You're a pain in the ass." It said that and lots more.

"Do I really smell that bad?" Janousek said, sniffing his sleeve.

"How come you get to stay in my newsroom when you're not writing anything for my paper?" Rice said. He hoped the Cleveland reporter would get that he was pissed.

Instead there was the snarky charm again.

"Professional courtesy," Janousek said. "Plus, I'm putting a local spin on my *Chronicle* story. Billard promised me a 'Special to the *Tribune*' byline."

"Christ," Rice said.

"Sometimes life bites the big patootie," Janousek said, turning to look at Rice again. "You could work with me. I'd make sure you got a byline in the *Chronicle*. It would look good on your résumé."

"I don't have a résumé."

Janousek shot a look at Billard who was at his desk, sliding a letter opener into an envelope. "You should," he said. "Don't get me wrong. I like this little rag, but you could get a job on any big-city paper. Or with the wire services. Maybe television."

"I'm going to talk to Kadish."

"I saw him on the line last night," Janousek said. "He's probably sleeping."

He was, but Rice didn't care. He banged on the screen door of Kadish's Lustron prefab home until the detective showed up in his underwear. Unshaven and angry.

"Leave me the fuck alone, Channon," he said.

"If you're going out again tonight, you've got to be getting up soon anyway," Rice said, gingerly stepping inside. "Think of me as your wake-up call."

Kadish puffed out his cheeks and blew fetid sleep breath over him. "You don't want to know what I think of you," he said. "Especially right now."

Rice heard an alarm go off toward the back of the house.

"What did I tell you?" he said. "I'll make some coffee while you get cleaned up."

While Kadish was in the bathroom and after he put some coffee on, Rice walked into his living room. Kadish's bulletproof vest and batting helmet were on the floor. His service revolver was resting on a small blond wood desk. The desktop had no desk chair and was empty of papers, bills, and everything but a lonely ballpoint pen.

He took a deep breath, looked around once, and walked over to the desk.

In a pull-out drawer Rice found a few months of paid utility and mortgage bills. A recent birthday card from the guys in the squad room was here also. It showed a drawing of a woman wearing only long black gloves, a ribbon tied sloppily around her midsection. Inside it said, "We know what you wanted for your birthday, but we didn't know how to wrap it."

Rice shut the drawer and returned to the kitchen to turn the gas down on the coffee. The percolator was chugging like an old Buick.

Kadish came out of the bathroom rubbing a dry towel over his hair, another one clinging to his waist.

"If that towel drops," Rice said, pointing at it. "You won't have to ask me to leave."

"I wish it were that easy," Kadish said. "I'd go to work naked."

"Your place looks like you just moved in yesterday."

"What? You're working for *Better Homes and Gardens* now?" Kadish's eyes surveyed the living room and stopped at his desk. "You got some bad habits, Channon."

"How's that?"

"You nose around a lot, but you need to learn when to turn it off," the detective said, rubbing the corner of his right eye, as though sorry he had to bring the matter up.

Rice saw that the desk drawer was not completely closed. *Stupid. And sloppy.* "I'm sorry," he said, trying to look repentant. "You're right. If I'd used your bathroom, I would have checked out the medicine cabinet."

"You want to know what's in there? I take a daily multivitamin and a shot of Geritol because the doc says I'm iron deficient. The dentist tells me I should take better care of my teeth, so you'll find some fancy toothpaste I don't use. There's a tube of Brylcreem in there because it makes my hair soft and natural."

"What do you shave with?"

"I use a Gillette Trac II razor because it's supposed to reduce facial irritation."

"Does it?"

"This is why you don't have any friends, Rice," Kadish said. "You treat people like shit and they don't trust you."

"I thought it was because I show up unannounced."

"You don't show any respect," Kadish said. "But for some reason, people tolerate you."

"I'm earnest," Rice said.

"Yeah, well, I don't know what that means," Kadish said. "But I want you out of my house."

"I want to go with you tonight."

The detective pulled a pair of boxer shorts from somewhere and nimbly slid them on while dropping his towel at the same time. The boxers had red horizontal stripes that made him look like narrow shelves covered his crotch.

"No. You might get shot."

"Nobody's fired a gun during the riots," Rice said.

"I meant me," Kadish said. "*I* might shoot you."

"You wouldn't say that if you didn't like me a little."

"I can't take civilians into a riot area. Those are just the rules."

"I'm not a civilian. I'm a reporter. Nobody will care if anything happens to me. I'll even wear my press badge, if it'll make you feel better."

Kadish pulled on a short-sleeved white shirt and struggled to button it over his belly. "So that's what earnest means," he said.

Rice went to the kitchen and poured two cups of coffee. He gave one to Kadish who said, "I like it with cream, no sugar."

"Drink it black today," Rice said, grimacing when the hot liquid hit his lips.

"What do you expect to find on the streets?" Kadish said.

"Answers," Rice said, and the detective laughed.

"Jesus, Channon, you're smarter than that. Or I thought you were. You're not going to find any answers. You're going to be too busy dodging bricks and beer bottles."

"I can't just sit back and watch."

"That's exactly what you should do."

"Maybe it'll all make sense when I see everything firsthand."

"We're not going to be your babysitter out there," Kadish called from the kitchen. This was followed by the plop of milk into his coffee. "I mean it. I'm not looking after you."

Rice joined Kadish in the kitchen, smiled, and spilled some milk into his cup also. "So you'll do it."

"Stop in my office about six, and I'll give you an armband so at least the good guys will know you're harmless."

"Does it have a bull's-eye on it?" Rice said.

"You'll stay behind the police riot line," Kadish said.

"Thanks."

"Leave the coffee cup," the detective said. "And get out of my house."

# { 41 }

A contingent of bone-tired Ohio National Guardsmen drew up in an uneven line across that part of Toledo Street that served as the unofficial boundary between the domain of hookers, dealers, and assorted layabouts, and Goodwater's merchant district.

The district's grimy bars, tattoo parlors, and pool halls disappeared closer to the heart of downtown. Instead there were bakeries, nicer bars, a few law offices, camera shops, and clothing stores.

Downtown Goodwater was the keep, the center of the castle. Sorry as it was, it had to be defended at all costs.

Mayor Sandy McMillan, stylishly grimy in his Eisenhower jacket, day-old beard, and soot-smeared cheek, explained the strategy at a briefing attended by senior officers from various law enforcement branches, three Cleveland television stations, and local media.

A reporter from the Lorain paper asked about fatigue setting in on the guardsmen who had convoyed overnight from the Akron truck strike.

“They'll be fine,” McMillan said. “They're trained to work under difficult conditions, even if they're a little tired.”

“They're civilians with uniforms and guns, Mayor,” Janousek called out. “Aren't you a little worried?”

The mayor ignored him.

Janousek chose to go with the guardsmen, telling Rice he believed their sector was most likely to see the biggest disruptions. Rice agreed. He, on the other hand, was already committed to go with Ed Kadish and second-shift officers on the far side of town, near the old high school. This area had seen a few car burnings and minor break-ins, but the mayor’s mother lived in one of the old two-stories nearby, and he believed a strong police presence would discourage anything more.

“Gonna be an early night for us,” Rice told Kadish as busses took the suited-up officers to their assigned sector. “The guardsmen are going to catch the brunt of it.”

Kadish lifted one eyebrow at Rice. “You want to go with them?” he said. “It's up to you. Won't break my heart.”

“No,” Rice said, watching the empty streets as the bus drove on.

“Two words, Channon,” Kadish said, apparently catching Rice's disappointment. “Interior lines. That’s what I want you to remember.”

“Why?”

"I know you were never in the service," Kadish said. "But that doesn't mean you shouldn't understand something about military strategy."

"Enlighten me, general."

Kadish opened up his big right hand. "Pretend this is a saucer." He touched his fingertip. "Our team is on the perimeter of the saucer right here." Next he touched his wrist. "This here is where the National Guard is staging. Are you following me?"

"Sort of."

"The bad guys are the coffee cup. They're right in the middle of the saucer." Kadish poked at the center of his palm. "They've got the advantage of interior lines. They can run and hit the National Guard and then, because they have a shorter distance, turn around and hit us on the other side of town. Those of us on the perimeter of the circle can't move as fast. We have farther to go. Can't react."

Rice looked out the bus window. He'd never seen so few people on the streets so early in the evening. "Interior lines," he said dully. "Got it."

The bus let off its passengers in front of the Eichel home. Ragged police tape still hung from the front porch. No one getting off the bus even glanced at the place.

No one except Rice.

Annike Eichel sat on the porch. She stood up when he looked at her.

He was surprised to see Arnie Corso, uneasy and paler than usual, strolling awkwardly in his direction. Kadish and the other cops off-loaded weapons, tear gas, masks, and other equipment. The sound of snaps and buckles and adjusted slings filled the early evening air.

Rice half expected to see Star Lightman or maybe one of his whores looking on. Instead, only a lone mongrel dog watched. It was skinny and wracked with sores, its long ratlike tail tucked between its legs as it crabbed sideways, away from the twenty or so police officers.

Arnie reminded Rice of the dog. Arnie may have been cleaner and free from blemishes, but he carried the furtive look of the sorry beast slinking toward a mailbox.

"You shouldn't be here, Arnie," Rice said. "Go home. Close the door. Take her with you." He thrust out his chin toward Annike, who hung back. "There might be trouble—"

"There *will* be trouble," Arnie said.

"Is that what she told you?"

"Annike?"

"Yeah, Annike. Who else would I mean?"

"I haven't heard her. I haven't seen her," Arnie said, casting a quick glance toward the cops who ignored him the same way they ignored the dog and the Eichel house. They looked grim and tired as they slapped magazines into weapons, tucked in pant legs, and retied boots.

"You don't see her?" Rice said.

"No."

Most of the cops wore batting helmets, although some wore only their soft police covers. One policeman wore a proper riot helmet with a clear faceplate. This officer—clearly the man in charge, although Rice didn't recognize him—nodded, and the line stretched the width of the roadway, slowly marching away from these uptown homes toward the Goodwater bowels and a possible confrontation.

Rice heard murmurs as equipment was readjusted, then just the *tromp, tromp, tromp* down Carlisle Street with its empty sidewalks, lifeless homes, and darkened windows. Kadish looked back, scowled when he saw Arnie, then motioned with his arm to summon Rice.

"Alexander's here," Arnie said. "He called me."

"Annike's Alexander?" Rice said. "I'm not seeing him. Listen, Arnie, I've gotta go. Did you hear what I told you? Lock your door. Stay home."

"Trouble. Lots of trouble."

"What are you talking about? What kind of trouble?" Rice asked. He saw Kadish wave a dismissive hand in his direction.

"Alexander's full of anger."

"Is that why Annike's here?"

"I don't know for sure."

"Why doesn't she toss a lasso around her poltergeist and tie him to the sink or something?"

Arnie looked surprised. "She's dead. Alexander's an orphan now."

Rice shot a look at the police line. It was marching with wary slowness. He could catch up to them quickly.

"Ghost orphans, for chrissake," he said, but he worried about the kind of ugliness that had been able to draw Arnie out of his apartment-cave. "So where's your orphan going?"

"Going where orphans always go," Arnie said. "To hang out with his brothers. To gain strength from them."

This time Rice physically shivered. He tried to remember what Kadish told him about interior lines.

"Go home, Arnie," he said.

# { 42 }

Often in the fall, after the trees were bare but before the truly ugly winter weather set in, a cold Lake Erie gale sometimes snatched up a handful of dead leaves, spinning them corkscrew fashion into the air.

Although it was summer, this thought was on Ed Kadish's mind as the line of officers from the Goodwater Police Department marched in resolute silence down Carlisle Street.

He couldn't feel a rough wind, but the hair rose on the back of his neck. He saw no leaves spinning in the sky, but a few sullen teenagers—heads down and swinging left and right like hungry foxes searching for moles—prowled the streets, walking in the opposite direction.

Then the wind kicked up, and Kadish felt the tension rise in the line of marching patrolmen. Older black men, and more of them, many sporting huge Afros, called out words that were mostly unintelligible.

"Easy," Kadish muttered. Others on the line picked up on the sentiment as the pace of the marching slowed without any prompting.

Nothing had been thrown yet, but a murmur arose from the spectators. "Pigs go home," one man shouted. This was followed by louder, braver voices calling, "Get out, pigs," as the gale picked up.

Now people in alleyways and other dark places began tossing sticks and small rocks at the marching line of policeman.

Something hit Kadish in the face, cutting his cheek. He instinctively reached down to his holster.

"By order of the mayor and the Goodwater City Council, you are directed to return to your homes and remain off the streets until nine a.m. tomorrow," the officer with the riot helmet said through a bullhorn. A well-aimed rock struck the bullhorn causing the patrolman to drop it momentarily. This was accompanied by hoots from the crowd, which now included women.

"Disperse," the man said, his voice now clipped and angry. "Disperse at once or you will face arrest and criminal prosecution."

Kadish felt foolish in his batting helmet, sweat dripping down both sides of his head. He would have hooted too if he were one of the rioters.

"These are *our* streets," one young black man said. He wore neat bell-bottoms with a yellow T-shirt and seemed out of place amid the rougher, hungrier elements in the crowd.

Now, the chant of "pigs get out" was picked up by more and more men in the crowd. The higher-pitched voices of women proclaimed, "This is our home," until the whole thing felt like an opera in which Kadish was an unwilling walk-on player.

A strong hand gripped his arm, and this time he reached for his nightstick before spinning around.

Rice Channon was out of breath. Instead of being angry, Kadish was worried. "Get out of here," he said. "Now."

"I know," Rice said, his face a sickly gray like dull linen. He held his hand lightly against the detective's back, probably not even aware he was doing so.

"Stay behind me," Kadish said. The line moved forward.

A disordered throng of protesters faced them. It was composed of young men, little older than boys, dancing broadly and taunting the cops. Another more ragged line behind them tossed bottles, rocks, and even a license plate at the advancing officers.

"Disperse now," the man with the bullhorn said, electronic feedback distorting the ignored message. Multiple lines of sweat spilled down his cheek.

Kadish felt the momentum of the protesters swell like a great wave ready to tumble, a second or two of stillness left before the crash of sand and foam.

Then the kid with the fancy yellow T-shirt and tailored bell-bottoms marched out in front of the line of taunters and poked a fading red rose—brown and losing its petals—into the barrel of the only officer holding out his weapon toward the crowd.

The officer jerked the weapon up sharply, and the barrel caught the flower-poker under his chin. Blood poured out at once, dripping onto the filthy street. When the man fell to his knees, another officer placed him in handcuffs.

That's when the wave of anger and frustration crashed hard against the solid shore of the Goodwater Police Department.

An older man pulled up the bleeding kid like he was a small bag of wet laundry. He jerked him free from the tentative grasp of the arresting patrolman.

A shouted order was called out twice, and the police line backed up a few steps. The men held their batons out and then renewed their forward march.

Kadish looked left and right. He sensed movement from the shadows, and it made his stomach churn. In Korea, his platoon had been flanked on both ends of their line by a Chinese Communist assault. It was only a double-timing support unit coming up behind them that prevented panic and an all-out rout.

"Lieutenant," Kadish called out to the heavily perspiring man in the riot helmet. He pointed at both ends of the line where quiet groups prepared to attack while the louder taunters in front kept the attention of the marching policemen.

"Halt," the lieutenant said, and the line, without any hesitation, stopped immediately. He broke the advancing line of officers into a second echelon behind the main line. This line turned ninety degrees and advanced on the groups threatening the unit's flanks.

More and more protesters attacked from the front, and even when batons cracked hard against torsos, shoulders, and sometimes heads, the line of screaming black men advanced. Behind them, lanky men took bats and bricks to shopwindows. Screaming women and children followed behind, fleeing with boxes of shoes and socks or cans of peanut butter and sacks of potatoes.

Despite himself, Kadish admired the military nature of their attack. The first squad blasted a hole and the second squad—women and children mostly—charged through it to clean out goods on the inside.

Laughing, angry men farther in the rear threw Molotov cocktails that usually fell impotently to the street. But sometimes the flames shot forth like untamed beasts, howling and consuming everything nearby.

Kadish watched as Rice ran to the shadows of nearby taller buildings, talking to the people huddled there. He looked safe, but Kadish knew he could not protect him.

The flames grew. Kadish heard the wail of fire engines, but they sounded far off and heading away from here. This block would burn tonight, and there was nothing Ed Kadish could do to stop it.

Something like laughter mixed into the roar of burgeoning flames pouring from a Laundromat.

A heavier shadow, like a cloud or a sharp line of lake storms heading their way, fell over the fire.

The lieutenant's barking was unintelligible, but the police line slowly moved back, leaving the angry rioters. And Rice Channon.

And the black thing overhead that seemed to feed off the flames below it.

# { 43 }

When Father Growden opened the rectory door, Arnie hunched over as he stepped inside. He looked around nervously.

"What's this about?" Growden said. He wore a white dickey beneath a light-green sweater. It made him look like an overmuscled schoolchild.

"Rice says you live in the spiritual realm," Arnie said, jerking his head when a Woody Woodpecker windup clock on the priest's desk made a vague cracking noise.

Father Growden gave up a tight smile. "That's the business I'm in," he said, spreading his hands wide as though displaying newly tooled belts or a bushel of vegetables. "Why so jumpy?"

"It's the poltergeist, Alexander."

"He's still in her home, right?"

Arnie bit at a fingernail while eying the clock suspiciously. “Not anymore. It's on the street. It's feeding.”

Growden knew the answer but asked anyway. “On what?” he said.

“The anger. The hatred. The confusion. All the bad stuff that makes him strong.”

Growden walked around the desk. “You’re sure about all this, are you?” he said.

“Does your church believe redemption comes through fire?”

Growden stared at him, trying to jerk his mindset toward this new place. “Purgatory is often seen as fire. Jesus himself said he came to light a fire on the earth. So fire can be a kind of purification,” he said. “Is that what you mean?”

Arnie began pacing, arms behind his back, less frantic now. Almost comfortable. “You know spirits are everywhere around us. Every one of us. Angels, guides, random souls who are drawn to us somehow. You know that, right?”

Father Growden's jaw clenched visibly before he let it go slack. “No.”

Arnie raised a hand, kept talking. “Okay, okay,” he said. “You're not ready for that. I understand. Just trying to find the borders, locate the corners.”

“What?”

Arnie stopped his pacing and turned to the priest, a warm smile that seemed almost mature grew on his lips. “Like a jigsaw puzzle. You dump the box then look for the corners,” he said. "Then you build in from there. That's what I'm doing."

"You know, Arnie, I believe you're sincere. But you still could be a complete wacko."

Arnie raised a finger. "Point taken," he said and began pacing again.

"What's any of this have to do with the riots?"

"I'm not sure," Arnie said. "Not positive, anyway. I think it's all mixed up with that woman's death and Alexander's escape."

Arnie squinted at the finely detailed molding outlining the perimeter of the office ceiling.

"I worry about him," he said, returning his gaze to the priest. "Now he's a man without corners. No place to work in from. No starting point."

"Rice, you mean."

Arnie laughed. "Yeah. Who'd you think I meant, Alexander?"

"I'm just trying to keep up, son."

"The death of Annike Eichel must have been very difficult for Alexander," Arnie said. "She created him, nursed him, and watched him evolve as some kind of psychic doppelganger. You know what that is, right?"

"Rhymes with schizophrenic," the priest said.

"What?" Arnie said, then forced a chuckle. "I get it. You think a person's got to be crazy to see their double."

"I think a lot of crazy people do," Father Growden said. "But this Alexander you're describing sounds more like the offspring of a troubled or confused mind."

"Not *any* mind," Arnie said. "*Her* mind. She's alone so she creates an invisible playmate. Isolation makes her confide in this playmate. All her fears. All her confusion. All her anger, her hatreds."

"What about caring? Love? Compassion?"

"Okay. What about those things?" Arnie said. "You tell me."

"Annike carried a sweetness in her. She's not going to spit out a vengeful spirit who's mad as all wrath."

"But the bad stuff, the dark stuff, it stuck to him. And she kept him around like a pet. And her murder may have been the worst of it. That broke the balance that kept him in check. Kind of an equilibrium." Arnie moved his hands up and down as though they were the two pans of a balance scale. "So Alexander bolted like a skittish horse."

"What about the books flying off shelves? Insects and bugs that came out of nowhere and disappeared?"

Arnie's smile was smug. "Play acting," he said. "Simply a frightened child working out his frustration."

"You *know* all this?"

Arnie raised his forefinger again. "But Alexander sensed the anger and the riots. He sniffed out that scent like a bloodhound on the hunt. He ran to it. I saw him today. Lots of anger. From cops, rioters. Alexander feels right at home."

"And what else?" the priest said.

"And he's growing stronger from it."

"How—"

"And more dangerous. Nothing to mitigate his actions," Arnie said. As he grew more excited, some spittle formed at the corners of his mouth.

Growden shook his head. "What's he looking for? What's he want?"

"Release," Arnie said. "He wants release, and he's breaking things and people on his way to finding it."

Father Growden looked around as though searching for a way out. Then he lifted two boxes off the floor and opened the one at the bottom of the pile. He pulled out a clerical black shirt from the box and a white tab from a drawer. After taking off his sweater, he put on the shirt and slipped in the white clerical tab at his throat.

He turned to Arnie and put an arm on his shoulder. "Go home," he said.

# { 44 }

“You look like your mother,” Tom Janousek said, sliding off Stacey’s body without even jostling the sheets.

She was annoyed at the comment, even as she was amazed at the man’s recuperative powers. They’d had sex two times already, and he’d only been here half an hour.

“That’s just silly,” she said, trying hard to keep her tone light and the hurt out of her voice.

Tom laughed at her as he got out of bed and pulled on what looked like a new pair of white briefs. Stacey wished she hadn’t used the word *silly,* but nothing could change that. Maybe that was why he was laughing. She turned on her side and made a petulant scowl at the wall, angry the man could do this to her.

“You’re a beautiful woman, Stace,” he said. “When I’m close to you after you’ve washed off all that paint and goopy eyeliner from your face, you're pretty as a spring day. Soft and natural. That's all I meant."

"What's that have to do with mother?"

"Older women usually dress to look like somebody they're not. They hide behind a mask. You're better than that."

Stacey felt her face flush, and she wondered if the blush showed on her naked back. She pulled the covers up around her shoulders. "Women look better with makeup. That's just a truth," she said without turning to face him.

Tom knelt on the bed, took her shoulders, and spun her around to look at him. "It's not a truth," he said. "That's just … *silly*."

Stacey flushed again when he said the word.

"You told Rice about us," he said, carefully working the tie on his shoes until the bows were precisely the same size. Then he gingerly touched his puffy right eye and winced.

"So?" She liked that he was surprised at her indifferent reaction.

"I told him I'd back off if he wanted," Tom said. "Because of your history and all. Might make working together difficult."

She sat up, the sheet falling off her breasts. He walked over to the mirror, toyed with his tie again, but barely touched his hair.

"How'd he take it?" he asked.

"He seemed surprised," Stacey said. It was fun to watch the reporter's eyes on her breasts as he looked at her in the mirror.

"Did he act hurt?"

"A little, maybe," she said, looking down at the sheets, wondering if she should change them before he returned this evening. "I thought he would be more mature, to be honest."

Tom sat on the bed. "It wouldn't have bothered *me*," he said.

"You're not Rice," she said, her look piercing. "He's more sensitive and more considerate. And moral."

"Like your mom," he said, grinning, seeming to know that would get to her.

She crossed her arms.

"You're such a modern girl, so very Mary Tyler Moore," he said. "None of it matters to me. Rice is the one sleeping alone."

"What time will you be back tonight?" she asked, her hunger for him already growing again.

"City's on fire, darlin'," he said. "I'll be spending tonight with the Goodwater Police Department and the Ohio National Guard. Maybe Rice too. I'll try to swing by sometime tomorrow. Once the flames die down, maybe we could go out again."

Stacey slid out of bed and put on a robe before he could get another look at her. Then she checked herself out in the mirror. She did look like a slimmer version of her mother, although her eyes were brighter. But without makeup she looked ... naked. She pursed her lips and shook her head. Then watched the sad acknowledgement from the face looking back.

"How's your screenplay coming?" she said without turning around. She could have been talking to the face in the glass.

"What? Oh, it's on the back burner for now," Tom said, moving behind her and putting both hands on her shoulders. He leaned over to kiss the side of her neck.

She tilted her cheek against his hand. "A lot going on in my little town," she said. Stacey looked into the mirror to watch his face, but he seemed uninterested in seeing his reflection.

"We should set up a bureau here," he said. "I'm going to mention it to my editor. Maybe Rice would take the job."

Stacey shook her head. "Won't happen."

Tom stood up straight. "Yeah, you're probably right. I don't understand him."

"Me either."

"And yet you still have feelings for him," Tom said. "Don't shake your head."

After Tom Janousek left, Stacey took a shower. Then she sat down at the vanity in her bathroom and studied her face in a way she hadn't for a long time. She was still young enough to pull off the natural look, but as she looked carefully, she detected laugh-line creases at her eyes, and light shadows that could also be creases forming at the corner of her lips. Her mother had prominent wrinkles on her forehead. That would be next, probably.

She picked up the copy of *American Home* magazine on the edge of the vanity. A fresh-faced model in a broad-brimmed beige canvas hat stared back at her. Stacey resented her assumption of every good thing certain to come her way.

An article explained how to create a more natural look through application of pastel shades to her eyes. She adjusted the lamp and leaned forward, then drew a stripe of light yellow just under the eyebrow on her right eye.

Women, she decided, were always kowtowing to men and their wants. Here she was, a single, emancipated and—to use Tom's own term—a Mary Tyler Moore kind of gal, trying to apply makeup so it looked like she was wearing no makeup. All because a natural look was supposed to be more honest.

The word *sweets* swam into her brain. Sweets. That's what she called Rice. What she still called him sometimes if she let the reins fall loose. Tom was right about that.

But if she truly cared about him, why had she begun a relationship with Roger while she and Rice were still dating? Stacey giggled as she carefully laid on a thick stripe of pink under the yellow on the center of her eyelid.

Of course, there had been a lot more than dating going on.

Rice was sexually insatiable. Once he'd become comfortable with the pairing of their bodies, he'd fallen on her like a diver plumbing the depths of some newly discovered sea. She'd fed off that, even as his intensity had frightened her some. Roger, on the other hand, had represented an island where she could drag herself ashore, take a deep breath, and regain her bearings. Eventually, that had grown into love—or something like it.

Her eyes still didn't look right. The article said she should extend the yellow stripe out toward the temples, but that made her look like a villainess in a Flash Gordon serial. Nothing natural about it.

She tried to recall what kind of makeup Annike Eichel wore. She always looked so crisp, so put-together in her photos.

Stacey thought about Father Growden and his relationship with Eichel. *That*, she said to herself, *was an odd pairing if ever there was one*. The atheist and the fallen-away priest. Could be a television sitcom.

Or a tragedy.

A frisson of lust tore through her, and she wondered if it was an aftershock from the satisfactory, if not wonderful sex with Tom Janousek.

She looked down again at the magazine. The paint-by-numbers directions said the next step was to spread an aqua blush along the crease of her eye and close to the lashes.

More pastels. For a moment she yearned to draw a blood-red streak across the entire width of her face as a great big *fuck-you* to the timid subtlety of pastel.

Instead, Stacey sighed, closed one eye, and spread the blue into a blend with the other colors.

"Pretty eyes aren't just prettily made up eyes," the article sermonized. "They have the special sparkle that comes from good health."

She tried not to think about Rice in a sexual way, but sometimes her weary or distracted mind betrayed her.

"The heart wants what the heart wants," her mother often said, as if she'd invented the stupid cliché. Of course, that didn't mean it was untrue.

Loving Rice was like standing on a big ice pond in new skates with nobody around to help you up when you fell. And fall she would. Eventually.

So she ran to Roger, the confident pretty boy with the swagger of a schoolyard bully who really didn't want to fight. He had none of Rice's soft lines. No poetry. No confusion. No doubt about where he was going.

Roger was the *un*-Rice, so when he asked her to marry him, she had to accept. She had to get off that ice pond and onto solid ground.

But it didn't take long before she was eager to jump back on the ice. Tom Janousek knew it before she did. He wasn't interested in her sexual power games. He simply fed on what was there and that seemed good enough.

She knew it was going to end with Roger. When he lost his job—the reasons still weren't clear—she didn't see it as piling on when she took that opportunity to call off the engagement. He expected nothing less since—in his own eyes and, he assumed, in hers—he wasn't worthy any longer.

Stacey blinked twice. The sloppy mess of dull colors on her eyelids didn't look completely awful from a distance. Roger would have hated it, of course. He preferred the conventionally made-up look of her mother. Pearls around her neck. Skirts that were stylish but not *too* short.

Tom Janousek? Nodding, grinning. Licking his lips maybe. She could already hear his whispered *nice* as he closed on her, stroking her cheek lightly with the back of his fingers.

But Rice, he was different. *What was it he had said?*

"I like that you move your knees when I kiss you," he told her once. "That your eyebrows raise—even when your eyes are closed—if I touch you just right. And that top button on your blouse twists almost by magic, then pops free to show that soft whiteness above your breasts. And sometimes I watch the flutter of your heart beating there."

"And if it's dark?" she asked, her breath catching.

Another kiss. He loved kissing her. "Then I touch the spot," he said. "And I feel the flutter in my fingertips."

Oddly, it was those words that ignited the panic in her. They were too rich. Too dangerous. She thought of the feral horses she once watched on Cumberland Island in Georgia many years earlier. Beautiful, but wild and unpredictable.

And she thought of John Keats, his honeyed prose like caramel sauce over her favorite French chocolate cheesecake. But the suffocating heaviness was there too. "My love is selfish. I cannot breathe without you," as he wrote to his worship object, Fanny Brawne.

And Rice too sucked the air out of her, inhaled her spirit somehow, made her afraid to breathe too heavily, lest he steal the life from her.

Stacey's cheeks were a little bit pink now, but it wasn't any cosmetic that made them that way.

"The special sparkle that comes from good health," she said aloud, giggling.

Even now, alone, she felt Rice's warm, scentless breath on her face, remembered the way he whispered in her ear while he touched her, nipped at her chin, her earlobes, her throat. Preparing to consume her.

"The skin on your eyelids," the *American Home* article explained, "is thin and delicate and contains no oil glands at all. This fragile area is dependent on you for lubrication."

So why was the weak blend of pastel shades feeling heavy and greasy on her eyes?

Stacey reached for a towel and wiped her eyelids until they were free of color, dry and pink from the rubbing. Then she filled the sink bowl with warm water and dunked her face in, scrubbing at her cheeks, her forehead, and her lips as though she wanted to leave all the artifice here, in this bowl, to be flushed away.

Better. Water dripped on the floor, but her face looked truly clean for once.

Damn him with his poetry and his touches and all those tentative things about him. He continued to eat away at her, swallowing her like the communion wafer she took on her tongue at Sunday Mass.

She was part of him now. She was part of his skin, his blood. And it didn't matter who else touched her. They were merely watchers.

"When it's time to remove your makeup, do it with anything *but* soap and water," *American Home* concluded. "The key word is *gentle*."

Twins, she knew, sometimes shared intuitions and premonitions. Maybe it was like that with Rice and her now. Her thumping heart along with a general clamminess on her face and hands portended *something*.

All the hunger she felt. It was real. It was natural. It was human.

Stacey grabbed a light shawl from her closet. Weather forecasts called for a cool night fog settling over the area tonight.

She slapped at the door on the way out. It banged impotently against the swinging safety chain as she walked hurriedly to her car.

# { 45 }

Father Growden looked like he was ready to leave. Like he wanted to be somewhere else in a hurry.

And for once, he wasn't happy to see Stacey.

"Here's the irony," the priest said, late-afternoon shadows rolling across his face. "Hunger can eat us whole. It can become us. Define us. Make us believe we're less than we are."

Father Growden pushed the boxes around his office in a busywork way, not accomplishing anything. Sweat broke out on his brow, but his expression was flat and without secrets. Stacey thought that desperate people preparing to jump off the ledge of a tall building must look this way.

"I gave into lust," she said in the same tone she might have used to order regular at the gas station.

Growden held up a hand. "Save it for confession," he said.

"But it's a kind of hunger," she said. "Isn't that what we were talking about?"

He took a deep breath. "We were talking about Rice Channon," the priest said. "Like we usually do. This is where I tell you he's dangerous and you tell me he's lost."

"Have I become that predictable?"

Another sigh. "I can't help you any longer, Stacey. You say Rice is lost? Fine. Me too. Talk to his friend, Arnie. I've got my own hungers to deal with."

"I worry about you," she said.

He put a clammy hand on her shoulder and smiled. "I have to wrap up some business," he said. "For me. For everybody."

—

David Paul Billard propped his body against a windowsill in the *Goodwater Tribune*'s newsroom and dropped his head so his hair pressed against the lowered Venetian blinds.

It wasn't quite dark, and when he looked up, he saw several spirals of smoke about a mile away in the riot zone. No visible flames yet. With the uneven fog drifting in, Billard expected he would have seen reflections of dancing fires if any were burning.

A few silent fire engines drove slowly down the street on the north side of the Tribune Building. He assumed they were positioning themselves closer to the riot zone in the event they were needed later on.

It was so quiet.

Of course, some of that was the fog. It muffled the sound of bells at gas station air pumps and the groans of maneuvering semis trying to avoid the riot area.

But people also seemed to speak quieter in the fog. Like they were watching a play or sitting in church waiting for the service to start.

A photographer hustled out of the photo lab with one of the paper's old Rolleiflex cameras slung around his neck.

No one else was in the newsroom. It was too early for stringers to return to write up reports of rural meetings of the Grange, the school board, or village councils. Too late for everyone else, even on a normal day.

Except on a normal day, he'd be home watching the *NBC Nightly News* and drinking the one highball he allowed himself each evening. He'd be reviewing his home-delivered copy of the *Tribune* one more time, pretending he was a factory worker at the nearby Ford Assembly plant reading it after a long day on the line.

This afternoon he'd called everyone together and handed out typed assignment sheets. Reporters were dispatched to fire stations, police offices, hospitals, and morgues. Photographers were given sectors to cover. He kept one photog in reserve at the Goodwater Bank and Trust Building, the tallest structure in town. He wanted a panoramic view of the city if it caught fire again. Even copy girls were called in and charged with delivering exposed film to the newspaper's photo lab for processing.

Yogi Broadback, a relentless boozer and the oldest reporter on the paper, was directed to stay close to Mayor McMillan and Phil Fortunato. For some ungodly reason, the mayor took a liking to the old drunk. So maybe he'd come up with something.

But he was really counting on Rice and Janousek to bring back the smell and sweat of a city under assault. They were both resistant to direction—and Janousek didn't really belong to him anyway—so he hadn't bothered assigning them specific tasks.

But Billard knew they'd cut to the heart of the rioting and wouldn't worry about being shot or bullied or moved out of the way.

And each would try to outdo the other, even if neither one knew it.

"Excuse me."

Billard had closed his eyes. When he felt a thick hand lightly applied to his shoulder, he turned around.

The man who touched him was maybe five ten but had broad, powerful shoulders that stretched the black clerical shirt tight across his chest. His grin was easy and unforced, as one might expect from a man whose size sometimes intimidated people.

"My name is Father Pete Growden. I'm pastor at Sacred Heart Church," he said, reaching out his hand.

"How can I help you, Father?" Billard said after shaking the offered hand. He returned to his desk, sat down, and put his glasses on.

"I'm looking for Rice," the priest said. "Rice Channon."

Billard grinned. "You are? Me too."

"So you don't know where he is?"

"I kind of know," the city editor said. He arched an eyebrow. "He doesn't get many priests looking for him."

Father Growden looked at his hands and rubbed a fat knuckle that looked like it had been bruised recently. "It's sort of hard to explain."

Billard took off his glasses and rubbed his nose. "Then you'd be smarter to come back tomorrow," he said. "You might have heard that we're expecting trouble tonight."

"It's not about the riots," Growden said.

"Okay. Whatever it's about, you should talk to him tomorrow."

"Do you believe in evil, Mr. Billard?" Growden said.

The city editor pushed out his bottom lip. He almost asked how this man of the cloth with the wrestler's physique knew his name.

"I'm in the newspaper business, Father," he said. "I've seen dead children in a ditch after a tornado threw them out of their home. I've met lots of crooked politicians. Once I watched a guy with a butterfly knife cut off pieces of his own flesh while smiling at me. Does any of that count?"

"Nature and politics running amok or simple insanity does not meet my definition of evil," Father Growden said.

"I'll defer to you on the definition," Billard said. "Mortal sins, venial sins, original sins. The faith knows what goes where. I'll let you decide which people's sins are evil and which are simply mischievous."

Growden smiled broadly and clasped his hands in front of him. "Another lapsed Catholic," he said. "I know the code words."

"How do you know I'm lapsed?"

The priest simply continued smiling.

"Okay, you want to talk about evil?" Billard said, standing up, hands on his desk. "I've got a little time. During the war, I worked on bombers. I'm talking about World War Two and not that mess in Korea. I pulled butchered young airmen from crippled B-17s. Eyes missing. Limbs. Spilled guts held in place with zippered flight jackets. These were boys lots younger than Rice Channon. They were fighting an evil that I believe was the worst ever faced on this planet. Pure darkness. The end of civilization. Some mornings I expected Jesus Christ himself to show up over the runway, floating down to earth and announcing he'd had enough and was going to end it all. Some afternoons after some of the uglier bombing runs, I prayed for it."

"But you stopped praying," Growden said. "Didn't you?"

Billard scratched his head with an index finger. "I guess I did. Stopped going to church services too. At the time, I blamed it on the fine Scotch whisky I drank too much of, the lucrative card games I played most nights. That and the disreputable company I kept. But I was probably just pissed that God hadn't destroyed the world. Or at least rid it of evil."

"But he did. Eventually."

"He took his sweet time about it," Billard said. "I give most of the credit to the Eighth Air Force and the US Third Army."

"Do you feel better telling me all this?"

"I do, as a matter of fact," Billard said. "Haven't been to confession in about thirty years. Is this where you give me absolution?"

"No. But you've got my pity."

"Keep it," Billard said. "I'd rather know what you're hunting down and why."

"It has to do with Annike Eichel."

Billard nodded. "A lot of people didn't like her. Thought she was the anti-Christ. Evil like that?"

"She was not the anti-Christ and she wasn't evil," Growden said. "But she was a focus for blackness. It distilled into something."

"What's *it*?"

"I'm not sure. Some people call it a poltergeist," Growden said.

"Rice told me a story about books flying off shelves at Eichel's home. Bugs crawling around. Would this be the same fella?"

"Rice sees ghosts," the priest said. "Or thinks he does."

"I've heard the rumors," Billard said. "I try not to think about it too much."

"He says he sees the ghost of Annike Eichel," Father Growden said, looking down at his hands.

"That so? Should be a simple matter to discover who killed her then."

"She's … She's not talking," Growden said. "But she communicated that this poltergeist might have been responsible. That he killed her."

"Rice forgot to mention that to me," Billard said. His face softened. "Listen, Father. You could come in here with photos and an interview written in magic ink. I still couldn't do anything with it. You're worried about Rice. I understand. But do yourself a favor. Go home. And talk to him tomorrow."

"I didn't say I was worried."

"What then?"

"I want to find this thing before he does," Father Growden said.

—

"Can I spend the night here?" Stacey said when Arnie opened his door.

He blushed at once. Stacey walked past him, unwrapped her light shawl, and draped it over one of the kitchen chairs. "Got a radio?" she asked.

Arnie closed the door, then pulled a red and white transistor radio from a desk drawer and flicked it on. Radio station WCGN was barely audible through the static. He turned the radio ninety degrees and the signal got stronger.

"I'll leave when things quiet down tonight," she said, touching his arm lightly. Another blush from Arnie.

"I don't have anything to eat but some soup and stuff," he said, without looking at her.

"I should have brought something," she said. He looked at her with a sideways glance as though she might bite. "I'm not hungry."

"Sit anywhere," he said.

Stacey smiled and sat on the couch. "Thanks, Arnie."

The news reports were spotty, but something about listening to the radio together in the dark seemed to calm her. Arnie sat on the far end of the couch. She reached over to him after they heard a report of a shooting in the riot area. She scooted closer to him and took his hand in both of hers.

Even though he was hungry and wanted to heat up some vegetable soup, Arnie stayed there on the couch with her.

The spirits left him alone, even after she dropped her head to his shoulder and began crying quietly.

# { 46 }

Because of the cancer, Kleavon Hayes had a hard time making it up the steps to Foster Ebner's home without pausing, each time taking deep, labored breaths.

Kleavon looked around the neighborhood. Most of the homes were white—like most of the residents—and more than a few featured two-story-high Doric columns holding up faux balconies. Back when Kleavon's body was hard from digging ditches and trimming trees, he could have smashed a baseball bat against those columns and they would have crumbled.

Emblems, he called them. Symbols that weren't real. This wasn't merely a large and beautiful home. It was supposed to mimic a plantation house, and all the slaves were out back.

Kleavon rang the bell, then turned around. Two cars filled with young black men were parked near the end of the street, but not *in* the cul-de-sac. That would draw too much attention.

In the gloaming dark, neither the cars nor their occupants were visible.

The door swung open, and the imposing figure of Foster Ebner looked down at him. Kleavon had forgotten how light skinned he was. "A cup of joe with double cream," Ebner used to say when anybody brought the subject up. Nobody did anymore.

The disgraced Public Works director looked left and right down the street. "What are you doing here?" he said. "You can't be seen here. It'll fuck up everything."

"You gonna invite me in?" Kleavon said.

Ebner grabbed Kleavon's arm and half lifted him into the house, then shut the door. Ebner looked out the side glass to see if any lights came on in the neighborhood. To see if anyone was standing on their porch, hands on hips, displaying dissatisfaction that not only did they have to tolerate their nigger neighbor, but now they had to tolerate his nigger friends as well.

But he saw nothing. No movement. No lights. Ebner spun around to confront Kleavon.

"I should kick your ass," Ebner said. The living room was large but sparsely furnished. Newspapers were scattered on the coffee table and across both braided wool oval rugs. The buffet and sofa were in the Early American style. Hurricane lamps with never-lit candles punctuated most of the horizontal surfaces.

"Did your house come this way?" Kleavon said, lifting up the edge of one of the rugs with his toe.

"Did he send you?" Ebner said. "Is that why you're here?"

Kleavon offered a wide smile and took a deep breath. He felt better now. He felt the momentum swinging his way.

"He likes surprises," Kleavon said. "And not just at Christmas. So he asked me to stop in, see how things are going."

"I talk to him. Not you," Ebner said. "He knows that."

"He's changed his mind. That's what I meant about surprises," Kleavon said.

Ebner dropped into the sofa, sitting on top of open newspapers lying there. He angrily yanked them from under his body.

"I don't like it," Ebner said. "Not now. Not today, especially."

"When shit goes down, that's when it's most important to keep your head. He figures you know that."

Ebner laughed. He almost seemed to relax. "He's not getting jammed like me. You and him just sit back and collect all the bread. But it's me whose dick's swinging in the air."

"He said he'd take care of you."

Ebner spread his arms and looked around his living room. "So I'm in a nicer prison than the one downtown. I'm still in the slammer."

"He's got other shit to deal with these days."

Ebner scooted forward on the couch, and the remaining newspapers floated to the floor. "This is the time to fix it. Right now," he said, slamming a fist into his open palm.

"While everyone is looking somewhere else. Get me out now."

Kleavon smiled. "Too risky," he said. "You gotta trust him."

"How many white men do *you* trust?" Ebner said.

"Just the one," Kleavon said.

He walked to the front picture window and peeked out. A fat guy across the street with no shirt and tight shorts moved a sprinkler to the other end of his lawn, a dead cigar stump clenched in his teeth.

"You're a dumb motherfucker, you know that?" Kleavon said.

"You can't talk to me like that," Ebner said, eyes narrowing. "You owe me everything you got."

"I don't owe you shit," Kleavon said. He was feeling a little breathless again so he sat down.

"Is that what you said to that reporter you talked to?"

"Rice Channon? I told him you were a thief. I told him you were pretty good at it. I told him I didn't like you."

"What did he say?"

Kleavon shook his head. "He didn't say much. I think he knew most of it. 'Cept the part about me and you not getting along."

"You didn't say anything about selling me that shit then."

"No," Kleavon said. "That's hitting a little too close to my bone."

Ebner laughed. "You just a dog runner. Nobody cares about that."

"You see, when I said you were a dumb motherfucker, this is what I meant," Kleavon said. Ebner's face reddened. "I was the one got ya that shit you shared with your ladies."

"And the acid?"

"That was me too. Our friend wasn't interested."

Ebner looked worried. He paced across the scattered newspapers. "I don't believe it," he said, half to himself, half to Kleavon.

"Wait 'til you hear the next part," he said. "When I met with the suppliers, I played nigger buying for the big nigger."

Ebner looked stunned. And confused.

"That would be you," Kleavon said, grinning wide and pointing. "And after selling to me for a while, these dealers started getting hassled by the pigs. I might have hinted that you were two-timing them. Might have even called the pigs myself. It was pretty easy."

"I'm going to break you into pieces and bury 'em under the doghouse out back."

Kleavon looked at his watch. "Better hurry," he said.

"The cops are coming here," Ebner said, nodding.

"No," Kleavon said, grinning again. "As you said, they're otherwise engaged."

Ebner took a step toward him. "I don't think cancer is going to kill you," he said, scratching his head. "I thought you were smarter than this."

"Is that so?"

"Why are you here?"

"Somebody—I'm not saying who—is curious about you. They want to know why you were poking that god-hating white woman. They said that was a stupid thing to do."

Ebner laughed but kept a wary eye on Kleavon.

"I told them stupid things is what stupid people do. I told 'em I wasn't surprised at all," Kleavon said.

Ebner shot out his right leg and knocked Kleavon's chair over. His head slammed against the bare wood—not the Early American braided wool rug—and dazed him for a moment. Ebner got down on all fours and leaned against Kleavon's throat with his meaty forearm. So when Kleavon came out of his daze, he immediately started gasping for breath and coughing. But he refused to look at Ebner.

"I always took care of you," Ebner hissed. "Before you started dealing and lying about it. Before you started playing toesies with the cops. I should off your sorry ass right now."

"If you choke me to death," Kleavon squawked, "I'll shit myself and you'll smell it all night long."

This made Ebner smile and he leaned back. Kleavon rubbed his head and his throat before coughing hard for a minute. Some of it was the cancer. The rest of it was on Ebner.

"I know things about you, just like I know things about everybody," Ebner said, returning to the sofa. He picked up a few newspapers and folded them neatly, like he was going to use one for a napkin later on.

"So these people—these curious people I told you about—they wonder if after you get the pretty white woman knocked up, why did you take that butcher knife and begin carving on her hoo-ha?"

"Annike had a baby in her belly?"

"You didn't have enough sense to use a jimmy hat," Kleavon said. "I wasn't surprised 'cause I know you, like I said, but our curious friends find it hard to believe you did all that."

"They can believe whatever they want," Ebner said. "Whoever they are. I got nothing to say."

"That's what I told 'em. They wanted me to come, though."

Ebner withdrew a stiletto switchblade. "I don't want to see you again," he said. "If I do, I'll put this thing in you. It'll be someplace where if you shit yourself or bleed, it won't be on my floor. If I were you, I'd be extra careful. Get out."

Kleavon was over his coughing and showed no expression at all. He looked out the window again. It was getting darker. The streetlights winked on around the neighborhood. He wondered if he'd smell smoke when he stepped outside.

"Cleaning up dirty business. We all gotta do it," he said and sighed. "But I wished you'd talked to me."

There was a clatter on the porch.

"The fuck?" Ebner said as Kleavon opened the door. Eight black men—most of them wearing brown leather vests over bare chests, two with huge Afros—walked in as if they had a room in the back.

Three of them jumped Ebner before he had time to react, pinning him down. A fourth had a stiletto knife that looked a lot like Ebner's. Numbers five and six unbuckled his belt and pulled his pants down. Number four sliced his penis and scrotum with two efficient strokes, like he'd had lots of practice, and jammed the package into Ebner's mouth until his muffled scream became a squeak.

It took only a minute.

Number seven withdrew a revolver and shot Foster Ebner through the forehead, blood draining fast like a bag of tears, ruining the braided wool rug.

Number eight checked the street, directed Kleavon to the door, and shut off all the lights. The streetlights on this side of the street had already been taken care of, so it was way too dark to see the parade of the eight killers and Kleavon Hayes get into their cars and slowly drive away from the big beautiful homes—most of them white, many with faux columns and one containing the corpse of Foster Ebner and whatever secrets he kept inside.

# { 47 }

Rice moved away from the security of the Goodwater Police Department line currently retreating from increasingly aggressive rioters on Carlisle Street. He took an alley to the next street over, which paralleled Carlisle and was practically vacant.

A stock boy at a mom-and-pop grocery was carefully stacking tomatoes on a street display, and two kids played stickball as though it was just another lazy summer evening.

When the kids weren't laughing, Rice heard faint screams and banging noises coming from Carlisle, but no gunshots. Not yet. A favorable wind kept the smoke and smell away.

The stock boy considered him briefly as Rice walked by, then returned to his tomatoes. Two blocks up, Rice found another alley—this one clogged with dented garbage cans—and he made his way back toward Carlisle but behind the line of rioters.

He saw two figures on the ground talking quietly.

The younger guy was the man who pushed roses into a police shotgun and took a barrel to his chin for his efforts. The older man was the one who had pulled him to safety after he'd been handcuffed.

"Did you see what they did to my boy?" the older man said. "They beat him for defending his home. That's all he was doing. Then they put these cuffs on him. Why, man?"

"They're scared," Rice said, kneeling down. He looked into the older man's eyes, trying to gauge his mindset, then back to the kid. Both of them seemed more frightened than angry.

Rice took out a lighter and flicked it into flame. He circled the boy's face with the light. "You lost a tooth, but you probably know that," he said. "That's where the blood's coming from. Can you move your jaw back and forth?"

The boy did. Then he nodded.

"You should see a doctor, but I think you're okay," Rice said. "You home from college?"

Another nod. "Bowling Green," the kid said, then touched his lower lip like it hurt to talk.

"Did you learn that flower trick at school?" Rice said.

The kid looked down, and a fat blob of blood dropped on his yellow shirt. Rice saw his tongue probe the space once occupied by one of his upper central incisors.

"Cops in this town don't understand a nonviolent gesture," the kid said, lisping a little.

"What's your name?"

"Claude," the boy said, looking up. He had dried tear tracks on his cheeks.

"Claude, did you see anything strange tonight?"

"Stranger than pigs carrying guns through my neighborhood?"

"Yeah," Rice said, running a hand through his hair. "Stranger than that. What about a black form like a shadow or a cloud?"

"There was fog tonight," Claude said before spitting out another glob of bloody saliva. "If that's what you mean."

"You know most of these rioters," Rice said. "Did they mention anything about seeing an unusual shadow?"

"We're not rioters," Claude said. "We're revolutionaries."

"Okay, Trotsky. You're a revolutionary. Did you or any of the other revolutionaries see anything odd tonight?"

Claude dropped his head and shook it.

"I saw something funny," Claude's father said. "On our way over here, I saw a priest kneeling down and praying. He was white but everybody let him be."

"That was a priest?" Claude said, turning to his father.

"I think so," his father said. "I thought he was just praying to heaven, but there was something over top of him. I thought it was black smoke from one of the buildings on fire. It was getting dark, but it looked … it looked —"

"Odd?" Rice said

Detective Edwyn Kadish walked up behind them, squinting as if the alley darkness was a bright light. The baseball helmet sat high on his head so the ear holes pressed against his temples.

"Channon," he said. "You in there?"

Rice moved toward him and stepped on an overturned trash can lid. He kicked it toward Kadish, and it slid up against the detective's shoe.

When he saw Rice emerge from the shadows, the detective smiled, but it dropped away quickly.

"What in the hell are you doing here?" Rice said, enunciating each word slowly.

"I wish you'd just stayed with us," Kadish said, taking off the too-small headpiece and massaging his temples before stowing the helmet under his arm. "If something happens to you, I'm the one going to catch hell."

"So you came to rescue me?" Rice said, a huge grin on his face. "Because you care. You big lug."

"I would have been just as happy dragging your bloody carcass to the morgue."

"How about taking the bracelets off this kid?" Rice said, gesturing toward Claude.

"Look at you," Kadish said, unsmiling. "*Bracelets*. Like you're some kind of street thug or something."

"He didn't do anything."

"Yeah, sure," the detective said, fussing with his keys until the handcuffs sprung open.

"He's just a kid."

"They're all kids. Guess that makes it okay."

Claude and his father nodded in Rice's direction, then scrambled away in the dark.

"I'm not saying that," Rice said.

Kadish took a deep breath and exhaled slowly. He scratched his neck, then quickly withdrew his hand.

"Did you happen to see Father Growden on your way over?" Rice said.

"You got a one-track mind, Channon. Murder ain't the only way people die in this town."

"That kid's old man saw him earlier. He said he was praying to a black cloud. I wonder what that could be about."

Kadish's eyes widened. "A black cloud like the one we saw in the Eichel kitchen?"

"Just repeating what I heard."

"Nah, I didn't see him. I interviewed him earlier though," Kadish said, dropping his head. "He spent a lot of time with Eichel. Time alone. He admitted it."

"So you think he did it too?"

Kadish licked his lips and looked at Rice with a gaze that was half a beat away from fury. "He's a priest," the detective said, his voice rising. He looked around. "He's a man of God."

"Are you trying to convince me or yourself?" Rice said. He shook his head and looked at his watch, like the bus was going to leave without him if he didn't hurry. "Growden's somewhere close by. I think he's communicating with that thing we saw. The bugs, the books. All that shit. He's the connection."

Kadish nodded over and over, and when he stopped, he seemed calmer. “Growden had an alibi,” he said. “He couldn't have been there when she was killed. That seems certain. But a part of me wonders if he—I don't know—*controlled* things from a distance. Like one of those guys working puppet strings behind a curtain.”

“Okay,” Rice said. “So Alexander’s the puppet. Growden is the puppet master?”

Kadish took to scratching his neck, not seeming to give a damn if it started bleeding. “Okay, I *did* hear that Growden had been seen over here. The rioters had started falling back. So I thought I’d take a look.”

“I knew you weren’t hunting for me,” Rice said. “You think Growden’s mixed up in the Eichel killing.”

The detective interlaced his fingers and smiled at Rice like an old uncle. “I was kind of looking for you. I was looking for anything. You were right. Ebner’s problems, Eichel’s murder, and the riots are all mixed-up together,” Kadish said. He tapped his head. “And the priest is involved too. That's what my cop noggin tells me.”

“So, what are you going to do about it?”

Kadish shrugged his shoulders. “I’ll investigate some more. Starting tomorrow. By the numbers. That’s the way it works in the cop business. But you,” he said, jabbing a sweaty finger at Rice. “Get off the streets and stay away from that goddamn priest.”

Kadish started shaking his head, his tongue darting out repeatedly like a serpent tasting the air. “I’ve already been away too long. I gotta get back,” he said.

# { 48 }

A month after Rice had taken over the police beat, a prisoner broke free from the inattentive cop restraining him—grabbed a stapler of all things—and bounded down the stairs swinging it at passing secretaries and defense counsels.

Almost everyone got out of his way. Rice Channon reached out and grabbed the guy's shin, using the prisoner's momentum to send him plummeting, chin first, into the bottom step.

"My hero," said a fat patrolman as he put the bleeding man in handcuffs. "Nine out of ten guys would have let him run."

After that, the cops stopped calling him a *news-paper-man* with the phlegmy articulation they used when being dismissive of journalists. Instead he became simply the cop reporter. Only later did he get the other name.

Kadish once told him he had a sixth sense like any good cop.

Unfortunately, the little voice seemed unsure this evening.

He pushed his way through the crowd of white rubberneckers watching the ebb and flow of rioters and police on Carlisle Street, and cut a path toward Cleveland Street. The rest of central downtown was empty.

He pulled out a cigar and stopped to light it, then nursed the tip into a respectable ash before moving on. That helped. Hurrying muddled the mind.

David Billard had told him that years ago when Rice had submitted a sloppy burglary write-up in his haste to beat the deadline.

"If the story's big enough, we'll hold the deadline," the city editor had told him. "If it's not worthy, we'll run it tomorrow. Speed is important, but getting the story right is essential."

He expected Billard was waiting in the newsroom. He'd want to know if the rioters were out of towners. He wouldn't care about floating poltergeists or praying priests.

Rice took a deep puff and inhaled. This concentrated the smoke's sweetness, but he didn't cough. He looked at the exhaled smoke and imagined it was Alexander.

Another puff from his cigar, another ascending smoke cloud. It moved away quickly, caught by a new wind. Maybe a fresh breeze would blow away the fog. Maybe it would carry Alexander off.

Then he saw them.

Father Pete Growden knelt in a dirty alleyway, one yellow light over a service entrance giving a surreal glow to his features. Alexander was there too.

The irregular black mass was directly overhead, vibrating like some droning amoeba-shaped motor. Growden lifted his head to study it. The heavy humidity settled on his forehead and cheeks and ran away, dripping onto the littered alley floor.

"The fog is causing a temperature inversion," the priest said without turning around. His voice was calm and steady, the way it was in his office. "The smoke from the fires is trapped. That's what we're seeing."

"He seems to like you," Rice said.

The priest turned his bulk slowly and stood up. He was holding a small book in his right hand. His smile was genial, and he seemed relieved when he saw who it was. "Didn't know it was you," he said. He turned and pointed at the cloud, still pulsing intermittently, and without any definable shape. "Do you feel the strength coming from it? It's … it's …"

"Seductive?"

"I was going to say powerful," Growden said, reaching up in a plaintive way, as if Alexander were a pet monkey trapped behind a fence. "But they're really two halves of the same thing, aren't they?"

"I never thought about it."

Father Growden nodded, still grinning, as if to reaffirm the truth of his pronouncement. He lowered his hand and began reading. “Banish from me all spells, witchcraft, black magic, malefice …” The wind picked up, snapping at the pages.

“I thought we were supposed to stay clear of supernatural things,” Rice said. “You told me they were dangerous.”

“Did I say that?” Growden said, looking dazed. “Well, maybe it’s like alcohol. If you’re a child, you should stay away, certainly. Are you a child?”

“I don’t know,” Rice said. He looked up at the floating thing, believing he could discern some pattern in the barely visible light and shadows. Was it a face? Then it looked like a torso with a wide, flat head.

“Your ignorance speaks to an intellectual honesty,” the priest said, his smile far too wide. “You can feel the darkness if you stand here. It’s no more dangerous than standing at the edge of a cliff when the wind is blowing hard. It’s exhilarating. And you’ll be okay if you’re careful.”

The priest touched Rice’s arm. His fingers were soft like a woman’s, surprising in such a powerful man.

“You and I make it grow,” he said, turning to Rice as if he expected him to be surprised by this. “And yet we can feed off it as well. It will make you stronger too.”

“Why were you praying just now?”

Father Growden moved closer—close enough for Rice to see the priest hadn’t shaved today—and threw an arm over his shoulder. The strength of Growden’s grip and the unexpected intimacy made Rice want to pull away, but he was held fast in place.

"Saint Augustine once wrote, 'Lord, grant me chastity and continency, but not yet.' It used to trouble me, that phrase. Like Augustine wanted it both ways," Father Growden said, then chuckled. "But now I understand it. I want to be good in all ways. Perfect as our Father in heaven is perfect."

The priest moved close to Rice's face, his breath carrying no scent at all, his whiskery cheeks rustling as his mouth moved. "Just not yet."

"Did you kill her? Did you murder Annike?"

Father Growden's smile faded but didn't disappear completely. It looked sadder, though. "She was afraid of this … this thing," he said.

"Alexander?"

"Yes. Like it was a living being. But look at it. It seems more like a barrier."

"An umbrella is a barrier, but it keeps the rain off," Rice said.

Growden's arm slid up around Rice's neck, grasping him in a manly way, like he was congratulating him for kicking the winning field goal in overtime. "That's the problem with Alexander," the priest said. "He feeds off you. He blocks the light. But he keeps the rain off. And he can make a weak man feel ugly powerful."

"So it was Alexander that made you kill her."

The priest moved deftly behind Rice, slipping his hands under his arms and around his neck, tightening the full nelson hold just enough to keep the reporter immobile.

"She was afraid of it," Father Growden said, grunting a little, as if the effort of holding the wrestling move was tiring. "But she fed off it and it fed off her. I saw it."

"Let me go, Father."

"She tried to fight it. Once, she stabbed at it with a knife and made it bolt, like an octopus would, I imagine. Scrabbling into the corner. I took the knife from her and it felt electrified. Very odd."

"Is that what you killed her with?"

"She was stronger than I. Emotionally. Morally," Growden said.

"This hurts," Rice said.

"It's only a nuance of the pain felt by our savior on the cross," the priest said, surprising Rice by easing up a little.

"I'm no savior. So maybe you could put me down."

"Don't be so modest," Growden said.

"I'm not following, Father."

"Listen to me," the priest said. "Are you listening?"

"Yes."

"Sometimes, you must go into the den to chase the bear. If you do that, you can be a special kind of savior."

"I'm getting light-headed."

"This is nothing," Growden said. "The rear naked choke can actually make you lose consciousness. Can even kill you when it's held long enough."

"Are you telling me you're the bear?"

"I'm trying to get your attention, Rice."

"Hard to focus right now."

Father Growden slid his meaty arms into a rear naked choke and began squeezing slowly.

"This isn't you," Rice said.

"I started learning about it after the tea and the wine were gone," the priest said, dragging the reporter through the grit on the ground. "As the last of that fine Joseph Drouhin Pinot drained away, everything that made Annike unhappy in her life dribbled out too."

"Let up a little," Rice said. Father Growden responded by leaning him against a service door but not easing his grip at all.

"When she talked about the blackmail and the drugs that she used sometimes—and maybe sold too, I don't know—she would blame Alexander. Then she'd blame herself. Like she didn't know. She was the most lost soul I ever met."

"I'll help you find a good lawyer," Rice said, recognizing the desperation in his words. The hollowness.

"At first I felt a buzz that I thought was the pinot noir talking. It snuck up on me so slow. It was arousing. Not sexually, but in a dangerous way." Father Growden paused, smacked his lips wetly. "I wonder if our Lord on the cross felt like you do, when my arm around your neck cuts off your air."

"You've made your point."

Growden chin-gestured at the dim bulb over the door. "See how it follows?"

The black cloud, which looked indefinable in the dark alley, squatted on the light.

It pulsed like it was breathing. Or thinking. Or getting ready.

"That's the way it would come over to Annike and me sometimes. Skulking in from the kitchen like a mean dog, hiding and ready to rip the flesh right out of you. Watching us laugh and sip our wine."

Rice worked his neck free a little and was able to take a deep breath before Father Growden tightened his grip again. "So—what?—the kitchen is the den? Alexander is the bear? What are you trying to tell me?"

The priest shook his head hard, smiled in an exasperated way. "I can't get the words right."

"Are you going to kill me?" Rice said, his voice croaking.

Father Growden stared at him a long time, still with the smile, but now it said Rice didn't get it, would never get it, and Rice thought he was right.

"He knows he doesn't belong here. Not on the streets," Growden said, his voice raspy. "Annike's gone, and he wants to escape from this strange place. Maybe you can show him the way."

"Hey, Priest," said another voice. Rice sensed many people standing there, all invisible in the shadows of this backstreet alley. Then a black man, heavily muscled, a leather vest around his bare chest like a fashion accessory, stepped into view. He carried a heavy revolver that looked blacker and more menacing than the man holding it. There was no white in his mouth at all. Rice saw him shrugging his shoulders—

first the left, then the right—as if he was venting nervous energy.

"You the killer, right?" the man holding the gun said. "But you gotta be. Why else would you be here hiding in the dark like you are?"

"We're not killers," Rice sputtered. *Stupid.*

"Talkin' to the preacher," the man said, wig-wagging the gun barrel like he was trying to flick Rice out of the way. "Been takin' what ain't his. Not what the good book says. Or maybe you mackerel snappers got a different book."

Rice heard a cough behind the man. The shape over the door was gone. Father Growden loosed his grip, and Rice collapsed at the priest's feet and crawled away.

Then the black man with the leather vest fired two shots into the priest's chest without changing his expression. Father Growden grunted. One more into his forehead. Growden dropped in a heap, his prayer book dropping out of his back pocket.

The black man no longer shrugged. He walked close to Rice, his mouth a black hole so empty the reporter wondered where his words came from.

"And you," the man said, tilting the revolver so the three casings tinkled to the ground. Rice dropped to his knees. He could feel the warmth from Father Growden's dead body. Heard the wind riffling the prayer book's pages.

"You," the man said again, holding the pistol to Rice's forehead, directly over his nose. "You should leave here."

—

Kleavon Hayes watched Rice Channon—still on his knees—drop his head to his chest and take two deep breaths.

"Killing a Catholic priest," Kleavon said to the gunman, wagging his head like an old woman gossiping over the clothes line. "Now we all be going to hell for certain."

"As long as he's the right one is all I care about," the gunman said, his revolver stowed in his pants, pressed against his flat, bare belly. He raised his eyes at Kleavon as though he expected an answer.

"Yeah, he is. He's that, for sure," Kleavon said. The prayer book pages next to the priest's body still fluttered in a wind he couldn't feel. "I've followed him. Followed both of them."

"Then we're just about done with Ohio," the gunman said. He had a way of talking without moving his lips much. "I'll drive."

"I'm the one supposed to drive," Kleavon said. "That's the plan. Shouldn't fuck with the plan."

"I'm fucking with the plan," the gunman said without raising his voice. A blue Ford Gran Torino was parked, head out from the alley. Two men waited in the backseat.

"Where are the others?" Kleavon asked.

"Gone," the gunman said. He struggled with the Gran Torino's trunk before it finally popped open. Then he pulled out his .38 Special and fired two rounds into Kleavon Hayes's chest. The old man dropped at once, wheezing heavily. The wheezing stopped when the gunman fired the revolver's last round through the center of Kleavon's forehead.

One of the men in the backseat got out, tossed his cigarette against the wall of a Sherwin-Williams paint store, and helped the gunman tip Kleavon Hayes into the trunk. They both cursed when the lid wouldn't close, and stopped talking when it finally did.

They passed a few still-burning fires on the way out of town. None of the rioters, most of whom were returning home, paid them any mind.

At a quarry ten miles outside the Goodwater city limits, they parked the car, and all three men searched the area with flashlights until they found the red 1969 Chevrolet Chevelle SS parked under a black cherry tree. Keys in the ignition.

The gunman unzipped a canvas bag on the backseat, counted the blocks of cash inside, zipped it up again, and tossed it in the front.

Then all three returned to the Gran Torino, rolled down the windows, and pushed the car carrying the body of Kleavon Hayes into the quarry. The splash was barely audible. They waited until the car sunk completely before getting on the highway to Detroit.

—

Colonel Markle trotted to Rice's side, dropped to one knee, the alley lights reflecting off his face shield, and peered into the darkness. Apparently satisfied no danger remained in the alley, he directed the dozen officers with him to spread out in a one-block radius of his position.

The police chief lifted his visor and looked at Rice. “You shoot him?” he asked, holding two fingers under Father Growden’s jaw.

“No,” Rice said. “I didn’t shoot him. Why would I?”

“I don’t know why you do half the things you do, Channon,” Markle said. “So who killed him then?”

“Some big colored guy.”

“Rioters? How many?”

“Not rioters,” Rice said. “Killers.”

Markle examined the body briefly. He gently moved the priest’s arms so he looked like he was sleeping on the pavement. Then he nodded. “You may be right,” he said. “Looks like a professional hit.”

“I thought you weren’t supposed to move a body until the medical examiner got here.”

“It won’t matter,” Markle said.

A police sergeant approached the police chief and knelt down. “Nobody out there, Chief,” he said. “Found these by that door.” He dropped three shell casings into Markle’s hand.

“After Father Growden was murdered, I heard three more shots,” Rice said, pointing vaguely in that direction. “Then a trunk slammed shut and the car drove off.”

A few moments later, a patrolman dropped three more casings into Markle’s hand.

"All six came from the same weapon, but there's only one dead guy, a priest with three holes in him," Markle said. "I wonder why they left you behind."

Rice stared at him, said nothing.

"So the killer likely shot two people," Markle said, rolling the casings on his palm. "And he used a revolver, a .38. But why did he leave the casings behind at all?"

"Because he's sloppy and stupid," the sergeant said.

"Maybe he didn't care if we knew what he did," Rice said, looking up. "Maybe he *wanted* us to know."

The sound of singing, rising in volume, came from the street behind them. Markle put the casings in his pocket, withdrew his sidearm, and led the patrolmen in that direction. Rice followed.

A row of black men and women, mostly older and marching with linked arms, were singing, "We Shall Overcome." Claude, the black college kid with the bloody shirt, was in the middle of them all, grinning, his face cleaned up now. His father stood next to him, singing lustily.

When the group saw the policemen, they began laughing and stopped marching. Claude walked up to Colonel Markle. "We're not part of the rioting," he said. "Our revolution is peaceful."

Markle holstered his weapon. He looked at Rice, then back at the marchers. "Revolution's over for tonight, folks," he said. "Let's clear the street."

—

In the dark and the commotion, Rice slipped away from Markle and stumbled toward the center of town. Still feeling weak, he caromed off walls and stopped to lean against a locked door or a shuttered window when light-headed.

His brain whirled, even as he staggered forward. *Did Father Growden murder Annike Eichel?*

Lights shone up ahead. Rice was close to the town square. It seemed like a safe place, an oasis, and he rushed toward it, still stumbling in his urgency, but less groggy than earlier.

*Why was Growden targeted? Why wasn't I?*

A streetlight up ahead. When Rice stood under it, his shadow speared out in multiple directions. One spike was darker and thicker than the rest. No matter how far he moved from the streetlight—even if he changed direction—that shadow pointed like a compass needle in the same direction, seemingly indifferent to the light source.

This shadow was darker than the night and always visible. When he stopped, it stretched out, like a dog pulling at its leash, eager to get home. Toward the mayor's office across from the square.

It was finally coming together. Observations. Questions and answers. Obfuscations. Shake them up and sometimes the truth appeared.

He thought about Father Growden and Ed Kadish, about Kleavon Hayes and Foster Ebner. Each one of them had something to say.

And what did Annike's spirit have to add? She seemed more and more like the crazy old aunt who fretted and wrung her hands but never actually *did* anything. Little more than a worrier.

Rice stopped, made himself pull out a cigar, light it slowly, and take a few puffs. It was quiet downtown, a few flower baskets squeaking as they swung from light poles. He took one more drag, then flung the cigar toward the purple and yellow pansies in the garden at the base of the town fountain.

His heart pounded. The mayor's office was brightly lit. He saw people inside shuffling back and forth, including Mayor McMillan and Phil Fortunato. He watched Phil pick up a phone.

Rice looked down at the shadow. It quivered like a little boy seeing the ocean for the first time.

Alexander.

*Was the poltergeist responsible for Growden's death? Is that why Annike Eichel mouthed his name?*

He saw Annike's spirit at the base of the steps to the mayor's office.

He watched the compass needle that was the shadow of Alexander detach, change shape, and slither snakelike up the steps and under the mayor's office door.

That's when he knew.

# { 49 }

Yogi Broadback, the tired old reporter with the droopy right eye, twisted his head to look at Rice when he walked into the reception area. His neck was so wrinkled and rusty, Rice half expected it to creak as he turned.

"The Ratcatcher," Broadback said with the loose grin of the not-quite-drunk. "Hiding out with the other faint hearts."

Mayor McMillan winced. He'd taken off his Eisenhower jacket, shaved, and washed his face.

"You've been out in this," Broadback said. "What's happening. We're not hearing shit."

As if to dispute this, a phone rang and Phil Fortunato answered it. He turned away to speak into the receiver. The next silence reinforced Broadback's appraisal of things.

"Father Pete Growden, a priest I know, was shot dead in the streets a while ago," Rice said to the mayor. "I just left him with Markle. He's dealing with some marchers."

McMillan coughed once. “The rioters got guns now?”

“I don’t think it was a rioter,” Rice said. He fell heavily into a vacant chair.

“A priest. Shit,” McMillan said. Everybody was quiet in the room.

“You know about the fires?” Rice said.

“On Carlisle?” Fortunato asked. He was off the phone now.

“Yeah. Where Ed Kadish is.”

“Is he okay?”

“Yeah. As long as he can walk backwards.”

“Christ.”

“Fire trucks are on the way to Carlisle,” the mayor said. Could have been talking to Fortunato. Could have been talking to Rice. “And now that Markle’s marching his unit in from the west, things are calming down.”

“Did you hear what I said about the dead priest?” Rice said.

The mayor looked down at the floor, seemingly talking to the cigarette ashes he’d crushed into the office carpeting over the years. “Yeah, we heard,” he muttered. “He’s in a better place.”

Quiet again. Everyone but Broadback looked down.

# { 50 }

"Foster Ebner's dead too," Mayor McMillan said. Even though he barely whispered, his voice sounded loud. The mayor studied Rice, his normally disapproving scowl gone for once.

Rice said, "Who killed him?"

"We've got a pretty good idea," Phil Fortunato said. "You make a mistake when you're an embezzler and you go to jail." He looked at his nails. "You screw up when you're a drug dealer, and somebody puts a .38 round through your head."

Mayor McMillan stood up and motioned Rice to follow him into his office. It was neat except for his ashtray, which was overflowing with crushed-out butts. The place smelled like a bar ten minutes after closing.

"I didn't want to say this in front of Jeanie," McMillan said. "Before they shot Foster in the head, somebody cut off his, um, privates."

"They sliced off his cock?"

"And his scrotum. Jammed the whole package into his mouth, probably while he was still alive. Let him think about it a minute, I guess, before they killed him," McMillan said. He giggled nervously, then caught himself.

Rice looked around, wondered where Annike went. "Think about what?"

The mayor looked up, surprised. "About what he did to the Eichel woman," he said, the old anger flaring up again. "Getting her pregnant. Didn't you read the *Chronicle* story, Channon?"

"Janousek's story didn't say anything about her being pregnant," Rice said, pushing the overflowing ashtray toward the mayor.

McMillan harrumphed. "I read it somewhere," he said.

"Not in my paper and not in the *Chronicle*," Rice said. "Maybe you read it in the coroner's report."

The mayor considered this for a while and then raised his eyebrows, as if allowing this might be so.

"Do you think Ebner's killers read the report?"

The mayor shook his head, slowly at first and then with increasing vehemence. "Nobody saw it but law enforcement. Family's got to sign off to release it, and we haven't located any family."

"Let me ask you this, Mayor," Rice said. "Who do you figure killed Annike Eichel?"

"Hell, it's obvious," McMillan said. "Foster killed her to hide the pregnancy. The druggies killed him because they knew his drug connections would come out in an embezzlement trial."

Phil Fortunato had quietly slipped into the room and took a seat against the far wall.

"So Foster Ebner was a drug dealer?" Rice said.

"It's the only thing that makes sense," Fortunato said. "Why else would they kill him?"

"Let me ask you this, Phil," Rice said, leaning forward in his chair. "Why's a drug dealer cut off Ebner's package and jam it in his mouth?"

"To send a message."

"Uh-huh," Rice said. "And what would that message be? Don't dick a white woman? Or don't get her pregnant?"

"I don't know," Fortunato said, the smile back. "Yeah, maybe both things. What does it matter?"

"Maybe it doesn't matter for much," Rice said. "You think Ebner's the murderer and maybe you're right. But do you really believe he was smart enough to be running a drug operation in this town? He was just a big bully scooping up the money the city left on the table."

Now it was Fortunato's turn to scowl.

"Father Growden was shot with a .38 also," Rice said.

Phil spread his hands and shook his head. "Well, that explains it then. Didn't you tell me he had some kind of relationship with Eichel?"

"I can't remember," Rice said.

"Druggies were using the cover of the riots to clean up business," Phil said. "You say Markle knows about all this?"

"I doubt if he knows about Ebner yet," Rice said. "But he knows about Father Growden's death. And maybe somebody else. I heard shots, but we couldn't find a body."

"*You* heard shots?" Phil said. "You're lucky you're not dead."

Rice saw Annike at the same time he saw the safety-service director's face turn sour. She looked ethereal as always but lovelier than before.

*Foster Ebner*, he thought. She smiled. He couldn't remember her smiling before. It melted away quickly.

She looked at the closed office door. Then back to Rice. Then the door again.

Rice opened it and saw Tom Janousek, hair a mess, face smudged and still sporting the black eye, step in with great dignity as though he had a big announcement to make.

"Well, Mayor, your boys did real good today," Janousek said to McMillan when the mayor returned to the reception area. "The National Guard came at the rioters from the north, and everybody broke and took off running. Then they bumped into Markle's platoon coming along Twelfth and the pack scattered like spilled marbles. Fire department came next, put out all the fires, and everybody went home to watch *Ironside* on TV. Is that the way you planned it?"

Mayor McMillan's face lit up in a sheepish grin. He slapped Janousek's shoulder. "I'm not going to pretend we didn't make some of this up as we went along," he said. "But we had good people and we had a strategy."

"Well, then that's the way I'll write it up," Janousek said, returning the backslap like they were old buddies sitting behind a full bottle of blended Scotch whisky, ready to bend elbows and catch up.

Ed Kadish came in next. The little anteroom was getting crowded.

"Detective Kadish," the mayor said, his broad face looking lit up already. "Everything good?"

"I think the worst is over," he said. "Streets are cleared. Fires are out. Just smoke and stink left."

McMillan shook his head, agreeing. "Arrests?"

Ed took his batting helmet off and scrambled his sparse head hair with his fingers. "No. Not that I'm aware of," he said. "I haven't spoken to Colonel Markle. I thought he'd be here."

"He's dealing with some kind of peaceful demonstration," Phil Fortunato said, looking to Rice. "He sent one runner but didn't have much to report. I figure he'll be here soon."

Janousek raised his eyebrows. "Unless he ran into more trouble."

That furrowed the mayor's brow. " I think the rest of the night's going to be quiet," he said.

Rice tapped Kadish's elbow and directed him to the one vacant corner in the office.

"Growden's dead," the reporter said. "Shot to death right in front of me."

The mayor watched the two of them while pretending to converse with Phil Fortunato.

"How the hell…? I told you—"

"And Foster Ebner too. Murdered in his own living room. And one other person, probably Kleavon Hayes. All professional hits," Rice said.

Kadish leaned against the paneled wall. His eyes were red when he looked at Rice. "What about you? How come you're still here?"

"I don't know," Rice said.

"You were lucky."

"Yeah, that's the consensus," Rice said. "But these guys—I'll give you a full description, not that it will matter—knew who I was. They made it pretty clear I wasn't on their hit list. They wanted to make sure I understood that."

Kadish shook his head and pursed his lips so hard, they became bloodless and white. "I'm going to need help on this one," he said. "I don't care how Markle feels about it. I'll call the state guys. Maybe the FBI."

"Save your nickel," Rice said, his voice just above a whisper. "You're supposed to believe the big drug dealers killed Foster Ebner, their local distributor, because he's under investigation for embezzlement. Because he might turn on them to get a better deal. They whacked off his boy parts because he got Annike Eichel pregnant and presumably told her about his drug operation."

"Maybe it's all the street smoke I inhaled. I'm going to be sick. I don't want to puke in this office."

"But hardly anybody knew she was pregnant. The autopsy was never released."

"You knew," Kadish said.

"Yeah, I did. So did you, the coroner, and apparently the mayor. Oh, yeah. Father Growden."

"Is that why they killed him?"

"Maybe. Or maybe they thought he knew something else and would spill."

"That makes sense," Kadish said.

"Yeah, it kind of does," Rice said. "But I think it's all bullshit. I think it's a smoke screen. They all died for nothing. This wasn't orchestrated by some scary black man sitting at a table with stacks of drug money in front of him. He wouldn't know about Eichel's pregnancy, and if he did, he wouldn't care."

"I don't know what to think."

"It's somebody local, Ed. Maybe in this room."

Kadish looked at the mayor and Fortunato. They were talking and laughing with Janousek.

"The den of the bear," Rice said. "That's what Father Growden called it before he died. I didn't know what he meant because he was trying to choke me to death at the time."

"What?"

"Alexander was there, Ed. Growden was trying to dispel him, but the thing started sucking the good out of him. I don't know how else to put it."

"So the priest tried to kill you?"

"Alexander tried to kill me. Growden was a kind of host," Rice said, waving his hand at Kadish to keep his voice low.

"But Father Growden was fighting him. Alexander needs a place to park his darkness. He followed me here, Ed."

"This is all madness. I told you to stay away from that goddamn priest," Kadish said. "Christ, listen to me."

"I gotta call my boss," Rice said. "When I leave to make the call, give me ten minutes and then come get me."

"The hell ..."

"Will you do it?"

Kadish scanned the room, then nodded.

"Hey, Phil," Rice said after working his way back across the room. "Can I use the phone in your office to call the newsroom? A little noisy here."

"Yeah, sure," Fortunato said. A stairwell behind the mayor's office led down to a tunnel to city hall. The safety-service director had an office in the tunnel. It was windowless, but it was large and provided easy access to both the mayor and the police department.

"Locked?" Rice said.

"No, hell no," Phil said. "Probably some coffee there too. Help yourself."

"Thanks."

The stairwell was lit and so was the tunnel. He could see Fortunato's office down on the left, the door open and the lights on, but it seemed dimmer than he remembered. Like some of the fluorescents had gone out since he was here last.

He shivered a little and went inside.

The black mung that was Alexander slid uneasily around the upper corners of the room, like the blob in a lava lamp.

Every now and then it moved over the ceiling lights causing the light to diffuse and send intermittent grayness across Phil's desk.

Annike was here, but Alexander paid her no mind. She looked at Rice without expression, her face still beautiful as before.

The door closed. Phil Fortunato stood, hands on hips, staring up at the poltergeist. Alexander drew himself into a ball, then started to squeeze into the seams of the ceiling tiles.

"I've tried like hell to get rid of that son of a bitch," Phil said, shaking his head. He reached into his desk drawer and pulled out a Colt Official Police revolver. He waved it at Rice. "Sit down," he said.

# { 51 }

"Did you make your call yet?" Phil asked.

"Nah, I was waiting for you," Rice said, eyeing the revolver as he spoke. "Wanted to clear up a few things first. Billard will scalp me if I get the story wrong."

Phil nodded and scratched his temple with the business end of the revolver. "Which story do you mean? I guess you want to talk about poor old Foster Ebner. But you missed this one, pal. That murder ain't never going to be solved. Probably out-of-town hit men."

"Is that right?"

"There's no one in this part of Ohio who kills like that."

"Sending a message in a special way, you mean," Rice said. "Isn't that what you called it?"

Phil sat in the desk chair and put the revolver in front of him. "You know, Rice, I always liked you," he said. "Nobody had to die, not like that anyway. If you'd just done your job …"

"*My* job?"

"You're the Ratcatcher," Phil said, grinning too widely. He was sweating now and rubbing his fingertips over the gun's barrel. "I laid the whole thing out in front of you. Ebner was embezzling from the city. Ebner was selling drugs. Ebner was balling pretty Annike Eichel and got her knocked up. It was all there for you. Front page story. Burnish your reputation. Big-city dailies try to hire you. Maybe a fat raise. Don't you want to be editor?"

"I don't work well with people," Rice said.

Phil nodded, sighed.

"It wasn't Markle who got me tossed off the police beat," Rice said. "It was you. And you're the one who told Janousek our two papers should work together on the Eichel murder."

"Is that a question?" Phil said.

"No. I managed to figure it out on my own. What I don't understand is why."

"I don't mind telling you," Phil said. "I always wanted you on the Eichel case. No. That's not exactly right. Taking you off the case. Putting you back on. It kept you off-balance. It made it easier to steer you. Then when you finally explained how you solved the case, everybody would believe you because, you know, you're that guy."

"And my boss went along with it."

"Not Billard," Phil said. "He's a prick. But you got other folks in management with skeletons. I rattled them. They did what I wanted."

"I'm pretty sure Ebner wasn't playing patty-cake with Eichel," Rice said. "Was she even pregnant?"

"Oh yeah, absolutely," Phil said. He closed one eye and lifted the revolver until it was pointed at the corner where the poltergeist shimmied but stayed in place. "I thought she was sterile. Aren't devils and demons sterile? I read that somewhere."

"Why would she have sex with you?"

Phil raised his eyebrows as he lowered the revolver. "I'll be honest. She wasn't happy about it. She was strong—those little ones often are—and I got the bruises to prove it. Well, I used to. I'm all healed now."

"And Annike's dead."

"Yeah," Phil said. Again with the barrel scratching his temple. He seemed almost wistful. "Despite everything, a sweet piece of tail. It's better when they're kicking and putting up a fight. The best part is when they just give up. It's like coming twice." He looked up, feigning a worried expression. "I'd rather you didn't use that last part in your story."

"Fuck you."

"See?" Phil said, waving the gun in Rice's direction and smiling. "This is why you're not an editor. No people skills."

Alexander moved slowly, like something from the deep sliding out from under a rock. He settled over Phil's head.

“Have you ever seen anything like that?” Phil said, waving the revolver like a wand. “I don’t know what the hell it is, but he likes me. Makes me feel—I don’t know—strong, *alive*. Like nailing a wild woman. You should have seen him when I was doing that slut atheist. My God, I think he was coming himself.”

“Did you share the story with Mrs. Fortunato?”

“What am I going to do with you?” Phil asked, grinning like Rice was a spoiled and mischievous child. Then he started shaking his head and waving the gun around again.

“I saw your bread crumbs,” Rice said. “But I ignored them because I’m prickly and like to do things my own way. Probably because I lack the people skills, like you said.”

“Uh-huh, uh-huh,” Phil said, nodding, kind of sad. Then he brightened. “Gonna have to shoot you, though.”

# { 52 }

Rice's heart skipped a beat and he blinked twice.

Phil held a collegial grin but his eyes blazed with an ugly glint. He lifted the revolver and slowly turned the cylinder, each click taking longer than the last.

Then he pointed the gun at Rice.

"You're going to kill me because I won't write the story you want?"

The sad smile was back. Like he was heartily sorry he had to do it.

"And you think *I* lack people skills," Rice said.

Phil lifted the gun and fired a round into the ceiling, right through the pulsing black mush. It didn't make as much noise as Rice expected. Alexander seemed unaffected.

"Did you see all the holes in the ceiling at Eichel's home?" Phil said, looking up at Alexander.

Rice shook his head.

Phil sighed. "Neither did the officers on the scene. Neither did Ed Kadish. Sloppy police work," he said. "I shot at that black cloud a dozen times or more. The first few times I thought I was just having a bad dream. Then I realized I'm *living* this dream."

He made a fist. "But it gave me the strength to do what needed to be done."

"So you're just going to shoot me, then drag my body out through the mayor's office?" Rice said. "I guess he won't mind, but some of the others might say something."

Phil laughed and shook his head. "Folks around here say you should have been a cop and not a newspaperman. But they're wrong. You should have been a comedian. Like Jackie Gleason. No, no. That skinny guy. What's his name?"

"Woody Allen."

"Yeah, that's him. New York City Jew boy," Phil said, and then he looked to his left. "There's a back entrance to the alley behind city hall. It's right over there, behind my coatrack. Looks like a closet. It's where we keep the Christmas decorations. If you pop open a panel behind the boxes, you'll find yourself in the alley. I took a van from impound and parked it back there. For when you showed up."

"People are going to wonder what happened to me."

Phil pushed out his bottom lip, shook his head, agreeing. "They will, they will. For a while. But like I said, our cops are shitty investigators. You're the only one who figured out what happened."

"Are you sure?"

Phil rubbed the blue metal barrel against his jaw and considered this. “Pretty sure. Kadish doesn't know. Not his fault. I steered him in a dozen bad directions. Just like I did with you. But he listened to me.”

“Well, you're his boss.”

“Yeah, that was probably it,” Phil said, dropping the gun barrel to his lap and smiling real natural now.

“Maybe he's starting to put it together,” Rice said.

Phil chuckled at that. “How'd *you* put it together?”

“It was the lawn mower guy, Kleavon,” Rice said. “He was the only one willing to talk with me about Ebner. Real eager.”

“Yeah, yeah,” Phil said, eyes wide like a puppy about to have his belly scratched. “Kleavon had a hard-on for Ebner.”

“Lots of people did, but he's the only one willing to talk about it.”

Phil spread his hands. “That's the way we planned it,” he said. “He's got cancer. Probably be dead within a year. So why not spill his guts? You had to believe him. Don't tell me you didn't.”

“No, I did, I did,” Rice said.

“And everything he told you was true,” Phil said, smiling warmly. “Ebner's embezzling from the city and he's got to go down for it. It was simple to add in the drug involvement. Tying in Eichel's death was the next obvious step. His drug handlers get nervous and ventilate his head. Believe me, nobody's going to miss the bastard.”

Rice nodded. “It was a sweet setup.”

"The best," Phil said. "Yet somehow you wouldn't go along with it. You fall into some fucking rabbit hole, start sniffing around, and now I've got to kill you."

Phil said it simply and without rancor. Like he was handing him a ham sandwich and telling him he'd already added mustard.

"So you killed Ebner and you killed Hayes, even though he was going to be dead soon, anyway."

"Couldn't take the chance," Phil said, looking around as if he had all the time in the world. "Might have lasted a year, year and a half. Might have got greedy. Can't tell with those jigs."

"I saw Kleavon at one of the early riots. I think it was last week," Rice said, trying hard to calm his thumping heart. "I thought he was there to get the kids to knock it off. Send them home before they got into trouble."

Phil cocked his head.

"But that wasn't what he was doing at all. He was urging them on. Here's a guy dying from cancer, and he's acting like the ringleader of the mob trying to burn his city down."

"And that didn't seem right to you?"

"Not even a little," Rice said. "I looked at the guys he was talking to and they were all big, muscular fellas. I bet they were in their twenties, but they were wearing the cut shirts and torn bell-bottoms, and a couple of them were wearing pimp Panama hats."

"Like Star Lightman wears," Phil said, grinning. They could have been joking over burgers and brews in the backyard.

"Yeah," Rice said, forcing himself to point at Phil to reinforce his words. "Except they were trying too hard. Like they thought this was how kids dressed now."

Phil gave a grim shake of his head.

"They were outsiders," Rice said. "So I think to myself, 'Do these guys work for Kleavon? Why are they here?' "

"Overplayed their role. Is that what you're saying?"

Rice pursed his lips and nodded.

Fortunato raised his weapon, smiled real ugly, and scratched his chin again with the barrel. Rice was starting to think some kind of spider had bitten him on the face. "You're not going to get a rocket scientist in this business. If they've got half a brain and can shoot straight, you're lucky," he said.

"Those guys from Cleveland?"

"Detroit," Phil said, nodding to acknowledge the good guess. "They're mostly well behaved. These guys were crazy but tractable. I thought they might stoke the fires of the riots. I needed the cover for everything else I had planned."

"Sure."

"Turned out the rioters didn't need much encouragement," Phil said. "And these guys were really just killers. Didn't know much about creating civil unrest."

"It all must have cost you a bundle."

Phil blew the air out of his cheeks, eyes wide. "That it did, but it was a big mess and it had to be cleaned up. It was only going to get worse."

He pulled a small bottle of something from a desk drawer and took a long swig without removing his eyes from Rice.

"So why didn't you buy into the drug angle? It made perfect sense," Phil said. He held up an admonishing finger. "But not *too* perfect."

He laughed and Rice pretended to laugh with him. Kadish would always say that after he'd arrested a bad guy. "It looks perfect, boss, but not *too* perfect."

"I mean, you had to dig to even find the drug connection. I didn't exactly lay it in your lap. You had to search a little, right?"

Rice thought he heard something moving in the hall outside the door. He thought of calling out, but that would most likely end the friendly discussion they were having.

"I thought the drugs were a legit thing, but I never saw them behind the Eichel murder."

"Now that's curious," Phil said. "You didn't make the jump from drug dealing to murder. I figured you would. Gotta tell you, I'm a little disappointed."

Rice raised his eyebrows and spread his hands. *Sorry.*

"I think Kadish was ready to believe it, though," Phil said, eyes wide as though looking for confirmation.

"Oh yeah, he did," Rice said. "That was fine with me. I wanted to go my own way, and he just complicated things."

Phil grunted, took another swig.

"It was something the mayor said when he lowered himself to talk to me, last week I think it was."

"Sandy don't like you," Phil said. "Thinks you're a smart-ass."

Rice nodded.

"You are," Phil said. "But that's okay with me."

He emptied the bottle and threw it into the metal trash can where it clattered noisily, louder than the earlier gunshot. Rice could see the label now. Johnnie Walker Red.

"The mayor told me he wanted to get out of town for a few weeks," Rice said. "Told me he was going to take a case of Black Label and hide out in your cabin at Pymatuning Lake."

"Sandy told you that?"

"I didn't make it up," Rice said. "When he realized he said it, he shut up in a hurry and wouldn't talk about it anymore. Then he pushed me out of his office. And here I thought you guys didn't like each other."

"He figures *my* cabin is a perk of *his* office."

"Now I know why you don't like him."

"Just one of the reasons."

"Anyway, after that I started snooping around like I do."

"It's your job," Phil said.

"You've got a five-bedroom, four-bath cabin on ten acres."

"I love that place. Don't go there often enough."

"You're a hard worker," Rice said. "The city doesn't appreciate it. You should get another twenty grand a year. I mean it."

"Right on, as the kids say."

"But you're not making enough to buy a big house like that. And you keep a new Buick there too, I understand."

"I got a rich wife."

"No, you don't. She was dirt poor, living on a farm with her alcoholic mother somewhere near Chillicothe when you met her."

"How'd you find all that out?"

"They let me keep a phone on my desk," Rice said. "It seems Mrs. Fortunato was heavy with child when you got married."

"It was the right thing to do," Phil said, rubbing the gun against his pants leg for a change.

"I've been watching you for a long time," Rice said. "I know you've got your eyes on the mayor's office. It would help if McMillan backed you."

"Almost a requirement. The party is strong and Sandy's real popular."

"Which makes it a damn shame that he doesn't like you," Rice said. "Just who in the hell does he like?"

"He likes Jeanie."

"So you're never going to be mayor. Doesn't seem fair since you've been doing all the heavy lifting during his tenure."

"That is true," Phil said, nodding.

"But you're an ambitious guy and the mayor, well, he's a little sloppy overseeing things. He likes to say he trusts his people, but he's just sloppy."

"That's no secret."

"And Foster Ebner has always been a little hinky. A cheat and a bully, sure, but was he really smart enough to run a big deal embezzlement scheme?"

"He's been at it a long time."

"Nickel-dime grabs," Rice said, scooting forward in his chair. "Kid stuff, really. Then he started manipulating contracts, drug involvement. He was working above his pay grade."

Phil let out a puff of air. "So?"

"So someone bigger, stronger, and smarter was behind him. Someone able to keep him in check."

"You want me to offer suggestions?"

"I considered the mayor, but holding the reins on a big, ugly black man would be too hard."

"He's more of a handshaker and backslapper," Phil said.

"Then there's Colonel Markle," Rice said. "He was my first choice. I actually hoped it was him. He's the only guy I know who's a bigger bully than Ebner."

"Self-righteous prick."

"And you think he wants to be mayor."

"Doesn't he?"

"No," Rice said. "He wants to be sheriff. That way he won't have to kiss babies. He can just ride his horse down Cleveland Street during the Labor Day parade. Maybe he'll wear his brand-new riot helmet instead of a cowboy hat."

"I didn't know that."

"He's still driving an old Studebaker. He dresses nice but has practically nothing in the bank."

Phil jerked back his head, surprised.

"True. I checked," Rice said. "It's possible he could be stuffing his misbegotten gains into a secret account somewhere, but I think that's unlikely. He's incapable of minding the books in his own department. Nope, Quincy Markle is no player in an embezzlement and drug racketeering scheme."

"I wonder who it could be then?" Phil said, eyes narrowing. But smiling

"So I was stumped for the longest time. Of course, this came after Annike Eichel was murdered. And then Foster Ebner is arrested for embezzlement. And now Foster is murdered. The city catches fire. Drugs, mayhem."

"It's chaos."

"And then Father Growden gets shot to death right in front of me."

"Did you shit your pants?"

"Almost," Rice said. "And your shadow friend in the corner was there too."

Phil began smacking his lips noisily. "Oh, he was feeding off someone. He's like that. Probably the shooter."

"I don't think so," Rice said, his voice rising. "I think he was there for Growden. But he wasn't feeding off him. Growden was sucking him in. Why'd you have him shot, Phil?"

"Eichel talked to him about our relationship. Or probably talked to him. Anyway, I couldn't take the chance."

"I think you were wrong about that. Your guys killed a man for no reason."

"Maybe," Phil grunted. He wig-wagged his gun at Rice. "But the killer let you live. He coulda shot you."

"Yeah, but then I couldn't write my story the way you wanted."

Phil smiled, his forehead speckled with sweat beads. He began massaging his temple and squeezed so hard a tear rolled out of his right eye and fell on his palm.

"I got a headache that never goes away," he said, wiping his mouth with the back of his free hand. He looked up at Alexander. "It's worse when that thing is hanging around."

Alexander dropped even lower. Phil raised the revolver and punched it into the air. The cloud remained just out of reach.

"There've been enough deaths, Phil," Rice said.

"Oh, I know, I know," Phil said. "It's bad for business. It hurts me when I have to kill someone. If you think I don't have a conscience, you're wrong."

"Okay."

"But there's lots of ugly in this world, Rice," Phil said. The haunted look came over him again. "Maybe this thing hangs around just to remind me what I always knew was there."

"How's that?"

Phil slapped at the air to emphasize each word. "Sucking the air out of everything that's good."

"I thought you said the cloud gave you strength to do what needed doing."

"Did I say that?"

"Just a little while ago."

Phil smiled. "Oh, yeah. You know, it wasn't always that way."

"What do you mean?"

"I paid a visit to Annike Eichel once I realized Foster had—I don't know—*feelings* for her. It made me sick to think of that ugly, smelly black cocksucker draping his body over her white flesh."

"That explains why your boys hacked off his man parts," Rice said. "But I think they were just pals."

"Pals, huh? I don't know what they were, but yeah, you may be right. That actually makes it worse, though."

"How's that?"

"Look, the two of them were sipping wine, toking weed, and dropping acid together," Phil said. "There's no way Ebner could keep from spilling about his extracurricular activities. She knew. She had to."

"That's a big leap," Rice said. "You killed her for that?"

Phil thought about this, tapped the barrel on his teeth, smiled in that ugly way again. The perspiration poured off him. "I made a couple of visits to her. I tried to dance around what Ebner might have told her. She just laughed at me and kind of flirted a little. And I'm a married man. She knew that."

"Beautiful woman."

"That she was," Phil said. "She had that kind of clear, porcelain skin you only see in movie stars. Absolutely unblemished. And that's what was so funny."

"How's that?"

"Because she was the devil, a demon goddess."

"You sure about that?"

"I should have killed her right then," Phil said. He looked at Rice. "I thought about it. Instead, I threw myself on her. Oh, Lord, how she screamed. Like a devil drenched in holy water. And that was the first time."

"How many more times did you rape her?"

Phil turned to Rice, his smile suggesting surprise. "Rape?" he said. "I only neutralized her … her degenerate nature. The drugs and sex and who knows what else."

"So what are you talking about? The first *what*?" Rice said. He wondered how much longer he could engage this crazy man.

"The first time I saw that black thing." Phil made a lazy circle over his head with the gun barrel. "It came out of her kitchen. Sort of dripped out. Terrified me. This thing is a living demon's shadow."

"Makes sense."

Phil pulled open his desk drawer, felt around for something, then slammed it hard when he couldn't find it. He sat back against his chair and put his hands behind his head.

"Yeah" was all he said. As if that was the answer to everything. His expression was blank. Rice wondered where the gun was.

"She seemed a little worried about Ebner," Phil said, his demeanor looking like the old Phil again. "She thought I might hurt him."

"Did she know about the deal you and Ebner had? About the embezzlement, the bullying, the drugs?"

"She never said anything, but she knew. She was smart enough not to say anything."

"But you left her alone. No more … neutralizing her?"

"You really are a smart-ass. I can almost forgive Sandy for hating you so much."

"I'm just trying to understand. You're a complicated man, Phil."

"I felt dirty, okay?" Phil said. "Is that what you wanted to hear?" His voice rose. "She was a godless darkness, a living symbol of everything wrong in this country, in this world. She knew about the drugs, the stealing, the rest of it, but her devil nature wouldn't allow her to admit to it. Not to me."

"Maybe she was just afraid."

A huffed laugh.

"What happened the last time?" Rice said.

At that, Phil's face darkened as if the last light inside had just winked out. "She knew she was pregnant," he said. "The doctors didn't know yet, but she knew."

"She told you that?"

"Yeah," Phil said. "She pretended shame, but she was delighted, full of a monstrous pride. What kind of beast would she bring into this world?"

"The beast was half-yours, Phil."

"What? No, you don't understand."

"Enlighten me."

"A good man could not impregnate that swine. I wanted simply to demean her, lower her, make her even more unworthy."

"And you felt that was your job?"

Phil lifted up the revolver which had apparently been on his lap. He pointed it at Rice's forehead and pulled back the hammer with agonizing slowness. Rice felt his bowels liquefy.

"Where'd you get the knife?" he asked.

"It was that black thing," Phil said, head thrown back like he was expecting rain. He eased the hammer back and lowered the gun. "Whatever made it real also made that abomination in Eichel's belly. They both came from the same hell place."

"So the black cloud twisted you somehow. Just like it had twisted Annike Eichel."

"He led me to the kitchen. Showed me a large, broad butcher knife under a spatula. It sorta sparkled when I looked at it."

Rice said nothing.

"The shadow followed me back to the living room and kind of covered me like a blanket," Phil said, eyes focused on something far away. "It wrapped around my shoulders and gave me power to finish the job."

Rice felt the horror in the room like it was another living body.

"I expected her to run. I wanted her to. But she must have known there'd be no getting away from righteous vengeance. I reminded her that she was a whore, a turd of Satan, the stink and filth and decay and …" Phil stopped. "I would not take her again."

Phil's voice dropped just above a whisper. When he spoke, he was so dispassionate, he could have been pointing out cloud formations to a curious child.

"For a devil, she smelled wonderful," Phil said. "It made me think of a late-summer cantaloupe. You know how sweet and fragrant they are when you first cut into them?"

*Jesus, God*, Rice thought.

"I don't think I killed her the first or second time I pushed the blade into her. I twisted and carved, and the gush of blood didn't come at first, but then—wow—I almost lost my grip on the knife. But I knew it was important to exterminate that thing growing inside. I cleaned her out all the way to the intestines. At least I think they were intestines." He smiled. "I'm not a doctor."

The ghost of Annike Eichel returned to the room, her hand on her belly.

Phil's changing smile was paternal now. "Tossed the knife into the Dumpster behind the five and dime on Cleveland Street," he said. "Nothing feels better than to be an honest instrument of a Higher Hand."

"You murdered her," Rice said. He thought the words might kill him.

"No, no, you're wrong," Phil said, waving the revolver like an admonishing finger. "Blood, gore, yes, that was part of it. But it wasn't an ending. It was a beginning. Like pulling a calf free from its dying mother. It was … warm. And quiet at the end."

With each word, Alexander's heavy shadow lowered farther. Phil closed his eyes and seemed to be recalling something from long ago.

Annike moved next to Rice, her mouth open wide in a silent howl.

Rice jumped out of his chair, slamming his shins on Phil's desk as he leaped over it. Phil's eyes opened wide as Rice reached for the revolver, wrapping his fingers around the barrel.

Alexander's blackness fell on Phil completely now, settling over him like a mucous bubble. Phil's dull eyes grew bright and unfocused, and the human part of him seemed to disappear.

Phil pulled back the hammer. His eyes grew wider still. He reached out, his left hand twitching, and Rice wondered if at last he saw her. The spirit of the woman he killed.

Annike Eichel dipped her head at the cloud bubble, and it pulsed once as though inhaling fresh air.

Someone called out Rice's name. Then Phil's.

But Phil wasn't there anymore. Alexander shrunk his airy black soul into a line that slid, wormlike, into a corner of Phil's right eye.

Phil's mouth unhitched and opened wide, his head rolling from side to side on his shoulders. A bearlike growl spewed forth from his belly.

In a single powerful motion, the Goodwater safety-service director pulled the barrel away from Rice's grip, then pushed it into his own mouth, and fired one shot up into his brain. It blew away a saucer-sized triangle of Phil Fortunato's skull and scalp, which dropped on top of the discarded bottle of Johnny Walker Red whiskey in the trash can.

Splinters exploded as the locked office door flew open. Ed Kadish, weapon drawn, lowered himself to a half squat. He held his aim on the dead body, bleeding, gore-covered, and still.

"I thought you forgot about me," Rice said once Kadish's breathing had slowed.

The detective holstered his weapon.

The body of Phil Fortunato leaned over in his chair. What was left of his head lay on the desk in a growing puddle of greasy blood.

Rice saw no sign of his spirit. No apparitions of Foster Ebner either. Or Father Growden.

The ghost of Annike Eichel, the shadow of Alexander, and every ugliness in the room seemed to be gone for good.

# { epilogue }

Stories published in the *Cleveland Chronicle* and *Goodwater Tribune* over the next three days all carried double bylines.

Rice Channon's name was first.

Tom Janousek wrote a few articles about the Goodwater riots, but those carried his byline alone and usually ran on an inside page. The big news was the embezzlement/murder/suicide involving Annike Eichel, various city officials, and of course, Phil Fortunato.

Although Rice had been there for the main event—Fortunato blowing out a piece of his head—he wrote the article as a straight news story. Janousek clucked at what he called false modesty, insisting the story would read better if Rice gave a firsthand account.

The Cleveland reporter wrote a mostly praiseworthy sidebar about the way Rice was manipulated and threatened yet managed to confront the bad guy in the end.

He did, Rice thought, a fine job with his account. Janousek ignored rumors, and included nothing about ghosts, poltergeists, bugs, or flying books. In the end, despite his loose hold on journalistic ethics, he left out what he hadn't seen personally or couldn't confirm through reliable sources.

Janousek did, however, provide numerous examples of Mayor McMillan's lousy governmental oversight and bad judgment.

Neither Rice nor his newspaper's editorial page attacked the mayor directly. It was enough to mention the mayor's "sabbaticals" at Phil Fortunato's elaborate lake home in Pymatuning.

The unstated subtext was "How did Rice Channon figure out something was fishy about the safety-service director owning a big house with a big car when the mayor didn't?" Rice satisfied himself with the knowledge that some future political adversary would doubtless remind voters of this question at a later date, if the mayor ever decided to pursue higher office.

The others were painted with broad but colorful brushes. Detective Ed Kadish was the dogged investigator. Quincy Markle was the hands-on leader with the steely glare. Father Growden prayed for the burning city and was struck down by a paranoid madman.

All of it was true, if lacking important details.

"Pete Growden helped me when no one else could," Stacey said, sitting at Arnie Corso's kitchen table a few days later. Both she and Rice had shown up separately without invite. Arnie seemed grateful for the company.

"So you were on a first name basis?" Rice said. "I didn't know that."

Arnie leveled a scoop of coffee grounds with a kitchen knife before carefully pouring them into the percolator on his range.

"About five minutes and we'll have fresh brew," he said, rubbing his hands together as if this was a grand experiment that had never quite worked before.

"Yes," Stacey said, jutting out her chin. "When you and I split up, I was in a funk. Father Growden and I spent a lot of time talking about it. We grew close."

Rice sniffed. "It should have been *me* talking to him."

"You're happier in your own company," she said, looking over at Arnie. "I was the one who was hurting."

"What about Roger? And Tom Janousek?"

She shrugged. "I want people in my life who will be there when I need them. That's one of the things Pete and I talked about."

"What did you learn?"

She flicked her hair and looked around the small apartment. "He said I didn't need anybody to lean on. Nobody to make me complete. He made me believe it too."

"Is that when you left Roger?"

"Yes, around that time," she said. "See, it had nothing to do with Roger losing his job."

"So you weren't leaning on Tom Janousek?"

Stacey moved her face close to his and smiled like she knew this next part was going to hurt. “I had a hunger. Pete understood that. He told me the trick is not to give in.” She shrugged. “Unfortunately, I did. But it’s over now.”

“Anybody else you feasted on?”

“I know it bothers you,” she said. “I’m sorry.”

“Don’t be,” Rice said. He tried to sneer, but failed. “I’m happy you’re stable and independent.”

A few minutes later, Arnie brought over the coffeepot, beaming like it was the Holy Grail.

“I put too many grounds in,” he said, placing a cup of coffee in front of Stacey. “It may be more robust than you like. Try cutting it with some cream.”

“It’s okay, Arnie,” Rice said, staring at Stacey hard so she had to look at him. “She likes it strong.”

“Normally I drink tea,” she said, ignoring him and blowing across the cup before tasting it gingerly. “But this is fine.”

Arnie tossed a bag of Oreos on the table. “These are the only cookies I got,” he said. “Mostly crumbs now, but you could eat them with a spoon …”

“Just the coffee,” she said.

“How is Roger?” Rice asked.

She put her cup down after taking a sip, then widened her eyes as if this was a trifle. “We’re going to his parents’ house tomorrow. His mother insists on being involved in the wedding plans.”

“So he’s got a new job?”

She ignored him.

"I have a sensation at the present moment as though I was dissolving," Rice said, blinking wildly, hoping it made a mockery of the words.

"I know you're throwing Mr. Keats at me again," Stacey said. "I don't care."

Arnie slammed a cupboard door. "Wait," he said. "I found some of those windmill cookies. They're great for dunking."

—

The following Wednesday Tom Janousek strolled through the Mosopelea Junior College Student Union, hands in his pockets and eyes squinting against sun coming through the skylight. Three freshman girls sipping on Cokes giggled as he passed their table. He tilted his head and gave a slight courtly bow, which made them giggle some more.

He found Arnie Corso at a table by himself, two books open in front of him, drinking from a cardboard carton of milk.

Janousek sat in reverse on the chair and leaned his arms on the back. "You're a hard man to find," he said. "All the harder because nobody seems to know who you are."

"Are you a process server?" Arnie said. "You don't look like one." He tilted the carton back and drank until all the milk was gone.

Janousek introduced himself. He told Arnie about the stories he'd written for the paper. About his relationship with Rice.

"I was hoping you might help me clear up a few things."

"Fire away," Arnie said. He smiled when the freshmen girls at the other table looked in his direction.

Janousek pulled out a notebook. "I understand you were with Father Pete Growden the day he died," he said. "Did you see the killers?"

"I've talked to the police about all that stuff already," Arnie said. "No, I wasn't there. He sent me away. He wanted to take the thing on himself. *By* himself."

"What thing?"

"Annike Eichel's poltergeist," Arnie said, eyes wide, disbelieving. "Didn't Rice tell you about him?"

"No. We only discussed things living on, you know, *this* planet. Did you tell the cops about this … poltergeist?"

"No," Arnie said. He began batting at the empty milk carton. "I told them I saw Father Growden earlier in the day. Then I went home. Stacey stopped by his office after me. That's all I know, okay?"

"Yeah," Janousek said, scratching his jaw. "That's what she told me."

"I knew about Alexander," Arnie said. "And I knew what the priest was going to do. Or try to do. I didn't tell the cops that part."

"Who's Alexander?"

"He's the poltergeist," Arnie said, exasperated. He looked ready to end the interview, but the girls smiled in his direction again.

Janousek put his pad away. "Did you tell them what Growden hoped to do?"

"I told them I didn't know why he went to the streets. I didn't say anything about Alexander. Or that Father Growden wanted to destroy him."

"So you lied to the police."

"You think if I told them about Alexander they would have believed me?"

"So why are you telling me?"

"Just a gut feeling that you should know."

"And the priest's prayers didn't work," Janousek said.

Arnie smirked. "Alexander's gone now and that's what Father Growden wanted. I think the priest sucked the life out of him, and what was left buried itself in Mr. Fortunato's soul."

"Does Rice believe all this?"

"Yeah, probably," Arnie said, now spinning the milk carton on one corner like a top. "We haven't talked about it, but he understands these things."

They talked a while longer, Janousek only probing the edges of the foggy world Arnie inhabited. He knew he wouldn't write about it, couldn't write about it. But he remained fascinated by the commentary of this odd man with the air and appearance of a dazed Eagle Scout.

"People tell me Rice sees ghosts," Janousek said.

Arnie stopped the carton spinning and shook his head, chuckling. "He *thinks* he sees ghosts," Arnie said. "People who experience violent deaths appear to him. Sometimes try to talk. That's what he says."

"What do you mean, he *thinks* he sees them?"

"He can't see my guardian angel. He can't see my spirit guides or any of the lost souls in my room," Arnie said. "Do you really believe he can see other spirits? Think about it. Does that make sense?"

Tom Janousek stared at him for a long time before he finally stood up and pushed in his chair.

"Delusional," he said.

Arnie Corso nodded in sad agreement.

Janousek thought of Arnie spinning his empty milk carton the same way he spun his story of angels, ghosts, and spirit guides. Round and round went the milk carton. Round and round went his story. None of it useful for anything at all.

—

Rice got the police beat again and kept the raise.

A sad, sick part of him thought it would be fun to share the news with Stacey and returning fiancé, Roger Ranscombe, but he never did.

When he spotted Roger on the street later in the week, the man's bouncy step was back, along with the confident air he wore like a shiny badge. Roger smiled when he saw Rice. He shook his hand heartily and seemed genuinely glad to see him.

Mitchell Joyce impressed Dave Billard during his brief time on the cop beat, so the city editor gave him city hall. The mayor liked the new city hall reporter and so did Jeanie. It made the job a lot easier. Mitchell was becoming the new Boy Wonder.

Earl Sugarman, the former assistant, was named the new safety-service director, and seemed to grow a backbone with the promotion. He remained friendly with Rice but didn't kowtow like before and stopped apologizing so often. Colonel Markle still intimidated Sugarman, but Rice thought that might change too over time.

Rice headed over to Martelli's after lunch because he didn't give a damn about anything these days. He slid into a booth in the back and let cold air from the overhead vent blow away the heat and stink from outside.

Pearl Clinton—also known as Tulips Kissin'—spotted him at once. She brought over a Black Label for him and a ginger ale for her. He thought her expression looked almost maternal. Then she slid in opposite him and her glorious legs bumped his under the table, jostling his libido.

"Darlin', you were almost a dead man," she said after taking a tiny sip. "You wouldn't leave me here drinking my ginger ale all alone?"

"Would you miss me?"

"You hurt me when you say things like that," she said, leaning over and planting a kiss on his forehead like she was taking his temperature with her lips. "You're the only white boy I really care for. I thought you knew that."

She touched her tongue to a cocktail napkin and wiped the lipstick off his face. "All those bad men messin' with my angel," she said. "But somehow, here you are."

"Here I am."

"You want to just sit and hold hands?" she said, reaching out to grab his free hand with both of hers. Cold as usual. "I could do that. It's slow this time of day."

"Do you like ice cream?" he said.

"Sure. Who doesn't?"

"When do you finish tonight, Pearl?"

She dropped his hand and sat up straight. "I opened the place today, so I get off early. About eight. Why?"

"There's an Isaly's downtown. It's open to ten, I think," he said. "Skyscraper cones. Chipped chopped ham sandwiches."

"I've been there." She had high cheekbones, and the light made her look like a contented tiger.

"You and me," he said. "We'll sit in someplace bright, and then we'll watch the night from inside for a change."

"Oh," Tulips Kissin' said, shaking her head slowly from side to side. Then she ran her long painted nails lightly across his cheek. "Honey, *honey* …"

# Acknowledgements

Thanks to my editor, Starr Waddell, for battling relentlessly against my ongoing war on grammar and punctuation. Any remaining errors are a result of my ignoring her guidance. Thanks also go to the two Jessicas who beta read an early draft and gave me encouragement and head slaps, as appropriate. My buddy Mark O'Brien did *not* buy me breakfast but did relate his experiences with law enforcement as a police reporter. It was much appreciated, but we're not eating at that place again.

I workshopped a first draft of the novel with many writers more talented than I at the Writers in Paradise Workshop. Thanks to Peggy, Todd, Bill, Nick, Craig, Kat, Sarah, Lily, Ashleigh, Colleen, and Kelly. Also Laura Lippman, a best-selling author and patient overseer of the class. Plus, she didn't hit me even once after I criticized one of her books at the welcome party. It wasn't my fault. They shouldn't serve wine at those things.

Dennis Lehane, when he isn't writing brilliant books, is a director and faculty member at the same workshop. He gave a thoughtful presentation and graciously answered my questions about avoiding anachronisms in historical novels.

My wife and best friend, Kea, gifted me the aforementioned workshop and also beta read the book. Thanks for being honest and shamelessly brutal.

And thanks to Mary, a sweet lady from South Africa, who just happens to be haunted by a spirit that she admits is freaking her out. She asked my help in getting rid of it. Although I couldn't work any magic, she gave me lots of background about guardian angels, spirit guides, and the wandering souls that invisibly populate our world. She also gave birth to Arnie Corso.

## ABOUT THE AUTHOR

Dennis Anthony has been a newspaper reporter, sailor, military officer, television news producer, public relations executive and publishing company owner. He and his wife live in Pensacola, Florida, but try to spend as much time as possible at their cabin on Lookout Mountain in Alabama.

Website: http://www.dennis-anthony.com

If you liked this book, please consider submitting a review on Amazon.com. Reader reviews are important to authors and much appreciated.

Thank you.

Printed in Great Britain
by Amazon